I HEART LONDON

Lindsey Kelk was a children's book editor and is now a magazine columnist and author of *I Heart New York*, *I Heart Hollywood*, *I Heart Paris*, *I Heart Vegas* and *The Single Girl's To-Do List*. When she isn't writing, reading, listening to music or watching more TV than is healthy, Lindsey likes to wear shoes, shop for shoes and judge the shoes of others. She loves living in New York but misses Sherbet Fountains, London, and drinking Gin & Elderflower cocktails with her friends. Not necessarily in that order.

To find out more about Lindsey's novels, sign up for the newsletter, read exclusive extracts and enter competitions visit www.iheartlondon.co.uk and follow Lindsey on Twitter @LindseyKelk.

By the same author

I Heart New York
I Heart Hollywood
I Heart Paris
I Heart Vegas

The Single Girl's To-Do List

Jenny Lopez Has a Bad Week
(novella only available on ebook)

LINDSEY KELK

I Heart London

HARPER

Harper
An imprint of HarperCollins*Publishers*
77–85 Fulham Palace Road,
Hammersmith, London W6 8JB

www.harpercollins.co.uk

A Paperback Original 2012

4

Copyright © Lindsey Kelk 2012

Lindsey Kelk asserts the moral right to
be identified as the author of this work

A catalogue record for this book
is available from the British Library

ISBN: 978-0-00-746227-8

Set in Melior by Palimpsest Book Production Limited, Falkirk, Stirlingshire

Printed and bound in Great Britain by
Clays Ltd, St Ives plc

MIX
Paper from
responsible sources
FSC
www.fsc.org **FSC C007454**

*Della, Beth, Sarah, Jacqueline,
Ryan, Emma and Rachael.*

*People always ask me who my Jenny is and
I tell them I'm lucky because I don't actually have
one, I have all of you . . . I would absolutely take
your diaphragm out if I had to.*

Not you, Ryan.

ACKNOWLEDGEMENTS

This never really seems enough but a thousand thank yous to Rowan Lawton – super agent/enabler/general favourite person. Samesies to Lynne Drew and Thalia Suzuma, thank you for being so patient and so helpful and generally helping this book (and all the others) exist. I can't thank HarperCollins enough – everyone in the UK, everyone in the US and especially everyone in Canada (especially, especially Emma Ingram and Paul Covello who I still owe $30). More thanks to Charlotte and Kasie at Marie Claire – working with you makes me happy.

There are so many people who deserve a thank you-slash-hug-big-drink for keeping me alive during the writing of this book: Della, Jackie, Sarah, Ana Mercedes, Beth, Ryan, Sam, Ilana, Rachael and, good God, loads more people. I'll thank you in person with booze. People I can't thank but were also important include The National, Camera Obscura, The Muppets, the cast of Breaking Bad and WWE Superstar, CM Punk. Long story.

Last but not least, I want to thank all Twitter buddies

for convincing me I'm not mad when I'm sat in a Vegas hotel room writing a book at four in the morning. Big shout out to #TeamKelk and everyone who has taken the time to say hello. It means a lot.

CHAPTER ONE

'I'm so sorry I'm late,' I babbled as I ran into the *Gloss* magazine office, unbuttoning my top as I pushed the door open with my arse. 'I had a Jenny emergency and lost my shoes and couldn't get a cab, and how come it's so hot today? Oh and my shirt is covered in crap but I think I left a T-shirt here so—'

'Ms Clark.'

My blouse was halfway over my head and my arms were tangled upwards in a dying swan when I heard someone who most certainly was not Delia Spencer say my name. The reason I knew it was not my colleague and friend Delia Spencer was because it was a man's voice. And it was one I had heard before.

'Mr Spencer?' I peeped through a buttonhole to see Delia's grandfather, owner of Spencer Media and ultimately my boss, leaning against Delia's desk with a very grim look on his face. Behind him, Delia sat in her squishy leather chair biting her lip and trying not to laugh. Neither of them seemed terribly impressed by my bra. It wasn't one of my best.

'How lovely to see you,' I said, trying to pull my shirt back down over my head as casually as possible before offering Mr Spencer a handshake and a dazzling smile. 'I'm very sorry.'

'Don't worry about it,' he said. Then he stood up, ignoring my hand, and walked straight into our tiny meeting room. 'I understand you had an emergency and are covered in crap.'

'And I lost my shoes,' I whispered to Delia with a wince.

'Happy Monday,' she whispered back, following her grandfather into the meeting room. 'Jenny emergency? What threat level are we on there?'

'Orange? Maybe even a lovely reddish coral. She's losing it. I had to intervene.'

'As long as she's OK now,' Delia gave me a sympathetic look and opened the door to the meeting room. 'There's a spare sweater on my chair. It doesn't have any crap on it.'

Delia had enjoyed my BFF, Jenny's downward spiral as much as anyone over the last few months. It had been six months since she'd broken up with her ex-ex and since then she'd been doing a fine job of ruining her life. That or she was auditioning for a role on the next *Jersey Shore*. I hoped that was it, she was definitely going to need a new job soon if she didn't sort herself out.

'Perfect,' I muttered to myself, hurriedly changing shirts and checking out my blouse for permanent damage. 'No good deed goes unpunished.'

'So the launch phase will take place in Q three so we can be out for fashion week, with *Gloss* on limited availability in New York,' I said, as confidently as I could. Out of the corner of my eye, I could see Delia nodding confirmation. Directly in front of me, Mr Spencer, my boss, formerly known as Bob, was not nodding. He was sipping coffee and fixing me with a gaze so steely I was fairly certain it could cut through a tin can. I concealed a tiny squeak and clicked onto the final slide of my PowerPoint presentation. Oh yes, I was a PowerPoint person now. 'Once we're out there and have established a solid audience, we'll launch on the West Coast in Q four, and then, Q one, we go nationwide with a long-term view to international expansion in Q three the following year.'

I was incredibly proud of myself. After a less than promising beginning, I'd got through all my slides without cocking up and I hadn't spilled a single thing down Delia's jumper. Things were looking up. Now all we needed was Mr Spencer's go-ahead and we were quite literally in business. I attempted my best *Wheel of Fortune* pose in front of the drop-down screen and gave my audience of two a dazzling smile. I was ninety-nine percent certain I looked deranged, but still, Bob was pulling his concentrated face and Delia hadn't kicked me yet, so I took that as a win.

'Interesting,' Mr Spencer said. 'Very interesting.'

Once upon a time, Mr Spencer and I had been best buds – he had brunched with me at Pastis, offered me dream jobs in Paris. We were total besties – but then I might or might not have accidentally called his granddaughter and Delia's identical twin sister, Cici, several very colourful and slightly unflattering names in an email and, well, punched her in the face at Christmas. After that, we sort of drifted apart. He'd given Delia and me a chance to get *Gloss* going, we had a small office in the Spencer Media building and some office equipment, and he had reluctantly agreed to support my visa application, but that was where it ended. There was no free ride in the Spencer family. Not if you saddled yourself with a foul-mouthed British girl who knocked out a member of your family at a Christmas party while dressed like a slutty Santa. It was a long story, but Cici totally had it coming. Delia agreed. Often. I didn't have a sister but if I did, I'd want one like Delia. Kind, thoughtful and cleverer than anyone who had ever been on *The Apprentice*. I did not want one like Cici. She was the Ursula to her Ariel, the coffee cream to her hazelnut whirl. Pure evil. But she was out of the picture. At least she hadn't actively tried to ruin my life for the last couple of months so that was nice. It was just as well, I had been busy.

At last, we were ready to go. We had a killer dummy issue, we had a business plan that made sense, we had writers on standby, we even had a retailer lined up to distribute for us. We just needed advertisers. And to get advertisers, we had to get Grandpa Bob to include us in the annual Spencer Media sales conference. Delia was convinced it was a lock, but I wasn't so sure. Yes, he'd stayed all the way through our presentation without nipping out to the loo or anything. And he'd only picked up his iPhone once; and there was no way he'd been on it long enough to be playing Fruit Ninja. Unless he was very good. Which he probably was.

'So you have a retailer on board?' he asked Delia.

'*Trinity*,' she confirmed. 'As you know, the second largest women's fashion retailer in the US.'

'And you'll be distributing through them directly?' he asked Delia again.

'We will,' she nodded.

'And is she actually barefoot?' He cocked his head in my direction.

Ohhhh.

'She is,' Delia confirmed. 'But she's also a very good writer, a fantastic creative planner and an absolute asset to your company.'

I tried not to blush. Shucks.

'Even if she is a little eccentric.'

I couldn't really argue with that. Even if it did take the edge off her original compliment.

'I know I'm going to regret asking,' Bob said finally, turning to face me, 'but what did happen to your shoes?'

'Well, I was at my friend Jenny's house –' As soon as I opened my mouth I knew I wasn't going to be able to stop – 'and I'd been borrowing her shoes, but she was just a big drunken weeping mess and she made me take them off—'

'You don't have shoes of your own?' Bob interrupted. 'I don't follow . . .'

'Maybe if we just deal with questions about the magazine right now?' Delia suggested. 'And let Angela's shoe situation resolve itself. Do you have any questions about the business plan?'

Bob looked at Delia, at me, and then his phone. 'No. It was very clear and concise.'

Delia beamed. 'Any questions about the creative?'

'None at all. You know more about that market than I do.'

'So any questions at all?' She straightened the collar on her sky-blue shirtdress. 'Now's the time to ask them, Grandpa.'

The stately, grey-haired media magnate leaned forward and rested his elbows on our glass conference table. 'In all honesty, Delia, I just really want to know why she isn't wearing shoes.'

Delia sat back, rubbed her forehead and gave me a quick, sharp nod.

'So . . .'

'That wasn't scary at all,' I said, spinning round and round in my office chair after Bob had left the office. 'What are we going to do?'

'It's fine.' Delia stretched her yoga-toned arms high above her head. 'He's going to say yes. There's no reason for him not to. I have a good feeling.'

'I'm glad someone has,' I said grimly. I didn't have any good feelings. I only felt like I had dirty feet and a craving for bacon. 'Then why didn't he just say yes?'

'Don't panic, Angela – I know my grandpa,' she said. Her confidence was somewhat reassuring. 'He never says yes on the spot. He likes to think about things, weigh up his options, but we've given him every reason to say yes. Besides, I know he wants me on the magazine side of the business. It's not like Cici is proving herself heir apparent to the business when he retires.'

Despite a lifelong ambition to work in publishing, Delia had avoided Spencer Media until we started working on *Gloss* due to her batshit mental sister already working at *The Look* magazine. But while Cici's ambitions only reached as far as stealing from the fashion cupboard and ruining the lives of British freelancers (*cough* – me – *cough*), Delia actually wanted to succeed. On the surface she was a blonde,

Upper-East-Side WASP princess, but underneath she was a fiercely ambitious uber-genius. She was basically Serena van der Woodsen with the brain of Rupert Murdoch, and she had enough self-confidence to make Lady Gaga look like she was a bit down on herself. God help anyone who got in her way.

'I just can't cope with the idea of this not working out.' I laid my head on the cool desk and peered at my iPhone. Ooh, some peas needed harvesting in my Smurf Village. 'If he doesn't go for it, then the last six months have been for nothing.'

'Not going to happen,' Delia said, enunciating each word with a clarity and confidence I couldn't even try to feel. 'Look, why don't you take the afternoon off? There's really nothing we can do now until he gets back to us.'

'I was going to try to talk to Mary about some new features ideas,' I said, twisting the emerald ring around my finger. Mary Stein, once we were officially off the ground, was going to be our editor. I was sort of surprised she'd agreed to it if I was being entirely honest. Mary and I had worked together on my blog when I'd moved to New York and I'd been nothing but trouble but I had a feeling she was itching to get off the blog and back onto a real magazine. That said, until we had full funding, she was still working on *TheLook.com*, but she made plenty of time to bitch out my ideas as often as possible. I loved her dearly. 'And I could do with looking at the website plans again.'

Delia smiled at me across the office. 'Do you realize you always do that when you're nervous about something? Twist your engagement ring?'

'I do?' I looked down at my diamond and emerald

sparkler and felt my frown turn upside down. 'I hadn't noticed.'

'It's cute,' she grinned. 'When you're stressed, that calms you down. Bodes well for the future, doesn't it?'

'I suppose.' It was a nice thought. 'I'm probably just terrified of losing it, though.'

'Speaking of engagement rings, I have something for you.' She pulled a thick glossy magazine out from her beautiful Hermès Birkin and tossed it across to my desk. It landed with a pleasing thud and spilled open on a page full of amazing wedding dresses.

'What is this?' I said, turning to the front cover. 'How do I not have this? I have all the magazines.' I did. There were so many stacks of glossies in my apartment, I'd started using them as coffee tables. It was all part of my wedding-planning procrastination. If I had the magazines, at least I was sort of trying.

'It's actually British,' Delia explained. 'I wore some of the designer's pieces when she did regular couture, but now she's doing bridal. They're amazing. I put a Post-it on the page you should look at.'

Regular couture. As if there were such a thing. I opened the magazine randomly to a painfully beautiful spread of painfully beautiful models wearing painfully beautiful wedding dresses. I ran my fingers over the glossy paper and tried to pretend I wasn't barefoot and wearing a borrowed jumper because I'd effed-up one shirt already today. How was I ever going to manage in a wedding dress?

'I marked the page with her dresses. Let me know if you want to talk to her – I'm sure she'd love to help.' Delia's eyes were bright and shining. It warmed my heart a little bit to remember that people could be lovely sometimes, especially after the morning I'd had. 'And if you need any help with a venue, just say. I have so many contacts. Although I'm sure you're fine. But really, just say the word.'

'I will,' I said, wiping some melting mascara away from under my eyes and added 'wedding venue' to the never-ending list of things I needed to worry about at some point in the future. Then delved right back into the bridal porn. Oh, the gloves . . . The vintage lace elbow-length gloves . . . 'We haven't got anywhere with planning yet. So far, all I know is what we don't want.'

'Which is?'

I couldn't tear my eyes away from the pretty pictures. 'Agadoo. Any sort of live animal. Our parents.'

'I don't know what an "Agadoo" is. I'm with you on the live animals, but I really don't know how you're going to get away with leaving your folks out of the proceedings.'

'Well, if I never tell them, they'll never know,' I pouted. 'Sometimes I think we should have got married in Vegas.'

'You know you don't mean that,' Delia said with a shudder. 'Vegas weddings are very 2008. How is Alex?'

'Recording.' I gave her a small smile. 'Always recording.'

Everyone I met thought it was super-cool to be engaged to a boy in a band. They saw nothing but gallons of champagne, midnight rock-and-roll adventures and sweaty on-stage serenades. The reality was far less romantic. We were more cider than champers, and the

9

most adventurous I got pre-dawn was deciding whether or not I could be bothered to get up for a wee in the night. And as for the sweaty serenades, well, I couldn't lie. There was something wonderful about hearing a song written just for you; but the actual process of pulling that song out of Alex's head and recording it so thousands of other girls could pretend it was written just for them was an incredibly painful process.

At the beginning of January, a glazed look had come into Alex's eyes and overnight he'd turned into a nocturnal creature. From the first deep freeze of the winter until the frost broke and the sun started shining in April, he'd been working on songs all night long and sleeping through the daylight hours. All of them. Now it was May and he was still at it. Every evening he'd emerge from the bedroom, confused and dishevelled, as the sun went down, only managing to focus when he picked up a guitar, a cup of coffee or the keys to the studio. It had been cute at first, but after the third time I'd had to take the rubbish out by myself, I'd been forced to slap him round the back of the head.

'Seriously, go home,' Delia commanded. 'I'm ordering you to take the afternoon off. Go home, see your fiancé, read your wedding magazines. And don't come back until you've got a colour scheme.'

'A colour scheme?'

'Go!' she ordered. 'You did really great this morning. You showed my grandpa your bra, you gave a very convincing PowerPoint presentation barefoot, and you handled an international Jenny Lopez crisis all before lunch. You get the afternoon off.'

When she put it like that, it did seem fairly reasonable.

*   *   *

10

The apartment was silent when I got home. Even though I'd been given the afternoon off by my kind of partner, kind of boss, I still felt like I had won something. Was there any better feeling than being at home when you were supposed to be in the office?

'Hello?' I called out, only to hear my voice echo back at me. No answer from Alex. Our place wasn't huge, but it was airy – floor-to-ceiling windows, open-plan rooms, wooden floors. It would be beautiful if it weren't such a shit-tip. There were takeout boxes everywhere, piles of magazines doubling as coffee tables and half-full, half-empty glasses resting on every surface. We were animals.

The answerphone flashed two messages which I purposely ignored; instead I went to wash my poor feet. The only people on earth who called the landline were my mother, because she was scared Skype was going to steal her soul, and telemarketers, because they had no soul to begin with. I was in the mood for neither.

Feet de-hobbited, I looked around the living room. The place really was a mess. When all I'd had to do in this world was write a blog, there had been hours upon hours to spend horizontal on the sofa, occasionally cleaning and watching the world go by. I'd spent days wandering through the city, dreaming about my next adventure, lost countless weekends on the Lower East Side with Jenny and our friend, Erin, and one too many cocktails. Now, with a few sacred spare hours, I was trying to shake the obligation to do the dishes while Erin sat at home with swollen ankles and Jenny, who had been dumped twice by the love of her life, was going off the rails faster than an underage *X Factor* contestant. I stared out of the

11

window in the general direction of her apartment, wondering if she'd made it into the office. The Empire State Building winked back at me in the sunlight. It was such a tease.

A loud yawn emanating from the bedroom made me jump. Alex was home. I turned the AC all the way up and turned my back on the dishes. It was hot already, too hot for late spring, and all I wanted to do was hop into bed beside Alex and snuggle up under a blanket, but it was hard to snuggle under a blanket when you were sweating like a horse. Opening the bedroom door slowly and quietly, I smiled at the sight of my comatose boyfriend sprawled flat on his back, right across the bed. His dark hair slipped off his forehead as he stirred and his pale skin looked practically translucent from his self-enforced seclusion. The T-shirt he had passed out in had twisted up around his body, and his legs were caught up in our crisp white sheets. It was adorable. And hot. The good kind of hot.

Part of me really didn't want to wake him. He looked so peaceful, and it was nice just to take two minutes out to stare at him without making him feel uncomfortable or making me feel like a pervert. Unfortunately, I was a clumsy cow who could only take off a pencil skirt by twisting the fastening round to the front, and sometimes, when that pencil skirt is stuck to your skin, twisting it round to the front is harder than you'd think. After wrestling with the hook and eye for too many seconds, I yanked it as hard as I could and triumphantly knocked myself right into the nightstand. My lotions and potions scattered and rolled around the room, crashing and clattering as they went. I froze, clutching the table and waiting for my pot of Crème de la Mer, a Christmas gift from Erin, to come to a silent standstill by the wardrobe.

'Morning, Angela,' Alex muttered without moving.

This was the problem with wearing lady clothes, as I had discovered. Taking them on and off again was hazardous to my health.

The bed was cool and the sheets were soft as I crawled in beside Alex. For a skinny boy, he was a great cuddle buddy. Broad shoulders and strong arms opened up and wrapped me up inside them as I sank into the bed.

'Hey.' He pressed his lips against my hair and yawned again. 'You're in bed.'

'I took the afternoon off,' I replied, pressing backwards against him, shivering with a happy. 'Thought it might be nice to see your face.'

'My face likes your face,' he whispered. 'Wait, it's the afternoon?'

Bless his sleepy, confused heart.

'You didn't come to bed until five a.m.,' I pointed out. 'So I suppose technically it's still the middle of the night to you.'

'You had a meeting today,' he murmured, reaching for my hand and entwining his fingers through mine. 'How'd it go?'

'I honestly don't know,' I admitted. One of the terms of our engagement was full disclosure at all times, which I had a feeling Alex was starting to regret. 'Delia says it will be OK, though. How's the record going?'

Alex fumbled for an iPod resting on the nightstand on his side of the bed and pressed it into my hand. 'Done.'

I rolled over quickly and kissed him square on the

13

lips. 'That's amazing!' I said, kissing him again. Because I could. 'You're really all finished?'

'You know I wouldn't let you listen to it if I wasn't,' he replied. 'I'm done.'

'Well done you.' I pushed my far-too-long-and-desperately-in-need-of-a-trim hair out of my eyes to get a better look at him. So pretty. 'I've missed you. What happens now?'

'Now I sleep,' he said, planting a kiss on the tip of my nose. 'For a really long time.'

'Sounds fair.' I helped myself to one more kiss. Delicious. 'And what happens after that?'

I really hoped he wasn't going to say touring, because I was very concerned I would be forced to tie him to the bed and never let him leave. No one brought out my inner crazy like that man.

'I was thinking . . .' His bright green eyes flickered open and the lazy smile I'd heard in his words found its way to his lips. I was such a smitten kitten. 'I might marry my girl.'

I pressed my forehead against his, completely incapable of keeping the biggest, brightest smile ever from my face. 'Well, that sounds nice,' I said. 'Do you have any sort of plan for that?'

Alex kicked the covers away to wrap his bare legs around mine and drew me closer. 'I have been putting a lot of thought into the honeymoon,' he said, rolling over until his warm body covered mine. This was the kind of hot and sweaty I was perfectly OK with. 'There's some stuff I kinda need to test out.'

It had been so long since we had used our bed for anything other than sleeping, snacking and the occasional *True Blood* marathon that I felt a mild panic come over me. I couldn't actually remember the last time we'd both been conscious and coital. I was so nervous, it was like the first time all over again. I was holding my breath and second-guessing my touches, but as I gave myself over to the melting feeling in my chest and the tingling in my lips, I forgot that it was daylight outside, I forgot that my underwear didn't match, and suddenly, without even trying, it was like the first time all over again.

Amazing.

CHAPTER TWO

I was half awake and completely naked when I heard my phone buzzing in my bag from the living room a couple of hours later. Alex had slipped back into unconsciousness – I chose to believe that my supreme sexual prowess had knocked him out – and so, nosy old mare that I am, I rolled out of bed and into my pants, grabbed my phone and crawled into the kitchen to avoid flashing the neighbours.

Naturally the phone stopped ringing as soon as it was in my sweaty paws, but straightaway I saw a terrifying number of messages and missed calls from Louisa, my oldest, dearest friend in the UK. I swiped my phone screen to open them, refusing to entertain all the horrible thoughts that were running through my head. Of course someone had died while I was at home blowing out work for an afternoon quickie; what else could possibly have happened? Louisa's texts didn't really give me a lot of information, just repeated the demand that I call her as soon as I could, and that only worried me more. Louisa and I Skyped once a week as well as texted as often as her baby schedule would allow, and I knew I hadn't missed a phone date. Since she had given birth to Grace a couple of months ago, we hadn't been quite as chatty as normal, so seven 'call me now' texts at what had to be ten-ish in the evening UK-time couldn't be good news. I fannied about with my iPhone contacts, trying to get it to call her back, but was cut off by an incoming call.

From my mother.

Someone was definitely dead.

Or someone was about to be.

With a very unpleasant feeling in my stomach, I reluctantly answered the phone.

'Mum?' I grabbed a tea towel from the kitchen counter and wrapped it around my chest. It just didn't seem right to be topless while on the phone to my mother. Thank goodness I'd put on pants. 'Is everything OK?'

The last time she'd put in an impromptu call was when my dad was in hospital after enjoying a recreational batch of space cakes at my auntie's house. Ever since, I'd been waiting for the call to say he was leaving her for the milkman or that he had defaulted on the mortgage to fund his crack habit. It was impossible to say which was more likely.

'Angela Clark, do you have something to tell me?'

The quiet fury in my mother's voice suggested that my dad wasn't in trouble but that I certainly was. And I was almost certain I knew why. Louisa's texts suddenly made a terrifying kind of sense as I put two and two together to come up with a big fat shiny emerald-coloured four.

'Um, I don't think so?' I answered sweetly. Because playing dumb had worked so well when I'd 'borrowed' her car in the middle of the night when I was eighteen,

17

only to return it with three exciting new dents. I thought they added character. She thought they added to the insurance premium.

'Are you or are you not –' she paused and took a very deep, very dramatic breath – 'engaged to that musician?'

Sodding bollocky bollocks.

It wasn't like I'd planned on keeping my engagement a secret from my parents, but circumstances had conspired against me. And by circumstances, of course I meant stone cold terror. I'd called on Christmas Day to deliver the happy news, but my mum had been so mad that I hadn't come home for dry turkey and seething resentment, and so mad that I was choosing to stay in 'that country' with 'that musician', that I couldn't seem to find the right way to tell her I had just accepted a proposal from 'that musician' to stay in 'that country' for the foreseeable. Then, as the weeks passed by, the more I replayed the conversation over in my mind, the less I felt like casually mentioning my betrothal.

'Am I engaged?'

'Yes.'

'To Alex?'

'Yes Angela. To Alex. Or at least one hopes so.'

She used the special voice to pronounce my fiance's name that she usually saved to refer to Sandra next door and Eamonn Holmes. And she hated Sandra next door and Eamonn Holmes.

'Well, at least I'm not going to end up a barren spinster.' Yes, dangling a grandchild-shaped carrot in front of her was a low blow, but needs must when the devil shits in your teapot. 'Surely?'

'Oh dear God, Angela, are you pregnant?' she

18

shrieked directly into the receiver before bellowing at the top of her voice in the other direction, 'David! She's pregnant!'

'I'm not pregnant,' I said, resting my head on my knees. I might be sitting half-naked on a dirty kitchen floor with a slightly grubby tea towel over my boobs, but I wasn't pregnant. As far as I knew. 'Seriously.'

'Oh Lord, I should have known,' she wittered on regardless. 'Moving in with that musician, never calling, never visiting. How far gone are you?'

'I'm not pregnant,' I repeated with as much conviction as I could muster while simultaneously trying to remember if I had taken my pill that morning. 'Mum, I'm not.'

'How far gone is she?' I heard my dad puffing his way down to the bottom of the stairs. 'Is it that musician's? Is that why she's engaged?'

'Oh, for God's sake.' Even though they couldn't see me, I couldn't resist an eye roll and emphatic wave of the hand. 'I'm genuinely not pregnant. Alex did not propose because I'm up the stick. To the best of my knowledge, it's because he actually wants to marry me.'

'Right,' she replied with a very subtle scoffing tone. 'Thanks, Mum.'

'Shall I book a flight? Do I need to go and get her?' Dad was practically out the door already. 'I'll have to go to the post office and get some dollars.'

'The post office,' Mum seethed. Another of her arch enemies. 'Go back upstairs. She says she's not pregnant.'

'She'd better bloody not be,' he said, just loud enough for me to hear. 'She's not too old to go over my knee. That musician of hers as well.'

19

I fought the urge to remind him I'd only gone 'over his knee' once, when I was five and had purposely gone into his room, walked into the garden and thrown his best leather driving gloves into the pond so we wouldn't have to go to my aunt Sheila's. I was a petulant little madam. But he had apologized when I was twenty-five and told me I was right to have done it because my aunt Sheila was a – quote-unquote – right pain in the arse.

'I can't imagine why else you would think the best way for a mother to find out her daughter is engaged – to a musician, no less – that she has never met and who lives ten thousand miles away is to hear it from the village gossip on the Waitrose cheese aisle.'

I had to admit she had a point there.

The thing was, ever since my seasonal no-show, the subtle digs at Alex and his choice of profession had become out-and-out abuse. By the end of January she had written him off as Hitler and Mick Jagger's love child. To most people, a musician was someone who played an instrument. To my mother, they had to be a lying, cheating drug addict whose only ambition in life was to knock up her poor, stupid daughter and then leave her destitute in a motel on the side of a highway with an arm full of track marks. It was a bit of a stretch. Alex didn't even like to take Advil for a headache.

'You told Louisa before your own family?'

Oh, Louisa, I thought to myself. Baby or no baby, you are dead.

'Look, I wasn't not telling you,' I said, deciding to take a different tack. And to get off the kitchen floor because my bum was completely numb. 'I just didn't want to tell you over the phone. It didn't seem right.'

Check me out – the dutiful daughter. For a

spur-of-the-moment excuse, I thought it was pretty good. I tiptoed over to the sofa and replaced the tea towel with a blanket. Very chic.

'Well, that's probably because it isn't right,' she said, still sounding grumpy, but I had a feeling I wasn't going to be disinherited. This time. 'We haven't even met this Alex character. It's not right.'

'He's not a character, he's a person.' I took a deep breath, imagining the cold day in hell when Alex would sit down for afternoon tea with my mum and dad. 'And you will meet him and you'll love him.'

'When?'

Oh cock.

'Soon?' I managed to make the word so high-pitched I swear the dogs next door started whining.

'Bring him home for my birthday.'

And it wasn't a question.

'We're having a bit of a do – nothing fancy, just something in the garden for the family,' she went on. 'And I want you there. And if he thinks he's going to be part of this family, he'd better be there too.'

I put my mum on speakerphone and opened my calendar. Her birthday was in three weeks. Three very short, very unavoidable weeks. It wasn't that I had forgotten, it's just that until Facebook reminds me someone has been born, it just doesn't register.

'It's a bit soon, Mum,' I said slowly. 'And the flights will be expensive . . .'

'Your dad and I will pay.'

There was blood in the water, and Annette Clark never gave up until she got her kill.

'For both of you. As an engagement present.'

'Right.' I felt very, very sick. Home. London. England. Mark. Everything I'd left behind.

'And you'll stay here.' She was really enjoying herself now. 'With your dad and me. Oh, Angela, you've made my birthday. David, get on Expedia, she's coming home!'

And at that moment, I knew two things only. The first was that I was going to kill Louisa. The second was that I was going to have to go to London.

'I didn't tell her,' Louisa whined into the phone as I hopped into a cab the next morning. The subway was down and I was already late for the office, having spent most of the previous evening drinking home-made margaritas while Alex stroked my hair and tried to talk me off the ledge. 'It was Tim. It was a mistake.'

'How did Tim manage to tell my mother I'm engaged?' I fumbled in my satchel for a pair of sunglasses. The sun was too bright and my hangover was too sharp. 'Is this because I broke his hand?'

Which I did. Almost accidentally. On their wedding day. I wasn't sure if he'd forgiven me in the two years since I'd fled.

'No.' Louisa sounded tired. I had heard that was one of the side effects of having a baby, and according to my mother I'd know all about that. 'He was in the supermarket and Mark's mum was in there and going on about how Mark was going to New York for some conference—'

'Mark?' I suddenly felt very sweaty. And sick. And violent. '*Mark* Mark?'

'Yes, Angela, Mark. You do recall? You were engaged to him for a million years?'

'So Mark then?' I said. 'I just wanted to clarify that we were talking about the same scumbag.'

'Yes, Mark.' The word had lost all meaning. 'So he

was supposed to be going to New York for this conference because he's just so important, and obviously Tim mentioned you were in New York, and obviously she couldn't help having a dig, and so he casually dropped in that you were engaged. He didn't mean to, honestly, and he had no idea she'd tell your mum. I mean, he didn't know your mum was in there as well, did he?'

'My mum is always in the supermarket,' I replied, watching Williamsburg rush by, giving way to the Polish shop signs of Greenpoint and assorted acid-washed denim ensembles. 'She lives and dies for Waitrose. I'm amazed they haven't given her a job yet.'

'Well, I just wanted you to know it wasn't on purpose. Really, he was trying to do you a favour,' Louisa bellowed over the *Top Gear* theme tune. 'He's totally Team Angela.'

'But getting back to the important things, Mark is coming to New York?' I didn't need to see my reflection to know I had no colour left in my face. 'When? Why?'

'I don't know,' Louisa sighed. 'He didn't get the details. He is only a man, babe. And you know they don't talk at all any more. It's not like you're going to bump into him, though, is it?'

'No.' I breathed out hard. My ex in my city. How dare he? Wasn't there a law against cheating ex-boyfriends coming within five thousand miles of you? 'It's just sod's law, isn't it? I'll be walking into work with my skirt tucked into my knickers and he'll just appear.'

'No he won't, don't be silly.' Louisa had a fantastic telling-off voice already. She was going to be a great mother. 'And even if he did, you'd just walk straight past him with your head held high.'

23

'Or scream like a banshee and kick him in the bollocks?' I suggested.

'Sounds perfectly reasonable to me,' she replied. 'God knows, I've thought about it.'

'It's a good job he cheated on me before I discovered my violent side,' I said, not even slightly meaning it. 'Louisa, why on earth are you watching *Top Gear* on a Tuesday afternoon?'

Louisa's voice strained as she hoisted up something heavy. I assumed it was the baby. 'I'm sorry, it's the only thing that stops her crying. I sometimes wonder what I'm raising.'

'A tiny female Jeremy Clarkson?' I shuddered. The idea of Louisa having a baby terrified me, let alone the idea of a baby that could only be placated by watching grown men with bad hair drive a Ford Mondeo into a caravan. 'You should see someone about that.'

'*Top Gear* and *The Only Way Is Essex*,' she sighed. 'Three months old and she's already a fake-tanned boy racer with a vajazzle.'

'I don't understand at least half of what you just said,' I remonstrated. The shop fronts slid into warehouses and the warehouses into the expressway before I finally saw the bridge and my beloved Manhattan in front of me. My blood pressure dropped just enough to make me sure I wasn't going to die in the car. Good news – they charged fifty dollars if you puked; I had no idea how much a stroke would set me back. 'And I don't think I want to.'

Louisa laughed. Which made the baby cry. Which made Louisa sob.

'Well, I know it's selfish, but I can't wait to see you,' she said. 'It's time you met this little girl of mine. It's been too long, Clark.'

24

'I know, I want to see her face.' I traced the Empire State Building against the window as we hurtled over the bridge. 'I just feel so weird about coming back.'

'That's natural,' she shouted. 'It's been a while, but, you know, you've got your visa now, you've got Alex – it's not like they're going to hold you at customs and never let you go.'

'Yes, I have Alex now, but he hasn't met my mum yet,' I replied grimly. 'And there's every chance my dad is going to tie me up with a hosepipe and lock me in the shed.'

'Yeah, he might do that,' she admitted. 'Or I might. I miss you so much.'

'I miss you too,' I said, feeling incredibly guilty for not meaning it nearly enough.

I did miss Louisa, I really did, but I missed the old Louisa. I missed our Friday-night wine dates and calling her during *Downton Abbey* to get a running commentary on the episodes that hadn't aired in America yet. No one took apart a period drama like Louisa. But things had changed. She had an actual live baby, and the way life raced around me now, it was hard to find five minutes to really indulge in a good sulk about days gone by. Between work, not planning the wedding, trying to stop Jenny from drinking New York dry and attempting to dress like a grown-up every day, I struggled to find time to miss anything other than sleep.

And I definitely wasn't in a baby place. I couldn't even see the baby place from where I was. Now that Louisa had Grace, things felt a bit strained. Sometimes she was all we talked about. Of course I knew it was the most important thing that had ever happened to her, but I felt stupid complaining about being a bit

25

hungover and the cost of handbags when Louisa now had to keep a tiny human being alive. I couldn't even look after a handbag, I thought, stroking my beloved and nigh on destroyed Marc Jacobs satchel with every ounce of tenderness I would show my firstborn child. Which, as far as I was concerned, it was.

'It'll be fine, you know,' Louisa promised. 'Obviously your mum's going to be an arse for the first couple of days, but your dad will be so happy to see you. And I want you to meet Grace. And I want to meet Alex. Honestly, Ange, it'll be great.'

'I suppose,' I said, trying to adopt her positive attitude. 'It's just been so long, you know? I feel like it'll be weird. Things are so different.'

'No they aren't,' she argued. 'Bruce is still doing *Strictly*, everyone's still obsessed with Percy Pigs and the world still stops for *X Factor*. Things are, in fact, exactly the same.'

I smiled. She was trying. And it didn't really make a lot of difference. I was going whether I liked it or not.

'It's not just that, though – there's work as well,' I said. Hopefully there was work. We still hadn't heard back from Bob. 'I'm working twelve hours a day. I don't know how I'm just supposed to take a week off.'

'People manage,' Lou replied. 'And you bloody should take some time off. It's not healthy to work as hard as you have been.'

I didn't like to say it might not be healthy but it was entirely necessary. When she had told me she was thinking about packing in work to be a full-time mum, I couldn't speak to her for a week. Not because I didn't agree with it as an option; it was just so far removed from the Louisa I knew. My career was important to me, but she was keen to tell me I couldn't possibly understand anything 'until I had a baby'. Grr.

'Do you promise to make me lots and lots of tea?' I asked solemnly.

'I do,' she replied with equal gravity.

'And to be nice to Alex?'

'You'll be lucky if I don't try to run off with him.'

'And that you'll be my alibi in case I accidentally murder my mother?'

'I'll do it for you,' she swore. 'Just get your arse home, Clark. There's a chav-obsessed shit machine here that's desperate for your influence.'

'I'm pretty sure you should stick with Grace,' I suggested. 'It's much more flattering.'

'Just get on a plane and call me as soon as you land,' Louisa replied. 'I'll pick you up from the airport.'

'Yes, you bloody will,' I said. 'Yes, you bloody well will.'

CHAPTER THREE

Tuesday and Wednesday were no better than Monday. No word from Mr Spencer on *Gloss*. No word from Jenny from the dubious liaison that had led to last week's meltdown. Lots of word from my mother on times and dates of flights back to the UK. Finally, after a very long day of spreadsheets and feature ideas and willing the phone to ring with good news from Bob, I fell through the door sometime after nine and noticed right away that all the lights were out. No Alex.

I buried my disappointment in a hastily downed glass of white and went to run a bath, shedding my Splendid T-shirt dress and French Sole flats as I went. While the bath filled with lovely lemon-and-sage-scented Bliss bubbles, I pulled my hair back from my face, scrubbed away the day and stared at myself in the mirror. It was two years since this face had been in England. Two years since I'd walked in on my fiancé shagging his mistress in the back of our car. Two years since I'd cried myself to sleep in a hotel room. Two years since I'd jumped on a flight away from it all and found myself here. Home. I frowned. Was I allowed to call New York home? I mean, I had grown up in England – my family was there, my GCSE certificates and *Buffy* DVDs were there. *Come Dine with Me* was there. Didn't home mean family and familiarity and M&S?

I washed my face, hoping to uncover a happier expression, but just uncovered a couple of fine lines around my eyes and a hint of sunburn across my cheeks. Hmm. Running my fingers lightly over my skin, I stared myself out, looking for something new. Same blue eyes, same cheekbones, same hair, if a little longer and blonder. Same Angela. But still not a flicker. For the want of an answer that would settle the butterflies in my stomach, I got into the tub. There were so few things you could rely on in life, but bubble baths, kittens and a quick game of Buckaroo were three things that would never let you down. Sadly, we were kittenless and there was no one home to play Buckaroo with.

Deep in the warm, soapy water, I closed my eyes and rested my toes on the taps. Heaven. Nothing could go wrong when you were in the bath. Until the day they invented waterproof iPhones, anyway. I spun my engagement ring around my finger with my thumb, rhythmically clinking it against the side of the tub. The magazine was good. Yes, we needed to get Bob's blessing, but like Delia said, there was no reason why we wouldn't. OK, so Jenny had gone slightly mad, but who could blame her? She would be fine when she'd had some time and I'd be there for her. And I was engaged. I was engaged, for real, to someone I loved. Someone who loved me. That was a pretty good thing. And as for going back to England, well. Hmm. I screwed up my face and sighed, eyes tightly closed.

'Man, what is that face for?'

I jumped a mile out of my skin, splashing white, frothy bubbles all over the bathroom floor and slipping back under the water in surprise.

'Alex,' I gasped, re-emerging with wet hair and a considerably shortened lifespan. 'I didn't hear you come in.'

'I'm not surprised.' My fiancé stretched in the doorway and peeled off his leather jacket, throwing it on the floor on top of my dress. We were a right pair of scruffy bastards. Thank God we had found each other. 'You looked like you were trying to solve one of life's great mysteries. Were you trying to work out what I Can't Believe it's Not Butter is made from again?'

'That was only once,' I grumbled, adjusting my bubble coverage. 'And you admitted you didn't know either.'

'No, I admitted I didn't care.' He corrected me with a smile and folded himself into a sitting position beside the bath. 'So what's up? Tough day at the office?'

'Actually no.' I leaned my head over to accept my hello kiss and resisted the urge to splash him. It was a very strong urge. 'Still just waiting to hear if Bob's going to let Delia present at the advertisers' thing. It's next month, I think, so he's going to have to make his mind up fairly quickly.'

'He's gonna say yes,' Alex assured me with a gentle stroke of my hair. 'You guys have put so much work in. He would be crazy to turn it down.'

'I know,' I purred. Stroking was nice. 'I just want it confirmed, you know?'

'I do know,' he nodded. 'So what was that face all about when I came in?'

Sometimes I hated our full disclosure agreement. Sometimes a girl wanted to sit in the bath and wallow like a mardy, hungry hippo. Now I was going to have to tell him all my ridiculous concerns and let him make me feel better. Stupid, clever, pretty boy.

'Just thinking about this whole going back thing,' I said, wiggling my toes at myself. 'Just stressing myself out.'

'Huh.' He rested his chin on the side of the bath and looked at me with bright green eyes. 'You know you don't have to talk about it if you don't want to, but I feel like it's getting to be a thing. What's up with you and your mom? What's with the big freak-out?'

Now there was a question. I thought about it for a moment, waiting for words to come out of my mouth. But they didn't. For the first time in my entire life.

'I mean, it's not like I don't have parental issues of my own,' Alex went on, filling in the silence for me. 'But you're gonna have to help me out. You don't want to go home or you just don't want to see her?'

'I don't know,' I replied. It didn't help, but it was honest.

'You guys don't get along?'

'We actually used to be all right,' I said, remembering all the Sunday dinners in front of the *EastEnders* omnibus. 'I mean, she's my mum. She's a pain in the arse, but I just – I just feel bad.'

Alex resumed the hair-stroking. 'Because?'

'Because I came here. I left her. And I know that, for all her moaning, she misses me, and I feel guilty. As much as she's a pain in the arse, my mum's always been there for me.' I couldn't help but think about Louisa's wedding. Who else would put you to bed and tell you everything was going to be all right immediately after you'd split up a ten-year relationship, made something of a scene and broken the groom's hand with a stiletto? Only your mother.

'The day you don't feel guilty about your parents will be the day the world stops turning,' Alex said. 'I think going back to visit is a good thing. Maybe it'll remind her you're still here. You're not on the moon, you're just a plane ride away. Maybe she'll stop guilt-tripping you so much.'

'Yeah, maybe.' And maybe I'll wake up to find a bacon sandwich winging its way past the window. Silly Alex. 'It just feels so strange. Like, I won't be welcome.'

'Well, that's dumb,' he laughed, pulling on my pony-tail. 'I didn't want to say anything, but I've already had two emails from Louisa and a Facebook friend request from your dad. They can't wait to see you.'

'Parents really shouldn't be allowed on Facebook,' I said, making a face and trying to smile. 'Please feel free to ignore it. I know they're excited to see me. And I'm excited to see them.'

'But?'

I looked around the bathroom. At the towels on the heated rail, at all my products loaded on the window-sill, at my boyfriend on the floor, and imagined my life for a moment without any of it.

'But I still don't want to go,' I said eventually.

'Because?'

'Because I left,' I said with a deep breath. 'And I'm scared that if I go back home to England, I'll have to give up my home in New York.'

Alex breathed out with a whistle. 'Wow.'

I turned my head to the side to face him properly and did not enjoy his expression.

'You realize that's the dumbest thing you've ever

said?' Alex asked. 'And you know, between you and me, you've said some pretty dumb shit over the years. It's not an either/or sitch.'

'I know,' I whined, dropping my toes back into the bath and flipping the bubbles around my feet. 'But you don't get it. When I came here, everything changed. I met Jenny, I started writing, I met you. I changed. I didn't like myself before. Before, I would just sit in my pyjamas and watch *Sex and the City* and wait for something to happen.'

'Angela, what did you do last night?'

'I sat on the settee in my pyjamas and watched *Sex and the City*, but that's not the point,' I replied. 'It's different. I'm different.'

'I do get what you're saying,' he started carefully, choosing his words, presumably to minimize the chances that I would pull him face first into the bath. He was treading a very fine line. 'But just listen to what you're saying. You are different now. Even if you get back and they're all the same. I know things weren't awesome for you before you moved here – people don't usually get on a plane and move to another country without notice if they're super happy with life – but what you have here, what you've achieved, no one can take away from you.'

I bit my lip and nodded.

'No one can take me away from you.' He reached into the bath water and pulled out my left hand, holding my ring up to the light. 'And no one is going to take you away from me.'

I felt myself blush from head to toe. Sometimes I still didn't quite believe it.

'We're going to go to London, you're gonna show everyone this ring, and I'm gonna knock your mom's socks off. By the time I'm done, she's going to love me so much, she'll be pushing you back on that plane. Back to New York, back to the magazine, back to all your friends and, like it or not, I'm going to marry your ass.'

'Yeah, whatever,' I said, trying to maintain my grumpy face, but it was hard when he was sitting there making sense and being adorable.

'So, list of reasons to be cheerful?' He squeezed my hand tightly. 'You're gonna see your mom and stop beating yourself up. You get to see Louisa and the baby. You get to see me being adorable with a baby. Your magazine is gonna kick ass and we get to go on a trip to London. I think that's pretty cool. I'm excited.'

There were a million good reasons to marry Alex Reid, but one of the best was his ability to talk sense and put a smile on my face when I couldn't see the lovely wood for the shitty trees.

'And if you don't tell me you're excited, I'm going to drag you out of that bath and throw you into the East River,' he declared.

'You're all talk, Reid.' I shuffled further into the bath, further under the bubbles.

'Is that right?' He leapt to his feet, all six-foot-something in skintight jeans and a battered old black T-shirt. 'You're asking for trouble now.'

'Fuck off and put the kettle on,' I yawned. 'I'll be out in a minute.'

'That does it. Get your ass out the bath and put the kettle on yourself.'

Without warning, he leaned over into the bath and picked me up. I reached up and grabbed around his neck instinctively, half the bath water following me out.

'Alex, put me down,' I squealed, dripping wet and completely and utterly naked. 'Put me back in the bath!'

'No way.' He held me tightly, so much stronger than he had any right to be, and ducked my flailing, sodden limbs. 'That's enough sulking in the bath for one day. It's time you made my dinner, woman.'

I couldn't argue for laughing, and, despite slipperiness, couldn't seem to wriggle away, so I let him carry me out of the bathroom, water dripping behind us, and throw me down on the bed.

'So we're agreed?' Alex asked, peeling off his piss-wet T-shirt and tossing it at me. 'You're going to stop being a dumbass?'

'Only if you get that bloody kettle on and clean up the bathroom floor,' I retaliated, finally getting my breath back.

'I knew marrying you was going to be a mistake.' He flipped me his middle finger and walked out of the bedroom. I sat on the bed, holding his T-shirt, then heard the kitchen tap followed by the click of the kettle. I smiled.

Things were probably going to be OK.

Over the next couple of days, due to Alex's enthusiasm and in spite of my mother's, I started to get excited about the idea of going home. In between frantic spreadsheet sessions in the office, I'd find myself fantasizing about sausage rolls or imagining a crazed rampage through the Marks & Spencer lingerie department. No one made knickers like M&S. And the more I thought about it, the more excited I was to take Alex with me. He was going to be my good-luck charm. After all, he was right – I had changed, and it wasn't like I would regress in the space of a couple of days to the same old mousey, housebound Angela whose idea of an exciting night out was a turn round Asda. We would go to London, I would parade him around like the show pony that he was and then we would come home. With enough bags of Monster Munch to warrant the purchase of a new suitcase. Or two.

When Saturday morning rolled around, I finally felt like myself again. There was a bounce in my step and considerably less need for Touche Éclat as I prepared for brunch with the girls. Jenny had been quiet all week, ignoring texts and emails, but according to Erin she'd got her shit together in the office, at least. Every day this week, she'd been on time, awake, seemingly sober and, most importantly of all, appropriately attired. Not only could no one see her underwear, but said underwear was covered by designer clothing befitting a label whore of Jenny's standing. I was relieved. I wasn't ecstatic that she was dodging my calls, but I was happy that she was at least functioning. And as a reward, today we were going to sit down with her in a public place, feed her full of scrambled eggs and suggest she get help moving on from Jeff. And hope she didn't punch me in the face.

I'd chosen a heavily patterned Marc by Marc Jacobs shift dress just in case she decided to launch her Eggs Benedict in my direction and had kept my make-up to a minimum. Nothing that couldn't be patched up while sobbing in a public bathroom. With one last deep breath and a quick practice of my resolved face in the mirror, I kissed a sleeping Alex goodbye and headed out to the train. Before we could stage our Lopez arse-kicking, Sadie and Erin had asked me to meet them all up town for my 'surprise'. I wasn't super-excited, mainly because it added thirty minutes to my journey and that meant thirty minutes' less sleep on a weekend morning. Plus, while I always told people I loved surprises, what I really loved was someone planning a surprise and then me finding out what it was before it happened. I was something of a spoilsport.

The entire week had been warmer than it needed to be and my deodorant was being sorely tested by the time I emerged on 77th and Lex. I was hungry. I was stressed. I was ready for brunch. What I was not ready for was two giddy blondes, one tall and skinny, the other short and round, humming with excitement outside a big, boring corporate building. The second Sadie spotted me, she started leaping up and down and squealing. This, in my experience, was never a good sign. She was either drunk or high or drunk and high, and I wasn't mentally prepared to deal with any of those things without a belly full of bacon. Sadie was Jenny's roommate. My replacement. My six foot, blonde, beautiful, genuinely had her photo taken for money model replacement. But that fact didn't bother me nearly as much as the fact that Jenny wasn't with her.

'Morning,' I frowned, looking to Erin for some sense. I got nothing. Instead I was bundled into a giant hug, made a little difficult by the bump, but this was one hell of a committed hug. 'What are we celebrating? Is Jenny sober?'

'Jenny isn't here yet.' Erin broke the hug and brushed my hair behind my ears. 'But she's on her way.'

'We have to go in before we're late,' Sadie said, giving me a smile so wide and bright I had to take a step back. I hated models. 'I am so freaking excited.'

'Excited about what?' I looked around, trying to

work out what had them so dizzy. If I didn't find something that would stop my stomach from rumbling in the next seven seconds, I would be snatching a bagel out of the hand of the very next passer-by.

'Oh, honey, we have a surprise for you.' Erin took hold of my arm and led me through the doors of the office building and straight into a lift. 'Sadie and I were talking, and we think it's high time you got your mind set on this wedding of yours.'

I didn't know what alarmed me more – the thought of Sadie and Erin having a meeting of minds or the fact that there had apparently been an Angela Clark Wedding Summit without Angela Clark.

'So we decided to hurry you up a little.' Her eyes sparkled brighter than my engagement ring.

'Just to give you a little inspiration.' Sadie dug her hands into her jeans pockets and tossed her honey-coloured ponytail over one shoulder.

The lift doors opened before I could wonder any longer and I was greeted with three words that simultaneously made my heart swell with joy and put the fear of God into my soul. Vera Wang Bridal.

'Oh no,' I whispered.

'Hell yes,' Sadie responded, pushing me out of the lift. 'Now, let's get your ass into a wedding dress.'

And suddenly I was incredibly thankful for the fact I hadn't had breakfast.

Ten minutes later, the three of us were perched on silk-covered clouds, masquerading as overstuffed sofas, in a giant dressing room while a very smiley, very enthusiastic assistant named Charise brought in dress after dress after dress. Except that 'dress' really wasn't an adequate word for anything in front of me. They were frothy concoctions of silk, tulle and the souls of unicorns, sewn together by kittens and carried here by a family of bunnies. They were amazing. They were a fantasy. I sat on my hands to keep from poking them. Didn't seem like the done thing.

'Sorry we kept it a surprise,' Erin whispered in an appropriately reverential tone. 'It was Jenny's idea. We know you've been so crazy busy that you haven't even started thinking about the wedding, so, you know, this just seemed like a good way to kick-start things.'

I nodded slowly. This was the second time in a week someone had tried to 'kick-start' my wedding planning with the lure of pretty dresses. I wondered if Alex's friends were tempting him out of the house with the promise of delicious meals only to bombard him with designer tuxedos. Probably not.

'We are still having brunch though, aren't we?' My priorities were poker straight.

'Believe me, I know how stressful wedding planning is,' Erin said, holding up both hands to emphasize her point while Sadie listened intently. Both ignored my question. 'And these are the fun parts. Honestly, by the day of the wedding, you're going to wish you'd just eloped.'

'I had a friend who got married. She was a model,' Sadie added entirely unnecessarily. All of her friends who weren't in this room were models. 'And she cried the whole time. Everyone thought it was because she was so happy, but it wasn't. She, like, totally freaked out. I had to talk her out of ditching him in the bathroom.'

'Sounds like my first wedding,' Erin agreed. 'I had to watch the video afterwards to actually see what happened. I was just panicking the whole time.'

Thanks to the massive number of mirrors in the dressing room, it wasn't just the girls who had the pleasure of my expression. If my eyebrows could get this high this quickly, I would never need Botox.

'But you'll be fine,' Erin said quickly. 'That's why we need to start planning now. Dresses first, then the venue and the catering, and then you only need to worry about the guest list. And you've got for ever, right? What are you thinking? Next summer? Next autumn?'

I opened my mouth but nothing came out. Guest lists. Venues. Dresses.

'Oh, you need at least eighteen months,' Sadie declared. Unmarried, twenty-three-year-old, single Sadie. 'At least. You won't get any decent venue with less notice than eighteen months.'

'Unless you do a Friday.' Erin shrugged and made a face. 'But you can't do a Friday.'

'Tacky,' Sadie confirmed. 'So what are you thinking?'

And that was the first time since getting engaged that I realized I wasn't just wearing this ring for a laugh. I was actually getting married. I was going to be a bride. I was going to put on a great big dress and mince down an aisle and make promises to Alex in front of lots of people, then eat a painstakingly selected meal that I would endeavour not to spill down one of these incredibly expensive dresses. I was getting married. To a boy. For ever and ever and ever. Gulp.

'Can I get you ladies some champagne?' Charise asked, hanging a fourth dress and glowing in our general direction.

'Yes please,' we answered in unison.

'I'll be right back,' she replied, backing out of the room. Obviously she could tell something was wrong because instead of cooing over the dresses and having a little cry like we should be, we were sitting in stony silence.

'Where is Jenny?' I pulled out my phone and jabbed at the screen. No messages, no missed calls.

'I knew I shouldn't have left without her.' Sadie rubbed her bare arm and frowned. 'But she's been OK the last couple of days and she was excited.'

'And she said she was coming?' Erin asked, dialling Jenny's number, hanging up and dialling again. And again. And again. 'You spoke to her?'

'I knocked on her door, I told her we needed to leave, she stuck her head out.' Sadie paused to reinforce her statement through the medium of mime. 'And said she'd be here, like, ten minutes after us. Now can someone please, for the love of Wang, start trying on dresses?'

'I can't try them on without Jenny here,' I said, reaching out to touch a puff of organza. I prodded it lightly with a fingernail in case it popped and disappeared. 'I can't.'

There was silence in the room while Sadie vibrated with impatience.

'I'll go and get her,' Erin said after a long, lustful look at an ivory satin bodice. 'You get started on the dresses and I'll go and get her.'

'No, don't be stupid.' I jumped to my feet. 'You're the size of seven hippos. I'll go.'

'But you have to try on dresses!' Sadie actually stamped her foot. It was like having a six-foot-two three-year-old in the room throwing a tantrum. 'Someone has to try on a dress.'

'So you try one on for me,' I said, tossing my satchel over my shoulder and heading out of the door. 'I'll be

41

back in fifteen minutes. Twenty tops. Don't drink all the champagne.'

Before Erin could heave herself out of her chair I was up and on my way out of the door, and I didn't breathe again until I felt the sun on my skin. I breathed in and out as deeply as I could as I stuck my arm out for a cab. The bridal salon had a soft, powdery perfume that had started to make me feel sick. It wasn't that I didn't want to try on the dresses. I was only a girl, after all, and what girl could resist wedding dresses? And these weren't just any wedding dresses, they were Wang. These were hardcore, triple-X bridal crack, enough to go to any girl's head. But it was the surprise element that was too much for me. A girl needed to build up to something like this; you couldn't just go in cold on Wang, for God's sake. I needed an hour or so with some magazines, a visit to the Bloomingdale's bridal floor, enough notice to make sure my underwear matched, that kind of thing.

I could still see each of the four dresses Charise had picked out dancing around in my head when I jumped into a taxi and gave them Jenny's address. There was the ivory one with the black ribbon waist that flowed down to the ground like a pile of very elegant used tissues. Maybe not for me. And then the one with the sparkly embroidered bodice that whispered Kim Kardashian a little too loudly for my liking. I didn't really want to celebrate my special day looking like someone whose last marriage lasted a whole seventy-two days. The whitest one looked a little bit like a very beautifully draped towel, and then there was the prettiest dress I had ever seen. Not the most mind-blowing, not the biggest, brightest or boldest, nothing that would change the world, but definitely the prettiest. I closed my eyes, wound down the window and took a moment to imagine myself waltzing around a candlelit ballroom wearing the delicately peach-hued mermaid dress, roses of tulle floating around my feet, wisps of silk brushing against my skin. It was beautiful and I could see it. But it just didn't feel like me. And it definitely didn't feel like Alex. I pressed my fingers against my forehead and nibbled on a thumbnail. It struck me this whole wedding malarkey was going to be harder than I'd thought, now I realized I hadn't really thought about it at all.

CHAPTER FOUR

'Jenny?'

I had decided against ringing the buzzer and let myself straight into the apartment with the key I had never bothered to give back – I wasn't about to stand on the pavement like a spare part if she had just decided she didn't fancy company. It was about time we got this intervention-slash-arse-kicking on the road.

Things had changed since I'd lived on the corner of 39th and Lex. Every surface in the apartment was now bright white, courtesy of Sadie and her Mariah Carey addiction to blinding surfaces. Unfortunately, that addiction didn't run as far as actual cleaning or hiring a housekeeper. If possible, their flat was a worse shit-hole than mine. Used-up cartons of coconut water (Sadie's) and empty pyramids of Coronas (Jenny's) lined the kitchenette, and the living room was artfully decorated with more clothes than you could find in your average Help the Aged. A cashmere sweater here, an Abercrombie hoodie there, seven Victoria's Secret thongs adding colour to the couch and an eye-wateringly beautiful Jason Wu dress being used as a rug. It hurt my heart to look at it on the floor, just begging to be picked up, nicked and then never, ever worn, given that it was at least three sizes too small for me. Sadie's and Jenny's wardrobes tended to bring out my inner klepto.

'If you're not here,' I called out, tiptoeing around a lovely-looking pair of YSL Tributes in, ooh, my size, 'I'll just help myself to that box of Godiva truffles you keep hidden on top of the cupboards.'

I stood outside her bedroom door, barely breathing, just to make sure I could in fact hear shuffling around. Unbelievable. She was in bed.

'Right, I'll put the kettle on as well,' I shouted, slamming the kitchen cupboards and bashing the kettle around. 'Nice cup of tea and an entire box of choco-lates. Probably just throw them straight up. Every single one.'

Now I was annoyed. She knew what we were doing today. She knew Sadie and Erin were taking me to try on wedding dresses, and she had decided to get an extra couple of hours' kip. What a bastard. I clambered up onto the kitchen counter, skirt up around my knickers, shoes kicked onto the floor, and grabbed around for a golden box tied in black ribbon on top of the cereal cupboard. It was dusty enough to suggest it had been up there for a couple of months, but it wasn't off-putting enough to stop me from tearing off the ribbon, chucking the lid on the floor and shovel-ling the chocolates into my mouth three at a time.

'Bloody hell, Jenny,' I yelled through the gooey chocolatey goodness. 'These are amazing. You should get your lazy arse out of bed before I eat them all.'

I contorted myself around to mash my tea, twisting over the sink to reach the kettle, and made a mental note to take up yoga classes soon. Again. And then stuffed another fistful of chocolates into my gob while trying unsuccessfully to pull my skirt over my knickers.

'Any left for me?'

If hearing a distinctly masculine voice wasn't enough to topple me from my countertop perch, spinning around to see a half-naked man grinning at me was. But that grin didn't last long. As soon as he recognized me.

Tyler.

I slapped a hand over my chocolate-filled mouth and inadvertently propelled myself over the kitchen counter and onto the living-room floor.

'Holy shit.' It took him half a second to compose himself before running around to help me up. I coughed, choking down a particularly chewy caramel. 'Bad spill. Did you break anything?'

For a couple of seconds I lay on the floor, dazed, wondering if I'd been hit by a taxi or fallen downstairs and woken up in a coma. Or purgatory. Or out-and-out fire and brimstone, seventh circle of hell. But no, here I was on the floor of Jenny's apartment, chocolate smeared all over my face and my less than best underwear on display, while my former boyfriend – no, that was too strong a word; former fling – loomed over me in his very best underwear with nothing on his face but a shit-eating grin.

'Annie?'

Oh, now that was just rude.

Tyler stroked his abs with an absent-minded hand and looked around the apartment with new eyes. 'I thought this place seemed familiar.'

'It's Angela.' I pushed myself upright and did the

best I could to put everything where it was supposed to be. Skirt over knickers, chocolate off face, hair – well, the best I could do was on head. 'I need to speak to Jenny.'

'Right, right. English chick. So this is weird, huh?' he shrugged, still smiling. Actually smiling broader and brighter if possible. What a wanker. 'She's in bed.'

I stared hard, willing him to vanish. Willing this not to be happening. Willing myself not to be true to my word and throw up all those chocolates.

'I guess I'll jump in the shower,' he said. His eyes twinkled in a way that, once upon a time, I had found incredibly attractive. At that moment it was all I could do to hold onto my New Year's resolution to punch fewer people. 'See you later, Annie.'

As Tyler sauntered off into the bathroom, I was frozen to the spot. My brain was a screaming mess of confusion and, for some reason, I really wanted a wee. But with the bathroom out of action, there was only one thing to do.

'Get up!' I ran into Jenny's room, spotted her sitting on the edge of the bed half dressed, and saw red. I picked up a pillow, flew at my best friend like a Britney scorned and proceeded to bash her about the head with it. 'Get up. Get out of bed. Get up now.'

'What? Angela, what the fuck?' She held her hands up over her face against my sad little assault. I was both weak and feeble. It didn't take more than a couple of seconds for Jenny to overpower me, grab the pillow and shove me across the bed. 'Why aren't you at Vera Wang?'

'I was at Vera Wang but everyone was so worried about *you*,' I howled from the floor beside the bed. 'I said I'd come and get you. But clearly there was no reason to be worried because nothing was wrong, you were just too busy shagging my ex to be there with me while I tried on wedding dresses.'

'What?' Even from my position on the floor, which badly needed hoovering, I saw the colour drain from her face.

'*Worst. Bridesmaid. Ever*,' I shouted.

'Seriously, what are you talking about?' Jenny reached down and pulled me up onto the bed. 'I was on my way, I swear.'

'Tyler.' Suddenly remembering there was someone else in the apartment, I lowered my voice to a hiss and stood up, too angry to sit beside Jenny on the bed. 'You slept with Tyler?'

'Uh, the blond guy?' All the colour she had lost came back in a bright red flush. 'You know him?'

'The blond . . .?' I went from being incredibly angry to incredibly worried in a heartbeat. With a side portion of pissed-off still hanging around for good measure. 'Jenny, I used to date him. Remember when I first moved here? Tall? Blond? Sleazy bastard?'

Jenny's eyes widened to the point where she made Disney heroines look a bit squinty.

'You?' I could see her searching for recollection. 'Tyler. You dated a Tyler. He bought you Tiffany.'

And then I saw her weighing up her options.

'And he was an asshole.' Jenny pressed her hands against her face and groaned. 'I met him in the bar last night. He seemed OK – he was funny. He was hot. I can't believe it's your Tyler.'

'Yeah.' My nervous energy ran out and I collapsed on the bed beside her. Then remembered what had happened in that bed and jumped back up. 'Jenny, this is really, really disgusting. As in, I want to have

48

a shower disgusting. Only I can't because the man we've both had sex with is in the shower.'

'Oh, man.' She doubled up, dropping her head to her knees. 'I'm gonna puke. I didn't know. How could I know?'

'I suppose you couldn't,' I admitted. 'But when you've shagged enough people to accidentally get around to the only other person in the city I've slept with aside from Alex, I reckon you've probably shagged too many.'

She rested her hands on her thighs, which I noticed were covered in jeans. And she had one sock on. And a tank top. And her phone, on the nightstand, showed the location of Vera Wang on Google Maps. So she really was on her way to meet me. After she'd finished shagging my ex.

'Angela?' she said in a soft, quiet voice I hadn't heard in a long time. 'I don't know what I'm doing. I don't know what to do.'

Taking a deep breath and trying very hard not to think about bed-based high jinks, I sat down next to her and wrapped an arm around her shoulders. Most of the time Jenny seemed like an Amazon to me, all long legs, shiny hair and glamour, but sometimes, when you took away the high heels and confidence, you remembered how tiny she really was. Right now, without so much as a swipe of mascara or an ounce of confidence, she looked like any other little lost girl with a broken heart.

'It's going to be OK,' I promised, pressing my lips into her hair and not even knowing whether or not it was true. 'I know things are hard, I know it hurts, but it will get better.'

'I want it to stop hurting so much.' Her voice broke

with tears as she spoke and it made my heart hurt for her. 'It's been so long and it doesn't change. I thought dating other people would help.'

'It just takes time,' I replied, hugging her a little tighter and letting her cry it out on my shoulder. 'There's no other answer. I wish there was. And I don't think rebound dating works. I know. I tried. With the man in the bathroom.'

This wasn't the time to point out that trolling bars for slut-bags wasn't the same as dating.

'Some days I just can't function,' Jenny snuffled into my arm. 'I wake up and it hits me that he doesn't want me, that he married someone else, and I just cannot get out of bed but I have to, you know? I have to, so I'm just a zombie. I just switch off. And I hate it. I want my life back.'

'Well, just don't do what I did and run away to another country.'

All at once, the snuffling stopped and she jolted upright in my arms. Her wet, snotty face was overcome with a lightning strike of an idea I already knew I wasn't going to like.

'That's it,' she announced, arms out wide. 'You are so smart!'

'Thank you?' I said carefully. I always found that kind of compliment was nice to hear but came at a price. 'What exactly did I do?'

'I'm coming to London with you,' she announced, downgrading my level of intelligence with every syllable. 'It's perfect. I need to get away from the city, you need protecting from your mom, your mom loves me, therefore I'm coming to London. With you.'

Now, it was true that my mum loved Jenny. When we were living together, the two of them spent a lot

50

longer talking on the phone than I did. For some reason, suburban mother-of-one, Su Doku-lover, Marks & Spencer acolyte and lifelong subscriber to *Take a Break* magazine had found a soul mate in the *Vogue*-reading, Agent Provocateur-wearing, Angry Birds-loving Jenny Lopez. She was the daughter she had always intended to have. While my mum and I got along just fine, she had always been a bit disappointed that I wasn't more of a girly girl. I'd never wanted ballet lessons, to play the flute or play with prams, pushchairs and baby dolls, even though they were forced upon me. I'd wanted to ride horses and learn guitar and read *The Secret Garden* until my eyes were sore, not sit and drink tea nicely with the Avon lady. She'd always adored ladylike Louisa and hoped she might influence my ways, and I genuinely believed the main reason she hadn't flown directly to New York and marched me straight onto a plane two years ago was because she was hoping some of Jenny's feminine super-powers would rub off on me. And they kind of had. I could walk in heels and not fall down (most of the time), I knew how to apply eyeliner without looking like a tranny or a member of Kiss, I could tell anyone why a Chanel 2.55 handbag was called a 2.55, and I had an uncontrollable, burning desire to possess one. I was quite the success as a woman these days, and a lot of that was due to Ms Jenny Lopez.

So it all worked aside from the fact Jenny's plan had one major flaw.

Alex.

Jenny and Alex were the two most important people in my life – my New York family – and while they were friendly when their paths happened to cross, I had learned my lesson and tried to keep them away from too much one-on-one time or unnecessarily intense situations. I loved them both and they both loved me, but each other? Love might be slightly too strong a word. It was one of the few things that fell outside our overshare pact, but I knew for a fact that Alex thought Jenny was a drama queen who brought most of her misery on herself. And Jenny, as my best friend and ultimate defender, kept Alex on a short leash just in case he ever, ever did anything to hurt me. It was a time-honoured relationship between boyfriend and bestie and we handled it just fine. But bringing Jenny along on a trip that already promised to be more painful than a girl's first bikini wax?

'It'll be awesome.' Jenny wiped her tears away on the back of her arm and offered me the beginnings of a smile. 'You can show me London, I can meet Louisa, I'll totally take all the pressure off the parentals so you and Alex can take time to hang out. It'll be so great.'

Not for the first time, I was completely lost for words. And not for the first time, I was completely unable to disguise the fear on my face.

'Angie, honey.' Just like that, Jenny was back. Her face shone and her eyes sparkled with conviction. 'I won't be any hassle and it's what I need. An escape, you know? Space. Time. Just a few days to breathe and empty my head.'

I sighed and nodded. How was I supposed to say no when she'd pulled me out of exactly the same situation two years ago? Besides, it was impossible to look at those big brown Lopez eyes and not give in. I often worried about what would happen if Jenny ever decided to use her powers for evil.

'Oh my God, I love you.' She bounced up onto her

knees and pushed me backwards, showering me in kisses. 'I love you so much.'

'Am I interrupting?' Tyler's voice rang out across the room, causing one sick feeling in my stomach to make way for another. I looked over to see him leaning against the door frame, a towel wrapped low around his hips. Given that my sexual CV was incredibly brief, I'd never been in a situation where I'd been in the same room as someone I'd boffed and broken up with and so I had no idea how I was supposed to be feeling. All I knew for sure was that I really, really wanted him to be gone. Preferably with a black eye. And a ruptured scrotum.

'So, is this a private party or can anyone get in on this?' he asked with a raised eyebrow, arms folded across his ridiculously hot body. Arsehole. How dare he stand there with his abs out. 'This is weird, right?'

'It's weird,' Jenny and I replied in unison.

'So would it be more weird or less weird –' he started to move towards the bed – 'if the three of us, you know . . .'

I had no words. Literally no words. But Jenny, luckily for me, was full of them.

'I don't know.' She stood up and pulled Tyler's trousers out of the pile of clothes at the foot of the bed. 'But I do know you're not putting these on right now.'

Jenny smiled. Tyler grinned. I grimaced. And then Jenny walked over to the window, opened it up and threw his trousers out into the street. 'Hey, Angie, toss me his shorts.'

It was hard to say who was more shocked. Tyler's jaw dropped at exactly the same moment as his towel, but now his nudity wasn't nearly as entertaining as the fact that Jenny was very busy throwing all of his clothes out onto 39th Street. You had to laugh. So I did. Long and loud and hard.

'What the fuck are you doing?' he demanded when he finally found his voice. 'Are you fucking crazy?'

Jenny dangled a very expensive leather loafer over the sill and cocked her head to one side. 'Wanna find out?'

Out went the shoe.

'Jesus.' Tyler looked at me, grabbed his towel and shook his head. 'You're both insane.' And with that, he ran out of the bedroom and out of the apartment.

By the time he made it onto the street, a homeless guy had already claimed his shirt and shoes, but fortunately, given the New York City decency laws, his underwear and jeans were still a crumpled mess on the sidewalk. Jenny and I leaned out of the window and waved down at him as he shuffled into them, flashing his backside to passers-by. Elbows on the windowsill, Jenny and I turned to look at each other.

'So – London then?' I smiled.

'London,' she replied with a grin.

CHAPTER FIVE

'I'm here, I'm here.' I threw myself through the glass doors of the *Gloss* office the following Friday, late as usual. For some reason, I'd decided not to waste money I didn't have on a taxi and had taken the subway, despite the fact that I had two suitcases and the world's biggest carry-on bag. Well, maybe not the world's biggest, but definitely not one of the smallest. I could easily steal Beyoncé's baby and carry it off in this bag. Which I totally would.

'Did I miss anything?'

'Just the coffee run.' Mr Spencer was sitting in my leather chair, a small smile on his face. It had been so long since I'd seen that smile that I actually shrieked in surprise. Bollocks. Yes, I was late into the office, but I wasn't late for the meeting. Why was he early? Who was ever early? Arses. 'I hear you're off to London, Ms Clark?'

'I am,' I nodded, attempting to regain my composure. And failing. 'It's my mum's sixtieth.'

He stood up and gestured for me to sit down. Which was nice of him, given that he was in my seat in the first place.

'I'm sorry it's taken me so long to get back to you, ladies,' he said, striding across our tiny office in two steps and settling himself on the edge of Delia's desk. For an older gent, Bob Spencer was still well put together, like he'd reached a certain age and decided he was just going to stick with that. He always reminded me a little bit of Ken Barlow, but less evil. 'Things are very busy right now, as I'm sure you can appreciate. The industry is going through a very difficult time.'

I settled into my chair, suddenly aware that I shouldn't get too comfortable. Where was Delia? Why was he talking to me when she wasn't here? There was only one possible reason – he was here to shut us down and she was crying in the toilets.

'I'm sure you remember I was a big fan of your work, Angela.' He smiled at me and I waited for the blow. Why had she gone to cry in the toilets without me? Selfish mare. 'You did some wonderful writing for *The Look*, and what you did with James Jacobs was really very good.'

Through the mediums of eyebrow raising and telepathy I tried to communicate to the boy dropping off our mail that Bob was talking about an article I had written about the actor James Jacobs coming out of the closet and Nothing Else. He replied with widened eyes with a very loud and clear 'Whatever, lady'.

'Thank you?' I brushed the floor with my toes and turned the chair very slightly from side to side.

'And Delia assures me my first impressions about you were correct,' he went on, continuing to stare me down. I took it all back – Ken Barlow would never be so rude. 'And that, possibly, Cecelia didn't exactly cover herself in glory when working with you.'

I took that as his very, very diplomatic way of saying that Cici was a batshit, cray-cray mental who should be locked up, but instead of correcting him, I made a small scoffing noise and concentrated on pressing the hem of my striped American Apparel T-shirt between my thumb and forefinger.

'So I have to be honest with you – I thought the presentation the two of you gave me last week was a little lacking.'

Finally we were getting to it. I felt tears prickle in the backs of my eyes and fought to keep them down. I have always tried so hard to keep tears out of the workplace. It was a very smart woman who said, 'If you have to cry, go outside.' Or a very intolerant one. Either way. But this was too awful. We'd worked so long and so hard on *Gloss*, and the feeling that it was just going to go away was almost as disappointing as thinking you had a packet of chocolate Hobnobs in the cupboard only to find nothing but two Rich Teas.

'There was a distinct lack of vision.' Mr Spencer raised his voice a little, presumably to ensure every word of his carefully put together 'fuck off and die' speech hit home. 'You weren't looking at the bigger picture. But that's what I'm here for. I am the bigger picture.'

Bigger *knob*, I thought to myself with a sniffle, but managed to keep the words to myself. Just.

'If we're going to launch a new print magazine in this climate, we need to make some noise,' he said. 'And you make noise by going global. Or at least transatlantic. Simultaneous US and UK launch. So what do you think, Angela? Up to the challenge?'

Huh. So I'd got it a bit wrong. As I desperately fought both disbelief and the urge to reply with the words 'fuck' and 'off', Delia pushed the door open with her tiny bottom and beamed at me, hands full of giant Starbucks cups.

'You're here.' She turned her back to her grandfather and gave me the biggest smile I'd ever seen on her face. 'Has Grandpa filled you in?'

'He has,' Mr Spencer answered for me. 'But Angela hasn't actually reacted in any way other than to gape at me like a goldfish.'

'I, um, I'm sorry.' Second attempt to gain composure in one day. Second failure. Delia set a large cup down in front of me and passed the second to her grandfather, gulping down the third as if someone was going to take it off her. 'I'm just sort of surprised. What exactly are you saying?'

'I'm saying I need you to sell this idea to the London office,' he said. 'And if you can get them on board, and you can get the exec team on board, you've got yourself a magazine. And not just a magazine but a franchise.'

'Oh. Right then.'

'You don't think you can do it?' Bob mistook my shock for terror. It was reasonable.

'Of course we can do it,' Delia replied. Life really was so much easier when people answered all of your questions for you. 'Angela means it's a pleasant surprise.'

'I do,' I said, remembering myself and nodding eagerly at Delia and then at Bob. 'That's exactly what I meant. We can absolutely pull off a transatlantic launch.' I felt like we were back in a Bob place now. Probably.

'Perfect.' Bob stood up, took one sip of his coffee, made a face and set it back on Delia's desk. 'I'll make an appointment for Angela to meet with the publishing team in London, and Delia, I'll send you the information about Paris. Ladies.'

And with a nod, he was gone.

Delia waited a slow three seconds before running round to my side of the office, knocking my coffee across the room and wrapping me up in a very tight, very excited hug. I squeezed back, even though I was still in a complete state of shock. The magazine was happening! There were Hobnobs in the cupboard after all! I needed to clean up that coffee.

'Holy shit, Angela,' Delia shouted as loud as her WASP-y lungs would allow, which wasn't really all that loud, and let go of my shoulders to do a little dance in the middle of the office. 'We have a magazine. We have two magazines. We're global, Angie!'

'I know.' I breathed out hard. 'I can't believe it. I mean, we've been planning it for so long, I can't believe it's actually going to come to life. We're going to print a magazine and people are going to be reading it. Fingers crossed.'

It was all a bit much. It had taken me six days to recover from the shock that I wasn't just walking around wearing a very pretty ring but was actually going to have to have a wedding and get married, and now I had to adjust to the idea that we really were going to have to write and publish a magazine, not just talk about it and put together pretty PowerPoint presentations.

'So I talked to Grandpa before you came in and the plan is that you'll meet with the London Spencer Media publishing team next week while you're over there, and I'll take the advertisers' conference in Paris.' She paused, took in the look of abject horror on my face, and recovered herself. 'Unless you want to do Paris and I'll do London?'

'Paris?' Not bloody likely, I thought to myself. 'You can take Paris. But, um, wouldn't you like to come to London too?'

'Love to,' Delia laughed, calming down slightly and settling into her desk chair. 'But the advertisers' conference is next Friday and I need to get everything together for that. Grandpa is going to schedule your meeting for Wednesday, maybe Tuesday? Keep it clear of your mom's party on Saturday.'

I nursed my coffee as though it were the Holy Grail. As long as I had coffee, this would all be OK. 'Tuesday?' I tried not to cry. Again. 'As in four days from now?'

'You're going to be totally fine,' she soothed from across the office. 'All you have to do is go in and give the presentation you've already given a thousand times to, what, three people? This is a formality. This is a hoop for us to jump through.'

I pouted. So she went on.

'People are already predisposed to be nice to you because their boss has told them to be.' I could tell she'd already switched into business mode and that meant she had no time to pander to my insecurities. When Delia turned on her monitor and started tapping away at her keyboard, she was almost never on Facebook. 'You're going to be amazing. You've been amazing so far, haven't you?'

In all honesty, I thought, so far I had been a liability. Sure, I could sing my own praises with regards to the creative side of things. I was happy enough to say I was a good writer, I had good contacts and great ideas and was perfectly capable of stringing together an attractive sentence. But in meetings? Not so much.

First, there was my uncontrollable tendency to be massively overfamiliar with everyone I met. Within fifteen minutes of our first meeting with Trinity's global marketing director, I was merrily telling him about my adventures with my junior school's guinea pig, Alex's terrible haircut and my intense love for *Les Misérables*. He'd only asked if I'd had a nice weekend. My mouth had a tendency to run away with itself. And that was before we took into consideration turning up to meetings barefoot, outing celebrities, almost blogging myself out of the love of my life and getting into catfights on stage at music festivals in France.

I had enjoyed quite the career.

'You're doing it, Angela.' Delia closed the conversation with her final say-so. 'And besides, this will give you a day away from your parents. That's got to be good news, hasn't it?'

She really was a very bright girl.

The rest of the day was spent obsessively reading over the *Gloss* publishing presentation, making to-do lists and ignoring text messages from my mother. I was booked on the 9.25 p.m. flight back to London. Alone. For all Jenny and Alex's promises of supporting me through my family reunion, neither of them was able to fly in with me. Jenny, having remembered that she actually had a job, had to manage an event for Erin and was flying out tomorrow. Alex had studio time booked to record live sessions for iTunes or B sides or something else band-related that I couldn't quite remember and was coming on Monday.

To be fair, I was struggling with everything I'd been told for the last five days because the only thing I could think about was London. One minute, I'd be super-excited about going. Share Topshop with Jenny, hug my dad, sniff Louisa's baby, generally show Alex off like a shiny new toy. But then I'd remember the flipside. For every trip to Topshop, there would be a cup of stewed tea with Aunt Sheila. For every dad hug, there would be a passive-aggressive dig from my mum. For every sniff of the baby, there would be a shitty nappy, and it was going to be very hard to show Alex off if my mother poisoned him five minutes after he'd entered the house. And given her cooking skills, she might not even do it on purpose. Of course, there was a chance everyone would just be happy to see me, and my mum would hand me the biscuit tin and forget that I hadn't been home in two years. There was just as much chance that the house would be picked up in a tornado during the night and dropped on top of a witch in the wonderful world of Oz.

As the office clock ticked towards five, I kept looking at my phone, waiting for the car service to buzz. So far I'd had five texts from Louisa detailing how very excited she was that I would be back on British soil in twenty-four hours, three texts from Jenny asking whether or not she should pack her Jimmy Choo over-the-knee boots, and one from my mum and dad confirming that it was supposed to rain so I should bring a coat. And if I didn't have a coat, I should get a coat.

I was looking longingly out of our twenty-fifth-storey window at the bright spring sunshine when my phone buzzed into life. The car was here. The end was nigh.

'Want a hand with your bags?' Delia piped up from her corner. I looked up and considered throwing myself on her mercy, begging her not to let me go, but it was no use. Not only had Delia been very vocal on the subject of me 'reconciling' with my mother all week, but she was now one hundred percent committed to me giving this presentation in London. I'd have more chance appealing to her twin sister's good nature.

'I've got them.' I closed down my laptop, heaved myself up out of my chair, grabbed my notepad off the desk and tossed them both into my satchel. It groaned with the weight, echoing my sentiments.

'What exactly do you have in there anyways?' she asked as she stood up, offering a hug in commiseration. 'It looks like you're packed for a month.'

'I have every item of clothing I own,' I explained, heaving the bags along the plush carpeting. 'And as many bags of peanut-butter M&Ms as I could pack. And a shit-ton of Tide pens for my mum. I feel like she'll like Tide pens.'

'Good call,' she said, hugging me quickly and shoving me towards the door. 'Even my mom loves Tide pens, and she hasn't as much as looked at laundry her entire life.'

I bit my lip and shook my hair out from behind my ears. 'It'll be OK, won't it?' I asked.

'You can call me any time,' Delia assured me, arms folded in front of her. 'You're going to kill at the presentation.'

'Weirdly, I'm not so worried about the presentation any more,' I muttered. I wanted to get changed. I shouldn't be wearing jeans. My mum hated it when I wore jeans. And I should have tied my hair up, she never liked it down. And all in the space of ten seconds, I'd regressed ten years.

'Your mom is just going to be happy to see you,' she replied, holding open the door while I shuffled through. 'You're going to be surprised.'

I pressed the glowing grey button to call the lift and looked back over my shoulder. 'Well, yes,' I nodded. 'That's pretty much a given.'

Obviously, my taxi did not get stuck in traffic and my flight was not delayed. As if that wasn't bad enough, when I got to JFK airport I discovered Alex had upgraded my flight. What a bastard. Before I could even think to tell someone I had a bomb in my shoe or fake a panic attack, I was on the plane and downing tiny glasses of champagne like they were going out of fashion. I swiped at the screen of my iPhone and reread Alex's last text. 'Be calm, be cool, don't punch anyone and I'll see you Monday. Love you.' I closed down the screen and closed my eyes. Easier said than done, Reid.

'Is there anything I can get for you?' A tall, blonde flight attendant in a smart red suit smiled at me in the dim cabin lighting.

'Oh, no, thank you,' I hiccupped. 'I'm fine.'

'Just let me know if there's anything at all.' She rested her hand on my shoulder very briefly and then disappeared, presumably to tell the rest of the crew it was OK, I wasn't going to drink them dry.

I had planned on sleeping through the flight, but I already knew I was too restless. Every time I closed my eyes, something started niggling. I'd spent the first couple of hours going over and over and over my presentation for *Gloss*. I'd spent the next hour eating peanuts. And then I'd gone over the presentation again. And I couldn't quite get my head round how much had changed since I'd flown the other way, out of Heathrow. I was proud of myself, I was. Two years ago, I'd been scared and alone and entirely directionless. Now I was so close to realizing so many dreams. Which didn't stop me being scared. The more you have, the more you have to lose.

And then there was the wedding. The non-existent wedding. Thanks to Delia, Erin and Sadie, I was really starting to worry about my lack of preparation. Maybe watching *Breaking Dawn* was a bad idea. Edward and Bella were making me feel bad. I switched off the screen and pulled out my notepad, along with the wedding magazine Delia had given me. Maybe if I made a list. Maybe if I had an idea of what needed doing, I'd be able to get my head round how to make it work for me. Dress. Guest list. Venue. Catering. Dog and pony. Bleurgh.

Where was that stewardess? Why had I said no to more champagne?

Number one, I needed a dress. Flipping to the pages Delia had marked for me to look at, my eyes popped. I had imprinted. Suddenly, life had new meaning for me. On the page in front of me was a light, frothy concoction of sheer beauty. Layers and layers of ivory skirts floated around the model, making it look like she was walking through a cloud, and a high slit up the front revealed a hint of leg, giving the dress an edgy look without seeming slutty. Up top, a delicate bodice gave her boobs that she quite clearly did not have. Models did not have boobs. I did not have boobs. It was simple. It didn't look like I would have to starve myself for six months to get into it. The slit led me to believe I might not trip.

This was the dress. I closed my eyes and imagined myself wearing it, getting married in it, and it was easy. I could feel sunshine on my skin, I could see Alex smiling at me, and in that moment, all I wanted to do was jump off the plane, grab Alex and march him down the aisle. Now I really wasn't going to be able to sleep.

Full of wedding beans, I picked up my pen, turned the glittery vampire wedding back on and started on the guest list. How come there wasn't a magical page in a magazine that would make this easy for me? Obviously Jenny, Erin and, I supposed, Sadie. Probably my friend Vanessa. Definitely Delia. Mary, if she would come. And Louisa and Tim would have to come over. And I assumed my dad would insist on bringing my mum. Alex's side was even easier to whittle down than mine. I drew a line down the middle of my notepad and added all my people to one side, then added Alex's band members Graham and Craig, his parents, his brother, his manager, and his slightly creepy old roommate who came over once every couple of months, brought himself two cans of beer and peed sitting down. I knew this because he left the door open when he did so.

So that was the dress and the guest list sorted. Who knew I would turn out to be a wedding planner extraordinaire?

I tapped the pen against the tray table, incredibly pleased with my progress. My seat neighbour, however, was not so pleased with the tapping. He raised his eye mask and gave me the frowning of a lifetime until I pursed my lips and carefully laid the pen down on the table. How dare he not care that I had just solved two-thirds of the world's most pressing problem? Global economic crisis be damned, I had a wedding to plan. So if I could pick a dress and sort out my guest list without slashing my wrists, where was all the drama coming from with other people's weddings?

66

Perhaps I was just supernaturally talented. I considered the likelihood of this while quietly judging Bella's wedding dress. My main thought was that it was very tight. Maybe incredible event-organizing skills would be my vampire talent. It must take a lot of organization to be a vampire these days. After a few minutes, I felt my eyelids getting heavy and began to doze pleasantly, losing myself in a dream where Alex's skin sparkled and my ex, Mark, crashed our wedding, howling at the moon. Although he was considerably less Taylor Lautner and considerably more *Home Counties Werewolf in New York*.

Hmm. I felt my earbuds slip out of my ears as I nodded off. No doubt about it, I was Team Alex all the way.

CHAPTER SIX

When I woke up, I'd missed the breakfast service and my several tiny glasses of champagne had added up to one big headache. Between my dehydrated skin and crumpled clothes, I was far from my most fabulous self and there was very little I could do about it between getting off an aeroplane and getting into a car. Louisa's car, I reminded myself, a little thrill of excitement splitting through my headache for a moment.

I pushed up the shade and looked out of the window. There it was, that green and pleasant land. OK, so it looked a bit grey and murky from the air, but that was probably just the drizzle I'd been warned about. Drizzle. A word I hadn't used in two years. It had never occurred to me before, but we didn't really have drizzle in New York; we had light rain, heavy rain or fuck-me-is-the-world-ending rain. But never drizzle. It was perfect really. Now I would have frizzy hair to match my grey, bloated face and scruffy clothes, and my mum could be entirely certain that I had spent two years peddling crack under a bridge and definitely not eating vegetables.

And then it appeared. The opening titles of *EastEnders* rolled out underneath me, the ribbon of river curling up and stretching out across the landscape, punctuated by large patches of green. My stomach slipped when I spotted the Houses of Parliament, the London Eye. I'd grown up a little less than an hour outside London, less if I managed to catch the fast train (I never did), but it always felt like a million miles away. Louisa and I used to sneak off on Saturdays and get the train to Waterloo, just to wander up and down the South Bank before buying chocolate and riding straight back home. (Nights out in the big smoke were verboten.) I'd always got a kick when the train rolled into Waterloo, even as an adult. The city always made me feel like a little girl. It was so much older and more serious than I could ever be. New York was a little more encouraging. Fewer men in suits stroking their beards and more women running around in high heels. Clearly it was the media's fault. London was defined by books and poems and centuries of words written by men. NYC had been culturally claimed by skinny-jean bands, cocktails and four ladies into Manolo Blahniks, brunch and Mr Big.

Passport control was painless and, thanks to a bargain I made with the devil for the soul of my first-born child, my suitcases all came off the carousel intact and unexploded. Forty minutes after we touched down, I was wheeling my bags through the exit and out into the wild. The first thing I saw was a Marks & Spencer Simply Food. The second thing I saw was my mother. Without exerting any control over my own feet, I stopped stock-still and wondered whether or not I had time to duck into M&S and grab a bag of

Percy Pigs before she spotted me. It was only after I'd considered this gummy treat that I realized my mother was in the airport and Louisa was not.

'Angela!'

Whatever time I'd had to recover myself was gone. I had been seen. And now my mother was waving like a loon, shouting my name and hitting my father on the arm. 'Angela Clark! We're over here! Angela!'

Wow. There they were. Not a hair on my mum's head had moved since Louisa's wedding or, to be more specific, since 1997. As much as I had prayed to find out I was adopted as a teenager, there was no denying she was my mum. We had the same blue eyes, the same dark-blonde hair – or at least we did when I didn't highlight the shit out of it – and the same tendency to go a bit pear-shaped when we got lazy. Which we both did. All the time. At her side, my dad was wearing the same old Next cardigan that he kept in the car in case it got a bit chilly. On one hand, it was sort of reassuring. On the other, bizarre.

'Are you deaf?' My mum marched towards me, handbag on her shoulder, arms outstretched. For one scary moment I thought she was going to hug me, but instead she reached out and rubbed a tough finger on my cheek. 'You've got mascara all under your eyes.'

'All right, Mum,' I said, nodding at her and wishing I'd put on more lip balm. 'Nice to see you, Mum.'

'Hmm.' She looked me up and down quickly. 'New bag?'

'Well, not really.' I looked down at my Marc Jacobs satchel and thought back to when it was new. 'But new to you.'

'I don't even want to know what it cost,' she said, turning on her sensible heel and taking off across the arrivals lounge. 'Come on – the car park costs a bloody fortune.'

'Yes, Mum.' I looked down at my handbag and, not for the first time, wished it could talk. It would have been lovely to get a quick reminder that I'd actually spent the last two years in New York and that they weren't picking me up from my first semester at uni.

'All right, love?' Dad patted my shoulder and took the handle of one of my suitcases. 'Flight all right?'

'Not bad,' I replied. 'Although I do appear to have flown into the Twilight Zone.'

'Eh?' Dad trundled after my mum, leaving me behind. *Twilight*? Your mum was reading that. Nonsense, if you ask me. I watched the film. Not my cup of tea but it passed an evening. Come on – I'm gasping for a coffee and she won't let me buy one at Costa now I've got a Gaggia at home.'

Not ready to discuss my mother's progressive choice of reading material or my dad's new espresso machine, I played the dutiful daughter, stuck out my bottom lip and did as I was told.

Home, sweet home.

'News, news, news.' My mum looked over her shoulder from the passenger seat to make sure I hadn't bolted out the back of dad's Volvo. Fat chance, since Dad had activated the child locks. 'You know Vera from the library?'

'Yes?' I was clutching my phone so tightly my knuckles were white. I didn't have a blind clue who Vera from the library was.

'Dead,' Mum announced. 'Cancer.'

And now it seemed I never would.

'Brian as well, from the butchers,' she continued,

looking to the heavens as though more dead people I'd never met were going to wave down and remind her they'd carked it. 'Who else? Well, Eileen, but you didn't know Eileen. Oh! Do you remember Mr Wilson?'

I shook my head.

'Yes you do,' she encouraged. 'He used to walk his dog past our house. Every day!'

'Ohhh,' I exclaimed dramatically. 'That Mr Wilson.'

'Dead,' she declared. 'He didn't have cancer, though. Something wrong with his pancreas, I think.'

'It was pancreatic cancer,' my dad said, snapping his fingers. 'Went like that.'

'Patrick Swayze, Steve Jobs and Mr Wilson who walked his dog past our house.' I stared out of the window. 'Pancreatic cancer certainly has claimed some of the greats.'

I was fairly certain I heard my dad turn a laugh into a cough, but it was covered up by my mother's continuing list of obituaries. To take the edge off it, I swiped my phone into life and checked for messages. Nothing. Nothing from Jenny to say she was on her way, nothing from Alex to say he'd lain awake all night sobbing into my vacant pillow, and, most importantly, nothing from Louisa to apologize for leaving me at the mercy of my parents.

'And her from the post office had another baby,' my mum carried on. We'd exhausted the funeral roll call and moved on to who had had a baby and whether that baby was in or out of wedlock. 'And Briony, who you went to school with – she's on her third. Third! Two different dads, though. And of course there's Louisa's little Grace. What a beauty.'

'Speaking of Louisa . . .' I leaned forward to rest my chin on my mum's seat. 'Where is she?'

'Oh, Grace was a bit colicky this morning and she couldn't leave her,' she replied as though my best friend abandoning me was no big deal. 'Your priorities change when you have a baby, Angela, as you will find out. You're not the centre of the universe, you know. Louisa has a husband and a baby and they always come first.'

That was my cue for major sulking. Mostly because while part of me knew she was right, another much larger part of me still thought Louisa should have let said husband take care of said baby, seeing it was a Saturday, and be at Heathrow as promised. Sinking back into the back seat of the car, I turned my gaze out of the window again and watched the motorway whizz by. It felt strange to be on the wrong side of the road. It felt strange not to see any yellow taxis. It felt strange to hear my mum and dad's voices and Radio 4. It felt strange to be in England. Every second we sped closer to home, we sped further away from New York. It was like it was all falling away, as though it had never happened. And that was a thought I did not want to even entertain.

'First things first – kettle on,' my mum stated, dropping her handbag onto the table like she always did while my dad went into the living room and turned on the TV like he always did.

I stood in the middle of the kitchen, clutching my handbag to my body, trying not to cry. That had definitely happened before, but it wasn't standard behaviour. I didn't know what exactly I was expecting from my parents' house, but nothing had changed. Not a single thing. The bright yellow wall clock was still running five minutes ahead. A box of PG Tips sat open next to the kettle, as always, even though the tea caddy was completely empty. The spare keys still sat in the hot pink ashtray I had made out of Fimo when I was twelve. The sun shone through the window, right into my eyes, reminding me to move.

'Are you going to stand there all day?' my mum said, turning to me and filling the kettle from the filter jug as she spoke. 'Are you tired?'

'Not really,' I lied. I was completely exhausted, but it was more that this was all too much to take in. I was suffering complete sensory overload and I was worried that if I went up to my room and found the Boyzone posters on the walls, I might lose it completely. 'Might have a lie-down in a bit.'

'Well then, we'd better hear the story,' she said, settling the kettle in its cradle and sitting down at the kitchen table, an expectant look on her face. 'Let's see it.'

For a moment, I thought she meant my end-of-term report, but then I realized she meant my engagement ring. Because I was engaged. To a boy. In America. I stayed frozen still in the middle of the room and held out my hand, fingers spread, eyes wide.

'I haven't got my binoculars, Angela,' she sighed. 'Come here.'

Reluctantly, I dropped my bag and moved over to the worn, wooden table. Same place mats, same salt and pepper shakers, same artificial sunflowers in the centre. Before I even sat down, my mum grabbed my hand and yanked it across the table. My dad bounded over like an overexcited teenager.

'Ooh,' he cooed. 'It's very nice.'

'It is, actually,' Mum agreed, sounding surprised. 'Shame he didn't bother to ask your father's permission, but still. At least it's tasteful.'

74

'Why wouldn't it be?' I asked. Mistake.

'Well, who knows what an American thinks is an appropriate engagement ring. You could have ended up with God knows what on your finger, couldn't you? Unless you chose it. Did you choose it?'

She almost sounded hopeful.

'I'm not marrying Liberace, Mother,' I pointed out. 'Alex chose it. All on his own. And it's beautiful. I couldn't have picked anything I'd love more.'

'I said it was nice.' She pursed her lips and brushed her grey-blonde hair behind her ears. 'And should I bother to ask when and where you're planning on getting married? Or are you going to tell me you've already run off to Vegas?'

A coughing fit was not what you wanted when you already felt post-plane pukey, but I managed to get over it and keep the conversation going and headed off any difficult questions. 'Early days,' I spluttered. 'But it'll be very low-key. Town hall, dinner, small party, that kind of thing. Don't bother booking St Paul's or St Patrick's.'

'What's St Patrick's?'

'The cathedral in New York.' I waved a dismissive hand. 'I just don't want all the drama. Something nice with all the important people and lots and lots of boo—'

It was scary how many of my own expressions I could see on my mum's face. This particular visage suggested she was not amused.

'Lots and lots of beautiful flowers.' I corrected. Too late.

'You're telling me your wedding is going to be a piss-up in a brewery. In a New York brewery.'

'I never mentioned a brewery.' This was true.

'But you want to get married in New York?'

'Not necessarily.' This was not entirely true.

'Angela.' Mum showed me the same face I pulled at our local Mexican place when they told me they had no guacamole.

'We haven't made any decisions. And it's not like you're on the no-fly list, is it?'

She looked down at her fingernails for a moment. 'Is it?'

Finally, she looked up and turned her blue eyes on me. 'So. This Alex.'

'Don't talk like I've just dragged him home out of the bins behind the supermarket,' I said. 'You've spoken to him on the phone, you've seen pictures, I've told you everything.' Obviously not everything. 'I've known him nearly two years.'

'And you knew Mark for nearly ten,' she replied, holding up a hand to cut me off. Just as well I was tired or I would have swung for her. 'I'm just saying, before he gets here, that you need to be careful. You've been away over there and I'm sure your head's been turned, but you're home now and I want you to think very, very carefully before you make any rash decisions.'

'This is about as rash as it gets,' I said, holding up my ring again. 'Mum, there's nothing to worry about. Alex is lovely. You're going to meet him and you're going to praise the day I met that man.'

'We'll just see about that,' she said, her lips pursed almost as tightly as my dad's. Clearly it wasn't just my mum who had a problem with me marrying 'an American'. Although, to be fair, my dad had never been that keen on Mark either. Or anything else with a penis that came within fifteen feet of his little girl. Bless him. 'And what's this about Jenny coming to stay as well?'

'She just needed a bit of a break,' I said, trying to suppress a yawn as the kettle rumbled to a boil across the kitchen. Dad got up to mash the tea without waiting to be told, just like Alex. These were the real signs of true and lasting love. 'There was this bloke and he was messing her around and . . .'

I paused, looked up and saw my mother's lips disappear altogether. 'And she was just desperate to meet you,' I continued, pulling a one-eighty and trying to get her back on side. 'As soon as I told her I was coming home to see you, she insisted on coming with me. Wouldn't hear of me coming without her. She totally loves you.'

'She totally loves me, does she?' She shook her head. 'Totally?'

Smiling, I pulled my hair behind my head, slipped the ponytail holder off my wrist and tied it up high. 'Totally.'

'You cut your hair.' Mum took her mug from my dad and placed it to her lips, steaming hot. Asbestos mouth, she always said. 'And it's blonder.'

'I thought it was quite long at the minute,' I frowned, flipping the length through my fingers. 'But yeah, I got highlights. I wanted it to look nice for the presentation. And your party.'

'I think we probably need to talk about this presentation, don't we?' she said. 'We don't know exactly what it is you're doing, you know.'

At last. A topic on which I couldn't fail to impress.

'It's a new magazine,' I started. 'Me and my partner Delia came up with the concept, and the publisher liked it so much they want us to launch it in New York and London at the same time.'

'Hmm.' Mum stared out of the window.

Not the reaction I'd been looking for.

'Bit risky, isn't it?' she asked. 'Don't you think, what with you getting married to a musician, that you really ought to stop playing around and think about a proper job?'

Oh. Wow.

'One of you should have something steady, surely?'

I didn't have an answer. I didn't have anything.

'So you don't like my hair then?' I asked. 'Bit too much of a change?'

I knew I'd made a mistake as soon as I'd said it. Aside from one other term of endearment starting with a 'c', *change* was the filthiest word in the English language in my mother's house.

'It's shorter than when I last saw you,' she pointed out, reluctantly going with the subject. 'And I'd have thought you'd have had enough changes of late without messing about with your hair.'

'I think it looks nice,' my dad said, placing my cup in front of me. My Creme Egg mug that had come with an Easter egg fifteen years earlier. 'Very "ladies in the city".'

'Thanks, Dad.'

I sipped my tea carefully and felt every muscle in my body relax. Louisa had sent tons of teabags to me in New York, so I couldn't tell if it was the mug, if it was the water or if it was just sitting in my mum's kitchen being talked down to by my parents, but this was the best cup of tea I'd had in two years.

'Get that tea down you, we haven't got all day,' Mum bossed, necking her scalding-hot cuppa as though she was doing an impression of Jenny with a Martini five minutes before the end of happy hour. 'Do you need to use the loo or can I go?'

'Why haven't we got all day?' I was confused. What was going on? Why wasn't I getting a beautiful, emotional family reunion? Why weren't there cakes? I thought I could count on at least a KitKat. At least. 'Why do I need to use the loo?'

'It's Saturday.' She stood up and looked at me like I'd gone mad. 'Just because you're here, the world hasn't stopped turning. Now, are you going to have a lie-down or are you coming with us?'

Every single atom of my being said have a lie-down. Everything I had learned in twenty-eight years of life said go upstairs and go to sleep. So obviously I picked up my handbag, waited for my mum to come out of the loo and followed her out of the front door.

'So I said to Janet, I'm not disputing the fact that you've been here since half nine,' my mum said, carefully weighing the difference between two courgettes, narrowing her eyes and placing the bigger one in a little plastic bag. 'I'm just saying I finished at three and I've got things to do. Why should I hang around late because she wants to leave early?'

'You shouldn't, love,' Dad confirmed, passing her a bag of King Edwards for approval. 'Do we need onions?'

'Get one big one,' she replied. 'I might do a spag bol tomorrow. For the American girl.'

It turned out my mother's idea of an emotional family reunion was a quick turn around Waitrose. At midday on a Saturday.

'I need to get some milk,' I said, walking away from the trolley without proper approval. This was tantamount to going AWOL – my mother looked like she was ready to court martial me right up the arse.

'I've got milk,' she said, waving her list at me. 'Why do you need more milk?'

Twisting my engagement ring round and round and round, I shrugged. 'I'm going to see if they've got any lactose-free stuff. Alex is lactose intolerant.'

Both my mum and dad froze on the spot. My dad looked like he might cry.

'It's not catching,' I said. 'He just can't digest milk easily.'

Mum pressed a palm to her chest and visibly paled, while my dad hung his head, presumably seeing visions of feeble lactose-intolerant grandchildren failing to return the football he had just kicked to them.

'The woman who did my colonic says I'm a bit intolerant too,' I added, waiting for a reaction. But there was none. There was only silence. Picking the list out of my mum's hand, I scanned it and popped it back between her thumb and forefinger. 'So we make a good pair. I'll get the stuff for the pasta.'

'Angela,' she said in her kindest, most pleading voice. 'You didn't really have a colonic did you?'

Sometimes, I thought to myself, it's kinder to lie.

'Yes, I did, Mum,' I replied. 'In fact, I've had two.'

And sometimes, I just couldn't be bothered.

If I wasn't disorientated enough from the overwhelming jet lag that kept threatening to take my legs out from under me, roaming around Waitrose looking for tinned tomatoes and spaghetti just about pushed me over the edge. The only thing that kept me moving was the lure of the Mini Cheddars I'd promised myself. I moved through the aisles of the supermarket like they were full of treacle, my legs heavy and tired. Dodging trolleys and pushchairs and what seemed like dozens of sixteen-year-olds in green uniforms with cages full of Old El Paso fajita dinner kits, I was on autopilot. Maybe I wasn't home after all. Maybe the plane had crashed and I was in purgatory. There couldn't be any other explanation for the way I was feeling, the way nothing had changed in the slightest.

Well, nothing had changed but me. I looked like shit. I stopped by one of the freezer cabinets to be quietly appalled at the price of Ben & Jerry's and caught sight of my reflection. Transatlantic travel did no one any favours. Even following Jenny's advice hadn't helped me; sometimes you can drink two litres of water, spend the entire flight getting up and down to go to the loo, smother yourself in Beauty Flash Balm and still deplane looking like you've flown in directly from a two-week vacation with the crypt keeper. My skin looked crap, my hair was greasy, and whatever long-lasting, no-smudge mascara I had been wearing was either missing or smudged. Because cosmetics companies were liars. Why couldn't we all just agree that bruise-like swipes of grey and black etched into the fine lines around your eyes were sexy? Why did we make life hard for ourselves? Maybe I could put it in *Gloss* as a trend. Maybe I could put it out of business before the first issue even got out.

'Angela?'

Oh no. I bit down hard on my dry, chapped lips and closed my eyes. Maybe if I didn't open them again, the voice would go away.

'Angela, is . . . is that you?'

How could this be happening? I'd been in England for less than three hours, I hadn't even had time to change my pants, and yet this – *this* – was happening?

Holding my shopping out as my last defence, I turned round, offering absolutely everything I owned to every deity ever conceived if they would open up a hole in the ground for me to jump into.

'It *is* you.' Mark, my ex-fiancé, stood in front of me, smiling. 'Wow.'

No disappearing hole. Just an arsehole. Five foot ten of cheating scumbag shithead gurning like the total bell end he was, holding onto a trolley as though he was going to charge me with it. How come he got a weapon and I didn't? I quickly looked around, trying to find something deadly. It was like *The Hunger Games* meets *MasterChef*.

'Hi,' I said. Thanks to my bushel of cheesy snacks I couldn't even put a hand through my hair, couldn't try to wipe away some of my errant eyeliner. 'Well.'

'Well.' He rapped his fingers on the handle of his trolley, keeping it ever so slightly mobile. 'Fancy seeing you here.'

'Fancy,' I replied. This was unfair in every way. I needed to have a very serious conversation with whoever was in charge about how incredibly shit my day had been going so far.

'Um, so this isn't New York?' He had always had a talent for stating the obvious.

Mark, like everything else I'd come across so far, hadn't changed a bit. His hair was still ever so slightly too long, his jeans were still ever so slightly too big, and he looked almost as uncomfortable as he had the last time I'd laid eyes on him. At least he didn't have a skinny blonde wrapped around his waist this time, so I suppose I should have been counting my blessings.

'I heard you were still there.'

'I am,' I said quickly, shuffling my shopping in my arms. 'I mean, not now, obviously. I'm back for Mum's birthday.'

'Of course,' he nodded, every moment growing more awkward than the last. 'I was supposed to be going this week, but the deal fell through and, well, you know how work is.'

It pissed me off that I did know. It pissed me off that he still existed.

'Yeah, I heard,' I said. And immediately regretted saying it. He smirked a little and shifted his weight from foot to foot.

'Jungle drums,' he commented and tried a laugh. It didn't take. When I didn't respond in any way, shape or form, he gave me his most earnest expression and leaned over the handle of his trolley. He was winning. 'It's good to see you.'

Unfortunately for Mark, I already knew he was a liar.

'Hmm.' It was all I could manage. I should have got changed. Here he was, all sparkly Saturday clean, and here I was in baggy jeans, a rumpled T-shirt and Converse. I wanted to run home, wash my hair, pull out my tightest dress and my highest heels and come back with my heaviest handbag, fill it with tins of tuna and smack him really, really hard around the head with it. Instead, I utched my shopping further up my body, trying to cover my face and failing.

'Well, it would be lovely to catch up, if you've got time?' he said unconvincingly, looking anywhere but at me. I squeezed my great big bag of Mini Cheddars so hard that the plastic bag popped open with the sigh I was trying to keep inside. 'This is weird, isn't it?'

'It's a bit weird,' I agreed. 'But it would be weird if it wasn't, wouldn't it?'

'Fair point,' he replied, shuffling backwards in his knackered old tennis shoes. 'It really would be good to catch up. I'm still on the same number. Text me or something.'

Tennis shoes. He played tennis. That's where he met her.

'Yeah,' I nodded, trying to get my hair to move. Why couldn't I think of anything to say? Where was my witty comeback? At least I had my hands full so I couldn't swing for the bastard. For every second we stood there, his patronizing smile getting smaller and smaller, I got angrier and angrier until I was at full capacity. And then I remembered pissing in his shaving bag and getting on the next plane to New York. Suddenly I didn't feel quite as bad. 'I've got to go. My dad's waiting.'

I think the last time I'd used that line on him, we were seventeen and snogging outside Karisma at three in the morning. How time flies.

'OK.' He reached out one very rigid hand and placed it on my shoulder for half a heartbeat before snatching it back. My eyes widened to the size of saucers and I jumped back involuntarily. 'Anyway, give us a call.'

Refusing to respond, I staggered backwards into the freezer door, dropping my shopping and sprinting for the nearest aisle.

'I thought you'd gone back to New York.' My dad's voice interrupted my heavy breathing as I peered round a rack of Kettle Chips, watching Mark standing there with his trolley, clearly embarrassed by the pile of abandoned shopping. 'Good God, girl, you've been gone for ever. Where's the pasta? Your mum's at the till.'

I turned to face my dad, and his blue eyes softened from a crinkled smile to a wary frown. 'Angela, what's wrong?'

'Can I have the car keys, please?' I asked quietly. I was not going to cry in Waitrose. There couldn't possibly be anything more pathetic than a girl crying in Waitrose.

'Of course you can,' he said, fumbling in his pocket and producing a bunch of sparkly silver lifelines. 'Are you all right?'

'I couldn't find the tomatoes,' I mumbled, wiping at my grubby face with the sleeve of my stripy T-shirt, which was pulled down over the fists I couldn't seem to relax. 'Or the Mini Cheddars. Or the pasta.' The fact that we were standing in front of about twenty-five bags of Mini Cheddars dented my credibility somewhat. My dad looked at me, looked at the snack aisle and then stepped to the side to look past me. I couldn't bring myself to see if he was still there, but my dad's angry bear growl confirmed that he was.

'Sod's law,' he said, pressing the car keys into my hand. 'Get yourself back to the car. I'll get your mum's things. Do you want anything?'

'No,' I whispered. 'Thanks, Dad.'

All I wanted was to go home. And that did not mean back to my parents' house.

CHAPTER SEVEN

Almost an hour after I'd slumped up the stairs and wrapped myself up in my childhood sheets, I was still wide awake. Cocking jet lag. I couldn't remember when I had been more tired, but every time I closed my eyes, I just saw Mark grinning at me and that cow trying to get a good look through the car window from behind him.

For the want of something better to do, I sat up, huffed, puffed, opened my laptop and re-read the *Gloss* presentation. Again. After fifteen minutes of soothing stats, facts and numbers, I quickly flicked through all the other important things online – personal email, work email, Facebook, Perez Hilton, Bloomingdales.com . . . I was halfway through the purchase of a half-priced Theory shift dress when it all became a bit too much and a tidal wave of jet lag swept me under. As I slipped backwards against the pillows, I caught one last look at myself reflected in the screen and prayed I would wake up looking less like Jabba the Hutt on an off day.

*　　*　　*

'Get out of bed, you lazy mare.'

My ears engaged before I could even attempt to open my eyes. Reaching out for Alex, all I felt was a cold, hard wall. The pillows felt wrong. And someone was eating pickled onion Monster Munch. I rolled over and pried open one eye to see Louisa leaning against my bedroom door in boyfriend jeans and a sky-blue T-shirt with her hair high on top of her head in a ponytail. In the blink of an eye, I was fifteen again.

'Fuck off, I'm tired,' I said with happiness in my voice, rolling back towards the wall. 'Leave the crisps. I'm also starving.'

'Good job I brought you some, then. You look shit.'

A crinkly packet landed square on my head and it was all the incentive I needed to force myself awake.

'Sorry I couldn't meet you at the airport.' Louisa bounded onto my bed like a golden Labrador and wrapped her arms round my neck. 'Grace hasn't been well and I couldn't leave her with Tim. He's such a wimp when she cries.'

'And where is she now?' I asked, returning the hug with such strength I was worried I might break her. At last, something good to come out of this trip. 'You didn't leave her in the car, did you? Because that's really bad parenting.'

'Your mum's got her,' she replied, breaking the hug to get back into her Monster Munch. I was relieved. I did the same. Precious, precious pickled oniony goodness. 'I need ten minutes away. You're safe.'

'Safe?' I jostled myself into a sitting position, pulling my T-shirt down over my knickers. 'You've given my mum a baby when my fiancé is on his way here to meet her for the first time and you think I'm safe? Her secondary biological clock will be going batshit.'

'Oh, yeah – fiancé.' Lou dropped her empty crisp packet on the floor, wiped her hand on her jeans and grabbed my engagement ring. 'Bugger me.'

This was the amazing thing about Louisa. I hadn't set eyes on the woman for a year, and before that I'd sort of, kind of, ruined her wedding, but here we were, sitting on my bed eating snacks and talking about boys like we'd just come in from a particularly dull GCSE history revision class. Some love affairs were just destined to last a lifetime. Any friendship forged in the fires of a Take That themed birthday party was in it for the long run.

'Yeah.' I held my hand out in front of me, splaying my fingers wide. Before plunging them back into the Monster Munch. As I said, some love affairs were destined to last a lifetime. 'The boy done good.'

'He has, he has.'

She stretched her legs out across the bed and looked around the room. Presumably she was as weirded out by the fact that my mother had kept it as a shrine to my difficult teenage years as I was. Why on earth anyone would want to preserve 'Angela: ages sixteen to eighteen' was beyond me. At least, she had taken down all the cut-out pages from the *NME* that I'd actually stapled to the wall. It was embarrassing all the same.

'Any developments on the wedding plans?' Louisa asked. 'Anything you need me to do?'

Obviously, after immediately changing my Facebook status from 'in a relationship' to 'engaged' (I'm not proud), the second thing I did after Alex proposed was to ask Jenny and Louisa to be my bridesmaids. They were my best friends – it made perfect sense. It just didn't make a lot of logistical sense. Aside from the fact that they lived in entirely different countries, separated by a not insignificant body of water, they were very, very different people. While Jenny was, when sober, desperate to get involved in the spectacle element of the wedding – the dresses, the party, the food – Louisa wanted to know about the chair coverings, the venue, the guest list. I assumed it was experience talking on her part: she knew which parts of wedding planning would drive you insane and she knew you had to prepare for the . . . unexpected. Cough.

'I've actually been thinking about it a bit more recently,' I admitted, gnawing thoughtfully on a monster claw. 'And it's freaking me out a bit. The idea of a wedding. Of actually walking down an aisle in front of people and doing that whole bit.'

'That's only natural,' Louisa shrugged. 'I wouldn't have got through it if it wasn't for you. It was the best day of my life. Before I had Grace, obviously.'

'Obviously,' I agreed.

'But at the same time, it was absolutely the most stressful. And that was before you hulked out and broke my husband's hand. If I had to do it again, I wouldn't go half as crazy. Just small, simple, close friends. Nothing else.'

'Are you trying to tell me you're getting divorced?' I asked through the trauma of finishing my crisps.

'There are days, babe, there are days,' she sighed. 'But no. I'll stick it out a bit longer.'

As a testament to just how well she knew me, Louise pulled a third bag of Monster Munch out of her handbag. 'One's never enough.'

'Imagine living in a world with no pickled onion crisps of any kind,' I said, diving in. 'Actually, imagine living in a world with no salt and vinegar crisps. It's a wonder to me that America has done as well as it has, honestly. I wouldn't have made it through university without salt and vinegar Hula Hoops.'

'You're the one who wants to live there,' she replied. 'These are the choices we make, Angela Clark.'

'There are a few things that make up for it,' I acknowledged. 'Brunch, Buffalo Wings, Combos, Lucky Charms. And, oh God, the pizza.'

'And there was me thinking you might mention your fiancé.'

'Well, obviously.'

We sat in silence for a while, inhaling the snacks. It was only when I'd scoffed the entire bag that I realized I hadn't actually eaten solids since New York. Entirely unnatural. Although my only real food option was my mum's cooking, so maybe I could stick it out the entire week.

'So, do you think you'll ever move back?' Louisa's voice was impressively breezy, but I could tell she'd been building up to this one. 'Long term, you know?'

'I really haven't thought about it.' I crossed my legs and pulled a pillow into my lap. Looking at the dirty grey smudges on the white linen, I could only imagine what a state my face must be in. Bless Louisa for not mentioning it. 'I was so worried I would have to come back when my visa was revoked that I literally put it to the back of my mind and locked the door.'

'Alex hasn't mentioned it?' Her breeziness faltered. 'When you got engaged, he didn't bring it up?'

'No.'

'I would have thought you'd have talked about all those things. When you would get married, where you would live, kids. I would have thought it was a bigger issue for you than most couples.'

'Why?' I took as subtle a sniff of myself as possible. Dear God I needed a shower. 'Am I missing something?'

'No.' Louisa rested her hand on top of mine and squeezed gently. 'It's just that you're English. Maybe you'd want to move back to England. Where your friends and family are. I would think he'd take that into account, that you both would.'

Hmm. Alex and I hadn't discussed where we would end up living. But then we rarely discussed where we were going to eat dinner at night before we left the house.

'It's just stuff you have to think about,' she said, leaning back against the wall. 'Tim and I had to go through it all when we got engaged. He wanted to go and live in Australia for a while, but we agreed we wanted to get pregnant before I was thirty, so we put that on hold. What are you going to do when you get pregnant? Where are you going to live?'

'Tim wanted to live in Australia?' I pulled a face. 'But he gets sunburnt walking out to the car.'

'I'm just saying you have to think about these things. Before you have a baby.'

'Tea?' My mum clattered through the bedroom door carrying two steaming mugs. She smiled lovingly at my best friend before frowning at me and picking up the three empty crisp packets from the bed. 'Are you staying for dinner, Louisa?'

'Um, I'm not sure, I've got to get Grace into the bath,' she hedged.

'We're having fish and chips. I'm sending David out for them in a minute, so just let me know,' she added.

'Oh, actually, it's only six, isn't it?' Louisa brightened. The promise of deep-fried food was almost as exciting as the idea of not having to eat my mum's over-boiled slop. It seemed almost impossible that she had spent forty years cooking dinner every day and had only got worse. Not that I cooked. Ever. There were too many different Mexican restaurants for me to try before I put anything in the oven. God bless America. 'I'll just feed her and then she'll go down for an hour anyway.'

'I don't know if I've mentioned it, but I cannot believe you have a baby,' I said, jumping up off the bed as soon as my mum had vanished and opening up my suitcase. 'How is that possible?'

'So, first your waters break, and then you spend twenty-four hours screaming at the man you love as a far too big living thing squeezes its way out of your vagina, and then—'

'Yeah, I know the logistics.' I cut her off, trying not to feel sick. 'I just can't believe you – you, Louisa – have a baby. Is she even downstairs? Does she even exist?'

On cue, something on the lower level of the house let out an ungodly roar.

'Yeah, she's real,' Louisa nodded without flinching. 'And if you can believe it, that's a happy sound.'

'Holy shit,' I whispered. 'Is it an alien?'

'I thought she was something from *Alien* when she was coming out,' she said as she curled up on the bed, rested her head on her arms and watched me unpack. 'You won't be able to cope.'

'I totally won't,' I said, still trying not to feel sick. 'No interest in it. At all.'

'In having kids?' Lou reached over the edge of the bed and started pulling things out of my suitcase and oohing approval. Or not, in the case of my pattered DVF wrap dress. That put that out of the running for my *Gloss* presentation then. 'Since when?'

'I didn't say I wasn't having kids,' I grumbled, shaking out a very creased blue silk Tibi dress. I was going to have to iron. Or at least my mum was. 'I just don't have any interest in the actual physical having of them. Why haven't we evolved past that yet? Why can't they just put me under, pop it out and wake me up when it's been washed and dressed?'

Louisa had a very peculiar 'not amused' look on her face.

'We haven't talked about it.' I threw the dress over the back of a chair by my dresser and moved on to my T-shirts. And by my T-shirts, I meant the band T-shirts I'd acquired from Alex and all the lovely kitteny soft Splendid tees I'd nicked from Erin and Jenny's office. 'We've literally just got engaged. I'm not going to ask him when he's planning to knock me up.'

She looked away and bit on an already chewed-down fingernail.

'And neither are you,' I commanded.

'Fine.' She went back to pulling stuff out of my case, purring over a pair of Gucci sandals. My post-Vegas treat. I settled back against the chair for a moment and took a better look at my bestie. It wasn't just her fingernails that were suffering. Her ponytail was covering up some pretty dodgy dark blonde roots and someone had been hitting the Batiste pretty hard. Of course there were baby-induced dark circles, and no, she wouldn't be slipping back into that twenty-four-inch-waist wedding dress again any time soon, but that was to be expected. What made me uncomfortable was seeing bright and shiny Louisa look so faded and tired. As if she was even less interested in having a baby than I had been five minutes earlier. Which was to say not interested at all.

'Really, Lou, it's not on my agenda right now.' I took my prized McQueen clutch, a January sale steal, from her hands and placed it on the dresser. 'Don't worry about me. Or Alex. Or our future awesome babies. They're going to be fine.'

'There's just so much to think about,' she sighed. 'I couldn't even start to prepare you. It's not just the baby – it's being pregnant, it's buying everything, it's trying to get ready for something you could never ever get ready for. The way it changes your body, your relationship and, oh God, the sleep.' She stopped for a moment and took a deep breath. 'And more than anything else, it's giving up silly, selfish stuff because it's not about you any more.'

'Silly selfish stuff?' I didn't think I wanted to hear the rest of this sentence.

'Running off to New York? Popping into LA for work, to Paris, to Vegas.' She pulled on the end of her ponytail, reading my mind. 'I haven't even got time to go to the hairdresser.'

'It's not like I would do those things if I had a baby,' I said, trying really hard not to be offended. 'But just because we're getting married doesn't mean we're going to have a kid straightaway. We've got stuff we want to do first. Alex has this record to tour, I have the magazine to launch. We haven't even set a date yet, remember?'

'I recall,' she said, ploughing headfirst into my underwear. 'I just think it's best to know these things before he puts a ring on your finger. Another ring,' she added when I held up my hand. 'What are you going to do when he wants to go off on tour and you're at home with a teething baby and no one to help? I won't be there. Your mum won't be there. His family don't live in New York, do they?'

'You really don't need to worry about me,' I promised, taking my days of the week underwear from her and pretending her disapproval was based entirely on my lack of baby-preparedness. Clearly I wasn't ready to have a child: I was still wearing children's pants myself. 'There is no bun in this oven.'

'But when there is, it'll be *American*, Angela,' Louisa said, a look of abject horror on her face. 'Your kid is going to have an American accent. It's going to go to American school. It's going to have American friends.'

The sadness in her voice made my stomach hurt more than my mum's shepherd's pie.

'And it's going to have an amazing British aunt,' I replied. 'And a brilliant British best friend in Grace. And wonderful British grandparents who take it off my hands every summer for six weeks.'

'Huh.' Louisa threw a balled-up pair of socks in my face. 'Maybe you have thought this through.'

'I can't think of a better reason to have an American baby. And my mum will be so happy. She's only had control of Grace for half an hour and she was bloody ecstatic when she came in here just now. Imagine her with my kid for two whole months.'

'Angela?' The bedroom door opened again, without a knock. This time it was my dad. It really was like being sixteen again. 'There's a taxi downstairs. Your mother told me to tell you the Americans are here.'

That 'A' word really was sticking in everyone's throat today.

'Wait, what?' I looked at my watch, looked down at my underwear and looked back at my dad. 'Americans? Plural?'

'Your mum says Americans, I'm telling you Americans,' he said, wandering back off down the hall. 'What do I know? It's only my house.'

There wasn't an awful lot of time to worry about who was coming down the drive because Jenny had smashed through the door and, from the sounds of it, taken it off its hinges before I had even had time to put my jeans back on.

'Is anyone home?' she yelled from the hallway. I looked at Louisa with wild eyes. She looked back, equally concerned. Someone had just let themselves into my mother's house. Someone she had never met. Blood would be spilled. 'For real, Angela? Annette?'

'She calls your mum Annette?' Louisa mouthed. 'I don't call your mum Annette.'

'You're not Jenny,' I explained, pressing my hands to my face. 'Do I still look shit? Oh God, I still look shit, don't I?'

'Yeah, but it's only your mate, it's not the Queen,' she replied. 'What's the big deal?'

'And you must be Jenny.' I heard my mum on the approach downstairs and leapt to my feet.

'Come on,' I said, pulling Louisa along. 'There's going to be hugging – you don't want to miss this.'

And I was right. I hurled myself down the staircase

just in time to see my mum give in to a giant Jenny hug. It's not that we weren't an affectionate family, it's just that our idea of expressing emotion was to be incredibly passive-aggressive when angry and gift each other with Penguin biscuits when we were happy, with a little light shoulder touch if we were particularly moved.

'Angie!' Jenny discarded my mother, who stumbled into the side table, arms out wide, and barrelled into me. 'Baby, it's been like, three days. What the hell – you look like shit.'

'I haven't got changed since I got here,' I told her as every ounce of breath was pounded out of my body. 'Or had a shower.'

'You do smell kind of funky,' she confirmed in a stage whisper. 'Maybe spritz a little something before Alex gets in?'

'I thought I might try and have a shower before tomorrow,' I replied.

'Tomorrow?' Alex appeared at the door, laden down with suitcases that I knew for a fact were not his own. 'What's happening tomorrow?'

'Alex.' My heart actually expanded to five times its normal size and threatened to explode then and there. Not only because I hadn't seen him for one whole night and almost two whole days, but also because he looked painfully adorable. While I was still wearing my skanky striped tee and by now extremely baggy jeans, Alex was wearing actual trousers, with an actual shirt and tie under his leather jacket. It was unnerving and extremely hot at the same time. Weird.

'Well, hello.' He smiled, put down the cases and opened his arms for my Jenny-inspired rush. 'What's going on?'

'Nothing.' I nuzzled into his neck, breathing in his Alexness, while trying to ignore my overwhelming Angelaness. 'Just, I thought you were coming tomorrow?'

'I was,' he said, breaking my dry hump and coughing loudly. 'But I figured why wait? We finished up recording early so I came out with Lopez. Which was a mistake.'

'Hey, just because you have no interest in fine cinema or social issues does not make me a bad travel buddy,' she rallied, punching him in the arm.

'*Breaking Dawn* and *Us Weekly* do not fall into the categories of fine cinema or social issues, Jenny,' he said, shaking his head and taking off his leather jacket. 'Learn some boundaries. And some taste.'

I stood in the middle of my Jenny/Alex sandwich and felt myself light up. Granted, I still needed a shower, a swipe of blusher and a change of clothes in the worst way, but just having them close to me made my heart beat a little faster, my smile shine a little brighter. It felt good. Or at least it did until my mum regained her composure and righted herself with the help of the coat rack.

'Mrs Clark, Mr Clark.' Alex dropped me like a hot rock and stepped over to my parents, holding out his hand. 'It's so great to meet you at last. I'm Alex.'

'Apparently so.' Mum took his hand and shook it with all the grace she could muster. Which wasn't much. My dad went completely silent but I saw his knuckles turn white as he accepted Alex's handshake. 'Come in, come in. David, get the kettle on. Tea, or will it be coffee?'

I winced as she spat out the 'c' word.

'I'd love tea,' Alex replied, following her into the

kitchen and throwing me a wink. 'Thank you so much.'

'Shit, son, coffee for me,' Jenny said, yawning loudly. 'I have to get me some caffeine.'

'I'll take the bags upstairs,' I called, grabbing a suitcase and Alex's weekend bag. Thank God one of them was able to travel light. 'Mine's a tea. Two sugars.'

'Pass me that other suitcase,' Louisa offered from halfway up the stairs. 'I'll give you a hand.'

Louisa. I'd completely forgotten she was there. But from her pale, terrified expression, I knew she had been watching. Her first sighting of Hurricane Jenny. God help her when she got to an actual one-on-one encounter. I passed up the second small-for-Jenny-but-giant-for-anyone-else suitcase, only pausing for a second to think how light it was for its size, and followed Louisa back up the stairs.

'I'm going to jump into the shower,' I shouted down the stairs. 'I'm literally throwing myself in and out,' I added to Louisa, who was still looking shell-shocked. 'Two minutes.'

For the first time, I was ecstatically happy that nothing had changed about my mother's house. I dashed into the bathroom, pulled on the shower cord, grabbed a spare razor from the mirrored cabinet and hopped under the hot water. It felt so incredibly good. Probably all the better for knowing that Alex was waiting for me downstairs, but still, really, really good. Five minutes later I was dry, deodorized and pulling on my pants in front of Louisa, much to her distress.

'Pass me that jumper,' I demanded, pointing at a pale grey Vince Henley sweater that was insanely comfortable and showed off just enough boob to make it cute enough for Alex but within the bounds of parent-friendly, and paired it with my black skinny Topshop jeans. Perfect. Well, I was clean and dressed.

'What are you waiting up here for?' I asked, swooshing bronzer and blusher across my cheeks and waking up my eyes with mascara. 'Your tea will be stone cold.'

'I was waiting for you,' Louisa said, colouring up. No need for blusher there. I stared at her while I whacked on half a tube of lip balm. 'What?'

'Nothing,' I answered, taking one last look in the mirror. That'll do, pig. 'Just not used to you being shy.'

'I'm not being shy,' she snipped. 'I was waiting for you.'

This was an interesting development. In all the years we'd known each other, Louisa had always been the one dragging me off into social situations I would otherwise have avoided. I even went to the same university as her to avoid spending three years sitting in a hall of residence watching *Buffy the Vampire Slayer* on my own. I still ended up doing plenty of that, but thanks to Louisa, I also played netball (badly), acted in the drama society (badly), and got wasted in the Student Union every other night (very successfully). But now here she was fiddling with her hair, hiding in my bedroom and risking missing a hot cup of tea. This was not my Louisa.

'Isn't your baby downstairs?' I asked with narrowed eyes.

'Oh God, Grace!' She jumped up and sprinted out of my bedroom faster than when my dad busted us with a bottle of Kiwi 20/20 and a VHS copy of *The Camomile Lawn*. (We were curious.)

I followed Louisa downstairs at a more leisurely pace. The excitement of my best friend and fiancé being in the same house as me was clouded somewhat by the realization that my best friend and fiancé were in the same house as my mother, but I couldn't hear anything breaking and no one was raising their voice, or at least no one was raising their voice any louder than usual (Jenny), so it couldn't be going too badly.

'Oh my God, how cute are you?'

I rounded the corner to see Louisa frozen to the spot by the kitchen door and a tiny human that I assumed to be Grace sitting on Jenny's lap. Dad was busily pouring out cups of tea and cutting up slices of cake as if his life depended on it, while my mum sat at the table and stared at Alex, trying to find something, anything, wrong. The subject of her visual interrogation was ignoring it all and smiled at me as though this was perfectly normal. It was quite the tableau.

'Grace.' Louisa faltered, turning to look at me for help. I could kind of understand. A stranger had her baby. And the stories Louisa had heard about said stranger were enough to have curled Grace's hair while she was still *in utero*.

'Jenny, stop trying to steal the baby's soul,' I said, gently pushing Louisa towards the table. 'Sacrificing her won't atone for your sins.'

Sulking, Jenny held out Lou's bundle of joy. The new mother grabbed hold of the baby and immediately relaxed. I leaned against Alex's open arm as it wrapped around my hip and watched ten years' worth of premature ageing slip off her face.

'Hi,' she whispered at the baby. 'Do you want to meet Auntie Angela?'

It was all too much. Jenny, Alex and a baby in my mum's kitchen?

I thought back to when I'd stood in this room the

morning before Louisa's wedding. I was carrying my bridesmaid's dress and strutting up and down the kitchen trying to get used to my heels, while Mark and my dad were looking at his car. The 'check engine' light had been flashing for ages and he'd decided to have a look at it on the morning of my best friend's wedding. And now here I was barefoot in jeans with a pair of tiny stick-hands thrusting at me, feeling considerably less stable than I had in the four-inch Louboutins.

'Can I hold her?' Alex piped up from the table, pushing away his tea. 'She's beautiful, Louisa.'

'Oh, of course,' she said, colouring up all over again. 'And . . . nice to meet you properly.'

'You too.' Smiling, he held his arms out for the baby and my legs almost gave way. Even my mum let out a little gasp. Jenny, of course, was stuffing her face with scones and completely impervious. Louisa rested a hand on my arm and gave me a sly grin.

'You're not even thinking about it though, are you?' she whispered as Grace gripped Alex's finger and giggled. He looked up through his floppy black fringe and waved her hand at me.

'Hey, Aunt Angela,' he said on behalf of Grace. 'I think you're weird because I'm awesome but you don't want to get in on this.'

And with that, my ovaries exploded.

'So, where are we going for dinner?' Jenny broke the tension with her usual charm. 'I'm super-hungry.'

'David was going to get fish and chips,' my mum replied, still completely discombobulated. It was actually amazing to see. 'Does that sound all right? We can get something else if you'd like.'

Annette Clark was actually deferring to Jenny Lopez.

Louisa squeezed my hand in amazement. So this was where we'd been going wrong all these years – asking permission, being respectful, worrying what she would say. All along we should have been telling her what was what. From the look on his face, my dad was having a similar realization.

'That sounds awesome,' Jenny said, glowing. 'Fish and chips. And tea! And scones. Awesome.'

'Naming everything on the table is going to get real tired, real fast,' Alex replied, still bouncing Grace on his knee and causing my womb to spasm uncontrollably. 'It sounds great, Mrs Clark. But let me and Angela go. You guys shouldn't have to go out of your way for us.'

'Well, if you're sure . . .' Once again, my mother relented. And smiled. Sort of. 'Angela knows the place we like.'

'She does,' I agreed. 'But I'm not taking Grace. Can you imagine anything more heartbreaking than a baby smelling like a chippy?'

'I should take her home.' Louisa picked up her cue and took the baby from Alex. I took the opportunity to poke her little round cheeks. And nose. And belly. It was sort of addictive. 'But I'll see you tomorrow?'

'Tomorrow,' I confirmed, kissing her on the cheek and kissing Grace on the head. So soft. So, so soft. 'Text me when you've got home.'

The front door shut behind Lou while Alex put on his jacket and stood up beside me.

'So, five cod and chips?' I grabbed my handbag from the counter and dabbed on more lip balm. I wasn't happy about leaving the house again before I'd been properly beautified.

'I'm sure you and I can share a chips,' Mum replied,

fussing over Jenny and buttering some bread. 'Surely you don't want a full bag to yourself?'

'Surely she does,' Jenny replied. 'But we've got to get her ass into a wedding dress, right, Annette? So it's sharesies on the chips, Angela.'

My mother laughed. Out loud. For people to hear. My dad remained silent.

'Come on.' Alex took my hand in his and pulled me towards the door before I Darth Vadered my mother to death. 'Show me where this chippy is.'

CHAPTER EIGHT

Outside, the evening was warmer than I'd expected, but I was glad I was wearing a jumper. Dad's garden was enjoying the early summer, and the smell of freshly cut grass and roses made me smile. Not only because it meant Mum had made him mow the lawn for my arrival, but also because it smelled of home. New York could smell of a thousand wonderful things at once, but the clean, glossy green smell of cut grass? Unless you followed one of the giant mutant mowers around Central Park all day, it was hard to find. But here it was, right by the front door.

'Who do I have to pay to see you smile like that more often?' Alex said, slipping his arm around my shoulders and placing a very gentle kiss on my lips.

'When do I not smile?' I asked, returning his kiss and holding him tightly. The sun was just starting to dip down low and, nap or no nap, I was fading fast.

'Seems like we've both been too busy lately.' Alex stretched his arms out so wide his shirt came untucked, showing just a hint of his hard, flat belly. 'There hasn't been nearly enough smiling.'

'Well, don't get used to it while we're staying in this house,' I said, grabbing one of his outstretched hands and pulling him down the garden path. 'Fish, chips and then bed.'

'I can totally get behind that,' he said as he followed me, holding on to my hand as we went.

The strangeness that had hit me in the kitchen followed Alex and me down the road and across to the shops. These were streets I'd wandered endlessly as a teenager. Suburban Surrey with its family-friendly cars and its privet hedges and its bright and sparkly net curtains. I'd walked back and forth from the library with my mum, arms full of books she thought were inappropriate but let me read anyway. I'd wandered around aimlessly in cycling shorts and baggy T-shirts with Louisa, eating Push Pops from the corner shop and wondering if the boys we liked liked us. And I'd driven up and down them with Mark, listening to him moaning about visiting my parents. Me and these streets had a lot of history. Alex clashed wildly against the four-wheel-drives and Little Tikes play sets that lay out on the lawns we passed. His shirt was too tight, his tie was too skinny, and he looked altogether too confident. Loose shoulders, long strides, black hair. He looked like a skyscraper in the middle of a row of semis.

'I'm so glad you came out early,' I said, speeding up my step to fall into stride alongside him. 'Is there anything you want to do tomorrow? We are sort of on holiday – we should do something fun.'

'You're not going to like this, but I think we should do something with your folks tomorrow,' Alex suggested. 'Look at it from their position. You just walked through the door, their house is full of loud Americans they've never met before and one of them thinks he's going to marry their daughter.'

'Thinks he is?'

'OK, *is* going to marry their daughter,' he said, pulling my left hand up into the air and waving my engagement ring in my face. 'But they're probably just as freaked out as you. We should, I don't know, go to some country pub or something. Or take them out for lunch somewhere. I want to make a good impression.'

'Alex, you've saved me from spinsterhood and you held a baby,' I said, trying to process his family Sunday lunch idea, incorporating Jenny as our overenthusiastic Labrador. 'You're golden.'

'I still think we should suggest it,' he insisted gently. 'Maybe we could invite Louisa – and it's Tim, right?'

'All right, slow down,' I said. My head was spinning and this time it wasn't from the jet lag. 'I think I need to eat before I start thinking about playing happy families.'

He gave me his sad but slightly impatient puppy face.

'Fine!' I said. As if I wouldn't have given in anyway. 'It might be nice.'

'That's my girl,' he said, swooping in and pulling my ponytail.

'But we are on holiday,' I repeated. 'And yes, while I know we need to see Mum and Dad, we also get to do fun stuff too. Just me and you?'

'Sure.' He nodded slowly. 'Although you have your presentation, right? And I said I'd go in and meet with the label while I'm here.'

'And everything's OK?' I asked. Any mention of the label worried me. Because in all honesty, I had no idea what the label really meant. 'They like the new record?'

'They do,' he confirmed. A pair of teenage girls across the street – Louisa and me ten years ago – turned on their high heels when they heard him speak. I ducked my head and grinned. He didn't notice, as ever. 'They want to discuss a tour sometime. But I'll have a ton of time to hang out. And you have Jenny to deal with also, so I don't think you'll miss me.'

'*We* have Jenny to deal with,' I corrected him. 'We.'

'Nuh-uh,' he laughed. 'I'd rather take your mom shoe shopping than handle that girl any more. Remember I just spent twelve hours with her. And please know that she spent at least six of those hours crying.'

'She did?' This was not good news. 'About Jeff?'

'About Jeff, about Sigge, about not having packed the right clothes.' Alex turned his green eyes on me as we paused and waited to cross the street. 'I tried to help, but honestly, I kinda tuned out after a while.'

'And no court in the land could find you guilty for that,' I replied. 'I just want her to be OK, but I have no idea how to help.'

'You can't,' he said, almost carrying me across the clear street. The lure of fried food always turned Alex into Popeye. 'People deal with break-ups in different ways. We both know that, don't we?'

After his last bad break-up, Alex had boned half of Manhattan and about a third of Brooklyn. After mine, I'd done a transatlantic runner. It was fair to say neither of us had dealt with our romantic let-downs well.

'We do know that,' I said with a sigh. 'And I know there's no magic switch, but I wish there was at least an off switch for the tears. She would kick my arse all the way to New Jersey if I cried as much as she has. She would tell me how bad it is for my skin, how I was giving myself wrinkles. How I was making myself look old.'

'So tell her that,' he suggested. I looked at him like he was stupid. Because that was a very stupid thing to say. 'What?' he asked.

'Are you insane?' I punched him in the arm for good measure. 'I like my life.'

'Point taken,' he said as we walked into the chip shop.

Armed with five cods, four bags of chips, two pots of mushy peas and, at Alex's insistence, a pickled egg and a can of Irn-Bru, I walked back into my mother's kitchen expecting to see a laid table, a bottle of vinegar and enough salt to give a horse a heart attack. Instead, I saw an empty table, a stack of plates and my mum standing in the middle of the kitchen in a hot-pink Diane von Furstenberg dress and six-inch black YSL Tributes. I didn't think it was unreasonable that I dropped the pickled egg.

'If the wind changes your face will stay that way,' Mum said. If I hadn't been so startled, I'd have been impressed that she was able to pronounce a coherent sentence while Jenny was doing her eyeliner. 'Do you like my new frock?'

'Your new frock?' I picked up the pickled egg along with my jaw.

'Yeah. I was in the showroom on Friday,' Jenny said, jumping in on Mum's behalf, 'and I saw this, and all I could think was, man, if I was turning sixty and throwing an awesome party to show everyone how much ass I still kick, I'd want to do it in this dress.

Maybe not these heels, but definitely this dress. So I brought it with.'

'Maybe not those heels,' I agreed. I felt like a disapproving parent. So this was what my mum was on about when I bought those black Chinoiserie wedges in the lower sixth. 'Maybe.'

'Angela brought me a stain-removing pen,' Mum told Jenny as they moved onto blusher.

'And she didn't bring me anything,' Dad chipped in, pouring himself a very big glass of whiskey from a very new bottle of Jack Daniel's. 'Jenny brought me whiskey.' He raised his glass to me.

'I brought you me!' I protested and held out my paper packages. 'And chips! And fish! And Irn-Bru!'

'Ooh, that'll go down a treat with the whiskey, actually.' My dad took the bags from me and cracked open the can. 'Now, get sat down before this gets cold.'

I sat opposite my mum and didn't even try not to stare.

'Are you all right over there?' she asked, accepting her plate of fried goodness from Alex.

'You look really nice,' I said quietly. And she did. Jenny had brushed her hair out to give it a little more shine than usual, and the make-up was delicate enough to bring out her features but not look obviously made up. She looked polished and, well, pretty. It wasn't something I was used to thinking about my mother. 'That dress suits you.'

'It's not something I'd usually wear,' she acknowledged, pulling the low neckline up a little. 'But it is going to be a party, isn't it?'

'It is,' Alex replied, joining us at the table with his own glass of Irn-Bru and whiskey. 'You look great, Mrs Clark.'

'Annette, really,' she replied, more than a little flustered. 'Thank you, Alex. Does anyone else want a drink? Jenny?'

'I'd actually kill for a Martini,' she said, yawning loudly. 'Or a beer? Just something to perk me up.'

'I think I might have a beer as well.' Mum teetered over to the fridge and came back with two bottles of Heineken. Mum? Drinking beer? In DVF and YSL? 'Angela?'

'Not for me.' I was too tired and too on edge for a drink.

Mum looked at Dad and smirked. Dad shook his head and looked away. I assumed they had a bet on how long it would take me to get ratted. Looked like Dad had lost.

'So, Alex.' Dad sat down next to my fiancé while Jenny elbowed me in the ribs and merrily chowed down on a chip, beer in hand. 'Tell me all about this band you're in. I've had a listen on the YouTube, and I must say, you're very good.'

To his credit, Alex brushed his hair away from his face, cleared his throat and gave my dad a very earnest nod. 'Um, thanks, Mr Clark—'

'David.' Dad took a swig of his boozy Bru. A very big swig. 'It's David.'

'OK, David,' he went on. 'We've been playing together for what, about ten years now? I met the other guys in school, so yeah, it's got to be at least that. And we just finished our fourth album, and yeah, it's really great.'

'You met in school ten years ago?' Mum choked on her chip butty. 'How young are you exactly?'

'School means university,' I translated. 'He's thirty. Thirty-one in July.'

111

'Oh. And I thought they spoke English,' she said into a napkin. 'Did you study music? Did you do well?'

So it was going to be the Spanish Interrogation of Alex over fish and chips. I squeezed his knee under the table, but he just patted my hand and shook his head. He was so good at this. How come he was so good at this?

'I studied architecture, actually, and yeah, I graduated top of my class.'

I knew that. Starter for ten.

'Class means year,' I interjected quietly.

'I went to RISD – that's in Rhode Island. It's a couple of hours out of New York. It's a pretty good school.'

That one I didn't know. Lose five points. Although I did know Seth Cohen applied to go there on *The OC*, so that was something.

Mum was nodding her approval, Dad was nodding into his booze, and Jenny just seemed to be nodding off. So far she'd managed to eat about three chips and her fish was untouched. I was giving her three minutes before I took it. Sharing chips with my mum, my arse. I was Hank Marvin. Jet lag, obviously. Not just general greediness.

'How do your parents feel about the music thing?' Mum wasn't giving up. 'I can't imagine I'd have been very pleased if I'd sent Angela to university to study law and she'd come home to tell me she was running off to join the circus.'

'I don't think it's exactly the same thing,' I remonstrated, jumping in to defend Alex before he could come up with a response. 'Not that I wouldn't have been an excellent circus performer.'

'You did spend most of Year Ten wearing clown make-up,' Dad chuckled to himself. I tilted my head to give him a glare. Oh, he was happy with that one. 'And Year Eleven. Remember when you wore pigtails for six months straight?'

'They were very popular,' I said clearly and loudly. 'It wasn't just me.'

'My folks weren't crazy about it,' Alex said, ignoring the sideshow. Probably best. 'But they understood. And I guess we thought the band would just be a fun side project until we got real jobs, but then we all moved to Brooklyn together and things sort of took off.'

'You lived with those guys?' Jenny scrunched up her face. Which was now laid on her forearm, on the table. 'With Craig? Ew.'

'Just for a little while,' Alex said, trying not to laugh. 'Living with Graham had some benefits – he's a pretty good cook. And it was that or go home to my folks.'

'And what do your parents do?' My mum was on a roll.

'My dad is in real estate and my mom does a bunch of mostly charity stuff,' he explained. 'She used to teach but now she's retired.'

I had a weird feeling that these were things I was supposed to know about my fiancé already. Alex never talked about his family. I knew he had a brother, and obviously I knew he had parents, but they weren't a regular topic of conversation. And by that, I meant he never, ever talked about them.

'And do you think you'll be doing music for a lot longer?' I could see my mum was trying really hard to keep an even expression, even though I knew the idea of telling her friends she had an architect for a son-in-law was much more appealing than saying 'musician'. 'Or . . . not?'

'I think it's something I'll always do,' he replied, hastily swallowing his food. 'But there's other stuff I'd like to try. I am incredibly blessed to be able to make a living out of playing music, but it's a huge commitment. Weird hours, lots of travel. I think it would be super-hard to be playing full time and raise a family.'

My mum, my dad and I all coughed in stereo, but when we came up for air there were three very different expressions around the table. My mum had the glazed-over look of love in her eyes, my dad gave the impression he was going to be sick, and I didn't know what to think. Or say. Or emote.

'Of course.' Mum reached across the table and rested her hand on Alex's wrist. He did not pull away. Or cry. 'That makes sense.'

Alex nodded, smiled and stuck a fork into his fish. 'This is really good, by the way,' he said, lifting it to his mouth. 'Almost as good as Angela's cooking.'

'She learned everything she knows from me,' Mum sang happily. I glared at my dinner. That was just offensive. 'Well, it's very nice to have you here, Alex. It is quite a relief to know Angela has found someone with his head screwed on.'

'Because my head isn't?' I asked. 'I'm sensible.'

'I don't think you can argue that someone who has a degree in architecture –' Mum gestured towards her new favourite person – 'is a less sensible person than you.'

Between being too tired to argue and wanting my mum to like Alex more than she liked Eamonn Holmes, I let it go. I wanted to run upstairs and show her my *Gloss* presentation. I wanted to show her last year's tax return that I'd completed all by myself. I wanted

114

to explain that I knew how to get from Sunset Park to Central Park on the subway inside half an hour without changing trains more than twice. I was sensible. I was smart. But this wasn't the time to point this out. Beside, there was deep-fried fish to be eaten and every vinegary mouthful tasted like heaven. I was two years clean on battered cod and that wasn't something I was OK with.

'Actually, I have something for you guys,' Alex said. He reached into his pocket, pulled out three shiny keys and placed them on the table. 'I figured you should have keys to our place. Just in case.'

Now he'd gone too far. Keys? To my house? They had better be fakes. They could open the White House for all I cared as long as they didn't fit the lock to our apartment.

'That's very thoughtful,' my mum said as my dad snatched them up and stuck them deep in his pocket before I could nick them back. 'Really, Alex, that's lovely.'

'Well, you're always welcome, obviously,' he said, loosening his tie a little. All the better to throttle him with. 'Angela's home is your home.'

I almost bit my tongue. My home was their home? News to me. Their home was my home, of course, but not the other way around. Bloody hell. Someone was getting a slap at bedtime.

'Uh, Angela.' Alex snapped me out of my rage trance and pointed across the table. At some point, Jenny had crossed the line from a bit tired to full-on passed-out and her head had rolled off her arm into her dinner. Nice. Nothing like a bit of fish in your hair to really set off a look. But just looking at her reminded me how tired I was, and in the blink of an eye, I could barely stand to blink my eyes.

'I'll take her up to bed,' I volunteered. 'I'm shattered as well, to be honest.'

'Right.' Mum jumped up from the table and took up her hostess action stations. It was her happy place. 'Angela, you and Jenny are in your room and Alex is in the spare room. I've put out extra towels in your bathroom. The pink ones are for you, the white ones are for Jenny and the blue ones are for Alex. There should be everything you need – I got extra tooth-brushes and things—'

'Wait.' I paused in my attempt to hoist Jenny's face out of the plate of grease. And accidentally dropped it back in. 'What do you mean Alex is in the spare room?'

'Angela, it's cool,' Alex said calmly, appearing at the other side of Jenny. 'Thanks Mrs . . . Annette. Super-thoughtful.'

'No, really. You want us to sleep in separate rooms?' I wasn't sure what I was more upset about. The idea of another night away from Alex or sharing a room with Jet-lag Jenny.

'Angela, don't be difficult,' Mum sighed as she started to clear away the half-eaten food. 'You're in your room, Alex is in the spare room.'

'You do know that we live together? And that we're engaged?' I leaned forward, both palms flat on the table. In my head, I looked all confrontational and Jeremy Kyle-ish, but in reality, I probably looked like I was just trying to hold myself up. Because I was. 'Do you think we've got separate bedrooms at home?'

'Angela,' my dad chimed in with his official 'warning' voice.

'Because we haven't.' I ignored it. 'And not just because we can't afford a two-bedroom apartment.'

116

'Angela.' The similarities between my dad's warning voice and Alex's warning voice were spooky. And slightly unnerving. The two of them were at opposite ends of the kitchen, one raising an eyebrow and carrying an unconscious New Yorker in his arms while the other sat at the table nursing his glass. Mum was busy stacking plates in the sink and practising elective deafness. Things really were just like old times, except I didn't feel like I'd gone back in time by two years; it was like I'd gone back in time by twenty.

'Oh, sod it. I'll see you in the morning.' I folded my arms and added under my breath, 'You bastards.'

'I heard that,' my mother shouted as I pushed past Alex and stormed up the stairs. I was almost as mad with him as I was with them, but if they wanted to treat me like a teenager, I would behave like a teenager. I was this close to locking my bedroom door and turning the loudest album I had owned at fourteen, *Spiceworld*, up to full blast. Instead, I headed straight for the bathroom and punched a bale of pink towels. How come Jenny got the white ones anyway?

I turned on the cold tap and held my wrists underneath. I needed to calm down. Clearly I was overreacting. Clearly being back in my childhood home was making me behave like, well, a child, but looking back at me in the mirror wasn't a fourteen-year-old running on Pepsi and cheesy Wotsits who couldn't control herself but a twenty-eight-year-old running on fried food and fumes who should know better. I turned off the tap, pressed a cool hand to my forehead and picked up a white towel to dry off.

OK, I was still feeling a little bit contrary, but I was ready to apologize. In the morning. It was so time for bed.

Dragging on the cord that switched the bathroom light off as I came out of the door, I bounced straight into the brick wall that was Alex's chest. Pressing a finger against my lips, he walked me backwards into the bathroom and locked the door behind us. Surprised but still not entirely awake, I perched on the side of the bath and stared at him in the dark.

'What?'

'What?' he repeated in a whisper. 'What? Really?'

'Yes.' I was pouting. I hoped it was too dark for him to see. 'What.'

'Don't pull that face at me, Clark.' He crouched down in front of me. 'What's gotten into you?'

'Me?' I was trying to whisper but my voice seemed to be set on fishwife hiss. 'You're the one who's so far up my mother's arse I can see you when she opens her mouth. What's with the keys?'

'It's a gesture,' he replied, placing a hand on my knee. 'I want them to like me and you're not helping. Or maybe you are. I feel like they like me a whole lot more than they like you right now. And they're not going to appear on the doorstep next week – calm down.'

'Don't tell me to calm down,' I said, pretending I couldn't feel the warmth of his palm through my jeans. It was off-putting. 'Because they bloody well will. Just to be awkward.'

'No one's being awkward but you,' he said in a stern voice. It was oddly sexy. 'I know you're tired and I know you're stressed, but you're gonna regret it if you fuck up this week. You haven't seen your family in two years, Angela – don't make this a bad time. They've missed you and I know you've missed them.'

I looked back at the towel bales and sniffed.

'Yes you have.' He nudged me and smiled in the darkness. Damn those blindingly white American teeth. 'So tell me what's up.'

'Everything's just so weird.' My voice sounded tiny even though it echoed around the tiled walls. 'I've been gone ages and nothing's changed. Nothing at all. They've even got the same soap.' I pointed at the fresh white bar on the side of the sink. 'But it's all so weird because things have changed, haven't they? I feel like I've walked into a reality show or something.'

'Things here might not have changed so much,' Alex answered after a second's consideration. 'But think about it. You have.'

Huh. That sort of made sense.

'Two years isn't such a long time if you're living the same life you've been living for the last fifty. Even the last five. But when you up and move to another country and change every little last thing, it's gonna seem kinda wacky when you come back to the place you left behind,' he went on. 'Especially when you come back and throw two arsehole Americans into the mix.'

I didn't want to smile but I couldn't help it. So this was why I was marrying him. My mum was right. He was sensible.

'It's like putting Mickey Mouse in a Dickens novel, right?' He squeezed my knee, pushing for a laugh. And he got it.

Alex reached up to push the hair back from my face. His fingertips rippled through my roots, sending shivers right through my body. I could have sworn I was a fat lap-cat in a previous life. 'So you're going to get some sleep and wake up in the morning all shiny and new, right?'

119

'Am I?' I wasn't quite convinced.

'Yes, you are.'

He pushed up on his knees and slipped his hands around my face, pulling me in for a long, soft kiss. In the dark, with his warm body against mine, we could have been anywhere in the world, and that's when everything suddenly made sense. Alex was my home. Now I'd got that, nothing seemed quite so strange.

CHAPTER NINE

Waking up in my bedroom the next morning was confusing. Waking up next to Jenny was even more confusing. Looking at my phone and seeing that it was almost midday was less confusing. I had been tired.

With a groan I rolled onto my side and threw my legs over the edge of the bed. The events of the day before came back to me in slow motion – the airport, the supermarket, Louisa, Louisa having a baby, Alex, Jenny. Me behaving like a complete child. Alex was right. It wasn't anyone's fault that I was pissed off. Maybe if I hadn't run into Mark, maybe if I'd had more sleep on the plane, maybe if I wasn't so stressed about the meeting. This week wasn't going to get any easier if I was just going to be a complete cock.

Freshly showered, freshly made up and wearing a fresh aqua-coloured Nanette Lepore sundress and brown leather flip-flops, I ventured into the kitchen with a smile on my face only to find it empty. Sighing, I pushed some loose strands of hair that had already escaped from my perky ponytail out of my face and put the kettle on. Tea. Tea made it all better. Because even if it was after twelve, it was too early to hit the cocktails. Unless – I looked over each shoulder – I made a quick screwdriver. It was Sunday, after all. I'd be brunching myself blind if we were at home right now and brunch meant a Bloody Mary at the very least.

I flipped off the kettle, pulled the vodka out from under the counter and poured a generous measure into my mug before topping it off with orange juice. Sip, sigh, relax. The perfect crime.

'Angela?' came a voice.

I jumped out of my skin and hurriedly hid the Smirnoff. As I did so, I noticed the brand new bottle of JD wasn't quite so brand new any more. In fact it was half empty. Father – for shame. So that's where I got my drinking problem from.

'We're in the garden,' my mother called. 'Bring the biscuit tin.'

Putting on my best McDonald's smile, I picked up the biscuit tin, checked it had Hobnobs in it and put my best foot forward.

'Morning.' I placed the biscuit barrel down on the wrought-iron garden table and showed the meanest teeth I could manage without looking like a Rottweiler. 'What are we up to?'

Alex, sitting opposite me in jeans and a David Bowie T-shirt that looked suspiciously like it had been ironed, smiled over his coffee cup.

'Afternoon,' Mum replied. 'We were just discussing where to go for lunch. Alex thought it would be nice if we all went out together.'

'That sounds lovely,' I said, taking a deep drink and trying not to shudder. Maybe it was a little bit strong. 'I've been dreaming of a Sunday roast.'

'Someone got out of bed on the right side.' Dad got up from his chair and kissed me on the top of my head. Thank goodness vodka didn't smell. 'Alex and I were almost as lazy as you. Late one, wasn't it, son?'

Son? Wuh?

'It was,' Alex confirmed. 'Your dad has some awesome vinyl. You never told me he was a rocker.'

'I didn't think a Phil Collins cassette made someone a rocker?' I turned to follow my dad as he walked towards his shed. Ahh, the shed. A man's last bastion of freedom.

'Are you kidding me?' Alex leaned across the table and yawned. 'He has *so many* records. I can't believe he saw Bowie in the Seventies.'

I looked down at Alex's T-shirt and leaned over to sniff it. It smelled of Comfort. And yes, it had definitely been ironed. 'Is that my dad's?'

'It was,' Dad called back. 'I gave it to Alex. Keep it in the family and all that. It's not like I've worn it in the last forty years.'

My good-girl resolve was being tested. My mum looked so calm, I would have put money on her having had a Botox-fest in the night, and my dad and Alex sharing clothes and staying up late listening to record . . . Perhaps it wasn't just me who was drinking in the day.

'We nearly did for that bottle of whiskey, as well,' Dad shouted. 'Drank me under the table, this one did.'

Ahh, so that's how Alex had moved up the son-in-law ladder so quickly. They had bonded over Seventies rock and got hammered. And my mum had seen him hold a baby without pulling a face or even slightly injuring it. Which was more than could be said for me. He was in. Relief washed over me. Or at least the buzz from my screwdriver did. I really did need to eat something soon.

'Is Jenny up?' Mum, complete with lipstick *and* mascara, reached for a Bourbon biscuit. 'We need to set off soon if we want to get a seat in the garden.'

'She's still fast on,' I said, waiting for someone to compliment my dress and wondering if my mum looked better than I did. I had relied heavily on the frock for impact. 'I'll go and ask if she wants to come. Garden looks nice.'

'Dad's been getting it ready for the party,' she said, looking incredibly pleased with herself. While my mother was one of England's leading martyrs, she also really enjoyed an opportunity to rub my Aunt Sheila's face in the fact that our garden was three times the size of hers. I would have found it sad if I hadn't been fighting exactly the same gene my entire life. It was probably why I was still so pissed off that no one had mentioned my very beautiful and not inexpensive dress. 'We're going to have a little marquee over there,' she said, pointing to a pretty grassed area between the two silver birches at the end of the garden. 'And Dad's going to turn the shed into a bar. He's a bit more excited about that than he should be.'

'I've been learning how to mix cocktails,' he called from behind closed doors. 'Just call me Tom Cruise!'

'Don't call him Tom Cruise,' Mum said in a low voice. 'Whatever you do. Right, Angela, are you going to check on Jenny? Poor girl, I hope she's not sickening for something. Lovely dress, by the way.'

I nodded, patted Alex on his criminally soft T-shirt and pattered back into the house. It was a lovely dress.

* * *

Jenny passed on Sunday lunch, or at least that's what I took her grunting underneath the covers to mean. I patted her on the top of the head, told her where my mum hid her chocolate and recommended that she shouldn't wander into sunny Surrey unaccompanied in case she was burned as a witch by my mother's neighbours. Then I closed the door.

The drive to the pub was uneventful. My parents were oddly quiet, even with each other, only breaking their silence when we passed someone from the garden centre who, surprisingly enough, might or might not have cancer. Alex and I were safely strapped into our seat belts on opposite sides of the back seat. It wasn't quite the same as a frenzied late-night make-out session in the back of a taxi, but there was something lovely about watching the English countryside rush by with the window down, holding hands with my boyfriend and hoping my parents didn't notice.

The garden at the pub was almost completely empty – just a couple of kids playing on the see-saw and the usual smokers hiding out in a corner. Everyone else clearly thought their proximity to the bar would get them served quicker. They were right. I was jealous, but on the other hand drinking in front of my parents had always made me uncomfortable. This was indeed quite the predicament.

'Now you're awake and not quite so mardy, do you want to tell us what your plans are for the week?' Mum asked, ordering a spritzer. Dad and Alex ordered pints. I went for a Diet Coke and made a secret deal with myself to sink a glass of wine at the bar later. Now that I wasn't quite so mardy.

'Not drinking?' Dad said in a slightly too high voice. 'Glass of wine?'

'I'm still a bit tired,' I said, crying inside.

'Not drinking.' Mum gave Dad a sly glance and raised her eyebrows. Did they know I'd already been on the vodka? Was there a marker on the bottle that I hadn't seen? Like when I was a teenager? 'Not drinking. So, plans? For the week?'

'Nothing much set in stone.' I pulled out my iPhone and checked my calendar. 'My meeting at Spencer UK is going to be Thursday now, I think, and obviously it's your party on Saturday. Alex has got some meetings, haven't you?' He nodded on cue. 'And I suppose Jenny's going to want to do the touristy things. Why?'

'Just interested,' she shrugged. The problem with my mum was that it wasn't what she said but what she didn't say that you needed to look out for. When she said she was 'just interested', what she meant was she wanted a complete itinerary of every waking second for all three of us otherwise she'd have us tagged like stray dogs. 'I've been doing a bit of thinking about the wedding.'

'Have you now?'

Alex kicked me very gently underneath the picnic table and leaned in towards me.

'I have,' she went on, pulling her shoulders back and clearing her throat. 'I was thinking about what you said – about keeping it small and just with close friends, and, well, what I thought was, why not have it here?'

'Here in the pub?' That didn't make any sense at all.

'No.' Mum took a deep breath. 'Here at home. This week.'

I felt Alex's thigh tense beside me but his expression never changed. Mum and Dad, on the other hand, were lit up like Christmas trees.

'Right.' I laid my hands flat on the wooden table and looked to the heavens. What pretty fluffy white clouds. 'You want us to get married this week?'

'Yes.'

'Even though weddings, on average, take about eighteen months to organize?'

'Yes.'

'And we haven't organized anything yet. Or got a licence. Or lost our minds.'

'So this is what I was thinking,' Mum went on as if I hadn't spoken, pulling up her handbag – a very tasteful Radley number complete with dangling dog – and producing a flowered notebook. 'We've got the party all organized for Saturday, the family is going to be there, Louisa is coming, your Jenny's here and you did say you just wanted something simple and no hassle. What's less hassle than this? It's all done for you.'

'Even if I didn't think you were completely insane,' I said, picking my words as carefully as I could, 'I don't have a dress. Alex doesn't have a suit here. And we have other friends as well as Jenny and Louisa. And what about Alex's family?'

'Uhh, I kind of mentioned something about not being so close with my mom and dad last night,' Alex said, laying a hand over mine on the table. 'And I guess I might have said they probably wouldn't be coming to the wedding?'

I turned slowly to give him the full power of my glare. 'So you know about this?' I asked. 'Is this your idea?'

'No,' he held his hands up just in case I was thinking about shooting him. And if I'd had a shotgun, I would have. 'I swear.'

'It's my idea.' Mum started tapping on her notebook with her pen. 'Angela, just think about it for a minute. You were the one that said you didn't want too much fuss. And what would be nicer than getting married surrounded by your family, at home? We've always had some money put aside for your wedding, so that's not a problem. I've already ordered lots of flowers – pink and white peonies. They're still your favourite, aren't they?'

'I don't hate peonies,' I admitted grudgingly.

'And I've ordered all your favourite food.' She looked down at her list. 'And I'm not making it. It's coming from a caterer.'

Now she was playing to the crowd.

'And I know we don't have a licence, but I looked on the Internet and what we could do is have your Uncle Kevin do the ceremony and then get the paperwork signed afterwards. I downloaded it all – it looks very straightforward.'

I hated the Internet.

'But the dress?' I looked at Alex for support, but he just shrugged and held up his hands again. 'I don't have a dress.'

'You're not telling me that between you, Louisa and Jenny you can't find a wedding dress in a week?'

She was right. If ever there was a crack team of bridesmaids preassembled on this earth, it was those two. But still. This was even more poorly thought out than Kim Kardashian's wedding. Her second wedding, anyway. I couldn't speak about the first; it wasn't covered by *E!*.

'I'm going inside to the loo, and when I come back I'm going to pretend this conversation never happened,' I said, standing up and attempting to extricate myself from the picnic bench without flashing my knickers. 'And when the waitress comes back, I want the beef. With everything.'

I stormed into the bar wishing I wasn't wearing a swishy lace sundress and stomped into the bathroom as violently as I could. I was in the mood for DMs and ripped jeans and flannel shirts and shouty suicidal music. Instead I was rocking a look that Zooey Deschanel might have written off as a bit too cute. I knew I shouldn't have spent ten minutes in the bathroom applying seventeen coats of mascara. No one ever believed Bambi when he was angry.

I peed furiously, washed my hands and tossed the paper towel into the bin. It didn't help. There was only one person who could help at a time like this.

'Hello?'

'Jenny.' I snuck out of the toilet and out through the front door of the pub. 'My mum has gone mad.'

'Like, Hulk mad, or crazy mad?'

'Like she wants me and Alex to get married on Saturday in the back garden mad.'

There was a silence on the line that I took to mean Jenny was also freaking out. Or at least watching visions of a Vera Wang bridesmaid's dress disappearing in a puff of smoke generated by Annette Clark.

'Angela,' she said slowly. 'That is a freaking awesome idea.'

'What?'

Had the entire world gone insane?

'Think about it.' Jenny's pace picked up. She was going to run with this. 'Your family is here, I'm here, Alex is here. Dude, it's so romantic.'

'Getting married in my mother's garden is romantic?' She'd lost me.

'Totally. It's like something out of a goddamn Nicholas Sparks novel,' she squealed. 'I love this. We'll get flowers, a ton of flowers, just fill the place up, and it's still six days away – that's a heap of time.'

'But it's not a Nicholas Sparks novel,' I pointed out. 'I'm not dying, I don't have amnesia and Alex isn't going away to war. This is stupid. Why don't you think this is stupid? What about Erin and Sadie and all of Alex's friends?'

'Please – they can get their asses over here,' she said, dismissing my concerns immediately. 'Do you have any idea how much money those girls have? More than you and I will ever, ever have. And I'm sure Alex's friends would come if he asked them. We can put them up in the house. Or maybe Louisa could help?'

Louisa. Why didn't I call Louisa? She would have shit on this idea before I'd got as far as agreeing on Uncle Kevin officiating. And in what way exactly was Uncle Kevin ordained? I'd work that out later. I had bigger questions right now.

'Angela, I think you should think about this,' she said seriously. 'You want a no-hassle wedding, right? This is a no-hassle wedding. And it's super-romantic.'

'I suppose it does give me six more days' notice than the last one I planned,' I said, sitting down on the low stone wall behind me. 'But it just feels wrong.'

'Everything feels wrong to you,' Jenny reminded me. 'Remember when I got bangs? You thought that was wrong too.'

'I don't think this is the same,' I huffed. 'And you did grow them out immediately.'

'Spending eighteen months planning a ridiculous wedding doesn't guarantee happiness.' She wasn't about to give up. Jenny had clearly decided which team she was on here and it wasn't mine. 'Look at Russell and Katy.'

'I was actually more upset about that than I expected to be,' I mused. 'But what if we can't find a dress? What about your dress?'

'Oh, please,' she scoffed. 'I could find me a dress blindfolded. Worst comes to the worst, I'll have something flown over. And if I start looking for you now, we could go shopping tomorrow. Thank God you had that stomach flu last month – you don't even need to lose weight.'

'So you'd be ready to call a stop to this if I wasn't at my target weight?'

'I'd call a stop to it if I wasn't at my target weight,' she replied. 'But I honestly think it's a good idea. We could make this super-beautiful. An English country-garden wedding. I'm seeing a loose skirt, maybe a deep V-front and back for the dress, your hair down, wavy, fresh flowers in a garland. I'm having a vision, Angie. I'm having a concept.'

'And I'm having a heart attack,' I said. 'Just don't get overexcited, OK? I haven't agreed to this. And Alex literally hasn't said a word.'

'Alex will do whatever you tell him to,' Jenny said with a yawn. 'Guy's whipped.'

Alex wasn't whipped; he just understood I was easier to manage when I was getting my own way. He wasn't afraid to kick my arse when I needed it. And if he wasn't into this, he'd tell me. 'I'll talk to you later. And don't eat all the Mini Rolls. I'm going to want seventeen when I get back.'

'What's a Mini Roll?' Jenny asked, excited. 'Are they better than the Penguin biscuits? Because I already ate, like, four of them. And what's with your bacon? Why is it weird?'

'Please leave some food for the rest of us,' I said. The last thing I needed now was a return trip to the supermarket. 'We'll be home in a couple of hours.'

'KK, bridey,' she said before hanging up.

At times like these there really was only one answer.

'Vodka, lime and soda please,' I told the bartender. He nodded with surly agreement, poured the drink and mumbled something about two pounds ten. I silently rejoiced at suburban British booze prices and then necked my drink. More vodka was absolutely what this situation needed.

'Could I get another, please?' I asked. The bartender looked at me as though I'd just asked him to punch his own mother in the kidneys and didn't move.

'If it's not too much trouble.' I stared him out until he started pouring. This damn dress.

The second drink went down slightly slower and my brain started to process everything that had happened in the last fifteen minutes. In all honesty, I was more surprised at Jenny's enthusiasm than my mum's suggestion. Looking out across the dark wood-panelled room, I considered the pros and cons. Pro: it would be an easy option. Con: I wasn't even slightly prepared. Pro: it would make my mum really happy. Con: it would make my mum really happy. Pro: I would be married to Alex. Con: . . . there wasn't really a downside to that one.

'Hey.' I looked up to see Alex walking across the bar. 'You OK?'

I nodded. 'Just a bit shell-shocked.'

'That one came right out of left-field, huh?' He gave

me a lopsided smile and sat down on a bar stool beside me. 'Your mom has this all figured out.'

'She was giving you the hard sell?'

'She was,' he confirmed. 'I think she's really freaking out about the idea of us getting married in New York without her.'

'I wouldn't do that,' I protested, taking another sip of vodka. 'I know I'm a shit daughter, but I'm not that shit.'

'Angela.' Alex took my drink from me, took a sip, pulled a face and handed it back. He hated sweet cocktails. 'If you want me to, I'll go right back out there and tell her never to mention it again. There's no pressure here. There's no time frame, there's no stress, as far as I'm concerned.'

'Thank you,' I said. I leaned in and placed a Sunday afternoon pub-appropriate kiss on his soft lips. 'The weird thing is, I'm not sure it isn't a good idea.'

'You're not?' He looked surprised.

'I don't know.' And I didn't. 'What do you think?'

He rested his elbows behind him on the bar, much to the annoyance of my friend the bartender, and looked at me with level eyes. 'I think it could be awesome. Like we're reverse-eloping.'

I looked at the bar and ran my fingernail along the grain in the wood, trying not to get overexcited until he'd finished.

'You know I'll do whatever you want to do. But that doesn't mean I'm just gonna sit back and go along with whatever everyone else says. I honestly think this could be great if we do it right. If we do it for us. And I'm not going to let you give into this just to shut your mom up. But if *you* want this, then we'll do it.'

'I don't think it's a terrible idea,' I repeated. 'And I

133

am sort of a bit excited about the idea of it. Maybe if I didn't have the presentation to worry about as well. Is it a terrible idea?'

'If you're not into it, we just say no,' Alex said.

'I think I am, though,' I whispered in case my mum was recording me somehow. 'Am I mad?'

'Maybe a little.'

'I'm an idiot.' I tried to get my head round what I was considering. This was definitely more of a tequila quandary and I was almost certain the Red Lion didn't have any Patrón behind the bar. 'I'm just asking for trouble.'

'I wouldn't have come up with this myself,' he admitted. 'But I just want to be married to you. I don't care if it's your mom's garden, the top of the Empire State Building, Vegas or the moon. I want you to be Mrs Reid, and hell, if that happens sooner rather than later, I'm not going to complain.'

'I'm not changing my name,' I reminded him.

'My wife the feminist,' he said, pulling me towards him and resting a hand on my bare back. 'This really is a cute dress.'

I ate up the compliment like Ms Pac-Man and felt my skin burn where his hand was touching me. 'So I'm thinking I go out there, refuse to commit to anything until I have asked many, many questions *and* eaten my dinner,' I said slowly, 'but maybe this might happen?'

'This might happen.' Alex's sleepy green eyes sparkled. 'And I'm with you whatever you decide.'

'We decide?' I amended. 'This has to be our decision.'

'Whatever we decide, then,' he agreed. 'I'm in.'

He was in. Whatever it was we were getting into, at least we were in it together.

CHAPTER TEN

By the time we got into the car to go home, I had a belly full of roast beef and Yorkshire puddings plus a head full of weddings. After talking to Alex, I had banned my mother from mentioning it again at the table and told her I'd think about it. I could see she was champing at the bit to pour out the rest of her argument, but she gave in. She knew when not to push, and I was fairly certain she thought she was getting her way. And, much like her daughter, she was always in a much better mood when she was getting her own way. Instead of talking dresses, party favours and first dances, we discussed the magazine launch, Alex's touring plans, Dad's shed and Mum's bitchy co-workers at the library. You'd think she worked for MI5 – it was ridiculous. The politics were less intense on *Question Time*.

Alex dozed in the back seat all the way, his iron constitution tested by the carvery option, while I imagined what a back-garden wedding might look like. It was definitely big enough, and I had to admit Dad's retirement had been good for the lawn. Either he'd bought shares in Miracle-Gro or he'd been investing every spare moment in that grass. Possibly because he was secretly growing weed somewhere; I hadn't asked yet. If I agreed to go through with this, I would definitely be bringing in a truffle pig to scout round the back of the greenhouse. So the venue wasn't a problem. And I had had a little internal swoon at the idea of peonies everywhere. And external catering. And perhaps this was the best way to avoid waking up in the middle of the night with wedding sweats.

And Alex seemed to be pretty into it, although I did feel a bit strange about his parents not being there, even if they didn't get along. And yes, Jenny was right – most of our really good friends probably could organize a last-minute flight to London; but his couldn't. They didn't own PR companies or come from rich, Upper-East-Side families – they were bartenders and baristas living six to a loft in Bushwick. I had a sneaking suspicion most of them didn't own passports. Or deodorant. But maybe we could have a party back in New York for them. It would be another occasion on which to wear my non-existent dress. And we'd probably have to do some City Hall stuff to make it legal anyway, so really I'd be getting two weddings with none of the hassle.

I looked over at Alex. He was smiling happily in his sleep. Years of catching a nap on a tour bus whenever he could meant he could sleep any time, anywhere. It was one of our shared skills and it made me worry for our kids. At least the odds were that they would sleep through the night pretty early on.

Calm down, Angela, I told myself. One step at a time. Yes, you're considering a shotgun wedding, but there's no actual baby involved. Thank God. But a wedding. An actual wedding. In six days' time. It didn't seem like such a bad idea sitting here in the car, looking at the man I loved. If only because whenever I got an uninterrupted gawk at my boyfriend, the devil on my shoulder popped up and started chanting 'lock it down, lock it down, lock it down'. I thought the engagement ring might have calmed that a little, but it hadn't. Well, I'd been engaged before. Not all sparkly engagement rings led to solemn wedding bands.

'Hey.' Jenny had been busy. I walked into the living room to find the carpet covered in magazines, sheets of paper and coloured marker pens. In the centre of it all, Jenny sat on the floor. Hair tied back, reading glasses that she didn't need though she swore up and down that they helped her concentrate better, she was waist-deep in paper products and staring intently at her laptop. Pinned to the wall beside her (with what I could only hope for Jenny's sake was something that wouldn't mark the wallpaper) was a chart titled 'WEDDING TIMELINE' covering seven days, starting with Sunday and running all the way up to Saturday, or, as it was now to be known, 'wedding day'.

'Woah.' Alex walked in, froze and walked back out, pulling me with him. 'Did I miss something?'

'I told her on the phone.' I creased my forehead in an apology. 'But I didn't say we were definitely doing it.'

'Well make up your mind quick,' he said, placing his hands on my shoulders, 'because as soon as your mom sees this, it's on. If you want to shut this down, we have to shut it down now.'

'OK.' I rested my own tiny hands on top of his. 'I'm not sure I do want to shut it down.'

Alex didn't say anything, just dipped his head in a barely noticeable nod.

'So if you wanted to do this, I think maybe I would want to do this.' I looked over my shoulder and wondered how long it would take me to regret those words. 'I don't hate the idea of being married to you before the week is out, if I'm honest.'

'That's really not the part that concerns me,' he replied, cocking his head to one side so his fringe fell in front of his eyes. 'I don't want you to agree to something you're being pushed into. You're too much of a people-pleaser and you already have the presentation to worry about this week.'

'Please!' I tried to laugh off his statement, but it was a little bit true. I did have a tendency to get myself into trouble out the goodness of my heart. Or at least for fear of Jenny beating me up. Because she totally could. 'But really, I think it could be lovely. Unless you're even a tiny bit not into it. At all.'

'I was kind of thinking about it in the car,' he admitted. 'And the only thing that's stopping me dragging you down the aisle and having your Uncle Kevin make shit official is the problem of getting Craig and Graham here. Kinda feels like they should be.'

'Agreed.' I breathed out. A part of me had been concerned that he would say he had completely changed his mind and was going to dedicate his life to becoming Justin Bieber's official Twitter chronicler. Although that was on my to-do list, not his. I shouldn't project. 'You really don't want to invite your parents?'

'I want to tell them,' he said, pulling me in for a hug and dropping his chin on top of my head. 'And my brother, I guess. But I don't think they'll come. And I honestly don't mind. We just don't have that sort of relationship. I don't want you to stress out about it.'

'You're telling me I shouldn't use this as an excuse to stage an elaborate, overly emotional reunion then?'

'I don't think so. My mom hasn't emoted since 1974. And that's one of the things my dad likes best about her.'

So his parents weren't overly demonstrative. Suddenly his laconic approach to life made a lot more sense. I broke the hug by slapping him on the arse, over-whelmed by a surge of excitement. My parents weren't exactly touchy-feely, but I'd definitely broken the chain.

'You really think you can keep a lid on this thing?' Alex nodded towards the living-room floor where Jenny was hard at work. 'This is our wedding – try to remember that.'

'What trouble can she cause in six days that she couldn't cause in six months?' I reasoned. 'And besides, Louisa is here. She'll help keep things sensible.'

'Good point.' He squeezed me tightly. 'The less time she has, the better.'

'And she's in a new country,' I added. 'She's totally at a disadvantage.'

'Angela, can you get in here?' Jenny called from her carpet office. 'I've been doing some research and I need you to narrow down some stuff so we can start placing orders.'

'Disadvantage, huh?' Alex released me from his arms and I reluctantly entered Wedding Central. 'No doves. That's all I'm saying. Anything else is OK by me.'

'No doves,' I agreed. That couldn't be too tough to avoid. Even Jenny couldn't arrange doves by Saturday. Could she?

'What was that?' Jenny looked up.

139

'No doves.' It couldn't hurt to make sure she knew. 'This is a dove-free wedding.'

'But there is definitely going to be a wedding?' Jenny scrambled to her feet so fast, her laptop fell onto the carpet and she didn't even blink. 'We're going to do this?'

'I'm not marrying you,' I fought off her kisses but accepted her hug. 'But yes. We're going to do it.'

'Angie!' Jenny jumped up and down, still attached to my neck. 'It's going to be awesome. I promise. Total dream wedding. The best.'

'Dream wedding?'

Mum appeared at the doorway and took a sharp intake of breath when she saw the state of her living room. This was more like her worst nightmare.

'Angie agreed, Mrs C!' Jenny let go of me and threw herself at my mum. 'We're having the wedding!'

'Oh, Angela.' It did seem a little strange that my mum was celebrating my agreeing to get married by hugging another girl, but I let it go. If her arms were busy hugging Jenny, she couldn't beat her senseless for making a mess of the wallpaper. 'Right, we've got some planning to do, haven't we?'

'We have,' I agreed. 'But I think I'd better go and see Louisa first, if that's OK?'

'Of course!' Jenny answered for both of them and I had a feeling it wouldn't be for the last time. 'Can I come with? We can bridesmaid-bond. And we really didn't get to chat yesterday. Because you didn't introduce us. Because you're rude.'

I couldn't actually argue that point.

'Fine. Can I borrow the car, Mum?'

'I'll drive you,' she offered. 'I need to pop to the shop for some things anyway.'

I knew this was a complete lie. The house was stocked to withstand a nuclear war, but she did not want me behind the wheel of her precious Toyota Yaris. Honestly, you have one little accident in ten years and they never let you hear the end of it.

'Fine.' I pulled my phone out to text Louisa while Jenny raced upstairs to grab her Proenza Schouler satchel. It made my bag look sad. My dad and Alex sat at the kitchen table, pouring out tumblers of whiskey. Watching them toast the wedding and clink their glasses gave me a happy.

'Best to stay out of it from here, son,' my dad said in a low voice. Just not low enough. 'Unless you really can't stand something, I recommend a lot of nodding, smiling and the occasional "yes, love". It's a lot easier.'

'Gotcha.' Alex sipped his whiskey. 'Good advice, Mr Clark.'

'You really are going to have to start calling me David,' he replied. 'Or Dad. If you want.'

I bit my lip and tried to hold in a little squeak. Good God, this week was going to be a trial for my mascara.

'Angie,' Jenny wailed from the bottom of the stairs. 'Move your ass. There's *no time.*'

'See you later.' I kissed Alex quickly on the cheek and waved at Dad. 'I'll be back so you can agree with everything in a couple of hours.'

'Can't wait.' Alex raised a hand. 'Take your time.'

'That's it,' Dad said, completely missing the sarcasm. 'Good work.'

For some reason, I was more nervous about telling Louisa I was getting married on Saturday than I was about the idea of getting married on Saturday. As we pulled up, Jenny was still grilling my mum on what exactly she had arranged and what exactly needed to be brought in 'logistics-wise'. Slightly flustered, Mum had sworn to have all the information ready when we got back home. I had a funny feeling she was going to go straight back to the house in order to create said information. The flower shop on the high street probably hadn't given her more than a 'we'll see you on Saturday' as confirmation, and that was not going to work for Jenny Lopez.

Lou's place looked the same as ever from the outside. The bright blue painted door, the wooden buckets full of pansies in the yard, the perfectly numbered and aligned wheelie bins outside, hinting at her OCD. It was my home away from home. I even had my own room for the nights when we'd done one too many bottles of white wine for me to stagger home. And for the nights when I just couldn't be arsed. It really shouldn't have been a surprise to me that my ex-fiancé was having an affair.

'Oh, it's super-quaint,' Jenny said, coming up the path behind me. 'And it's a house? Like, a full house?'

'It's a full house,' I nodded. 'It has many rooms. And two toilets. And there are only two people living in it.'

Jenny seemed puzzled. 'Doesn't Louisa have a husband?'

'Yes.' I looked at her like she was mad.

'Then three people?' Jenny looked at me like I was mad.

'Three?'

'Grace?'

Oh yeah. Grace.

'So two people and a baby,' I corrected myself.

142

'I know this is a controversial statement to you,' she said, straightening her hair, 'but babies are people too.'

'Whatever,' I mumbled, mirroring her last-minute grooming. 'She hasn't got an iPhone. She's not a person.'

I knocked on the door, expecting Lou to be ready and waiting, but instead we hung around on the doormat for a couple of minutes, Jenny's excited face turning quickly into Jenny's impatient face and me starting to freeze. Late afternoon in May required at the very least a cardigan. I had no such thing. Stupid beautiful sleeveless dress. I wondered whether or not Jenny would be able to whip me up a wedding dress with pockets. I hated having cold hands.

Eventually the front door rattled into life with the sound of someone struggling with a chain and swearing like a trooper behind it.

'Oh, hello.'

Louisa's husband, Tim, opened the door. Tim and I went back. Way back. Throwing-up-on-the-night-bus back. But the last time I'd seen him, I'd broken several bones in his hand with a shoe and so I could understand why he wasn't swooping in for a hug. Not that Jenny was going to give him a choice.

'Hi, I'm Jenny.' She flung both her arms around his neck and squeezed tightly. 'You must be Tim.'

Jenny's theory, presumably stolen from Oprah like most of Jenny's theories, was that hugs and physical contact made people feel closer to one another more quickly and therefore established trust. What Jenny had failed to realize was that she was in suburban southwest London, and hugging strangers made you seem like a developmentally challenged child. Tim immediately backed off and made as if to bolt down the hall.

'You have a beautiful house,' Jenny called after him automatically before turning to me and making a 'crazy' face. I nodded. He was a bit.

'Louisa's in the living room with Grace,' he shouted back at us. 'I'll make tea.'

'He's so well trained,' I said, only to walk straight into my best friend breastfeeding on the sofa. 'Oh God, I'm sorry.' I slapped a hand over my eyes and promptly tripped over a Fisher Price baby gym. The carpet, like everything else, smelled ever so slightly like baby puke, and my six drinks of the day threatened to make a return visit.

'Get your ass up. You can't walk down the aisle with a broken leg,' Jenny said, dragging me up off the floor while I tried desperately to keep my eyes averted.

'I'm not going to look any better with your finger-prints embedded into my arms, am I?' I said, shaking her off and trying to ignore the throbbing pain and giant gash in my knee. 'Bloody hell.'

'Hello, Louisa, how are you, Louisa? I'm very good, thanks. And you?' Lou sat serenely on the settee, still nursing Grace and staring at both of us.

'We haven't actually been properly introduced.' Jenny shook off the moment's drama and held out her hand. Louisa looked at the hand, looked down at the baby she was holding and looked back up at Jenny.

'Now's not a brilliant time for handshakes,' she said, not even a little bit amused. 'Angela, have you finished trying to destroy my house?'

I settled into an armchair, rubbed my knee and looked around. It would be a pretty difficult task to destroy it, as far as I could tell. Louisa's cream-coloured palace had been transformed. And when I said transformed, I meant decimated. Order had been overthrown by the chaos of primary-coloured pieces of plastic, boxes and boxes and boxes of nappies and never-ending stacks of baby wipes. Everything in the room looked as if it would be sticky. Jenny sat awkwardly in the other cream armchair and tried to contain herself. I didn't think I'd ever seen her look so out of place.

'Had enough of your mum already?' Louisa handed a very full, very red-looking baby to Tim, who swooped in for burping duties. 'Did Alex head for the hills?'

'Not quite,' I said, waiting for her to put her boob away. This was all very uncomfortable. And not just because of the boob. I couldn't remember a time I'd been in Louisa's house for more than three minutes without being offered a biscuit. I knew that baby was going to ruin everything. 'So, you know Saturday?'

'Your mum's party?' She gazed lovingly at Grace as she threw up all over Tim's shoulder. 'We're coming. We've been briefed. We've bought a card.'

'Well, technically, yes – it is still her party. But now it's sort of also kind of my, um . . .' I looked to Jenny for support. 'Wedding.'

The room went so quiet, I could hear *Songs of Praise* on next door's telly.

'Your what?'

'It's a long story,' I said, even though it wasn't really. 'But Mum's got it into her head that she wants us to get married at home, and, well, long story short, we think it's a good idea.'

'We think it's an awesome idea,' Jenny added eagerly. 'It's going to be so much fun.'

'So when you say "we", do you mean "we", you

and Alex or "we", you and Jenny?' Louisa's voice was cool. She was pissed off with me. 'Because it doesn't sound like something you would come up with. Because it sounds stupid.'

It wasn't as if I'd expected Louisa to jump up and down with joy – I'd thought she might need a cup of tea and maybe a ginger nut to digest the news; but this was a little bit harsh.

'Hey, I wasn't even there,' Jenny jumped in before I could defend her. Not that Jenny ever needed defending. 'It was Annette's idea. And Alex agreed to it. Then Angela called me to ask what I thought, and I told her, like I just told you, it's an awesome idea. Awe. Some.' She sat back in her armchair and glared at Louisa with a venom usually reserved for the woman who snatched up the last pair of Jimmy Choos at a sample sale. This wasn't ideal.

'Oh, Angela called you, did she?' Louisa folded her arms and gave me a level glare. I would have been more upset but her boobs were leaking and I was glad she had adopted the grumpy stance.

'I did.' I gave up on Jenny and started on my defence. 'And I was going to call you, but I knew Jenny was at home on her own and you were busy here with Tim and the baby and—'

'No it's fine, we were very busy,' Lou said, cutting me off. 'We're always busy. Having a family keeps you very, very busy. I know you two wouldn't understand.'

Ouch. Jenny pursed her lips and looked at the floor. Under normal circumstances she would have ripped Louisa a new arsehole for that comment, but I could see she was on best behaviour. In all honesty, I was a little bit disappointed because I kind of wanted to punch her in the boob myself, but I didn't think I'd get away with it. Instead I took a different approach.

'So, would this be a good time to ask you to be my bridesmaid?' I presented her with jazz hands and as bright a smile as I could manage.

'Are you actually serious?' Louisa sat forward on the edge of the sofa and leaned over to take my hands in hers. 'We're talking about a wedding, Ange. Which means a marriage. Which is a pretty grown-up, serious thing to do. This isn't another of your wacky adventures, you know?'

'Wacky adventures?' I pulled my hands away. Since when were my adventures wacky? 'What's that supposed to mean?'

'Just what I was trying to talk to you about yesterday,' she said, actively trying to pretend Jenny wasn't in the room. Tim had already shown his good sense and left with Grace. 'This isn't like running off to New York or punching girls out in Paris – you can't laugh it all off, come home and just pretend it never happened. Marriage is a big deal. I don't want you to take this lightly.'

'I've been engaged for six months,' I pointed out. 'No one's pretending anything never happened. I realize it's a little bit sudden, but that doesn't mean I'm not taking it seriously. We're adults making an adult decision.'

'Then look at it this way,' she said, trying another approach. 'People spend months planning weddings. I just don't want you to rush this and regret it for the rest of your life.'

'Some people like planning things for months,' I countered. 'I'm not one of those people.'

That much was true and she knew it. Louisa and

Tim were engaged for two years before their wedding, and that was only just enough time for Louisa to put everything together. Every weekend for twenty-four months I had endured cake tastings, dress shopping and a seating plan so complicated that it would have challenged Stephen Hawking. It was going to be a whole lot easier with two tables and a trough full of Monster Munch. I hadn't told Jenny about my trough fantasy yet.

'Louisa,' Jenny piped up in as gentle a voice as she could muster. 'We're gonna make this the most awesome wedding ever. Sure, it's going to be a hectic week and I'm going to work you both like bitches, but it's going to be great.'

'Is that right?' Lou leaned back into the sofa, giving me the dead eye.

'I know we can pull it off if all three of us work together,' Jenny bargained. 'You're the local, you've done this before, you're key to this. I'm not going to lie, I'm clearly the most awesome events planner who ever lived, but I can't do this without you.'

Whatever magic Jenny had worked on my parents appeared to be casting its spell over Louisa. Her hard expression softened and she dropped her head against the back of the settee before letting out a loud groan.

'I want it on record that I am completely and utterly against this,' she said, staring up at the Artexed ceiling that I'd been on at her to get rid of since she'd moved in. It was bloody horrible. 'But I'm clearly going to have to be the voice of reason in this thing, aren't I?'

'Pretty much, yeah.' Jenny was entirely serious. 'So you're in?'

'Of course I bloody well am,' she replied. 'But where do we even start?'

'With wine,' Jenny said, grabbing stacks and stacks of paper out of her giant bag. 'We start with so much wine.'

'That I can help with,' Louisa said, pushing herself up off the sofa and heading for the kitchen with a spring in her step.

Two hours later we were all sprawled on the carpet, surrounded by the results of brainstorming under the influence. Weirdly, I wasn't putting it away as quickly as anyone might have expected. Possibly because I'd eaten half a side of cow at lunch. Or possibly because the wedding jitters were cancelling out every other emotion I'd ever experienced. All I wanted to do was curl up in a ball with Alex and wake up wedded. Was that too much to ask?

'So, so, so.' Jenny attempted to bring order to the room by waving around an empty bottle of Shiraz. 'We have a list, OK? We're agreed on this?'

'Read it again.' Louisa's alcohol tolerance had diminished considerably from before she was pregnant, I noticed from behind my great big glass of red. Still my first, still full. She was hiccupping after one glass, and after two was agreeing with anything and everything Jenny said. The old drunken Louisa was far more bolshy, but for the sake of getting things done, the new compliant version was probably a good thing.

'Without having talked through the logistics with Annette, I'm figuring we're still going to need to look into the table dressings and centrepieces as well as arranging music and a dance floor for the party,' Jenny said, looking down her list as she sipped her wine. 'Plus I'm kinda dubious on the catering and the booze provisions, but I feel like they're going to be easier to take care of than some other stuff.'

'Agreed,' Louisa nodded. 'I can take care of the catering. And the booze.'

'And we need to deal with the cake. I figure that's going to be a tough one.'

'There's a woman.' Lou waved her hand towards the window. 'She lives around the corner. She makes everyone's cakes. I'll call her in the morning.'

'A woman?'

For once, I knew exactly who this incredibly loose description referred to. Mrs Stevens had been making the neighbourhood's celebration cakes for the past thirty years and did a fine job. If fruit cake, vanilla sponge, sugar roses and ribbon were your idea of a fine job. While I was pretty sure they weren't Jenny's, I was pretty OK with it. As long as I got my trough of Monster Munch.

'She did mine,' Louisa replied with an edge to her voice. As predicted, Jenny didn't look utterly convinced, but I saw her put an 'L' next to 'cake' and we moved on.

'So then it's simpler things like a memory book for people to write in, pens, disposable cameras, any decorative touches we think of, invitations and RSVPs.' Jenny paused to click onto another window. 'And we've already sent the email out to everyone in the US. There's no one else here you want to invite?'

By everyone in the US, she meant Erin, Sadie, Mary, Delia, James, Craig and Graham. There wasn't time for handcrafted paper engineering and a calligrapher, much to Louisa's dismay. I would have been perfectly happy with a Facebook invite, but Jenny said the least we could do was a proper Evite and follow up with paper invitations on Monday. So obviously we ended up with the Evite.

As for UK guests, Mum had already invited the family, so that was taken care of, and there really weren't any old friends I was desperate to have around me. I'd always been a bit rubbish at keeping things going, and since I had been a borderline recluse during the last couple of years I'd lived in London, Mark had claimed any friends I might have thought were my own. Such were the trials of (a) working freelance and (b) only having 'couple' friends. No work buddies to come on to your mum or tell lairy stories about Christmas parties at your wedding reception. The relief. Of course, there was a measurable part of me that wanted Mark at the wedding. I wanted to take the high ground, show that I was a big enough person to want him at this special day in my life. And I was going to look a hell of a lot better than I had in the supermarket. Besides, he really needed to meet Alex. And then go home and cry in a corner about how hot he wasn't. But maybe those didn't add up to enough good reasons.

'Then we need wedding rings, outfits for the wedding party – groom, father of the bride, mother of the bride, bridesmaids.' She stopped for emphasis. 'And of course the bride.'

'Oh.' I snapped back to attention. 'You mean me.'

'Well, yeah. You.' Jenny tutted. Clearly I was in trouble for not paying attention. 'You're gonna need shoes and underwear and jewellery and hair and make-up, although I can totally do the hair and make-up myself. Then all we have left is photographer/video-grapher, party favours and a honeymoon suite. Oh, and I guess we have to send Alex's ass somewhere the night before the wedding.'

'I've got a friend of a friend who does make-up,' Louisa suggested. 'And I think her boyfriend is a photographer?'

'So I'll do the hair and make-up, but we do need a photographer,' Jenny said, simultaneously acknowledging and ignoring everything Louisa said. 'Someone to do all the standard shit, but someone who'll do cool reportage stuff too. I'll talk to Erin. And Mary. They may know some people.'

'I could ask my old editor at the magazine,' I added. 'I know most press photographers don't do things like weddings, but you never know.'

'You never know.' Jenny pointed at me with a pen. 'Good idea, Angie.'

If I were a dog, my tail would have been wagging. I loved knowing I'd done well. I also loved how excited and engaged Jenny had become. It was ages since I'd seen her so involved with something. With anything, actually. If I'd known all it was going to take to knock her out of her funk was a shotgun wedding in another country, I'd have organized it months ago.

'Don't forget the hen and stag dos,' Louisa added with an attractive slur on 'stag'. 'Although this might have to count as your hen do since we're going to be so bloody up against it.'

'Dude, if hen night and bachelorette party mean the same thing, there's no way we're missing that shit,' Jenny corrected her. 'I will make time. I will make an extra day in the middle of the week if I have to.'

'Well, I do have some ideas,' Lou shrugged. 'Just things I was thinking about when we were planning all my stuff. Things I thought would work better for Angela when she got married.'

'And I've got a ton of ideas too,' Jenny said, getting

excited again. 'A London bachelorette! This is going to be so awesome.'

'Ladies,' I interrupted. 'Really, the hen night is the least of my concerns. Can we just make sure I'm not getting married in Primark's finest and walking down a non-existent aisle to the romantic yet tinny sounds of my cassette deck first?'

Both of my bridesmaids looked a bit put out.

'I put music on the list,' Jenny pouted.

Louisa brightened. 'You could always wear my wedding dress?'

'With all the love in my heart, I'm going to pass on that, thank you,' I said, finishing my wine. 'And the same goes if my mum even hints to either of you that I should wear hers. That woman got married in a fancy tablecloth. And I'm being nice by calling it fancy.'

'Well, that's our list.' Jenny scribbled down a few last notes. 'That's the how, what, where and when. What I really need to know now is how you want it to feel. What does your wedding look like?'

I wasn't sure, but I knew what my face looked like. Completely blank. What did my wedding look like? I was suddenly reminded of a very awkward session with a career counsellor Mark had organized for me one birthday (the old romantic). They'd repeatedly asked 'what does success look like to you?' I didn't know it could look like anything and was therefore quite thrown. Luckily, Louisa spoke both professional and American and was able to translate.

'How do you imagine your wedding, Ange?' She patted Jenny on the flank like a knackered racehorse. 'When you close your eyes and see the whole thing, what's it like?'

In order to answer her question properly, I rolled

onto my back and closed my eyes, holding my empty wine glass against my belly. My wedding.

'It's really simple,' I said, imagining myself in the delicate, flowing white dress from Delia's magazine, hair loosely tied back, a hand-tied bouquet of white peonies and flat, sparkly shoes that I knew Jenny would never allow. 'Very classic and unfussy. Elegant.'

'Nice.' I heard Jenny scribbling away at her pad. 'Keep going.'

'And Alex is in a black suit. Is that OK?'

'Not really,' Lou answered.

'Whatever you want is OK,' Jenny replied, overturning Louisa in a tone that couldn't be questioned.

'Well, I'm sure he'll know what he wants to wear,' I carried on, hoping to avoid a confrontation over Alex's wardrobe choices. We'd been doing so well. 'But yeah, there are loads of flowers everywhere. White and pale pink peonies. On the tables and in vases. And lots of candles and fairy lights so at dusk we can make it all twinkly.'

'Oh, that's gonna be pretty.' Jenny scribbled some more. 'Anything else essential?'

'Music.' I wanted there to be dancing. 'But I want Alex to be in charge of that. Or at least consulted, please.'

'Got it,' she replied reluctantly.

'And I just want everyone to be really, really happy and chilled out.'

'As far as I can tell, as long as we get you a frock and enough champagne to sink Wales, we should be all right,' Louisa reasoned.

'Sounds good to me.' I couldn't deny that the big party of my fantasy involved me and Alex surrounded by flowers and candles and fairy lights whilst necking champs.

'I think it's time to call it a night,' Jenny said, all business, hopping up off the floor and bundling away her planner. 'I say we reconvene in the morning when I've talked to Angela's mom, and then, tomorrow afternoon, we've got a dress to find, ladyface.'

'You think we'll find it in one day?' I popped the bubble of my designer dress fantasy. I wasn't going to fall in love with something else if I was still clinging to the idea of a dress I'd only ever seen in a magazine.

'Maybe two days,' she said with a reassuring tone. 'Louisa only just did all this stuff. You know all the best boutiques, right?'

'She knows literally all of the boutiques,' I answered for her. 'From Brighton to Edinburgh.'

'We only went as far as Nottingham – don't exaggerate,' Louisa said as she waved us out into the hallway. 'And yes, I'll dig out the numbers for the bridal places tomorrow. And all the other stuff. Don't worry. Tim'll drive you home. *Tim.*'

Her husband ran down the stairs as fast as his legs would carry him, car keys in hand. Either he was psychic or he'd been waiting for us to leave for some time.

'I'm not worried,' Jenny said with confidence. 'There's never any need to worry when you have a plan, and we've got a hell of a plan.'

'Hitler had a plan,' I muttered, wiping errant mascara flakes from under my eyes. '*X Factor* contestants *always* have a plan. Doesn't always mean it's going to work out.'

'Hitler didn't have my commitment to a vision,' Jenny said, her eyes flashing. 'Don't sweat it.'

'Right, I'm going up to bath Grace.' Louisa kissed

us each on the cheek. I was so, so relieved to see the two of them getting along, I could have cried. It had occurred to me that they might not. 'And I'll talk to you in the morning.'

'Talk in the morning,' I said with a wave and followed Tim out to the car.

'Hey, Jenny,' I said, following her into the back seat. 'Before we actually start calling people and buying things, do you think it might be a good idea to run some of this past Alex first?'

She pulled a very unpleasant face for a moment and then sighed loudly. I wasn't sure if this was professional Jenny who didn't like to be second-guessed or drunk Jenny who didn't play well with others, but either way, you'd have thought I'd just asked her to give Alex a kidney. 'Jenny.' I tried to echo her stern face but I just wasn't as good at it. 'It's his wedding too.'

'And I'm already allowing his douchebag friends to come along,' she replied. 'But fine. You can tell him what we've agreed. And tell him he needs to get his ass into a suit. I don't want to have to babysit that motherfucker in a tailor's. I know the dude can dress himself.'

Woah. High praise indeed.

It took around seven seconds for Jenny to ascertain that my mother's plans for the catering would not meet the 'simple, classic and elegant' theme of my wedding. I happened to think sausage rolls were completely classic, but Jenny wasn't having any of it, and it wasn't a battle I was interested in fighting at that moment. She was throwing around words like 'arancini' and 'beignets' when I skulked up the stairs and shut the bathroom door before texting Alex. A couple of minutes later, the door opened up and a very handsome black-haired gentleman appeared.

'Is this where we hang out now?' he asked. 'Because your parents have, like, three times the number of rooms we have at home. We don't have to have our one-to-ones in the tub.'

'It's the only room in the house with a lock,' I explained from my seat on the closed toilet lid. 'Admittedly it's not the sexiest.'

Alex smiled and pulled on the light cord, blacking out the bathroom. The street lamps outside cast orangey shadows across the white tiles and gave out just enough of a glow for me to see him swooping in for a kiss.

'Of course, there's a chance I'm wrong,' I said, catching my breath. 'Fun afternoon with my dad?'

'He had a really great nap,' he said in between kisses to my face, my throat, my shoulder, my collarbone. 'I went for a walk, did some reading, actually played around with some new song stuff. There was a guitar.'

'Ahh, that's mine,' I replied. 'From my Britpop phase.'

'Nice.' He clearly wasn't interested in hearing about my Britpop phase. It was best that he didn't, to be honest – those flares did me no favours, and I think we were both far more interested in what he was doing at that precise moment. 'I don't know if it's all this wedding planning, your dad's Scotch collection or being made to sleep in separate rooms, but I'm going kinda crazy over here.'

'I need to talk to you about the wedding,' I squeaked. This was entirely unacceptable behaviour for my mother's bathroom, but so entirely necessary. 'I have about a million things we need to decide on.'

'As long as you're there, I'm there and we end up married, I am super-cool with everything else,' he replied, hands searching in the darkness. I couldn't help but be slightly dubious, but he did seem far more interested in getting my dress off than choosing between bone, cream or ivory table coverings. 'I want what you want as long as I get you at the end of it.'

'That's not true and you know it.' I was trying to keep my voice even, but being dragged onto the floor and straddled by your fiancé who you haven't so much as touched in three days makes it very difficult to keep yourself in a serious place. 'Jenny wants to bring in goats as ring bearers.'

'Sounds amazing.'

'And do liver and onions for the reception.'

'My favourite.'

'And we're going to get Lionel Blair to dance me down the aisle.'

'I've always liked his work.'

'Do you know who he is?'

'No.'

The bathroom floor was not the most comfortable place for a romantic assignation, but it was difficult to argue with Alex's insistence. Every stroke of his warm, strong hands swept away a wedding worry. Where would we hire glasses? Didn't matter. What if we couldn't get a cake made on time? The guests would get Fondant Fancies and like them. And a wedding dress? Meh. I'd rock up in a bin bag and save myself the hassle.

'How long do you think we've got before they come looking for us?' Alex whispered, although how I was supposed to concentrate on what he was saying when all I was aware off was the sound of his fly popping open was beyond me.

'Not long enough.' I pressed my lips against his and tried to pretend I hadn't just kicked over a can of Mr Muscle as I wrapped my legs around his waist. 'So shut up.'

'Yes, ma'am.'

I loved it when he did as he was told.

CHAPTER ELEVEN

Monday morning was bright, sunny and filled with bird song. Unlike me. Fifteen seconds after opening my eyes, I vaulted over Jenny and hurtled into the bathroom, face first into the toilet.

'Angela, are you OK?' Mum knocked on the bathroom door that I'd kicked closed with impeccable parental timing.

'I'm fine,' I called, ignoring the echo of the toilet bowl. 'Just ate too much yesterday.'

And worried too much. And was jet-lagged too much. And did it on the bathroom floor too much. Maybe that last one didn't add to my nausea, but it certainly didn't help me get enough rest.

There was a brief silence while she did some motherly calculations. 'I'm going to make you some dry toast,' she announced. 'That always helped me. Come downstairs when you can.'

Pulling up my T-shirt, I rested my bare back against the cool tiles and closed my eyes. Weddings really were the answer. Somehow, in the space of twenty-four hours, I'd managed to press Jenny's reset button, reawaken the bridezilla within Louisa and find a way to stop my mum being mad when I puked the morning after night before. And whatever fire it had lit under Alex was fine by me, even if I was never going to be able to look at the bathmat in the same way again.

'Angie, did you vom?' Jenny didn't bother to knock, she just barged through the door in her vest and knickers combo. Fingers crossed my dad was already down the garden; I didn't need him having another funny turn. 'Are you sick?'

'My stomach is just a bit unsettled from too much excitement,' I explained, heaving myself up. 'I'll be fine once I've eaten.'

'Oh.' Jenny looked disappointed. 'I was going to say don't eat. You know, trying on dresses?'

'Right.' I never thought I'd be thankful for throwing up. 'I suppose. Although I'm not actually going to be able to lose weight between now and the weekend so it might be better to get something with a bit of give.'

Jenny shook her head so very slowly, never taking her eyes off me. 'You are so lucky I'm here. Get downstairs – I'll be fifteen minutes. And no carbs!'

That was the toast out the window, then.

The kitchen table was set to feed an army of thousands, but as far as I could see, it was just me, Alex and Jenny who were eating. Dad was nowhere to be seen and I knew Annette Clark never made it past eight a.m. without her bowl of All-Bran. It was just after nine-thirty – nearly tea and biscuit time.

'I hope you're hungry.' I sat beside Alex and squeezed his hand under the table. He leaned over to kiss me, a full-on hands in hair, lip-to-lip, filthy snog while my mum was busy removing half the contents of the fridge.

'Not for that.' I pushed him away and ignored his chuckles as my mum turned round, laden with jars of jam.

'Well, you've got some colour in your cheeks, at least,' she commented, placing everything Robinsons had ever created on the table. 'Ready for the dress shopping?'

'Ready as I'll ever be,' I said, taking a banana and ignoring her frown as well as her Dorothy Perkins Special cropped trousers. They did her no favours. We'd been through this. We Clarks were short-legged women and few things hated us as much as Capri pants. She never listened. 'Don't fancy toast.' Really, I just didn't fancy getting my arse kicked when Jenny came downstairs.

'Jenny gave me a list of things to do,' Alex said, putting his hand over his mouth while he chewed his toast and pulled a piece of paper out of his pocket. 'This is what I'm in charge off. I'm pretty psyched.'

Music (PA tbc – JL)
Suit (liaise with JL re: color scheme)
Stag (liaise with JL re: timings)
Write vows (submit to JL by Thursday p.m.)
Rings (confirm with JL)

I looked up at him, wide-eyed.
'That's it? That's all you have to do?'
He nodded like a big, happy dog.
'And basically she's going to do it all for you?'
'I'll be amazed if I'm actually allowed to write my own vows.' He brushed something off his plaid shirt.

'And Graham called to say they're coming out tomorrow, so that's pretty cool.'

It was pretty cool. There were several worries gnawing away at my insides and one of them was that Alex's friends were going to miss the wedding and that wasn't right. I still didn't feel great about his parents not coming, but Alex wasn't a baby – he knew what he wanted, and if he didn't want them there, he didn't want them there. I'd meet them eventually. Probably.

'I wish my list was that short.' Mum sat down with her fifth cup of tea of the day. 'Have a look.'

Mum's list was triple the length of Alex's and her jobs were twice as difficult or five times more depressing. She had the pleasure of hiring and overseeing cleaners, confirming RSVPs, making sure we had the right number of glasses for water, wine, cocktails and the champagne toast as well as all the correct flatware and table settings. There were also a million other dreary tasks involving toilet paper, napkins, trash cans (I had to translate on that one) and cloakroom storage. As far as I could tell, after I'd crashed out Jenny had spent the entire night working out every last possible necessity for Saturday and then picked out every single one of the most boring jobs and assigned them to my parents.

'Your dad is in charge of chairs and tables.' Mum sipped her tea and rubbed the burgeoning bags under her eyes. 'He's gone to B&Q on a recce.'

'Did Jenny approve B&Q?' I asked, wild-eyed. White plastic patio furniture did not emanate elegance and class. Simplicity, yes – but not in a good way.

'No,' she hissed. 'And I told him he should check with her. But he said once I'd got a tablecloth on them, you wouldn't be able to tell. But I'm not in charge of tablecloths, Angela. How am I supposed to cover up a contraband table if I'm not in charge of tablecloths? Tell me that?'

This was quite the predicament. On one hand, I was very happy that my wedding was clearly in good hands and would in no way be a right royal cock-up. On the other, I didn't really want to have to forfeit my honeymoon in order to check my parents in at the Priory.

'It'll be fine, Mum,' I said, feeling a bit distracted, as I wondered about what was going to be on my list. 'She doesn't know what B&Q is. Just don't tell her. And don't get anything from Ikea, whatever you do. She hates Ikea.'

'Are we ready?' Jenny appeared at the door fully dressed, fully made-up and carrying her handbag, notebook in hand. I immediately noticed she was wearing my green silk Marc by Marc Jacobs shirt as a dress and the same brown leather sandals I'd worn the day before. Not that I wasn't excited that Jenny had stormed my wardrobe, but it was a little odd. And I could almost see her knickers. Plus that meant another outfit I'd brought for the Spencer Media presentation that was out of the running. Obviously I was planning to wear it with trousers. At least until the presentation started to go badly. 'Angela, you need to get dressed.'

'So do you,' I retorted, sulkily putting down my banana. It was a poor rebellion because I was marching upstairs to find clothes before she even poured herself a coffee.

'Well, if she's going to steal my clothes,' I thought, slamming the door shut and stamping a foot, 'maybe I'll borrow some of hers.'

Living in my teenage bedroom was making me behave like a teenager, and teenaged Angela was a petulant little mare. Safely shut inside my bedroom, I opened up Jenny's suitcase, excited about what treats might be inside. Maybe a little Chloé shirt dress. Or a Missoni maxi. Even a little Alexander Wang mini dress – the weather was nice enough. I'd get myself warmed up for wedding-dress shopping by doing a bit of bargain hunting in Jenny's suitcase.

Or, I realized as I sat back on my heels and stared into the empty depths before me, I'd be shit out of luck. Flipping the zip-up compartments back and forth, I tried to work out why Jenny's suitcase contained absolutely nothing but several pairs of underwear, two bras and a pair of Havaianas. Hmm. Dragging her other case out from under the bed, I opened it up to find her jeans from the day before, the leather leggings she'd travelled in, two dirty T-shirts, a neon-orange Stella McCartney clutch, five bottles of flesh-toned nail polish and a battered copy of *How To Get The Love You Want*.

'Maybe she unpacked?' I pondered out loud, trying to work out where she was hiding her stuff. My clothes were in the wardrobe and there was nothing of hers in there. 'Maybe I'm just being stupid?'

It wouldn't have been the first time.

'Angie, get your ass down here,' the world's lightest packer bellowed from the bottom of the stairs. 'And make sure your underwear matches. And is nice. And don't wear pants. And freaking hurry up.'

By pants, I assumed she meant trousers. And by nice, I assumed she meant not falling apart. And by hurry up, I knew she meant be ready already.

Well, I told myself. Today should be fun.

*   *   *

165

'Should I be leaving Alex alone at home?' I asked no one in particular from the back of my mum's car, simultaneously checking my emails. I was all over multitasking. I was going to be the best bride, best editor, best darn Angela I could be. I had also had a lot of coffee. 'He's going to go stir crazy. I should be doing stuff with him.'

'He's got shit to do,' Jenny replied from the front passenger seat. She'd called shotgun, much to my mother's horror. It took a little while to explain that Jenny just wanted to sit next to her and had no intention of shooting her. 'And so have you.'

'I feel bad about leaving Grace with my mum.' Louisa rested her head against the headrest of the back seat and pulled a sad panda face. 'She wasn't right this morning.'

I tried to look sympathetic, but really, all I was thinking was that Lou looked so much better now she'd washed her hair and put on some make-up. She looked like herself again in a fine-knit baby-blue jumper and white skinny jeans. Even Jenny had approved her on-trend outfit, and my mum had commended her ability to wear cashmere without getting spit-up all over it.

'I'm sure we won't be long,' I lied, scrolling through my emails.

It was incredibly early in NYC, but I already had two messages from Delia. Mostly about work, but also to ask if I was seriously getting married on Saturday or had she driven me mad with too much pressure at work. And also where we were registered. She was an angel. Or at least she was until I got the second message that confirmed they'd moved the *Gloss* presentation to Friday. Perfect timing. I was meeting with the editorial team in the morning while Delia would be in Paris, presenting to the sales team, in the afternoon. Happily, it meant she would be able to make the wedding on Saturday. It also meant I would be spending the day before my wedding trying to convince a room full of people I didn't know that they should back my hopes and dreams. But no big deal.

'We are going to be super-long,' Jenny corrected me. 'We're not going home until we've ticked everything off this list.'

Louisa rolled her eyes as Jenny waved a piece of paper over her shoulder. 'We're going to be for ever,' she confirmed. 'Don't you remember buying my dress?'

I did remember. I would always remember. It took fucking ages. But that was her dress; this was my dress. Also known as the most amazingly awesome, beautiful, sexy yet tasteful, flattering and breathtaking dress of all time. Which we were going to find off the peg on a Monday afternoon.

'You're excited, though?' Lou asked with a smile. 'This is the fun part.'

'I am,' I nodded, sliding my favourite wedding mag out of my poor satchel. I might be feeling bad about leaving Alex, but I felt even worse about subjecting this shagged-out piece of leatherwork to all the beautiful designer dresses it was going to have to face today. 'I've been looking at stuff. And I really love this one. I know we won't be able to find exactly this, and I know these dresses take months to make, but I love it. Really love it.'

'Lemme see.' Jenny twisted in her seat and yanked the magazine out of my hands before Louisa could even cast an eye over it. 'It's cute,' she agreed before tossing it back and almost taking out Louisa's eye. 'But

I'm really seeing you in something more loose and flowing? To go with the garden setting? Like maybe Lanvin. Or Temperley, because you know, you really should wear a British designer.'

'I guess?' It made sense. I just needed to see some dresses before I made any decisions. I wanted to see them all, and I wanted them to make me look thin, but I really didn't want to have to try on too many or walk around too much. Bridezilla? Maybe. Lazy? Absolutely.

'I think it's gorgeous,' Louisa said quietly, stroking the page. 'I can absolutely see you in it. Any thoughts on the bridesmaids' dresses?'

I looked at Jenny. Olive-skinned, dark hair, brown eyes. I looked at Louisa. Pale skin, blonde hair, blue eyes. Jenny with her Latina bombshell curves, Louisa with her willowy long limbs. Eep.

'I'm thinking neon.' Jenny came alive in the front of the car. Her arms flailed around wildly while Louisa shook her head at me in silence. 'Neon Zac Posen. Something that pops against the garden. Tangerine is supposed to be The Colour this year. We could so rock a coral number. Or a Matthew Williamson flapper number. Or, you know, something a little more edgy.'

'At least it's going to be easy to get Grace a dress,' Lou said, flicking her phone into life and waving around the screensaver shot of her baby. Who I still hadn't actually held. Or spoken to. Or looked directly at. It was too much pressure – I was sure I was going to break her or ruin her in some way. 'Do they make neon Zac Posen flower-girl dresses?'

'Flower-girl?' Jenny hauled herself around again. 'We're doing a flower-girl? We're having a baby at the wedding?'

'She's not *a* baby.' Louisa sat up straight. 'She's *my* baby. She's Angela's goddaughter, and yes, of course she's coming.'

I shrank further into the corner of the car, eyes clapped to my iPhone, wrapping my cardigan around me and wondering if any part of my Urban Outfitters sundress was made out of Kevlar.

'Look, Jenny,' Mum interrupted loudly. 'There's Harrods. And Harvey Nicks.'

'Omigod.' She span round and leaned across my mother, who somehow managed to keep the car on the road. Jenny unfastened her seat belt and scrambled about in her seat like an overexcited puppy. 'Holy shit, it's for real,' she squealed.

'It is,' I agreed, pleased that the flower-girl debate had been postponed. 'Weird, that we're in London, isn't it?'

'Yuh-huh?'

Jenny and I stared out of the window while Louisa studiously ignored us both. It still felt strange to be in a car watching winding streets, big red buses and cheery Underground signs rather than numbered streets pass me by. I missed the yellow taxis and the green light-up subway signs and the endless street carts that would almost definitely give me food poisoning, but I was buzzing to be back in England. And to be buying a wedding dress. And to be full of coffee on an empty stomach.

While Jenny bounced around in the front, I took a look at the list she had furnished me with before we got in the car. She had assured me it was open to discussion, but that she hadn't wanted to overwhelm me with tasks when I had a presentation to take care of and a wedding to be at. Most of my to-dos were to do with resting, deep-conditioning my hair and not touching my eyebrows. I was shameful at eyebrow maintenance. But I was in charge of writing my own vows and I'd been given a questionnaire to fill in regarding colour schemes, cake options, cocktails and party favours. Slightly odd but totally manageable. My involvement was also required on the seating plan. A little scary. And I also had to drink six glasses of water a day and stay off the booze. Completely unrealistic.

'How many appointments did you two manage to make overnight?' I asked, silently chanting the number one over and over in my head. In my dreams, we were going to walk into the shop, I was going to fall in love with a dress and we were going to be murdering Topshop along with some very tasty pie and mash within the hour so I could go home early, cuddle up on the sofa with Alex, write our vows and eat as many Percy Pigs as it took me to throw up the sausage and mash. Never let it be said that I didn't have a plan. 'Surely nowhere is open yet?'

'Please, everyone has BlackBerries or iPhones, doll-face,' she said, bashing me in the head with hers for effect. 'Louisa sent me a bunch of numbers. We have three appointments confirmed and I'm just waiting for Browns to get back to me. I think they're going to be the best.'

I watched to see whether or not my mum flinched at any of this information, but she just carried on, eyes on the road. There had been very little talk of who was paying for everything beyond her rash declaration in the pub, but if Jenny was making appointments at Browns Bride, we really were going to have to get everything else from B&Q. It wasn't like Mum and Dad were short of a few quid – I always got the feeling they had considerably more put by than they wanted me to know about – but I didn't want to take advantage. Not Jenny's concern, obviously.

'Of course, this would be way easier back in Manhattan, but we don't have time.' She looked back at her mobile. 'And Erin can't get us a dress shipped in time. So London's just gonna have to come through.'

'London will do very well indeed, I'm sure,' Louisa said. 'It was good enough for me.'

'And I'm sure you looked great,' Jenny replied, almost too quickly, with a condescending smile. 'Really.'

Louisa's eyes flamed and she stared daggers into the back of Jenny's head. What a fantastic start we were off to.

Several hours and not a single sausage later, Jenny, Louisa, me and my mum had trekked the length and breadth of London looking for The One. It turned out it was considerably easier to locate your one true love on a planet of six billion people than it was to find your wedding dress in a city of six hundred wedding dresses. It was fair to say I was feeling a little defeated. We'd been to all the heavy hitters – Browns, Pronovias, House of Fraser – and nothing had been right. Either the dresses didn't fit, or they didn't have my size in stock, or I didn't like it, or Mum didn't like it, or Jenny downright hated it. Louisa loved all of them. For the sake of everyone's sanity, I'd taken to distracting her each time we walked into a shop with a hunt for a veil I had no intention of wearing. It seemed to be working.

We were all trailing behind Jenny somewhere in Mayfair, Mum muttering about me getting married in a bin bag if this carried on, while the New Yorker continued to stride around the city as though she owned it. The theory that planning a wedding in a city she'd never visited before would slow Jenny down had proved fatally flawed. Nothing slowed Jenny down. Nothing but five Dirty Martinis or her ex-boyfriend, and I was prepared to bring up neither. It was getting late – almost four – and I knew Mum wanted to be back in the car before rush hour and, more importantly, back in the kitchen before teatime. If she didn't get home before six, Dad would get into the biscuit tin and it would be all over. I couldn't be responsible for a divorce this close to a wedding.

'Hey, Jenny.' I stopped in front of a tiny white-fronted boutique and pressed my sweaty little palms against the glass. I hadn't had so much as a Mr Whippy and the weather was so much warmer than I had expected. 'What about this store?'

'It's not on the list,' she replied, looking more than a little harassed herself. 'And we're running out of time.'

'Ooh, it looks nice.' Louisa opened the door and beckoned me inside. 'Let's have a look. Come on, Jenny – it'll only take a minute.'

'But it's not on the list,' Jenny whined, placing her hands on her hips. 'I don't have time to waste on a whim.'

'I've read about this place,' Louisa said, letting the door close carefully and staring her right back down. 'And we're going in.'

Jenny's jaw tensed.

'Maybe they'll have a dress for Grace,' Louisa suggested.

Jenny's skinny shoulders shot up around her ears.

'We don't have to.' I stepped away from the window and towards my old roommate. 'We have all the appointments Jenny's made. And this isn't on the list. Let's go to the next place.'

'No.' Louisa folded her arms over her sweater. 'I want to go in here, Angela. We're going in.'

'Did she just "no" me?' Jenny shook her head as though she'd been slapped. 'Have I been no'd?'

I held my breath. I was trapped in the middle of high noon at the not OK corral.

'Right, shall we all just go in and have a look?' Mum said, breaking the tension and pushing past the bridesmaid showdown. 'While we're here?'

'Let's.' Louisa gave Jenny a triumphant smile and followed Mum in. 'I don't think they stock Zac Posen, though, so you might want to wait outside.'

This was not my dream come true. I knew Louisa and Jenny were very, very different people, but I had hoped they would overcome their rabidly diverse personality traits and be nice to each other. I didn't expect them to be sharing a bed at a sleepover by now, but I didn't want them bickering in the street when I needed both a dress and a wee.

'We wouldn't have put up with this shit in Kleinfeld,' Jenny muttered under her breath, pushing past me and into the shop.

The second we walked through the door I was transported. It wasn't that the dresses in the other stores weren't wonderful – they absolutely were – but I'd been completely overcome with the same panicky feeling I'd had in Vera Wang. The dresses were too big, too elaborate, too someone else. I wanted to be Monique Lhuillier with all my heart, but I wasn't. I knew this mostly because I'd tried on two of the dresses and fallen over in both. I might be Romona Keveza if I tried extra hard not to spill anything and wore some very restrictive underwear, but I was definitely too fat for Lanvin and absolutely too short for Temperley. Some of the dresses had been beautiful, just not on me. Others had been downright ridiculous. Apparently the 'in' trend for weddings was one part Princess Di, two parts Lady Gaga. In fact, even Lady Gaga would have rejected half the lace-covered, overgrown tutus I'd been shown on the grounds of them being a bit too much. And the assistants were even worse – so pushy and almost certainly medicated. (I was only jealous.) But this place didn't seem too bad. For a start, there was only one woman in the store and she was scoffing a Mars bar and reading *Heat* magazine while wearing a floral romper and listening to the Ramones. We were a long way from Berketex Bride.

'Oh, hello.' She leapt to her feet and jammed the magazine under the counter. Everything in the shop was painted white – the walls, the shabby chic furniture and display cases, even the floorboards. Shop-girl stood out against it all with her red lipstick and matching red hair. For no reason at all, I wanted to give her a big hug. 'Can I help you?'

'I hope so.' I pulled my hair back into an anticipatory up-do. I had a good feeling. 'I need a wedding dress.'

'It's all I'm selling.' She waved her arms around. 'I'm Chloe, by the way. Want me to pick some stuff or do you just want to browse?'

'If there's something you think?' Woah. Someone in a bridal shop giving us the option to browse . . . this was amazing. But without even turning round to see

Jenny, I could feel her prickling. This was not the approved bridal couture experience. There was no soft, piped music, no chilled champagne flutes, no chocolate truffles. White, obviously. (And none for me.) What there was was three racks of gorgeous-looking dresses and a large white screen at the back of the space, where presumably I would be trying on. It was small, friendly and unpretentious. It was exciting.

'So it's a little last-minute and I don't know what your set-up is,' Jenny broke in, taking over. As Jenny tended to. 'But she's getting married on Saturday and we need a dress.'

'Well, I can sell anything off the rack.' Chloe turned and eyed me carefully. 'I've got loads that will fit you. You're a ten?'

'There or thereabouts,' I nodded, already shedding my cardigan.

'What sort of wedding are we looking at?' She started pulling dresses down and hanging them on another rack at the back of the shop. 'City chic, country garden, Westminster Abbey?'

'Country garden meets city chic,' Jenny replied. 'Simple, elegant and classic.'

'And I really like this dress,' I said, taking my life in my hands by interrupting and waving my creased-up magazine in Chloe's carefully made-up face. 'If you've got anything like that, I'd love to try it.'

'Oh, Sarah Piper? I went to St Martins with her.' The girl smiled and grabbed two dresses from the opposite wall. 'That's an amazing dress. I don't have it, though. It's next season.'

I tried not to be too disappointed. It was a little much to ask.

'I've got a couple of hers from last season, though. And between you and me, I think they're better. What do you think?'

What did I think? I thought I was going to cry. Both dresses were exquisitely beautiful. One was a faded blush colour, an incredibly simple silk number with a high halter-neck that draped into an open back with a dropped waist and long, flowing skirt. I wasn't sure I would do it any favours, but for a brief moment I thought about ditching Alex and having that dress's babies. Until I looked at the other one.

Sweet baby Jesus. It was perfection.

'Can I try this?' I pointed at it hesitantly, holding my hands very close to my body, afraid to get too close in case she said no. The success of my entire wedding, all of my future happiness, depended on this dress going over my arse.

'You surely can.' She put the other back on the rack and led me towards the back of the shop. 'Give us a minute,' she said to my restless bridal party. 'This is an easy one to get on.'

It wasn't often I enjoyed taking my clothes off in front of strangers, but in this instance I couldn't get naked fast enough. I wanted that dress on my body as soon as.

'You can wear a bra with it,' Chloe said as I held my hands over my head with barely contained glee. 'If you get one of those convertible or racer-back ones. AP have a couple of nice bits. You can't do a corset, though.'

'I really don't want a corset,' I whispered, hoping Jenny couldn't hear me. The cool silk slipped over my skin, like a happy sigh. 'I want to be able to eat at my wedding.' Provided there would actually be food. We hadn't discussed that yet today. I was sure we would.

'This is perfect, then,' she said, turning to the back of the dress and fiddling about with some unseen fastenings while I stared impatiently at a covered mirror, trying to knock off the white muslin with previously unexplored telekinetic powers. 'The waist-line is fitted, but it only needs a pair of relatively contained pants rather than full-on Spanx, and the back really shows off your arms. You'd be surprised how many people look terrible in this. It wouldn't work if you were super-busty, but I think it looks really great. Just needs a couple of alterations and I can easily sort them by Saturday.'

Never in all my days had I been so happy not to be 'super-busty'. Chloe took a step back, frowned, then furnished me with a pair of spike-heeled silk sandals and a couple of white gold bangles, loosened my hair and pulled it over one shoulder in a messy cascade.

'And you're done,' she smiled. 'I love my job.'

She walked over and yanked the muslin cover away from the huge three-way mirror and clapped. I couldn't breathe. The long, layered silk skirts swished around my legs. There was a long slit up the front and hidden pockets at the sides. Pockets! A tightly fitted waist gave way to a slightly looser bodice with a high round neckline that slid over my shoulders into a narrow ribbon of a racer-back. The fabric widened as it trav-elled down my back until it met up with the skirt, wrapping me up in the physical embodiment of joy. This was a serious dress that had come to party. And it fitted. The magical secret zips all went up and once I tried I could very nearly breathe just like a normal person.

My feelings for the last dress had been lust. Maybe I thought I wanted its babies, but really I just wanted to give it a good seeing-to and send it home the next morning. But this dress . . . This dress I wanted to take home to meet my parents. I wanted to take it to dinner and make sure no one ever hurt it. If I wasn't getting married, I'd buy it to do the dishes. This was the dress.

'Oh, Angela.'

Louisa, Jenny and my mother appeared beside me in the mirror, but while I felt transcendentally happy, all three of them were sobbing as though someone had just told them they had terminal cancer of the puppy. Mum pressed one hand over her mouth and flapped the other madly in front of her, trying to wave her tears away. Louisa was having an out-and-out hysterical meltdown, while Jenny just nodded, tears streaming down her cheeks.

'That's it,' she shrugged, pulling her notebook out of her bag and crossing off her list. Score one for Clark. 'You look amazing, Angie.'

'Doesn't she?' Chloe stood to one side, her arms folded. 'Well, that was easy.'

'Great job with the accessories.' Jenny reached out for my arm to take a closer look at the bangles. 'These are beautiful.'

'I love my work,' she said again, pulling out a tray of more bangles and handing them to Jenny, the semi-professional magpie, for perusal. 'I'd need to take it up a little bit, maybe take the waist in a touch, but I could deliver it on Saturday morning. The wedding's in London?'

I switched off while the rest of the bridal party remembered themselves and went back to business, discussing timings, pricing and the finer logistics of the transaction. Instead of worrying about whether or not there was time for a final fitting, I lost myself in the mirror. I had a wedding dress. For my wedding. To Alex. Holding my left hand up to my chest, I smiled at the emerald as it twinkled against the fabric. All I needed now was for the rest of the week to work out as simply.

CHAPTER TWELVE

Wedding HQ was completely deserted when we got home. Alex had texted to say he was meeting some friends and some people from the label and might be out late. Dad was out somewhere rattling through his list of jobs, Mum went to have a lie-down and Jenny immediately bunkered down in the living room, going through emails, ticking off boxes and colour-coding spreadsheets. Louisa had vamoosed the second we'd got out of the car, citing the fact that she was missing her baby too much as the reason for not having time for the cup of tea she'd been moaning about for the last two hours. I had a sneaking suspicion it wasn't so much that she missed Grace as that she wanted to be beyond Jenny's shouting distance.

I sat at the kitchen table in semi-darkness, resentful of my ordinary clothes. Stupid sundress. Rubbish cardigan. But Jenny said there was no such thing as wearing in a wedding dress, so I was stuck with my everyday ensembles until Saturday, when it would arrive shiny and new and at a length that wouldn't cause me to break my neck. Sigh.

'Jenny?' I shouted from my seat, too depressed to walk into the living room.

'Angela?' she called back, too deep in wedding-related Pintrest boards to raise her head.

'Do you want to do something?' I couldn't cope with another evening in the house. I'd been here for three days and I was desperate to get out. And possibly get drunk. The day had been trying, to say the least. 'We could go back into town, get dinner, see some sights?'

'Sightseeing and dinner is scheduled for Wednesday,' she replied instantly. 'I've got too much to do. Why don't you go write your vows?'

Forcing myself out of my chair, I peered into what used to be my parents' living room. There seemed to be some semblance of order to the stacks of paper and charts that Jenny had created, but it didn't make any sense to me. A bit odd when you considered this was all for *my* wedding.

'Are you all right?' I asked, perching on the arm of the sofa.

'Sure.' She was concentrating on what looked like a drawing of the garden, Sharpie marker in her mouth, laptop by her side. 'Everything's on schedule. Sadie and Delia are coming. Erin and Mary can't make it. No word from James.'

'No, I don't mean with the wedding,' I said, although I did really want to know what all the different marked-off areas were for. CF? Was that a chocolate fountain? It had better be. 'In general. Are you OK? You seem a bit, I don't know, tense.'

'Is this about Louisa?' She turned to look at me. 'And the baby?'

Good grief.

'No, it's about whether or not you're all right,' I

181

repeated. 'You've been so up and down lately, and now you're, like, super-focused business Jenny. I sort of thought planning a wedding would involve more cupcakes and giggling than shouting at each other in the street.'

'So it is about Louisa?'

'I do want you two to get along,' I said, choosing my words carefully. 'But mainly I want you to have fun. I want us all to have fun.'

'We're doing the bachelorette on Wednesday, after we buy the bridesmaids' dresses,' Jenny said, shrugging as though she didn't know what I was talking about. 'We'll have fun then.'

Awesome. Jenny had scheduled in some fun. I was super-mad at Alex for going out without me. Not that I couldn't call him and tag along, I was sure, but I hated feeling like a clingy girl. I'd never really been one of those; I was far too lazy.

'I'm going to make a coffee.' She stood up and pushed past me into the kitchen. 'Or at least what your parents call coffee. You want one?'

I shook my head and waited until I heard the tap running before diving across the room to take a look at her computer screen. Well, there was a wedding, all right. I just wished I didn't recognize the groom. Jeff. I couldn't help but feel her ex-boyfriend's recent winter wedding in New York was a strange resource for researching a last-minute, London-based garden party ceremony, but then Jenny was strange. She'd thrown herself into planning this wedding to get away from thinking about Jeff and had only succeeded in trapping herself in this horrible, hateful little bubble. I turned away from the laptop and went back into the kitchen, trying to feel something other than bride envy.

For a complete asshat, Jeff had thrown one hell of a classy wedding. His missus wasn't a patch on my Lopez, though.

'Sure I can't tempt you out for a drink?' It had to be at least forty-eight hours since she'd imbibed, and that was just weird. 'We could just go to the pub round the corner? Drink away my jitters?'

'You're having jitters?' She span round, hurling freeze-dried coffee granules across my mother's spotlessly Swiffered floor. 'What? You can't!'

'Not jitters!' I backtracked wildly. 'I just meant, you know – grr, argh . . . weddings. We should open a bottle of wine, at least.'

'I can't drink when I'm working,' she said, pressing a hand to her heart in relief as she went back to making a very strong, very unpleasant-looking cup of coffee. 'You know that.'

In my defence, I didn't know that. From what Erin had told me, she loved to drink while working. Or at least work while drinking. And besides, she wasn't working, was she? Unless I was paying for this. I really hoped I wasn't. All of my money was tied up in important investments. Like my shoes.

'We're not technically working,' I said, trying to put the emphasis on 'technically' as politely as I could. 'We're kind of on holiday. We could go out for a little bit.'

Jenny put the kettle down and turned to face me, looking as though she was about to explain something very difficult to someone very stupid.

'Angie, honey. This stopped being a vacation when you asked me to organize a wedding for you with six days' notice. You wanna get drunk or you wanna get married?'

Well, that seemed like a stupid question. I wanted to get drunk, then I wanted to get married, and then I wanted to get drunk again. Wasn't that how this worked?

'I just don't want you to spend your week off stressed out over a spreadsheet,' I said with as much diplomacy as I could muster. 'That's what work is for.'

'I'm fine.' She stirred her coffee with her pen and poured in a distinctly unfine amount of sugar. 'Totally fine. Just let me get this done, OK? I'll be finished up for the day in a couple of hours. I have to call some guy called Carluccio about the catering. We can talk party favours when I'm done.'

'Jenny.' Time for the big guns. 'Where are your clothes?'

Her shoulders seized up and the sugar kept pouring.

'I was looking for something and your cases are empty.'

I could count on one hand the number of times Jenny had been lost for words in the years since we'd met. In her case, silence was not golden. Silence was a precursor to some God-almighty display that made *American Psycho* look like *The Tale of Peter Rabbit*. I shouldn't have asked that question when she was so much closer to the knife drawer than I was. But instead of savagely attacking me with a cheese grater, she turned to face me with a completely impassive expression, sipped her coffee and walked straight back into the living room without a word.

'Right.'

I left her alone and ventured into the conservatory, where I spotted a light on in Dad's shed. A shadow was moving around inside, and my heart started beating faster. If someone was stealing his Flymo, I was going to lose my shit. Today was not the day to mess with me.

'Why do you always approach potential robberies without proper shoes,' I admonished myself as I strode across the lawn barefoot. If there was a man in my dad's shed stealing power tools, I probably should have mentioned it to Jenny. Or at least brought my phone. I wasn't going to be much competition for a shed robber and it was going to be difficult to walk down the aisle if I was dead. And my mum would be well pissed off now she'd paid for the dress.

I cracked open the door with a polite cough and waited to get bashed in the head with a leaf blower. 'Hello?' I stepped inside and offered the burglar my most charming smile. But instead of finding an opportunistic teenager in a balaclava, I found my dad sitting down. Rolling a spliff.

'Oh. Hello, love.' He froze and looked around in the semi-darkness. 'Just doing some wedding stuff.'

'You're getting stoned for my wedding?' I was as morally outraged as it was possible to be while feeling utterly misplaced as a human. Teenagers got high. James Franco got high. Allegedly. Parents definitely did not get high. 'Are we serving space cakes for dessert?'

He looked down at the tin, which no longer contained mints, curiously strong or otherwise, then leaned back in his chair. 'Just don't tell your mother.'

'You've let me down, you've let Mum down and, most importantly, you've let yourself down,' I said, shunting a pair of secateurs along so I could sit down. I sighed. 'Mum doesn't know you're a secret stoner?'

'I'm not.' He closed up the tin, stashed the Rizlas in a drawer and gave me what was supposed to be a reassuring smile. I would have been more reassured by my credit card bill. 'It's not as if I'm high as a kite every day. Sometimes I get a bit wound up. And the doctor says it can be good for some people.'

'Yeah, people who have like serious health problems or dodgy doctors in California, not a slightly annoying wife.'

'Slightly annoying?' Dad snarked. 'You have been away for a long time. Anyway, today was just a bit trying, and listening to all that old stuff from the Seventies with Alex – well, it put me in the mood. And I thought you were still out.'

'My wedding has driven you to drugs.' I pulled up my legs and hugged my knees. 'Sorry.'

'Not so much your wedding as your little friend in there.' He nodded towards the house. 'I never thought I'd meet a woman more dedicated to keeping me out of trouble than your mother. Have you seen the list of jobs she gave me?'

'I haven't,' I admitted. 'But feel free not to worry. She's got some stuff going on – it's not about you. She won't kill you if you haven't got the right carpeting for the marquee.'

'Won't she?'

'Well, she might.'

We sat in companionable silence for a moment as I imagined Jenny chasing my dad around the garden in a bridesmaid's dress with his Black & Decker strimmer.

'It's nice to have you home, love.' He reached over and patted my knee. The Clark family equivalent of a sloppy kiss. 'I have missed you.'

'I've missed you too,' I said, surprised at how much I meant it. 'And Mum.'

'Really?' He didn't look convinced.

'Well, I've missed you.'

'And is everything all right?' Dad pulled out another tin, one that actually contained mints, and offered me one. 'Work really is OK? You're all right for money?'

'We're fine for money,' I confirmed. 'I'm not exactly buying an apartment in the Plaza, but I'm not stony broke. And yes, work really is good. I think. It might be the first time I can ever honestly tell you I love my job. It's going well and I'm not living in my overdraft.'

'You've been telling me you're not living in your overdraft for ten years,' he said, popping his own mint and putting away the tin. 'So that doesn't exactly fill me with confidence.'

'But this time I really mean it,' I laughed, thinking about that first exciting bank statement all in black ink. 'Things really are pretty good. Definitely better than OK.'

He gave me a steady look with his grey-blue eyes, hands on his knees. 'You'd tell me? If there was anything you needed to tell me?'

'Like what?' I couldn't work out whether he was genuinely worried about me or just tapping me up for some harder drugs. I was only on season one of *Breaking Bad* and I hadn't seen *The Wire* at all. I didn't know all the codewords.

'Anything,' he said, rubbing his thumbs together awkwardly. 'Even if there was something you didn't want to tell your mum. Or you thought we wouldn't want to hear. You know you can tell me anything.'

'I know I can tell you anything because I've got awesome blackmail material on you now.' I kicked the drawer where he'd hidden his stash. 'But really, there's nothing. I am ecstatically happy about everything that's happening in my life.'

'Well, that's good enough for me, then. Alex seems a good lad.' Dad straightened up a bit and dropped the serious chat. 'We've had a chat and it looks like he's got his head on his shoulders. Even if he is a musician.'

'Even if he is a musician,' I repeated. 'So Mum isn't going to stand up and refuse to let me marry him at the last minute?'

'I'll tie her to her chair,' he promised. 'He's sensible, he's not a penniless busker and he's clearly mad about you. He's a bit too handsome for my liking, but he does laugh at my jokes. I can't really ask for anything else for my little girl.'

This was good news. I loved my dad, I loved Alex, so there was no bad here.

'And it's probably better for my heart to get this whole wedding thing out of the way quickly. I couldn't have managed a year of listening to your mother debating whether or not to invite that woman down the road who looked after you once when you were seven.'

I frowned. I did not want that woman at my wedding. She was a cow and wouldn't let me watch *Blue Peter*.

'I did wonder one thing, though.' Dad fiddled with a screwdriver for a moment. 'You know I've always been a big fan of brass bands.'

I did know that.

'And I've been playing a bit with one from down the road.'

I did not know that.

'And I'm sure it's not in Jenny's theme or anything

and you can just say no if you want to say no because it's very silly, but one of the boys mentioned it might be a nice idea if we could play at the reception. For you. Just for a bit.'

Oh. At some point while I'd been away, my dad had become an adorable trumpet-tooting stoner. I pressed my hands against my mouth and tried to choke a sob before it emerged.

'It's silly. Your mum said it was silly. Jenny's got a string quartet or something planned, I know.'

'She has?' I wondered what else Jenny had planned that she hadn't mentioned. 'Whatever. If you want to play, then you should play. I want your brass band at my wedding.'

Now there were eight words I never thought I'd say. And I didn't entirely mean them, but who could say no to their dad, in his shed, when he's choking up and you're having your most emotional moment since he took you to your Brownie promise-making ceremony? So we'd have a brass band for half an hour. It might be fun.

'I'll let the band know.' He puffed out his chest with pride. 'They'll be chuffed to bits. And your mother will have to eat her words.'

'We all know how much she loves that,' I said. I hoped this wasn't going to come back to bite me in the arse. I knew Alex would be into it – he loved any kind of music stuff – but Jenny wasn't going to be amused, and it seemed like my mum wasn't completely won over by the idea. They'd better bloody be good.

'I just wish you were staying longer,' Dad said, clapping his hands on his knees as he stood up. 'But I know you'll be off living your life over there as soon as you can get away.'

'Not as soon as I can get away,' I replied, looking up at him in the dim glow of the shed. He looked well. Happy. 'I mean, we'll stay long enough for it not to be impolite. At least until the toasts. But then we're gone. Obvs.'

'I suppose I'm just going to have to get on a plane and come over, aren't I?' He bent down and kissed me on top of the head. 'Alex tells me there are some very interesting whiskey bars in New York, and I do want my grandson or daughter to know who I am.'

Huh? Grandson or daughter? And I knew giving them those keys was a bad idea. Alex was going to get a slap when he got home. If he came home.

'Well, I don't just want to be "that old man in the photo".' He opened the shed door and gave me a wink. 'Although I suppose I haven't got a lot of choice in the old man part.'

'I guess not?' I sat in silence and watched my dad stride off up the garden, back towards the house. Well, at least he approved of my choice of man. And he was pro-grandchildren. Even if I wasn't. I was quietly wondering whether or not the brass band would have time to learn any of Alex's songs when my phone trilled softly into life inside the pocket of my cardigan. A quick glance at the screen showed a UK number that seemed familiar but which I didn't have stored. And I answered. Because I was stupid.

'Hello?'

'Angela?'

Of course I recognized it. I'd dialled it almost every day for ten years.

'Mark.'

'You're still here, then?' He sounded nervous. He should.

'Yes?' I took a deep breath and then puffed out my cheeks to stop myself from spurting out a torrent of abuse.

'Right, well, I . . .' He took a deep breath of his own. 'What are you doing tomorrow?'

'Stuff.' Excellent comeback, Angela. Just classic.

'OK. I thought maybe you might want to get a coffee? Catch up a bit?' It sounded like he was walking – his breath was coming harder than it needed to. I looked at my watch. Hmm – seven on a Monday? He'd be on his way to the tennis club. And I hated myself for knowing that. 'I've got the day off, so maybe we could get lunch or something.'

'Maybe.' The word was out of my mouth before I could control it. 'Coffee maybe.'

'Brilliant.' He sounded relieved, I could tell. Which begged the question why he was bothering in the first place. 'I'll pick you up at about eleven.'

He hung up before I could come to my senses and tell him to go fuck himself. Hard. With a cactus. I sat and stared at my phone, willing it to do something other than remind me it was my move on Words With Friends. So when it actually started ringing, I nearly shat myself.

'Hello you,' I answered immediately. It was Alex. 'What's happening?'

'Hey,' Alex crackled down the line. 'How was today? Did you get a dress?'

'I did, and it's incredible,' I confirmed, unsure how much I was allowed to tell him. 'Did you write your vows?'

'Not yet,' he replied. 'But your dad did ask if I wanted to get high with him in the garden.'

I looked over at the secret drawer and sighed.

'I passed.' From the sound of car horns, sirens and overwhelming background chatter, Alex was outside somewhere far away from me. The garden was quiet and calm and deserted. And it was making me tense. 'Anyway, I just wanted to let you know, I'm gonna stay over at Steven's place tonight. We're on our way to some place in Shoreditch and he lives pretty close by. We're meeting the label people then maybe we'll see a show.'

'Steven?' I didn't want to come across as though I was sulking. Even if I was. 'He's not with the label?'

'He's a friend,' Alex sort of explained. 'You want to come meet us?'

I did and I didn't. I did because I wanted to kiss the taste of talking to Mark out of my mouth, and I didn't because it would take me at least an hour to get over to Shoreditch. Also, I was a little miffed that Alex had cooler friends in my city than I did.

'I'm going to pass.' I weighed up the options of a bath and bed against getting dressed up, getting on a train, getting on the tube and talking to Shoreditch twats for the remainder of the evening. Williamsburg yes, East London no. I wasn't nearly cool enough. 'I'm sad I'm not meeting your friends, though.'

'You're so not an East London girl,' Alex replied, demonstrating worryingly accurate telepathy. 'And for that, I am glad. Anyway, I emailed Jenny and had her put him on the guest list for Saturday. You'll meet him then. In your awesome dress.'

'There isn't a guest list for our wedding.' Kind of a lie. 'There isn't going to be a bouncer.' As far as I knew. 'You can invite anyone you want, you know that.'

'Yeah, I guess,' he said. 'I'm gonna go – I'm almost at the bar. See you tomorrow?'

'See you tomorrow,' I agreed. 'Have fun tonight.'

'You too.' He lowered his voice just a touch. 'I love you.'

'Love you too,' I managed to squeak before he hung up. I stared at the wooden walls of the shed and pouted. 'Fun is scheduled for Wednesday.'

While Alex was out enjoying himself, I sat in Dad's shed until the sun disappeared altogether, trying not to think about agreeing to meet up with Mark or my impending career moment so I could concentrate on imagining how wonderful the wedding would be. The garden was big – more than big enough for the marquee Mum had described that would be set against the silver birch trees at the back of our lawn. The miniature herb garden would be perfect for photos, and Dad's green-house was full of bright, beautiful flowers. I hoped I could convince him to let me open it up for cocktails.

I mentally dotted tables and chairs all across the lawn around a big, open dance floor lit by candles, fairy lights and the last light of the sunset, and saw Alex twirling me around, his tie loosened, my hair undone, everyone laughing. It wasn't fancy, it wasn't uptight. It would be lovely. If everything went right. And there was no way it wouldn't with Jenny in charge. Remembering I needed to slot Dad's brass band in there somewhere wiped the dopey smile off my face somewhat, but it couldn't be that bad. It was just one compromise. It wasn't like we were having clowns or ice sculptures of Scooby-Doo. And it might be fun. Or at least it would be over relatively quickly.

I added Jenny and Louisa to my imaginary wedding, trying to cosmic-order the perfect bridesmaids' dresses. I had decided that if I could get them in the right dresses, everything else would work itself out. And if it came to it, I'd wear a pair of Primark flats and trash my credit card on Loubous for them both. There was nothing designer shoes couldn't overcome. And as I knew from first-hand experience, they made a great weapon if necessity called.

My stomach rumbled at the thought of whatever Jenny was ordering from Mr Carluccio, which I assumed to be the Carluccio's restaurant down the road and not an actual man. Although I'd be pretty happy either way. We'd talked about doing something more picky than a sit-down regular meal. This pleased me. It allowed for greater gluttony on my part. We'd also talked about a great big mountain of cupcakes instead of a wedding cake, but that hadn't been approved quite so quickly. Louisa was worried Mrs Stevens wouldn't know what we were talking about, and it was too late in the game to expect her to watch the entire box set of *Sex and the City*. As in there literally weren't enough hours between now and the wedding for her to watch them all.

As well as allowing me to indulge in wedding fantasies, hiding in the shed meant I avoided going back into the house. I didn't know what to say to Jenny, and I couldn't cope with Mum and Dad cowering in terror in the kitchen. I'd sent Louisa a couple of texts, but she wasn't replying. Brilliant. It was five days until my wedding and I had petrified parents, two bridesmaids who weren't speaking to me and an errant fiancé who was probably being pawed to death by girls with asymmetrical haircuts and lots of ironic tattoos. Maybe I should have dragged my ass east.

Rather than sit and sulk, I decided to be productive. Or at least semi-productive. I crept back into the house, snuck upstairs, bypassing whatever hysteria was occurring in the kitchen, and skulked into my room to check over the *Gloss* presentation for Friday's meeting. Delia had sent over a few pages of updates and I wanted to be completely on top of my game. At that exact moment, the only game I felt on top of was Hungry, Hungry Hippos. I pulled out my phone roughly every fourteen seconds, tapping out the beginnings of texts to Louisa, to Alex, even to Mark. I didn't want to go for a coffee with him. I didn't want to see his face. But I did want him to see mine as long as mine looked really good. So good that he would spend every second of the rest of his life wondering what had made him make such a terrible, terrible mistake.

So we'd meet for coffee, I'd show him lots of pictures of Alex, and I'd look fabulous. It wasn't that I wanted him to be unhappy, I just wanted to be happier. Considerably happier. In a big way.

There was nothing weird about that, was there?

CHAPTER THIRTEEN

'Mum?'

No reply.

'Dad?'

Nada.

'Jenny?'

Nothing. The house was completely empty. Tuesday morning was grey and dull, no hint of sunshine behind the heavy dark clouds. I told myself the weather was getting its nonsense out of the way before Saturday, when it would be blue skies and blue birds and lots of other lovely blue things, like – well, I'd think of something. Blue Nun, maybe. Even if it was a fair few hours off cocktail o'clock.

A note on the kitchen table explained that Dad had gone to rehearse with his band and Mum and Jenny were out. No details. No information of any kind. Just out. But Mum had scribbled a P.S. that there were some boxes of my things in the back bedroom cupboard that needed sorting out when I had a minute. Brilliant. Going through boxes of knackered four-year-old Primark T-shirts and that purple pair of BHS culottes

I'd clung onto since 1997 was exactly what I felt like doing.

I'd had no word from Alex. Being the wonderfully trusting girlfriend that I was, I assumed he was hanging out at his friend's house and not wallowing up to the eyeballs in English groupies, but I sent him a quick text anyway just to make sure he knew how much I loved him and to let him know I was going out for coffee with a friend. I just casually forgot to add the words 'ex' and 'boy' to that sentence. I'd tell him later. It wasn't a text-appropriate conversation and besides, he trusted me like I trusted him.

It was pretty easy to convince myself that the two hours I spent primping before Mark's arrival were hours well spent. It was good pre-wedding prep – essential conditioning and moisturizing that couldn't be overlooked.

I went for a simple look – loose, softly waved hair and very delicate make-up, just enough to make me look bright-eyed and bushy-tailed. The outfit was more trying. When Mark and I were together, I existed exclusively in jeans, T-shirts and knackered Converse so I didn't want to show up in Alexander Wang glitter trousers and a leather corset, but I did want to show him how much I'd changed. Since the weather was threatening to be rubbish, I went for a little grey Paul & Joe Sister bird-print dress, a gift from Erin's pre-baby wardrobe, and a pair of my mother's black tights. Thank God she always kept spares. I added some ballet flats, the knackered old denim jacket I'd systematically destroyed through two years of sixth form and my equally knackered Marc Jacobs bag, which I had managed to destroy in under two years, looked in the mirror and declared myself 'OK'. The dress was pretty but the jacket played it down. The bag was clearly designer but the battering it had taken told you I wasn't precious. Or careful with my things. I just hoped it was OK enough to get me through.

The doorbell rang and I held myself back, trying to ignore my racing heartbeat.

'This is closure,' I told myself, pacing down the stairs step by step. 'This is closure. This is screw-you-my-life-is-amazing closure.'

I opened the door to find Mark standing there on my doorstep just like we were sixteen and felt my stomach flip. Just not in the good way.

'One minute.' I held up a finger, slammed the door shut in his face and raced into the downstairs toilet to throw up. Well, there went breakfast. I was going to have no trouble getting into my dress on Saturday. I cleaned myself up, gargled with Dad's disgusting Listerine and went back to the door. There really was no getting out of this now.

With an added, just-puked glow, I opened the door again, offering Mark what I hoped was a dazzling smile. 'Sorry,' I said, pushing him out of the way and locking the door behind me. 'Forgot something. Shall we go?'

'And so we decided to start our own magazine.' I kept my eyes safely on the road ahead of me as we pulled up alongside Richmond Green in Mark's Range Rover. The same Range Rover. I couldn't look at the back seat, also known as the scene of the crime, and I couldn't quite bring myself to look at Mark. Even I knew beating him to death wasn't a good idea while he was at the wheel, despite what the devil on my shoulder was suggesting. 'So that's what we're doing.

It's called *Gloss*. I'm going to be in charge of the website and work with the editorial team on the actual magazine too. It's good. It's going to be good.'

'Sounds like you've been busy,' Mark commented, reversing into a parking spot and turning off the engine. 'I wish I had half as interesting a story for you.'

Up until the car stopped, it wouldn't have mattered if he'd been crowned King of England – I hadn't let him get a word in edgeways. I'd always been a nervous talker, but this was ridiculous. Every second of silence seemed to turn back time. From the moment I'd got into the car, everything had started slipping away – New York seemed like just a memory. Alex? No one but a boy in a band I saw one time. Jenny? A figment of my overactive and extremely fashionable imagination. The whole thing made more sense as a fever dream I'd had after falling asleep listening to MTV and reading *Grazia*. Sitting in my old seat, in my old car. Mark was still wearing the same aftershave. It was all I could do not to rest my hand on his thigh, just like old times. I didn't want to, it was just habit. A bad habit. How did people cope with break-ups without leaving the country? I tried to picture my apartment, my walk to the subway, the Manhattan skyline waiting outside the window, but it felt like I was looking at someone else's photographs.

The only way to bring it to life was to keep talking, to force it to exist. Only the more I talked it up, the less realistic it seemed. Mark certainly seemed to be having trouble believing me. And why should he believe me? I was that lazy, dumpy girlfriend who sat on his sofa churning out sad little stories about mutated amphibian ninjas to scrape out a living. That Angela would never have done half the things I had done. At least, she would never have survived them.

'Sit outside?' Mark asked, snapping me out of my confusing pity party. 'Pint?'

'Yeah,' I nodded, following him over to a picnic bench by the Cricketers. Once upon a time, it had been 'our' pub. I wondered if it was still his. He vanished inside the darkened bar and I pulled out my phone to check for messages. Nothing but a quick text from Louisa, reinforcing the feeling that I'd imagined every event of the past two years. I spun my engagement ring around my finger as I read the message – she was crying off any bridesmaiding for the day because Grace was sick. I wondered if she really was ill or if Lou was just sick of me and Jenny, but I'd promised myself I'd make it up to her at the hen do anyway. As soon as I worked out what I was making up for exactly.

Richmond was as calm and peaceful as it always was. I gazed out across the green and thanked the sun for trying to shine. It wasn't quite all the way there, but, like me, it was giving it a go. I remembered all the summer Saturdays Louisa, Tim, Mark and I had spent on that lawn with a picnic basket. Well, first with bags of McDonald's and bottles of cider and then with Tesco bags full of baguettes and brie and those mini bottles of prosecco, and then eventually a proper wicker basket, picnic blanket, real glasses and everything. Or at least, Louisa and Tim had bought us the set for Christmas before we broke up. I figured Mark and Katie were using it now. I was destined to remain a plastic bag person. I'd only break a real glass anyway.

'Here you go.' Mark appeared with a pint in each hand and two bags of Kettle Chips hanging out of his mouth. 'They didn't have salt and vinegar.'

'S'fine.' I took the bag of Spicy Thai. 'I'm used to it. They don't have them in America.'

'Fucking hell.' Mark opened the Sea Salt and laughed. 'How do you survive?'

'I manage,' I replied with narrow eyes. His over-familiarity was irritating. 'So, what have you been up to?'

'Work mostly.' He chomped on a crisp thoughtfully, blue eyes looking to the heavens for a better answer. 'Banking's not the best place to be right now. The hours are just as bad but the job security's gone. Bonuses are down, perks are off the table completely. Do you know, I have to work until nine now before they pay for a car to get me home?'

'That's just terrible,' I said, trying to look sympathetic. 'You couldn't just get the tube like a normal person?'

'After nine? Back to Wimbledon?' He looked as though I'd just proposed he walk barefoot across the Sahara. 'I remember a time when you wouldn't leave the house unless I promised to come and collect you in the car.'

'Well, as the great Gary Barlow once said, everything changes,' I retorted, sipping my pint. And it was disgusting. 'I only really take the subway now. It's just easier.'

'I still can't believe you're living in New York,' Mark said, smiling his easy smile and shaking his dark blond head. 'Sounds like a lot has changed. For you.'

'It has,' I agreed, mentally preparing my speech. 'It's good—'

'Never really been a big America fan,' he said, cutting me off with a rap on the table. 'Vegas maybe. LA's all right. But New York's not for me. I can't see how anyone can stand it. Terrible place.'

'How so?' I asked coolly. Really? He was going to sit there and slag off my city?

'It's just so rush-rush-rush.' He waved his arms around his head and gave a mock shiver. 'Dirty taxis, overpriced restaurants, terrible beer. And the people? What a bunch of arseholes. They all think they know better.'

'I actually think the people are really friendly,' I said, turning my glass round on the spot. 'And it's not such a rush once you get into the rhythm.'

'Or if you don't get off the settee?' He laughed again then tried to choke it off when he saw my face. As it happened, I spent a very healthy amount of time on the sofa, but he didn't get to make a joke about it.

'Well, New Yorkers can be as friendly on the sofa as English people are on the back seats of their cars,' I said as calmly as I possibly could. Mark spluttered and spat a mouthful of beer out onto the pavement. 'That's quite friendly, isn't it?'

'Angela.' He wiped his mouth with the back of his hand and remembered his stiff upper lip. 'Do we have to?'

'Oh God, you're so English.' I couldn't help but laugh. It felt good. I sat up, leaning my elbows on the table and looked him in the eye. 'Mark, I don't care.'

'I know it wasn't ideal, the way it happened,' he said, wiping stray spots of ale from his chin. 'I never wanted it to work out that way, but things with me and you, they were—'

'Seriously,' I cut in before he said something he would regret. 'Really. I don't care.'

I wasn't sure if it was true, but I certainly didn't want to hear the excuses he'd been working on for two years. This, I reminded myself for the umpteenth time, was closure, not revenge or retribution. I didn't need to hear his whining, I just needed to show up, look amazing and leave the bigger person. Not physically bigger, though; I had lost a bit of weight.

'Good to know.' He sipped at his beer again with caution. I let him finish a whole mouthful before I started talking again. Just in case. If he spat on my dress, I would have to kill him.

'So, I'm engaged.' I splayed my fingers out on the table and let the ring twinkle against the dark wood. 'Not to you.' I clarified.

'I assumed we were officially off when I found your engagement ring in a bag of piss,' he replied crisply. I looked up suddenly. Oh yeah. I did that. 'So who's the lucky chap?'

'It's a funny story,' I started with suspicion. I knew Louisa and Tim must have mentioned Alex to him – there was no way it hadn't come up in conversation over the past two years, even if they didn't exactly hang out often these days. And he totally already knew I was engaged – his mum would have been on the phone to him faster than *Gossip Girl* when she found out. 'You know that band Stills? We saw them at the Garage years ago.'

'Don't remember,' he sniffed. Ha. I had him on the ropes.

'Well, we saw them,' I carried on, moving in for the KO. 'Anyway, I met this guy in a coffee shop one day and he turned out to be the lead singer. And then he turned out to be my fiancé.'

'You're getting married to a bloke in a band?' Mark did not look nearly as beaten as I would like. In fact, he was trying very hard to cover a very smug expression. 'Really, Angela?'

'Really, Mark.' I was confused. 'And that's funny because?'

'It's just a bit of a cliché, isn't it?' He started helping himself to my crisps. That shit wouldn't fly when we were together and it certainly wasn't going to fly now. I snatched the packet back. 'You bugger off to New York with a cob on and shack up with a musician? What, do you think you're Sid and Nancy?'

'That's an interesting way of looking at what happened,' I sniffed. 'Although I suppose I did have "a bit of a cob on" at the time. But I'm not just shacked up with a musician, I'm getting married. And hopefully not knifed to death in the Chelsea Hotel.'

'I don't want you to think I'm being an arsehole,' he said, trying to reach across the table and cover my hand with his. 'But I'm trying to make you see sense here. You can't run off to New York and marry a rock star on the rebound. That's not how life works.'

'I'm not on the rebound,' I screeched, entirely unconcerned about the old couple at the neighbouring table. 'This didn't happen yesterday. I'm not a sixteen-year-old groupie.'

'Will you calm down?' Mark hissed across the table. 'I forget how long you've been gone. You've clearly spent far too long with the Americans.'

'Or just enough time away from you,' I countered. 'Don't talk to me like I'm a child.'

'Then don't behave like one,' he snapped back. 'Don't be so stupid. Do you really think this man is going to marry you? He'll probably have moved when you get back or your keys won't work and all your stuff will be on the street.'

'Given that he's here with me and we're getting

married on Saturday, that seems unlikely,' I said triumphantly.

Mark gave a quick demo of his famous goldfish impression, with bonus opening and closing. I swept a stray piece of hair out of my face and folded my arms. Ah-ha. Have that, you bastard.

'You're getting married on Saturday?'

'Yes.'

'And that's why you're home?'

'Yes.' Well, sort of.

'Were you going to tell me?' He had suddenly gone very pale. 'If I hadn't called?'

'Would it matter?' I felt myself flush opposite him. 'It doesn't matter.'

'Of course it would matter,' he mumbled, pushing crisps around in the open packet. 'Don't be stupid.'

'Stop calling me stupid.' I was losing my temper incredibly quickly and that was not part of my be the bigger man plan. 'You don't know me. You don't know what you're talking about.'

'Yeah, I do know you Angela,' he said, raising his voice. 'I've known you since you were sixteen. I know your mum, I know your dad, I know you're allergic to penicillin, I know you put two sugars in your tea even though you tell people you only have one, I know you love reading those crappy celebrity magazines in the bath for hours on end, I know you won't go out in flip-flops until you've painted your toenails.'

He paused for breath and turned down the volume slightly.

'I know you would go out and buy me Lemsip at the first sign of a cold. I know the smell of mushy peas makes you yak but you never complain about me having them. I know *Watership Down* makes you cry.

I know that you were my first and I was yours and this is just the stupidest thing I've ever heard.'

I didn't know who was more stunned – me or the old couple beside us.

'Does he know all that?' Mark pressed his lips together in a thin, tight line. 'This Alex?'

'He knows I get easily upset at the death of cartoon rabbits and that I'm thoughtful enough to buy cold medicine when needed, yes,' I replied in a low voice. 'But I don't think he's terribly concerned as to who I lost my virginity to.'

Mark stood up with a start. 'I meant you were my first love. But whatever.'

He clambered out of the table, kicking it as he went and spilling his unfinished beer everywhere.

'Oh, I say.' The old man beside us winked at his wife.

'Drama,' she replied, lifting her gin and bitter lemon.

'Oh, bloody hell.' I snaffled a handful of crisps and legged it across the road after him.

'And I'm the one who got all American and dramatic?' I ran up behind Mark and gave him a good hard push in the back. 'What was that all about, you woman?'

He carried on walking in silence until he was right in front of the car and then turned around with a face like thunder.

'You're an idiot,' he said in a perfectly calm voice. 'I hope you know that.'

'As it happens, I do,' I replied. 'But I don't know what that's got to do with you.'

He huffed and puffed for a moment, looking left and right before grabbing my shoulders and shoving me roughly against the car.

'What the—' But I wasn't given a chance to finish my question because Mark had his tongue so far down my throat, I was pretty sure he could feel my liver. It was hardly the most romantic moment of my life, but for a couple of seconds, it was my life again. My old life. He smelled the same, he felt the same – it was too much.

'What are you doing?' I pushed him away and hit him with my satchel. 'What is wrong with you?'

'What are you talking about?' He covered his head with his arms and cowered behind the bonnet of the car. 'I thought you wanted me to!'

'Why would I want you to kiss me?' I continued to beat him for fear of another attack of the lips. I paused to wave my left hand in his terrified face. 'I'm getting married on Saturday, you fool.'

'And you come out with me, all dressed up, with bloody make-up on.' He spat out the word and waved a hand around in the general vicinity of his face. 'And I'm supposed to think you don't want me to kiss you?'

This was tricky territory. Because I did want him to *want* to kiss me, but I didn't want him to follow through with it. I wanted him to think about it, then go home and have a little cry in the bath. Now he had created all kinds of fun problems. Now I had to tell Alex. Now I had to tell my mum. Now I had to pick up all the tampons and lip balms that had fallen out of my handbag. Who needed seven lip balms and only three tampons? Me, apparently.

'Of course I didn't want you to kiss me!' I tried ever so hard to morph into the spitting dinosaur from *Jurassic Park*, but for some reason I couldn't quite manage it. 'Don't be ridiculous.'

'So what did you want?' He smoothed out his shirt

and shook out his shoulders a couple of times. 'Apart from to mess with my head?'

It was all very Danny Zuko in *Grease*. I tried very hard not to shout, 'You're a fake and a phoney and I wish I'd never laid eyes on you.'

'I wanted . . .' My mind was completely empty. I couldn't tell him I wanted closure. I couldn't tell him I wanted him to feel stupid. I certainly couldn't tell him I wanted him to go home and listen to whatever music boys listened to when they were sad and wish he'd never ever cheated on me. So I told him the biggest, stupidest lie I could think of.

'I wanted to invite you to the wedding.'

'I would love to,' he replied through gritted teeth.

'Wonderful.' My eyes widened and my throat felt tight. Cockingtons. 'I am so glad.'

'Are you now?' He smelled a rat. Or at least the busted bottle of Coco Mademoiselle that lay at my feet.

'I would be honoured if you would attend,' I said very slowly and clearly. 'You and your lovely girl-friend.'

'You want me to bring Katie?' His eyebrows shot up so high it was a wonder they didn't get caught in the engines of a passing plane. 'To your wedding?'

'Sod it, why not?' I had already destroyed the happiest day of my life by inviting this bell end; I figured I may as well push it as far as possible. Besides, there was no way she'd come. Right? 'The more the merrier. Please do tell her it's a fancy occasion, though, so if she can keep her knickers on, that would be bril-liant.'

'I'm sure she'll do her best.' Mark continued to stare straight at me. 'You really have changed, you know.'

'Thank fuck for that,' I said, stooping to gather my belongings as gracefully as I could without flashing my gusset to the world. 'I'll see you on Saturday.'

My dignified exit and refusal of a lift home meant that I had to get the train back. And having to get the train meant I had to get a Starbucks. Soothed by the globally recognized menu, I sipped at my venti latte and texted Alex to tell him we needed to talk weddings when he got home. And then I texted Louisa to tell her I needed to talk to her as soon as. And then I texted Jenny to tell her we needed to do some more work on the seating plan.

This had not been my most successful day. I got home and changed into my pyjama shorts and one of Alex's T-shirts, hoping his common-sense DNA might rub off on me, and settled down to sort through the boxes my mum had left in the back bedroom. Self-inflicted punishment of the worst kind – I was going to have to confront the ghosts of fashions passed. Thank God Jenny was out.

The first box was easy to deal with. Lots of H&M strappy dresses I'd worn with lots of little greying H&M T-shirts underneath. The odd Warehouse shift, a couple of pairs of worn-through leggings. I pulled a huge fluffy jumper out of the pile and put it to one side. It held many happy memories of cuddling up on the couch with Louisa and half a pint of Ben & Jerry's. The second box was full of books. I made a mental note to have them shipped before we headed back to the States. The last box was less easily dealt with. Instead of finding a pile of sad clothes or a stack of classics, I found everything else I'd left behind. This box was full of me. My *Little Mermaid, Bring It On*

and *Buffy* DVDs. A collection of Benefit make-up cata-
logues, so often lusted after and rarely used. Half a
dozen theatre programmes, my scrapbook of tickets
and flyers of all the gigs I'd gone to. And underneath
them, three large blue suede photo albums. The
collected volumes of Angela and Mark. It hadn't
occurred to me that he would have packed these up
with my things. These weren't my things, they were
our things. And I didn't want them. I pulled them out
and rested all three in my lap for a moment. They
were heavy.

I pulled a hair-tie from around my wrist and twisted
my hair up on top of my head before I opened up the
first album. The first thing that hit me was how young
I looked. And how terrible my hair was. I always
thought I looked pretty good for twenty-eight – I stayed
out of the sun, I wore sunscreen – but there was
something in my face in these pictures that no amount
of product could put back. I flicked through the pages,
watching me and Louisa grow up. Dancing in the
garden, dressing up as the Spice Girls, both of us on
horses, Louisa on a horse and me standing beside one
in a cast. And then the boys appeared. After a couple
of pages, the pictures moved on to just me and Mark.
Messing about for the camera at uni, our holiday in
Seville where he proposed, the day we got the keys
for our house. Slowly, as I moved on to the last album,
I noticed that there were fewer and fewer photos that
had been deemed album-worthy. The first few pages
were crammed with photos of us with our cheeks
pressed tightly together, arms thrown around each
other like the world was ending. But by the end there
were just one or two photos of us with strained smiles
and no touching. This was what people meant when

they said a picture spoke a thousand words. I just hadn't been listening at the time.

Underneath the albums were stacks and stacks of cards. I leafed through them, occasionally flicking them open to see the faded inscriptions. It wasn't until I felt the hot water dripping on to my knees that I realized I was crying. It wasn't just the birthday and Christmas cards I'd collected over the years, it was everything. All the Valentine's cards we had sent to each other. Every little love note. The anniversary cards, the postcards, the just-to-say-I-love-you cards. How did shared belongings automatically become possessions of the girl after a break-up? Why did we have to suffer the burden? I couldn't believe he'd discarded all of this so easily. I'd spent hours writing out these notes, these love letters, and at the time they'd meant everything. I'd assumed they'd meant the same to him. Apparently not. Maybe Katie didn't want them in her house. Or maybe Mark didn't care to be reminded of his past mistakes. Either way, it was harsh.

I picked up a pale pink heart and stared at it. I didn't need to open it to know what it said – I had the words memorized. This was the first Valentine's card I'd ever sent. For a second, just a second, I wondered what would have happened if I hadn't left England. If I hadn't run away. Would we have worked things out? Would I have fought for Mark? Could we have been happy?

I piled the cards back in with the books and wiped away my tears with an unattractive sniff. Maybe inviting him to the wedding wasn't a silly idea; maybe it was a downright stupid idea.

'Hey girl.' Alex knocked gently on the door and

stood in front of me in last night's rumpled clothes. 'What's up?'

I looked up, tears streaming down my face, grey traces of mascara staining the backs of my hands. 'Hi.' My voice was thick and sad, even though I was trying to smile.

'You OK?' His face creased with concern and he was on his knees by my side in moments. 'What's wrong?'

I wanted to hold it all together and tell him I was fine. I wanted to be completely reassured by his presence, by the fact that we were getting married in mere days, by the knowledge that Alex would be by my side for the rest of my life, but I couldn't. I wasn't. Seeing Mark, reading these cards, looking at ten years gone by wrapped up in blue suede had stolen my voice. They had stolen my faith. All I could do was press my lips tightly together and let my eyes burn.

'What are these?' Alex took the card out of my hands and opened it up. He read it, looked at me and read it again. Then he closed it and put it back in the box. 'You getting cold feet on me, Clark?'

I shook my head and smiled but I couldn't quite form the words I needed to. Instead I pressed my head into his chest and let out the last couple of whimpers while he stroked my hair.

'This is all your old stuff,' he asked, poking the box with his foot. 'Yours and Mark's?'

I noticed an edge to his voice when he said Mark's name – just a very slight crispness that never really made it into Alex's approach to life. There was a chance my news wasn't going to go down especially well.

'Yeah,' I whispered, clearing my throat. 'Mum asked

me to go through the boxes but I didn't know what was in them. Sorry, I just got a bit, you know, sad.'

'You don't have to be sorry for being sad.' He kept stroking my hair and holding me close. 'It must be weird to see all this stuff.'

'Yeah,' I agreed, scrunching up my face. I just had to bite the bullet. 'And I saw Mark too.'

'You did?' The stroking stopped.

'And I sort of invited him to the wedding.'

'You did?' Suddenly he wasn't holding me quite so tightly.

'It was stupid, it just came out.' I pulled away and looked up at him but his expression was completely unreadable. 'He called to see if we could catch up and I thought, you know, it'd be all right because we've both moved on and it would be good to see him and stuff.'

'Right.'

'But it was a bit weird.'

'Uh-huh.'

'So I invited him to the wedding.'

Alex rubbed his eyes and blinked a couple of times before setting his emerald eyes on me. 'Just so I'm straight here – you hung out with your ex, it got weird and *then* you invited him to our wedding?'

I squeezed my nose and swiped my smudged eyes again.

'Yes.'

'Then did you call Solene and invite her along to completely destroy any chance of this wedding working out?'

Solene. AKA Le French Bitch. AKA Alex's ex. AKA my nemesis. Well, one of them, along with Cici and Mark's girlfriend. I hated having three nemeses at

213

twenty-nine. It was too many for someone who wasn't a master spy.

'I did not call Solene – I don't have her number,' I replied. My joke fell flat. Besides, I did have her number. It was saved in my phone under 'evilbitch-fromhell' just in case. 'It was stupid, I know. It just came out. But I'm sure he's not going to come.'

'Did he say he's not going to come?'

'Not exactly,' I admitted. 'And I also invited his girlfriend.'

'Angela.' Alex leaned back against the spare bed, looking at me with tired surprise. The way a teacher might look at a pupil who has been eating the papier-mâché. Again. 'Do you want him at the wedding?'

I looked at the photo albums, the scrapbooks and half of Clintons Cards' warehouse piled up in the plastic storage box in front of me. 'Well, it's not like I want him to give me away.'

'And it's not my dream come true to hang out with your ex on our wedding day.' He put his arm back around my shoulders and pulled me into his chest. His heart rate was definitely up, and not in a 'let's do it on the bedroom floor' way. 'We both know what happened when you met mine.'

We did know. The short version of that story was 'nothing good'.

'And I don't want to come off as the jealous type,' he said, kissing my hair and holding me tightly. 'But I kinda am.'

I tilted back to drop a kiss on his lips. 'Me too.'

This didn't appear to be a good time to tell him about the attempted snog, and really, what was the good in him knowing? Mark had taken a kicking and it wasn't like anything had really happened. This was definitely one of those better-off-not-knowing things.

'This one is easy,' Alex said, dropping the cover on the storage box and clicking it tightly closed, ignoring my sharp intake of breath. Was he going to suggest disinviting him? Had he forgotten I was English? 'Just call him and tell him he can't come.'

'There's no way he'll come,' I promised. 'He's stupid, but he's not that stupid.' I really hoped I was right. He was pretty stupid.

'And all of this stuff? The cards, the photographs, all of it – ancient history,' he said, pushing the box underneath the bed with his foot. 'No more tears over the past. As of Saturday, it's you and me for good. No ex-boyfriends, no ex-girlfriends, just me and you every single day, exactly like it should be.'

'Just me and you.' I bit my lips, trying to put some colour into my face that wasn't a variation on grey. 'Sounds nice.'

'I guess I should add a proviso for the fact that we're never going to get rid of Jenny.' He rolled his eyes. 'And I figure it's only a matter of time before Craig ends up living on our sofa.'

'And now you've given my dad some keys, I'm pretty sure he's eyeing a move over,' I added.

Alex laughed and unwrapped his arms from around my neck. He gave me a gentle push backwards and we looked at each other quietly for a moment.

'I think you should wear that to the wedding,' he said. 'Suits you.'

'Might have to if the dress doesn't get here.' I pulled the faded black T-shirt out and looked at it properly. Hmm. Mum wasn't much for AC/DC. 'Have you got your ensemble sorted?'

'Your dad wants to take me to some place called

Westfield?' He stretched out a denim-clad leg and poked me with his Converse. 'Is that a good thing?'

'Westfield is a good thing,' I confirmed. 'Dad wanting to spend every waking moment with you is just adorable. Bromance of the century.'

'Right?' Alex's mouth curled at one corner. 'If he weren't giving you away, I'd figure he'd challenge Graham to a duel for best man.'

'He might still. Don't think he's nearly as taken with me as he is with you.'

'Angie! You have a wedding present!'

The front door opened and Jenny's voice screeched up the stairs at exactly the same time.

'I love it when she proves my point,' Alex said as I jumped up and vaulted over him towards the door. 'How come it's not *our* wedding present?'

The reason it was my wedding present and not ours became immediately apparent as I rounded the bottom of the stairs. Expecting a ribbon-wrapped box or something sparkly at the very least, it was more than a bit of a surprise to see a strapping six-footer standing in the kitchen.

'James!' I bounded up to my buddy and leapt into his arms. He spun me round the kitchen and dipped me low into a dramatic Hollywood kiss. As was the way with his people.

'You made it!' I dropped to my feet and settled into a more conventional neck-breaking hug. 'Why didn't you email?'

'Because I'm shit,' James Jacobs replied. 'So I thought I'd just stop in and say hello. Hey, dude!'

He gave Alex a far more manly hug as he appeared behind me.

'Glad you could make it, man,' Alex said, clapping him on the back.

'Is it me,' I heard my mum whisper to Jenny, 'or does he look ever so familiar?'

It wasn't just her. Aside from being my very favourite homosexual in the whole world, James was a very famous actor. I'd interviewed him in Hollywood and after a bit of a shaky start and accidental global outing, we'd become firm friends. He'd even collaborated with Alex on a couple of film scores for some independent movies he was working on. I'd read an article in which James claimed coming out had given him a 'new-found creative freedom', but I had a horrible feeling it was more to do with not being offered the romantic leads and hard-man roles he'd taken on before the world knew he preferred boys to girls. Sad. But he seemed happy; that was enough for me.

'Right, get yourself dressed – we're going out for cocktails,' he said, slapping me on the arse and turning to flash his million-dollar smile at my mum while I hopped from foot to foot, clapping. I was excited. 'You ladies will be joining us, of course? And Alex?'

'Oh.' Mum held a hand up to her throat and blushed. Actually blushed. 'I don't think you want me out on the town with you.'

'And I promised David I'd go suit-shopping with him and Alex,' Jenny said as the initial excitement wore off and the cold curtain fell around her again. 'You guys go.'

'Yeah, suit shopping,' Alex confirmed. 'Take a shot of Jack for me?'

I was sort of pleased Alex couldn't make it, this was definitely girl bonding territory, but Jenny wasn't getting out of it that easily.

'Jenny, they can dress themselves – they're grown-ups. They've got ninety years of getting-dressed experience between them,' I pleaded, hanging off James's hand. 'Or they can wait until tomorrow and we can all go.'

'And should you be having cocktails?' Mum remembered her place and gave me a stern look. 'Really?'

'Just one.' I waved away her motherly concerns and turned back to Jenny. She looked like she was wavering. 'Come on. We'll go somewhere brilliant. Won't we go somewhere brilliant?'

'We'll go somewhere brilliant,' James confirmed. 'Come on, Lopez. I've got a car outside, and if you really must, I'll have you home by midnight – you won't turn into a pumpkin.'

She scrunched up her face and looked down at her notebook. 'I just have so much more to do.'

'Jennifer Lopez.' James put on as stern a voice as he could manage. 'I demand you come out with us. Besides, if this one is going to insist on getting married, I'm going to need you as a wingman.'

Apparently that was exactly the wrong thing to say. Jenny's eyes froze over and she took a step back towards the living room. 'You guys go. I'll see you tomorrow morning. Louisa is coming over at ten.'

'I've got to say,' Mum said, nodding towards the closed living-room door. 'From all your stories, I thought she was going to be more of a wild one.'

'Well, she is.' James gave me a concerned glance. 'What's going on?'

'I'll tell you in the car.' I felt my shoulders droop, kissed Alex lightly on the cheek and started for the stairs. 'I'll be back in two minutes.'

'So, Mrs Clark.' James turned his charm up to one hundred percent. 'It's just you and me.'

I didn't think I'd ever heard my mum giggle. First time for everything.

CHAPTER FOURTEEN

'Where are we again?' I cowered behind James as we pushed through a narrow bar, following a ridiculously attractive waitress to a 'quiet table in the corner'. Of course it became wildly apparent as soon as we sat down in our big leather armchairs that it was the most visible position in the entire bar. 'It feels east.'

'It is east.' James nodded at the waitress and passed me the menu. 'It's Loungelover. It's nice. Shut up.'

'There's a hippo's head on the wall.' I rubbed my turquoise skinny jeans and wondered whether I should have gone with a dress. Everyone else seemed to be wearing dresses. And heels. And all of the make-up.

'Yes, there is, but we'll get to that after you've explained to me why exactly you think you're getting married on Saturday?'

'Because I am,' I replied, perusing the cocktail menu. 'And not that I'm not ecstatic, but how come you're here?'

'Aside from the irresistible allure of being your bridesmaid?' James cocked an eyebrow at my 'you're so funny' expression. 'Fine, pink doesn't suit me anyway. I was here visiting the family. My dad's been ill.'

'Oh God, I'm sorry.' I put the menu down and reached sideways to give him a mini-hug, but he shrugged it off before it reached full snuggle status as only a man can do.

'He's fine,' he said, taking up the menu. 'Or he will be. It's fine.'

'Spoken like a true Yorkshireman,' I said, taking in my surroundings. The bar was ornate – lots of chandeliers and giant champagne flutes filled with flowers – but any excessive elegance was balanced out by old iron gates that separated out the bar, curious anatomical posters on the walls and, of course, my new friend, hippo head. It was part cocktail bar, part nineteenth-century doctor's office, and all London.

'What's going on with Jenny?' James smiled brightly at the waitress, summoning her in a heartbeat and ordering a bottle of champagne. 'I didn't think that girl was capable of turning down a drink. Has she gone mad? Did she take a blow to the head?' He lowered his voice conspiratorially. 'Is she in AA?'

'Not quite, but she is being really weird.' I shook my head and rolled up the sleeve of my slouchy soft ivory sweater. I was practising not spilling anything down white clothing. 'The last couple of months she's been on this mad bender, and ever since we got here, she's just gone into crazy planning mode over the wedding. She won't drink, won't entertain a conversation if it's not about place cards. She made my mum take her to the Carphone Warehouse to get a Bluetooth headset yesterday. She bought a clipboard. The girl was in London within a half mile of Selfridges, and she wanted to go to WH Smiths and buy highlighters.

And then, just in case that wasn't random enough, I went to look in her suitcase the other day and she hasn't got any clothes with her. Seriously, none. Just, like, three pairs of pants or something.'

'English or American?' James looked concerned.

'English,' I confirmed. 'And when I tried to talk to her, she just shut me down.'

'You think she's jealous? Of the wedding?' he asked as the waitress brought a bottle of Veuve Clicquot to our table along with assorted appetizers we had not ordered but I would be eating. There were definite perks to hanging out with James. 'Maybe she's not organizing anything. Maybe she's secretly planning to bring it all down.'

'Don't even jest about that,' I said, vaguely wondering what it would mean to have Jenny as an enemy while I shoved shrimp tempura down my throat. I would need something stronger than champagne if that was the case. 'No, she's still not over Jeff. Although I have to say I wouldn't have thought organizing a wedding would be particularly good fun for her right now.'

'The heart wants what the heart wants,' James shrugged, pouring out the champagne. 'Sounds to me like she's punishing herself. And punishing you into the bargain.'

That didn't sound like a lot of fun. I took my drink and forced a half-smile for James.

'To you and your upcoming nuptials.' He waggled his eyebrows. 'Get it down you, I have to tell you some scary things about the wedding night.'

'Well, I am wearing white,' I replied, letting the bubbles fizz around in my mouth. Oh, champagne, I thought happily. At least you are always consistent. 'Obviously.'

'Just remember to try to relax,' he replied, relaxing into his chair. 'It only hurts more if you're tense.'

'How would you know?' I scoffed before choking on a gyoza. 'Scratch that. Do not elaborate, I don't want to know.'

'I'm just trying to prepare you for married life,' he said, slouching over the arm towards me. 'Husbands have certain expectations.'

'So, James –' I didn't want to find out where he was taking this conversation – 'how's *your* love life?'

'Good, actually.' He brightened noticeably and sat up straight. 'I'm seeing someone. It's very new so I don't want to jinx it or anything, but I like him. He's based in New York, as it happens, so hopefully we'll be able to hang out more when you get back.'

'That's good news.' I tried to ignore the group of girls at the next table who were taking sly pictures of James on their phones. Mostly, I just didn't want to be in them. 'Do you have pictures? Facebook?'

'He's not on Facebook.' James hid behind his hands and peeped out between his fingers. 'He's old.'

'How old?'

'Forty-seven.'

I made a very unattractive squealing sound, a little bit like an angry pig, and slapped James on the arm. 'Look at you dating a grown-up!' I cackled. 'I'm so proud.'

'Yeah, shut up.' He coloured slightly and dropped his head so that his longish curls covered his eyes. 'He's nice. It's nice. Strange but very nice. There's no drama.'

'Please, I'm all for drama free and nice,' I said, looking up at the hippo head and hoping he wouldn't fall. 'I'm happy for you.'

'Good. But that brings me back to my original question,' James said, popping a spring roll into his mouth. 'What's with the shotgun wedding? Are you knocked-up?'

'Would I be drinking if I was?' I held up my glass, more to point out it needed refilling than anything else.

'I don't know – maybe you're planning to be a terrible mother.' He topped me up and went back for another spring roll. 'Or maybe you just want to make sure it isn't too big and doesn't wreck your vajayjay. Drinking early on tends to make them pop out smaller.'

'Thank God you are physically incapable of giving birth to a child,' I said, trying not to think about where he'd picked up that nugget of wisdom. 'No, I'm not pregnant.'

'So it's just your common or garden spur-of-the-moment backyard wedding?' he said, looking disbelieving. 'Is he going to turn you into a vampire?'

'I'm not pregnant, I'm not dying, Alex isn't dying, as far as I know, no one else is dying.' I held out my fingers and ticked off the reasons one by one. 'I'm not doing it for a green card and I'm not being turned into a vampire or a werewolf or a fairy or any other mythological creature. As far as I know.'

'It's just a bit weird.' James flashed our neighbours a dashing smile and turned back to me with a bored expression. 'They know I'm gay, don't they?'

'Even the Pope has accepted you're gay,' I replied. 'And generally speaking, he's not so OK with it.'

'Is Alex gay?' he asked eagerly. 'Has he seen the light? Is that why you're trying to lock it down?'

'I'm not trying to lock it down,' I argued, even though I absolutely was. 'We came home for my mum's birthday and she suggested we get married while we're here and, I don't know, it just sort of made sense. The idea of a big wedding, church, reception, staged pictures? It just freaked me out. I never wanted that.'

'Doesn't mean you want this, though,' he said. 'Your wedding is a big deal – it's not something you should rush. I didn't realize it was something you could rush unless you were in Vegas, and I think we've already taken that option off the table, haven't we?'

'We have,' I acknowledged, shuddering at the memory. 'But this is different. It's going to be very simple – just small, no arseholes, lots of dancing and as much food and drink as can be arranged between now and then. As you have seen, Jenny is on it.'

'I'm just playing devil's advocate, as always.' He pushed the last spring roll towards me and I gladly ate it. 'But I think you're going to regret not taking your time with this. What if there are things you think of afterwards that you wished you had had? You don't get a wedding do-over.'

I chewed thoughtfully.

'At least, I hope you won't, because I love Alex.'

Damn spring roll. I was being silenced by Asian fusion tapas.

'Although I suppose you could do a Heidi and Seal and renew your vows every year until you get it right.'

'Or until you get divorced,' I said with my hand over my mouth. I couldn't wait to speak another second. 'If they can't make it work, who can?'

'Maybe you are on to something.' He crossed his long, denim-clad legs. 'Perhaps the never-ending tread-mill of wedding planning was what finished them off?'

'I heard it was because he was a knob, but who knows,' I said, rejoicing silently in the knowledge that Alex was in fact not a knob, but then I wasn't going to be accused of being a swimsuit model any time soon. As my friend and swimsuit model, Sadie, liked to point out. Often. 'I never wanted to spend a year looking at venues and freaking out over guest lists or any of that. It's the marriage that's important to me.'

James pretended to waft tears away from his eyes and then stuck his fingers down his throat. 'Don't make me vom. Of course the marriage is important, but since your most shallow friend has apparently gone mad, I'm here to tell you that the wedding *is* important. And anyone who says it isn't is a cock.'

'Of course it's important, but—'

'No buts,' James cut in. 'There are no buts. The wedding is what defines the marriage. It sets the tone. It's the cover of the book. And everyone judges a book by its cover, including you, so you can shut your yap.'

'But there isn't anything about this wedding I'd change,' I countered. 'If I'd had ten years to plan it, what we've decided on is exactly what I want.'

'Really?'

I stopped for just a second. I definitely liked the dress. And the cupcakes were still in play as far as I knew. And I had seen a couple of sacks of tealights in Dad's shed. So far, so Angela.

'Do you even know what's happening at your wedding?'

'Uncle Kevin is officiating, and my dad's brass band is playing.' I took a long sip of champagne. 'And my ex may or may not be in attendance.'

'Sounds amazing.' James looked into his glass. 'Dress?'

'The most amazing dress ever,' I rallied. 'It's a Sarah

226

Piper. We managed to get one off the rack. It's being altered right now.'

'You're wearing a store sample dress to your wedding?' He looked horrified. 'That hundreds of other people have tried on? Dozens of sweaty brides-to-be who have tainted your dress and then had their own, very own, no-one-has-ever-touched-it-but-them version made for their big day?'

Oh. I hadn't thought about it that way.

'Their big day that was not happening in their parents' garden to the soundtrack of *Brassed Off* in front of an audience of shitty exes?'

Bugger.

'And Jenny is allowing that to happen?'

'It's the dress I want,' I replied, silently changing the tense of my statement. It was the dress I had wanted. 'Stop being a dick.'

'I'm not being a dick.' James reached over, shaking his head earnestly. 'Angela, Angie. I think everyone has got a bit carried away with this and someone needs to give you some perspective. This. Is. Your. Wedding.' He enunciated each syllable as though I was struggling with the English language. 'This is the day of your dreams. From what you've told me so far, it does not sound like the day of your dreams. It doesn't sound like the day of anyone's dreams. Maybe your dad's. Maybe. If he didn't like you very much.'

I retreated into the back of my seat and stared straight ahead.

'What has Jenny got planned for the food?' he asked.

'I don't know,' I answered stiffly.

'But it's going to be sit-down service? Or a buffet? Or appetizers?'

'I don't know,' I said again.

'You don't know who's catering?'

'I'm just going to the bathroom, I'll be back in a minute,' I said, standing up. I walked blindly down the bar with no idea where the bathroom was and kept going until I couldn't hear James shouting after me.

Instead of finding a toilet, I found myself out on the street, hyperventilating ever so slightly. I looked at myself in the window and breathed out slowly. I was overreacting. James was being dramatic and overly romantic and ridiculous. But if anyone was supposed to be dramatic and overly romantic and ridiculous about my wedding, shouldn't it be me?

I thought about my beautiful dress and the moment we'd met. She was so beautiful and white and virginal, but now . . . all I could think about was all the other girls she'd whored around the store with. How many other brides-to-be had she twinkled and winked at before me? What a slut. And I couldn't believe James had even brought up the 'b' word. As if Jenny would subject me to a buffet. This was a classy, elegant wedding. With a brass band. And a shop-soiled dress. And my ex. And God knew what else.

There had definitely been moments when I'd questioned my sanity over the wedding, but this was the first time I could say hand on heart that I was regretting my decision. A powerful punch hit my stomach as I thought about what that meant. What would happen if I went home and told everyone I'd changed my mind?

No. I shook myself down and glared at my reflection. He was just being a drama queen. It was all going to be absolutely fine. Better than fine. It was going to be wonderful. And he was missing the point, which was that, at the end of it all, I was going to be married to Alex. If that wasn't enough for me, I didn't deserve any sort of wedding. I ought to be married in a hessian sack outside a McDonald's with four half-eaten McNuggets for a wedding breakfast.

'I'm sorry.' James stood up when I got back to the table. 'I'm being a tit. A horrible tit. I just want you to have a perfect wedding, that's all. After the Vegas debacle, I just want things to be perfect for you.'

'I know.' We sat down and I emptied my champagne flute and nodded. 'I do know.'

'But you know me. Westminster Cathedral wouldn't be good enough as far as I'm concerned.' He emptied the champagne bottle into my glass. 'And I'm sure your dress is nicer than Middleton's.'

'It is,' I sniffed. 'Loads nicer, actually.'

'I didn't care for hers.' He looked around, waiting for the Beefeaters to carry him away to the Tower. 'And I bet it was a right pain in the arse to get in and out of.'

'Probably.' I agreed with him, but I wasn't in the mood to let him know.

'Angela, I'm sorry,' James whined. 'I am. Your wedding is going to be amazing. If only because I'm there. I'm kidding. It's going to be brilliant and you're going to look spectacular and there's no way on God's green earth Jenny would subject you to a buffet.'

The bar seemed to get very close and quiet as my resolve crumbled.

'But what if she would?' I burst out, completely incapable of holding the words in. 'What if it's shit? What if it's pickled onions and cheese on sticks and music on a ghetto blaster and hot orange squash in plastic cups?'

James turned to me and gripped both my arms in his hands.

'Angela Clark. We both know those things will never happen. But if they did –' he cut off my whimper with a raised voice. If people hadn't been looking at us before, they were now – 'If they did, they would be fabulous. Ghetto blasters are very retro, and plastic cups are kitsch. And don't pretend you're above a pickled onion cheddar cheese hedgehog, because we both know that's not true.'

'It's true,' I lamented. 'I ate nearly an entire jar yesterday when no one was home.'

'Your wedding will be the proverbial shit,' James said, raising his glass and necking it in one gulp. 'So let us celebrate that fact by getting shmammered.'

'And so I basically have a live-in puppy sitter,' James said, picking up one of several shots of tequila from the table. We had realized it was much quicker to order them four at a time than to keep bothering the waitress. We were so polite. 'I just couldn't send them back to the shelter.'

His eyes glazed over and he burped loudly. And then he giggled. How he'd managed to stay in the closet so successfully for so long was beyond me.

'You're so drunk.' I took my lip balm out of my handbag and attempted to apply it to my lips. It took me two passes but I eventually made it. 'It's embarrassing.'

'I don't know what you're talking about,' James slurred, slamming a shot glass down on the table. 'You're more drunk than me.'

'So not even,' I replied, hoping I wouldn't have to prove it. 'I'm just tired.'

'Whatever.' He stretched up his arms, waving at the waitress and revealing his abs to the bar. The collective swoon was audible. 'You're going to have to improve your stamina before Saturday night.'

'Will you stop making wedding-night jokes?' I asked, rolling up the arms of my sweater. It was really warm in the bar. That or I was, in fact, drunk. 'I've totally done it already. Just don't tell my mum.'

'I'm just saying.' He gave me a goofy grin. 'Who knows what kinky shit he's been saving for married life? Most men wouldn't rush down the aisle just because their fiancée's mum suggested it. I reckon he's dying to start demanding his messed-up maritals.'

'You're a knob,' I declared with the utmost eloquence.

'Dungeon, maybe.'

'Shut up.'

'Or maybe he's a cross-dresser.'

'Shut. Up.'

'If you won't, I will,' he said. 'I've said it before and I'll say it again – I would break that boy of yours in two.'

'I'll be sure to let him know in case I get cold feet,' I hiccuped. 'I'm sure if I rejected him, he would be so devastated he would have to resign his heterosexuality, so you might be in with a chance.'

'So I'm going to go for a slash.' James stood up and every girl (and half the guys) in the bar fainted. 'And then we need more champagne. That one's dead.'

Our waitress had turned the empty bottle upside down in the ice bucket, confirming we had run dry. I tried to signal at someone to get another, but strangely enough, without a movie star sitting beside me, I was invisible.

Or at least I thought I was.

'Hi.'

I looked up to see a strange man smiling at me. Instinctively I looked around to see who he was talking to, but nope, it was just me and hippo head.

'Hello,' I replied when he sat down next to me.

'Your friend gone for long?' he asked, taking James's seat.

'Oh,' I said, eyes widening in realization. 'James.'

'James?' The guy stretched out an open palm to shake my hand. 'I'm Lewis.'

I shook back. Good handshake – firm, solid, backed up with good eye contact. And he was cute. Not as cute as James, but then very few people were. I wished I'd seen the forty-seven-year-old mystery man so I could make a call. 'I should tell you, James has a boyfriend.'

'He does, does he?' Lewis moved the chair a little bit closer to me. 'Is he here tonight?'

'Oh no.' I shook my head a little bit too hard and had to wait for the room to stop spinning. 'Not here.'

'Do you think James would mind if you and I had a bit of a dance?' He stood up, still holding onto my hand. I looked over at the bar. A spontaneous dance party had sprung up around us, presumably because someone somewhere had seen fit to play *Papa Don't Preach* and therefore there really was no choice but to dance. 'I'll bring you back in one piece, I promise.'

I followed him out to the makeshift dance floor, laughing. Gay dating rituals always seemed a bit odd to me. Guy likes guy. Guy approaches guy's girl. Guy charms socks off girl. Girl then approves guy-on-guy communication. Girl ends up doing shots at the bar on her own. The girl really never won in these situations unless you counted one turn around the floor to classic Madonna as winning. Which I did. Lewis was a good mover, spinning me carefully, wheeling me in and out of his arms. I tried desperately not to bump into people around us, not to stand on his feet and generally to remain upright. I wished Jenny and Louisa were with me. I made a sketchy mental note to put this bar on the agenda for my hen, but since I'd already forgotten what it was called, that was going to be a bit difficult.

'You didn't tell me your name,' Lewis shouted into my ear, spinning me in close and swooping me low to the ground. 'Or do I have to ask James?'

'It's Angela,' I shouted back. 'But if you just need an excuse to talk to him, you can ask him anyway.'

'I'd much rather talk to you,' he said, wrapping his arms around my waist and coming in very close. 'Actually, I'd much rather not talk at all.'

For the second time that day, an unwelcome tongue stuck itself down my throat, forcing me to resort to bag-related violence. Lewis was the worst gay ever. I squirmed out of his arms, gave him a filthy look and turned on my heel to march back to the table. Except that I couldn't quite work out where the table was.

'Angela?'

I turned around, trying to match James's voice to a face in the crowd, but I couldn't make him out. I brushed my fringe out of my face and squinted, determined to find my man.

'Oh shit, Angela. How drunk are you? Jenny is going to kill me. Probably.'

A pair of strong hands wrapped themselves around my waist and hoisted me up off my feet.

'James, I want to go home,' I groaned. Dancing had

been a bad idea. Lewis had been a bad idea. 'That man tried to kiss me.'

'I saw, and we're going home,' he confirmed, hoisting me into a fireman's lift. 'Thank God you're wearing jeans.'

'I thought he was gay,' I shouted over the music. 'But he wasn't.'

'Your gaydar is about as good as Elton John's wife's,' he replied, patting me on the legs. 'You probably think that kid on *Glee* is just going through a phase.'

James called over a waitress and ran his credit card through the machine, adding a healthy tip to our bar tab, all while I stared at the floor over his shoulder. The ends of my hair swayed gently, creating a fringed curtain of blurriness around all the pairs of shoes that passed me by.

'Now.' We walked outside and the cold night air hit me like a cold kipper in the face. 'Remind me where home is.'

'Kent and North Eighth,' I muttered as he lowered me down to the ground and wrapped my arms around his neck. A big black car stopped in front of us and rolled down its window. 'Take the Williamsburg bridge and then it's the first exit.'

'Oh dear.' James opened the car door and rolled me inside, hopping in after me. 'This is going to be fun.'

'I'm going to have a little sleep,' I said, lying down across his lap. 'Do you want to sleep over?'

'No, I do not,' he said, combing my hair off my forehead. 'I'm totally leaving you on the doorstep. As soon as I find the email with your address so I know where that doorstep is.'

'James?'

'Yes?'

'Do you think I should get married?'

He didn't reply.

'James?'

'Since you won't remember this anyway, married in general, yes,' he said quietly. 'On Saturday, no.'

'I think you're right,' I yawned. 'It's Kent and North Eighth. Night, Jim.'

'Night, Angela.'

CHAPTER FIFTEEN

Wednesday began just like Monday and Tuesday had begun. With my arms wrapped around a toilet bowl and my face a delightful shade of green and grey with a hint of purple under my right eye. I had a vague memory of James delivering me into Alex's arms embarrassingly early, blaming my incapacitation on some dodgy shumai for the sake of my mother. It would have been cute if it weren't so sad – I was almost thirty and still worried about getting grounded. Ten years ago, she'd have grounded me. Today she'd be cancelling my hen night.

Stretched out on the bathroom floor, my stomach twisted at the thought of a hen night. Firemen and L-plates and sugary cocktails and assorted penis-decorated accessories – no thank you. But that wasn't me. And it wasn't Louisa or Jenny. This was going to be a hybrid bachelorette bridal shower hen do with my mother in attendance. And the bride-to-be was incredibly, incredibly hungover. How bad could things get?

I wiggled my big toes, testing my ability to move

without vomiting, and tried very hard not to think about anything that had happened the day before. Everyone was allowed an off-day. And to kiss two men who weren't their fiancé. The rest of it was just cold feet. Today I felt fine. Today I was excited again. Or at least I would be once I had regained the ability to form a coherent emotion beyond 'bleurgh'.

The kitchen was full of voices when I rolled downstairs, happily receiving sweet tea and dry toast from my mother. She really was taking my daily vomiting terribly well. Absence made the heart grow fonder and all that. Alex was in the conservatory on his mobile and gave me a slow, single nod. Jenny and Louisa were sitting around the table bickering over Jenny's laptop, while Dad ate his Shredded Wheat and read the paper in the middle of it all. He looked quite happy.

'I'm not trying to be difficult. I'm just saying I've known Angela all my life and I've been planning her hen night just as long.' Louisa, all shiny curtain of corn-silk hair and sleeveless green sundress, crossed her arms in front of her. 'And this is what she'd want.'

'And I don't know what she'd want?' Jenny asked, back in her jeans and one of my T-shirts, which she'd knotted at the waist. 'Because I didn't know her when she was twelve? Dude, I lived with her. I've seen her face almost every day for the past two years. I totally get a say in this.'

'Now now.' Mum placed cups of tea down in front of them both and put a hand on each girl's shoulder. 'Why don't we let Angela decide?'

They looked up in tandem, surprised to see me standing in front of them. I raised a hand and sat down with trepidation. 'So what's the plan?'

'What did you do to your face?' Jenny leapt up and

started poking my bruised cheek. 'Holy shit, Angie, you have a shiner. How am I going to cover that up?'

'Get off.' I slapped her hands away and covered my face with my hand. 'It'll be gone by Saturday. I tripped.' I demonstrated tripping with my hand for everyone's benefit. 'I'm fine. Stop worrying. What is the plan?'

'The plan,' Louisa jumped in, 'is to do afternoon tea at the Ritz, then pop into Topshop before we go and see a show – I was thinking *Les Mis* – then get fish and chips on the way home.'

Les Mis. My secret shame. That did sound pretty good. And I was very pleased that Louisa appeared to be talking to me again.

'That is *a* plan,' Jenny said. 'And if we were sixty-year-old nuns, it would be awesome. No offence, Missus C. Not interested.'

My mum looked a bit confused as to why she should be taking offence, but she was too busy staring at Jenny's exposed midriff to pay a lot of attention to what was being said. As was my dad.

'I don't really care whether you're interested or not,' Louisa said, and she really didn't look like she did. 'When I had my hen night, me and Ange talked about these things. Didn't we, babe?'

'We did,' I agreed hesitantly. We had mostly talked about them because I was trying to convince her a spa day was a much more fun option than pole-dancing lessons. As it turned out, that lesson would have been more useful to me in later life. 'But let's just hear what Jenny has in mind?'

'What Jenny has in mind is to head into the city, hit the shops, hit a spa – I've been looking at this awesome place, the Sanctuary, that Erin recommended – get cocktails at the Soho House and then dinner somewhere awesome, maybe Nobu? And then hit up a karaoke bar. Lucky Voice looks pretty fun.' She gripped my wrist tightly. 'They have tambourines, Angela. You get your own tambourine.'

I was finally facing my Waterloo. This was my very own *Sophie's Choice*.

'That all sounds very exciting,' Mum said, not helping in any way. 'I've heard the Sanctuary is very nice.'

Louisa shot daggers across the table. 'I've heard it's fine.'

'But we all know how much Angela loves a show.' Mum waved her white flag. 'Even if she pretends she doesn't.'

'I've stopped pretending, actually,' I sniffed. 'But I know not everyone appreciates musical theatre quite as much as I do, and I don't want to drag you all out to something you won't enjoy.'

'It's your day, dear,' Mum said, draining her teacup and going over to the kettle to top up before adding in a slightly lower voice, 'And it's not like you've let other people's feelings get in the way of your decisions before now.'

I chose to ignore her and went back to the battle of wills happening at the table. How was I supposed to choose? Spas were lovely. Restaurants were lovely. Cocktails were less tempting at this moment. Karaoke was wonderful. Musicals were the best things on earth ever. And shopping? I loved shopping! This was just mean.

'Do you think we'll be able to get in at these places?' I asked, trying to narrow down the field without having to make an actual decision. 'Won't the Ritz and the Sanctuary be busy? And will *Les Mis* have tickets?'

'I called the Ritz – they're going to call me back,' Louisa shouted out first. 'And you have to be a member of *Soho* House. You can't just pop in.'

'Please.' Jenny pounded her coffee and gave Louisa a filthy, filthy look. 'I am a member.'

'There is one other thing,' I said, attempting to cut the tension by buying their attention. 'We still need to get your bridesmaids' dresses. And shoes. And I need to buy you presents.'

'I have a shortlist.' Jenny tapped her bloody notebook, ever-present at her side. 'I figured I could go and get them tomorrow once you'd approved the colours. I mean, you don't really need to be there when we pick them up, right?'

'What am I doing tomorrow?' I couldn't believe they hadn't backed down at the mention of presents. And I was pretty sure I did need to be there when they picked up their dresses, otherwise only one would return. My two best friends were turning into the bridal equivalent of *Highlander*. There could only be one.

'You and Alex have an away-day,' she replied. 'Don't you look at your schedule?'

She pointed towards a piece of paper pinned to the fridge, separated out into days of the week and highlighted in five different colours for me, Alex, Jenny, Mum and Dad. I hadn't looked at it. I'd assumed it was a bin rota or something. Blimey.

'Don't you think it would be fun to buy them together?' I suggested as gently as possible. 'I think I would really like to be there. Come on, it'll be fun.'

I knew I was taking my life in my hands going off plan. I also knew it absolutely would not be fun if it was anything like the wedding-dress shopping. And it would be exactly like the wedding-dress shopping, except that instead of buying one dress for one person, we'd be buying two dresses for two people who hated each other and had completely different taste. It was bound to be a wonderful experience. Jenny eyed Louisa's understated knee-length dress, and Louisa stared at Jenny's knotted T-shirt and skin-tight jeans. On anyone else it would look like Nineties fancy dress; on Jenny it just looked obscenely sexy. But we were definitely going to find something they would both agree on. Right?

'At my hen do,' Louisa started, 'we did a scavenger hunt and that was brilliant. We could do something like that.'

'I'm sorry, are we at camp?' So Jenny was not sold on the idea of a scavenger hunt. 'Are we fourteen? Did you play spin the bottle also?'

'I'm going to make a decision.' It was time to take charge. And to interrupt before Louisa confirmed that yes, we had in fact played spin the bottle with a stag do we met at Tiger Tiger. Sad times. 'We're going to Selfridges to look for dresses for you and shoes for all of us. Then we're going to go to the Ritz for afternoon tea, and then we're going to see a show, and then we'll go to karaoke. Does that work?'

Looking at their faces, you'd have thought I'd asked them to spend the day down a coal mine whipping orphans and eating lard sandwiches.

'I'm going to get dressed.' I took their silence as assent. 'And then we'll go. All right? Good.'

That was that then.

'You've got to be kidding?' Louisa turned to me and threw her arms up in the air. 'She's joking, isn't she?'

I sat in the corner of the dressing room, a sweaty,

crumpled mess, and closed my eyes. On one hand, this was the first time I'd seen Jenny smile since Sunday and I wanted to keep that expression on her face. On the other, I didn't really see a red, knee-length, gloss-finished strapless dress working out as my bridesmaids' dress. On Jenny it looked provocative but sophisticated at the same time. On Louisa it looked like she was auditioning for *Pretty Woman 2: Sometimes it Doesn't Work Out.*

'She isn't,' I said, sipping water from a bottle. 'But she also knows I'm never going to go for it. Take it off, Jenny.'

'At least it's fun.' She pulled down the zipper and stood in the middle of the room in nothing but her knickers. While Louisa was more than happy to pop them out for breastfeeding purposes, she clearly was not comfortable with Jenny parading around half naked for bridesmaiding duties. And to be honest, I wasn't ecstatic about it, either; just used to it. 'That looks like a dish rag.'

'It's Dolce & Gabbana,' Louisa protested in defence of her floral-patterned prom dress. 'How is that a dish rag?'

This had been going on for well over an hour. And that was just the trying-on bit. We'd been in Selfridges since eleven and it was almost two. The first hour had been spent bickering back and forth on the shop floor, Jenny dismissing all of Louisa's picks as 'safe' or 'boring' or just plain 'pieces of shit', while Louisa wrote off everything Jenny picked up as 'attention-seeking' and 'trannytastic'. It really was ridiculous. They were both impeccably well-dressed women in their own way, and Jenny was a bloody stylist, for God's sake. She could make Snooki look sophisticated if she chose to. I knew she was pushing Louisa's limits just to see what she could get away with, but this wasn't the time or the place. Still, it was nice to see the spark back in her eyes, even if there was a chance Louisa was going to punch it right back out again.

'Right.' I grabbed my sad bag and pointed at the massive pile of discarded dresses in the middle of the room. 'I'm done with this. I'm going out there to find your dresses and possibly have a quick wee and get a coffee, and when I come back you're going to try on the dresses I give you and then we're going to get some food because, goddamnit, I'm almost ready to start eating again.'

Outside the changing room, my mum sat fiddling with her phone. 'Are they done, dear?' she asked, not taking her eyes off the screen. 'Are we leaving?'

'No, but we're nearly there.' I pulled my own phone out of my bag and checked for messages from Alex. 'Everything OK?'

'Just playing Scrabble with your aunt Maureen.' She didn't even look up at me. 'I'm winning.'

'Of course you are.' I didn't doubt it for a second. Even if she wasn't, she'd cheat. 'I'll be back in a minute.'

Between the two of them, Louisa and Jenny had pretty much plundered every single dress on the floor of Selfridges, and I was starting to feel like I was suffering from couture blindness. I couldn't see the wood for the trees. There was only one thing for it – I needed a palate cleanser. Bags and shoes. Bags and shoes. Riding the escalator downstairs, my eye was immediately drawn to a bright orange satchel sat on top of a mirrored cabinet. It screamed Jenny. And beside it, a classic tan leather version that politely announced itself as perfect for Louisa. I twisted my bag until it rested on my bum so it couldn't see its rivals and headed straight over. They were the perfect bridesmaids' gifts. I loved bags, Jenny loved bags, Louisa loved bags. And the satchel was quintessentially English while still being high fashion enough for Jenny to want to show it off on the streets of Manhattan. It wasn't so big as to be obtrusive on the tube, but Louisa could definitely fit a couple of spare nappies and a packet of babywipes in there. I tried not to think about all the things I could carry in one. Totally big enough for an iPad. Perfect for meetings. So shiny and new . . . 'No, don't worry,' I whispered to my Marc Jacobs. 'I'm not replacing you.'

As if it could be done.

'Aren't they lovely?' An assistant breezed into view and picked up the orange bag, waving it under my nose. Foul temptress. 'And they're so practical. And classic. And—'

'It's fine.' I stopped her in her sales-spiel tracks. 'I'm sold. Can I get one of the orange and one of the brown?'

'We've actually just got these new ones in today,' she said, reaching under the counter and producing a black, shimmery patent leather version. She tilted it back and forth under the store lights, letting it shimmer until I was hypnotized. I felt like Mowgli. 'I love a bit of glitter.'

I looked at my satchel, the tarnished gold fixtures, the scratched and worn leather. It wasn't ruined, I told myself – it just gave the bag character. It got better with wear and tear. Although maybe if it had a little glittery British cousin, it would be able to recuperate a bit. So really I'd be helping to prolong the life of one bag by buying another. Before I could even finish arguing with myself, my credit card was out, screaming with the weight of the purchases, and all three bags were bought. It was far too easy.

A quick stroll around the make-up counters and an accidental dip into the chocolate shop later and, considerably calmer and poorer, I was headed back up the escalators and deep into the pits of hell. And that's when I saw it. The perfect bridesmaid's dress. And someone else was holding it.

'Excuse me.' I tapped her on the shoulder and smiled brightly. 'Could you tell me where you got that dress?'

The woman – tall, with black hair wrapped in a severe bun, lots of lipstick and very little time for my nonsense – held up two identical dresses. They were a blushing ivory colour with a V-neck and a great big black bow tied around the waist. Organza ruffles tumbled over themselves until they reached a pretty, scalloped hemline that I figured would hit both Jenny and Louisa around the knee. I felt like the Terminator. Target assessed and confirmed.

'It's Notte by Marchesa,' she replied, even though she clearly thought communicating with me was beneath her. I hoped I didn't have chocolate in my hair. Or puke. I wouldn't be surprised if the wedding party hadn't bothered to mention that to me this morning. Personally, I would have been put off being rude to someone with a black eye. You could never tell what injuries the other person had walked away with. 'They're designer.'

'Can you point me in the right direction?' I fought to keep the smile on my face and pretend I hadn't heard the second part of her response. The implication was very clear. They were expensive designer dresses that I couldn't possibly afford. Just because I was dressed like a tramp did not mean I didn't have the cash to back up my questions. Hadn't she seen *Pretty Woman*? Wasn't that law now?

'These were the last two.' She started edging away and actually made a little tutting sound as though I was holding up an empty bowl and saying 'Please, sir, I want some more'.

'Because I'm shopping for bridesmaids' dresses.' I jumped in front of her, eyes on the prize. 'For my wedding. And these are perfect. I don't suppose you know anywhere else that might stock them?'

'I don't work here.' It was a miracle she could actually see the dresses, she was looking so far down her nose at me. 'Ask someone who does.'

I watched as she walked away carrying my perfect bridesmaids' dresses and suddenly saw red. They were *my* bridesmaids' dresses. If I had those dresses, everything else would be perfect. Even if I didn't know what sizes they were, how much they might cost or whether or not Jenny and Louisa would actually like them. All I knew was that cow wasn't having them.

'I don't suppose there are that many people buying two of the same dress,' I said loudly, making her jump as she added another two dresses to the pile on her arm. 'Are you buying bridesmaids' dresses?'

The woman turned and looked at me with complete disdain. Maybe I had been in America too long. Chatting to a stranger in a shop? Shocking.

'No.' I watched her decide whether or not to explain to me what she was doing. She opened her mouth, probably realizing I'd sod off sooner if she told me. 'My daughter is making a film for college and she needs identical dresses for when they get ruined. It's about zombies. Or something. They have to be pale so they show the blood.'

Two things occurred to me. One, I hated her and her daughter. Two, there was no way on God's green earth was she taking these dresses and covering them in fake zombie shit. I looked at her once again. She was bigger than me. She was less hungover than me. She was wearing considerably higher heels than me. Without thinking about it, I snatched the dresses out of her hand and sprinted across the shop floor. Thankfully, and possibly due to the massive amount of Botox in her overly made-up face, the mother of the wannabe zombie movie auteur stood in shocked silence behind me. I ran like the wind, smiling at shop assistants as I went, my big yellow shopping bag bashing against my legs. 'Hi, Mum,' I gasped, throwing open the door and crashing into the changing room. 'If a tall, black-haired woman comes this way, you haven't seen me.'

'Righto.' She never took her eye off her phone.

'Try these on,' I panted, hurling the dresses at Jenny and Louisa, who were still bickering loudly. They were both staring at me, Jenny in a bright yellow Grecian goddess gown, Louisa wrapped in a pretty pink strapless shift.

'Do it!' I ordered. 'Fast!'

Nothing motivated mardy bridesmaids like a maniac bride. They did as they were told instantly. And the dresses were perfect. Completely, one hundred percent worth the fashion hit-and-run.

'Angie, they're beautiful.' Jenny preened in front of the mirror before testing out some suspect dance moves. 'Marchesa?'

'Notte by Marchesa,' I confirmed. 'And we're saving them from a fate worse than death.'

Louisa pulled her hair into a loose ponytail and fluffed the layers. 'I love it,' she said with a smile. 'It's so pretty.'

'Excuse me.' There was a sharp knock on the door before it opened to reveal a harassed-looking sales assistant. 'I don't suppose you've seen—'

She stopped mid-sentence, looked at Jenny and Louisa smiling in the Marchesa dresses, looked at me, hair a mess, more than a little flustered, then bit her lip and smiled. 'Never mind.' She started to close the door. 'Nice dresses.'

I held a finger to my lips to shush Jenny and Lou and pressed my ear to the door. My two best friends gripped my arms tightly.

'She came this way, with my dresses. She just snatched them.'

The voice of the enemy.

'Our dresses? She wants our dresses?' Jenny looked at me with horror. 'She can't have them, Angela, she can't.'

'Be quiet.' Louisa hushed her with a slap to the back of the head. 'She'll have to pry them off our cold, dead bodies.'

'Sorry, not in there,' the assistant chirped. 'I can't think what happened.'

'I'm sure I saw her run in here.'

'Nope. Sorry, can't help.'

The three of us stood in the changing room clinging to each other.

'I'm sure we can find something else for you.' The assistant's voice faded away and two sets of footsteps, muffled by plush carpeting, followed. 'Come with me.'

I leaned back against the wall and looked at the girls. They looked awesome.

'Totally worth it,' I said, collapsing onto the floor.

'This is nice,' Mum commented as we took our table at the Wolseley, armed with several giant Selfridges bags. 'Much nicer than the Ritz.'

'Yes.' I nodded, at Louisa, who still looked upset. 'The Ritz is just overhyped. I've heard it's better here anyway.'

'I really thought they'd be able to fit us in.' Lou busied herself by studying her menu while she spoke. 'I mean, it's a Wednesday afternoon. How busy can it be?'

'We could have gone to the Soho House,' Jenny said, brushing her long curls out of her face. 'Although this is nice. I guess.'

No one replied. Mum, myself and Louisa were too busy reading the menu, wanting a wee and wishing Jenny dead respectively. Whatever sisterly love had been generated by the perfect bridesmaids' dresses was lost when we were turned away from the Ritz for not having a reservation. The Wolseley was hardly a poor runner-up, but Jenny hadn't stopped whining about all the places she could have taken us. First she wanted to jump in a cab and head to the Sanctuary, then it was Harrods, and now we were back to her obsession with Soho House. And nothing was offending Lou more than the fact she insisted on putting a 'the' in front of it whenever she mentioned it. Which was often.

We ordered the afternoon tea for all of us, everyone choosing a different tea, and then sat in silence. It wasn't necessarily an awkward silence, but it wasn't the most comfortable.

'We're ticking a bunch of stuff off the list today,' Jenny said when the steaming silver teapots arrived. 'Dresses, shoes, underwear. We're, like, almost entirely sartorially sorted.'

After sneaking out of the dress department, we'd done brisk business in shoes, choosing black chunky Jimmy Choo sandals that would set off and toughen up the black bow on their girly dresses. I'd opted to destroy my mother's credit card with some crystal-studded Louboutin platforms that I already knew I'd need to trade for the matching leather sliders I'd convinced her to purchase at the same time. I was in shoe heaven. Added to that, I'd forced everyone into Stella McCartney lingerie, not that it was a terribly tough job.

'I'm gonna have to go through our make-up tomorrow and see what else we need,' she mused, adding to her to-do list. 'I really should have done that before now.'

'I did say I could probably get a make-up artist,' Louisa said. 'And a photographer. Have you got a photographer?'

'Oh, like you could get us into the Ritz?' Jenny asked with feigned innocence. 'And yeah, I have a photographer.'

I wanted to head-butt the table, but since I already had a lovely black eye coming through from my adventure over James's shoulder the night before, I didn't bother. Why was she being such a cow?

'We really felt like the make-up artist made a big difference at my wedding.' Louisa had clearly decided to fight this battle. 'Also, I was going to talk to you about maybe having a play area for the babies?'

'Multiple babies? Did you have another one when I wasn't looking?' I asked.

'No, but other people will be bringing their kids, won't they?' Louisa looked to my mum for confirmation.

'Your cousins have got children.' Mum was clearly reluctant to get involved, either because she knew we were headed for a fight or because she was losing her game of iPhone Scrabble – I couldn't be sure which. 'But I don't know if they're bringing them.'

'I'm just going to say it.' Jenny prepared to make a declaration. 'Kids make a wedding difficult. Sorry, but it's true.'

'At my wedding, we had loads of kids.' Louisa flashed her wedding ring as though to prove a point. 'And it was great.'

'Alex texted me to say Craig and Graham have arrived.' I changed the subject fast. God forbid that someone would ask me what I thought about who should be in attendance at my wedding. But actually, I didn't know how I felt about having kids at the wedding. Mostly I was worried about sticky hands getting marks on my wedding dress. And that was just my sticky hands. 'They're going to play a show tonight or something. That's their idea of a bachelor party.'

Mum and Louisa looked up at me.

'Stag do,' I translated. 'I think their friend's band is playing a concert, so they're going to tag on.'

'Do you want to go?' Louisa asked. 'I'd like to see them play.'

'Actually, yeah. That's a really good idea.' I brightened at the idea of seeing Alex on stage. It was a treat that I never got tired of. 'I'll ask him where it's going to be.'

'You can't crash your fiancé's bachelor party.' Jenny pulled my phone out of my hands. 'And you can't spend your bachelorette night watching your fiancé play with his band. That totally defeats the object.'

'It does?' I said, deflated.

'Of course it does.' She turned off my phone and handed it back. Cow. 'You're supposed to wear something inappropriate, get wasted and dance up on some hot piece. You can't do that in front of your man.'

I didn't bother to mention I'd already accidentally done that the night before. Instead I just shook my head and gave a rueful smile.

'All good suggestions, but I think I'd rather go and see Alex play.' I was trying very hard to keep things light. 'Let's see what he says.'

'If you want to go and see Alex play, that's what we'll do.' Louisa was speaking to me but looking at Jenny.

'Whatever. We're still going to karaoke,' Jenny said, adding something to her notebook that I couldn't see. 'And to the Soho House.'

'Will you stop fucking calling it *the* Soho House?' Louisa screeched with a sudden vehemence that made me drop my teacup. 'It's just *Soho* House. There is no *the*.'

Christ on a bike.

'That's what they call it in New York,' I interjected before Jenny could retaliate. There was no need for blood to be spilled over afternoon tea. We'd already dropped an F-bomb. 'They call it *the* Soho House. It's like to-mah-to to-may-to.'

'Tomahto tomayto bollocks.' Louisa slammed both hands down on the table and stood up. 'I'm sick of you defending her. She's not a child – she doesn't need babying.'

'I know,' I whispered, not really sure what to do.

'I'm not defending her. I'm defending . . . American language usage?'

Even I didn't buy that.

'You are defending her.' Louisa started gathering her things and wiping away stray, angry tears. 'You do whatever she tells you to. It's pathetic. Yes, Jenny, no, Jenny, three bags fucking full, Jenny. Why don't you just marry her and be done with it?'

'Lou, calm down.' I started to panic as people began whispering. 'Sit down, please.'

She stopped for a moment, arms half back in her cardigan, handbag in hand.

'Hey, Louisa.' Jenny cocked her head to one side and picked up her water glass. 'Did you throw a tantrum at your wedding, too?'

And that was that. Without another word, Louisa threw her bag onto her shoulder, knocking one of the teapots flying across the floor with a tremendous clattering racket, and stormed straight out of the door.

'Well done,' I said, turning to Jenny. Now I was furious. 'Well bloody done.'

'Me?' Jenny opened her eyes wide. 'What the fuck did I do?'

'I think someone had better go after Louisa,' Mum said quietly. 'And someone probably needs to apologize to the manager.'

'I think Jenny probably needs to apologize to everyone she's ever met,' I snapped, trying to wriggle out from behind the table. 'I'll be back in a minute.'

I turned to point at Jenny with as much threat and rage as I could muster. 'And don't you dare eat my scones.'

In the seventeen seconds it took me to get outside, Louisa had vanished. In the thirty seconds it took for me to turn my phone back on and dial her number, she'd either turned hers off or got on the tube. Either way, I was buggered. Back inside the Wolseley, Mum was trying to pacify Jenny. I could hear her bandying around phrases that included 'fuck Louisa', 'fuck London' and the all-encompassing classic, 'fuck this shit'. If Louisa had dropped the F-bomb, Jenny was detonating an F-nuke. It was the Hiroshima of expletives. I had nothing to better it with. Instead, I stood beside the table with my hands on my hips, basking in the warm glow of every sodding nosy mare in the place staring at me.

'What?' Jenny shrugged.

As befitting such a stiff-upper-lip establishment, our spilled tea had not only been cleaned up but had been replaced. In New York, we would have been dragged out onto the street by our hair or applauded, depending on the borough. Here, we'd been given cake. Lovely England.

'What?' I rammed a mini-scone into my mouth to stop it from saying something it might regret. Dear God, that was good. 'You are unreal.'

'I'm just trying to make sure your wedding isn't some provincial, red-neck shit-show.' Jenny's face started to turn red. 'It's not my fault your best friend wants to turn your wedding into a pre-school tea party. Angela, she wanted to hire a clown. A. Clown. I didn't tell you, but yeah – a clown.'

I didn't know what to deal with first. The way Jenny spat out the words 'best friend', the concept of my wedding being a provincial shit-show, or the clown. There would be no clowns. Luckily, Jenny gave me a more pressing concern to manage.

'You know what.' She stood up and knocked over

the new teapot. Had she learned nothing from Louisa's exit? 'I'm through with this. Deal with it yourself. Book your own PA system. Find your own serving crew. If you can hire someone to organize outdoor fucking fairy lights with three days' notice, then good luck to you. Screw all of this.' With a final flourish, she stared straight at me, stuck out her chin and slapped one of the sterling-silver cake stands across the table before turning on her heel and tracing Louisa's steps right out of the front door.

'Oh, I say,' Mum muttered, reflexively catching a flying egg and cress sandwich. 'Maybe we should have gone to the spa.'

'So they could drown each other?' I suggested.

'Oh yes. Maybe not.' She raised her eyebrows and sipped her tea. 'You'd better go after her. God knows what trouble she'll get herself into wearing those jeans.'

It reassured me somewhat that when Jenny had just trashed a two-hundred-pound afternoon tea, smashed a teapot, broken a cake stand and made more of a show of herself than my mother had ever considered possible in her worst nightmares, her main concern was that she was loose in London wearing low-riding jeans with her midriff showing. She gave me a tired smile, rubbed her forehead and waved her hand for me to go.

'Before you lose her.' She pulled her handbag onto her lap. 'I'm getting used to this now.'

CHAPTER SIXTEEN

I dashed out into the street, looking in every direction for Jenny. Unlike Louisa's Batman-esque exit, Jenny had gone for a less subtle approach. I followed a trail of destruction and scared-looking shoppers that Godzilla would have been proud of until I found her bellowing at a man handing out copies of the *Evening Standard*.

'Jenny!' I shouted, picking up my pace in case she decided to bolt. But my run wasn't enough. As soon as she laid eyes on me, Jenny stepped into the street, right in front of a black cab. Of course he was too busy staring at her tight, toned belly to be upset, and when she hopped into the back seat and slammed the door shut, he just did as he was told.

'Oh, bloody hell.' I flagged down the next passing cab and threw myself in. 'Can you please go after the cab in front?' I asked as politely as I could.

'Eh?' He turned in his seat to give me the once-over. Whatever the first driver had seen in Jenny, I seemed to be sadly lacking.

'Follow that taxi!' I shrieked, hoping volume would make up for hotness. Apparently it did.

'Yes, madam,' he replied, gunning the engine into life and charging off down the street. 'Although I feel like I should tell you these things never end well.'

'They never really start that well either, do they?' I reasoned, madly dialling Jenny's mobile. 'So it shouldn't be such a shock to people.'

'You're right about that,' he said, throwing me around the back seat as he took me towards the twisting, twirling streets of Soho. 'Most people aren't that clever though, are they?'

'Too true,' I agreed. 'Too true.'

The taxi driver kept on talking at me while I kept on calling Jenny. We whizzed down Piccadilly, almost killed someone crossing against the light outside Boots on Piccadilly Circus and kept on going. It was still daylight, but the billboards were all lit up like a teeny tiny Times Square. They made me want a Coke. We kept going, matching Jenny's driver light for light, and I was simultaneously grateful and terrified for my cabbie's lax attitude to the laws of the road.

'Looks like your friend's headed towards the river,' the driver said as we span through Covent Garden. 'And I don't go south of the river.'

'Really?' I held tightly onto my seat belt. 'I always thought that was a cliché.'

'Well it is,' he admitted with a big attractive snort. 'But I'm not going over Waterloo Bridge. So that's that.'

There was no way I was getting out of the taxi until I had Jenny in my sights. This was my first and hopefully last dramatic car chase through the streets of London. Also, there was no way I'd pick up another cab at this time of day on the Strand. I tried to decide whether I should lead with desperate lady tears or angry lady shouting, but a couple of seconds later my decision was made for me.

'Hang on, she's getting out.' The driver swerved to the side of the road without so much as the honk of a horn and pointed to the cab in front, where Jenny was indeed spilling out onto the pavement and shouting at her driver. 'Problem solved. Twenty quid.'

I threw some notes at him and jumped out, trying to grab Jenny before she ran. But she didn't run, she turned and faced me with an epic pout on her face.

'Are you OK?' I pushed my hair out of my eyes. It was windy on the bridge. 'What's wrong?'

'I haven't got any cash and asshat here doesn't take credit cards.' She flicked her head quickly and I could see she was trying not to cry.

'Oh.' I pulled another twenty out of my shrinking stash of cash and paid the driver, ignoring his obscenities and flipping him the middle finger as he drove off. 'They don't take cards here in taxis.'

'Yeah, I got that.' She wiped at her face and turned her eyes to the water. 'It's like being in the freaking past.'

'This isn't really the spot to dispute that,' I said, resting my elbows on the railings and looking out at the Houses of Parliament in the fading afternoon light. I considered explaining about the Addison Lee app to her, but that just seemed a bit much. 'Are you OK?'

'No, Angela.' She joined me at the railings and kicked at them with my ballet pump. 'I'm not OK.'

'Just checking.' I watched the water sparkle with sunshine, covering up all of its deep, dark, murky secrets.

Neither of us said anything for the longest time. Jenny occasionally huffed, puffed and turned to gaze in the opposite direction, taking in the Tate Modern and Somerset House before turning back round. I just flipped once, smiling softly at St Paul's. The last time I'd seen him, he'd been mid-makeover, his walls covered in scaffolding and soot. It had been a little bit sad. I'd always loved St Paul's, but to see him so brought down and not living up to his full potential was tragic. Now he was all freshly scrubbed and shining brightly – the last two years had been good to him. We had a lot in common. Sort of.

Jenny's phone rang with an old school bell and she pulled it out of her Proenza Schouler and visibly shrank back. I leaned back to get a better view of the screen. In big, bold letters it said 'Jeff'.

'Oh, Jenny.'

I watched a shadow fall across her face, her eyes sparkling with reactionary excitement before her expression collapsed in on itself and her lip began to tremble.

'He's been calling again?'

She nodded, brown eyes locked on the phone's screen until it faded back to black.

'Have you been talking to him?'

She nodded and waited for the screen to flash back into life. It did.

'Oh, Jenny.'

I wished I had something more insightful to say, something helpful and wise that would make her answer the call and tell that douchebag to go back to the bowels of hell whence he came and never darken her door or her phone again. When Jenny and I had first met and Mark had kept calling me, I'd thrown my phone into the Atlantic Ocean. So I shouldn't really have been surprised when Jenny pulled her arm back and tossed her phone into the Thames. It was becoming something of a habit.

'Oh.' I watched it sail through the air and then vanish into the water in silence. It really was a very expensive way of playing transatlantic pooh sticks. I couldn't help but imagine our phones in Ariel's cave of land-dwelling wonders, but I did manage to keep that image and accompanying song to myself. 'Jenny.'

'I'm sorry I was a bitch to Louisa,' Jenny said, never taking her eyes off the horizon. 'I don't know why I said – well, I guess I don't know why I said any of it.'

'She'll be all right,' I replied, having no idea whether or not it was true. 'Everybody says things—'

'No, she's right. Stop defending me.' She cut me off with a bittersweet laugh. 'You're doing it right now. You're like my mom. Except my mom wouldn't stand up for me the way you do.'

I didn't have anything to say so I didn't say anything. She was right. I'd been defending her when she was totally out of order.

'I'm probably jealous of her,' she said with forced breeziness. 'Husband, baby, first dibs on you. Whatever.'

I clicked the band of my engagement ring on the railing of the bridge, desperately biting my tongue. 'You don't need to be jealous of Louisa,' I blurted out after a whole three seconds of keeping it in. 'You're successful, smart, funny, gorgeous. I can't think of anyone on earth who wouldn't be jealous of you.'

'Wow.' Jenny pulled all her hair back into a loosely tethered topknot. 'Holy shit.'

'What?'

'We have totally traded places,' Jenny looked at me with an incredulous smile. 'This. Us.'

Dozens of people walked around us – tourists taking in the views, commuters on their way back to Waterloo making the most of the warm weather. None of them were concerned with me and Jenny and our roundabout lives.

'You know, when we met, you were this lost little girl.' She was smiling again. 'I figured you'd last maybe two weeks? A month? And I was all "Oh, I'm going to have to babysit this broad and hold her hand until she runs off home to Mommy", but man, I was wrong.'

She tucked a strand of hair behind her ear and let the tears start falling.

'You took hold of that city with everything you had and you didn't let go. You said you wanted to be a writer and now you're a writer. You wanted to make it work with Alex and you're getting married. You needed a visa, you found a way to get a visa. You don't let anything get in your way. You're amazing.'

'But I couldn't have done any of those things without you,' I said quietly. It was always strange to have someone lay your life out in front of you, especially when it was from a perspective you weren't used to seeing it. 'If you hadn't been there at the beginning or at the end of the day or on the end of the phone. I couldn't have done any of it on my own.'

'But you did do it on your own,' she argued. 'Just own it. Just for one minute drop the "Oh, I'm just so ditsy and all these crazy things just happen to me" act. Just know that everything you have now you have because you made it happen.'

There didn't seem a lot of point in arguing with her.

'I was standing in my room at home with my suitcases open, packing for this trip, and I just lost it. I don't even know what I put in there. Nothing seemed right – everything was just totally wrong. Everything. I just figured, if Angie can do it in New York, why can't I do it in London? But I can't. I can't do anything right because I'm not you. You fuck up and everything falls perfectly into place. I fuck up and the love of my life marries another girl. I fuck up and I lose my job. I'm still living with a roommate at thirty-one, for Chrissake.'

She took a deep breath and cracked her knuckles noisily.

'And what have I actually done while you've been off conquering New York? Quit one lame-ass job, went to LA, failed. Came back to be a stylist. Failed. Had to get a job from my best friend, which I'm fucking up royally. Reconciled with my ex, who dumped my ass. Met a great guy, cheated on him with my ex, who then dumped me for the third time, married his new girlfriend and is now trying to get me to meet up so we can what? Get into some nasty little affair where he messes with my head for another six months and then leaves me on my own, thirty-two and alone and hopeless and lonely and used up and—'

'Right! Enough's enough.' I slapped her arm hard to cut her off. She grabbed at the spot and rubbed it, looking at me like a lame puppy. 'If we really have switched roles, that makes me the Oprah in this scenario, and I'll be buggered if I'm listening to your pity party for one more second.'

'It's not a pity party when it's true,' she rallied, prepping for a second slap. Which she got. 'Stop hitting me.'

'Stop sulking then. You're talking shit, you do know that?'

'What part of what I said isn't true?' she demanded. 'What part of my life is kittens and unicorns and rainbows?'

'I'm not disputing you've had a rough time of it,' I replied. 'But you're letting the Jeff thing colour it all. You left your job at the Union to follow a dream. Brave. You went to LA and you were a success, Jenny – you got work. How many people actually get work? No one. Then you came back because New York is awesome and LA lives on salads. No shame there. And the job with Erin was hardly a hand-out. I'm not saying she didn't help you out in the beginning, but if it was just a charity gig, why did she promote you? You killed your styling business to put full-time hours into that job. And she would have fired you by now if she didn't believe in you. Erin is hardcore. We both know that.'

'Still doesn't explain why I've been such a tool over Jeff,' she muttered. 'I would never let you act this way.'

'Maybe we haven't completely swapped places, then.' I nudged her with my hip. 'Because I don't think I could have stopped you. God knows I tried. But there's not a lot you can do when you love someone.'

She opened her mouth to say something, but a heartbreaking sob came out first. I hated to see Jenny so helpless. She was my rock. When everything else went to shit, she stood firm and proud and full of bullshit psych 101 advice, but when she fell apart, I had no idea what to do. London walked around us, giving a slightly wider berth than before, and I wrapped Jenny up in the biggest hug I could manage and let her cry it out.

'I do love him. Even though I know everything I

know, I just love him so much,' she whispered after the sobs had died down into tremors. 'And I don't want to any more. I want to hate him. But I just keeping having "what if" moments. If I hadn't cheated on him, would we still be together? Would we be married now? I'm thirty-two in July. I thought I'd be married. I thought I'd have kids. I feel like such a failure.'

'How could you possibly think you're a failure?' I smoothed her hair back from her forehead. I knew that topknot wouldn't hold for long. 'You've done so much.'

'Please,' she sniffed. 'We both know none of it matters if you don't have a boyfriend. None of it.'

It was hard to hear her say that, and while I absolutely, one hundred percent did not agree with her, I knew I couldn't argue because I was the enemy. I had a boyfriend, and anything I said would either sound patronizing or be a lie.

'Your definition of success is your definition,' I said carefully. 'You can't help who you're in love with, but you can help what you do about it.'

'You've been hanging out with me too long.' She pulled up her T-shirt and wiped her eyes, revealing the edge of her bra and causing a businessman to fall off his fold-up bike. 'I'm sorry. I've been such an asshole.'

'You've have been an asshole,' I agreed, remembering not to defend her. 'But I know you were trying to help. I did spring the wedding thing on everyone, and I suppose I did just let you take it all over. It can't have been easy.'

'It would have been easier if I'd let you and Louisa help me,' she said. 'And it would have been a whole lot easier if I hadn't just launched my phone off a bridge.'

'So we'll get you a new phone.' I made a Jewish-mother clucking noise. 'And we'll beg Louisa's forgiveness together. Tomorrow. When she's cooled down.'

'We shouldn't go see her now?' Jenny looked genuinely upset. 'I feel like a total shit. I should, like, buy her flowers or chocolate or an hour with Michael Fassbender or something.'

'Maybe we'll get her *Shame* on DVD,' I suggested. 'But no, she'll need a night to calm down. Trust me.'

'Oh, I do,' Jenny sighed. 'Doctor Angela.'

'Doctor Angela is prescribing a cocktail,' I took her hand in mine and swung it around. 'Doctor's orders.'

'OK. If it's doctor's orders,' she shrugged, squeezing my hand tightly and spinning away from the bridge and back towards London town.

'Lezzers.' A particularly angry man on a bike swerved around us.

'Better a lesbian than you, asshole,' Jenny shouted after him.

And she was back.

'You really think it's a good idea to go?' I asked, pinballing off the walls of the toilet cubicle I was currently using as a changing room. 'We're not too drunk?'

'There's no such thing as too drunk,' Jenny said considerably louder than she needed to. 'It's your bachelorette. We didn't even do shots. We didn't even start yet.'

I was drunk, but not nearly drunk enough for her statement not to worry me. The last seven or so hours had been a blur of cocktail-crawling and drunk shopping. I remembered Dirty Martinis at Dirty Martini, mojitos at Freud, something in a teacup at Bourne &

Hollingsworth followed by a smash and grab in Topshop. Now we were in the toilets of the Social, changing out of our jeans and T-shirts into what Jenny referred to as the 'banging' bachelorette outfits we'd picked up. I'd ordered food, but I couldn't remember whether or not I had eaten it. Or what it was. Or where we'd been sitting.

I emerged from the cubicle, resplendent in a silver sequin minidress with a kick-ass flippy skirt that span when I did. Jenny followed me out in a purple mesh bandage dress that just about covered everything that needed covering with slightly thicker fabric. Jenny looked disappointed.

'You look hot.' I pointed at her fluffed-out hair. 'Really hot.'

'It's pretty cute.' Jenny dropped her chin and checked herself out in the mirror. 'I need so much eyeliner. So much.'

'No way. We're good. We're good to go.' I applied lip gloss with a heavy hand and passed it over before leaning into the mirror. 'Can you see my black eye?'

'Sadie gets into town tonight. She wanted to meet us.' She layered on several coats of gloss and pouted, ignoring my question. 'But I don't have my fucking phone.'

'I'll text her,' I promised, drunk enough to lie, sober enough to know I wouldn't. 'James was going to meet us too. We'll meet them after. We have to go.'

'Yeah.' She ran her hands down her curves and revisited her opinion. 'You're right. And we're going to be a thousand times hotter than anyone else there tonight. You know that, right?'

'A thousand. At least.'

*　　*　　*

As it turned out, not only were we a thousand times hotter than anyone else in the Garage, we were a thousand times more overdressed, and the venue itself was a thousand degrees Celsius. I crashed down the stairs into the main room where I'd spent hours of my life nodding to random indie rock bands and cast an eye about for Alex. As luck would have it, my extremely high heels made me at least three inches taller than anyone else in the room, so he wasn't hard to find. I grabbed Jenny's hand, pulling her away from the blatantly underage blond boy she was fluttering her eyelashes at, and yanked her across the room.

Alex was surrounded by the skinny jean, plaid shirt brigade, and had I not been properly sauced, I might have felt a little self-conscious in my sequins. But I was and I didn't. I hovered around his elbow, waiting to be noticed. I coughed quietly and gently tugged on Alex's sleeve, keeping Jenny tethered with my other arm. She orbited around me, making happy noises. At least I hoped they were happy.

'Alex?' I tugged a little harder on his leather jacket. 'Um, hubs?'

The rest of the group looked at me over his shoulder with varying degrees of suspicion. I gave them a big wave, swooping my hand in a broad arc. 'Hi, guys.' Alex turned round, all bemused expression and expertly messed-up hair. Only I knew it had taken him half an hour and half a tub of Tigi Bed Head wax to make it look so effortless.

'Hi, mirror ball.' He took in my outfit and stroked my hair. I immediately pulled back and messed it back up again. 'You found me.'

'Always will.' I nuzzled his neck and found my happy place. 'Happy bachelor party.'

'Happy bachelorette,' he replied as his entourage dispersed. 'You have a fun day?'

'I had an interesting day.' I kept a strong grip on Jenny's hand as she barrelled around behind me. 'You will note I am one bridesmaid short.'

'I will note that,' he agreed. 'Should I ask?'

'I'll tell you tomorrow.' I couldn't face telling the story without at least seven more drinks in me. 'What time do you go on?'

'I'm just waiting for the guys.' He looked over at the door and then at his watch. 'They should have been here by now.'

'Can I get you a beer?' I asked. I had dry mouth. Bad sign. 'I'm going to get some . . . water?'

'I'm good.' He kissed me on the forehead and slid his hand down to my waist. 'Shouldn't you be getting oiled up by strippers or something?'

'I'm going to strip you down later.' I traced a finger down his white shirt in a terrible attempt at being sexy. 'And um, dance?' I felt like being a little bit sick in my mouth. It was hard to act the temptress when you looked confused and your boyfriend was laughing at you.

'At your mom's house?' He looked scandalized. 'I'll get the cooking oil and meet you in your dad's shed.'

'It's a date.' I turned on my heel and sashayed away, only tripping once. Result.

'Two shots of tequila and two beers.' Jenny slammed her fist on the bar before hoisting herself up on top of it. 'I can get them if you're busy.'

'No need. Get your arse off my bar,' the bartender said, giving her a light push back down onto the floor and replacing her bottom with two bottles of Corona. She landed on her feet like a cat and rewarded him with a smirk and a twenty-pound note. That I had given her. It was expensive to drink in London.

The club was busy and the music was loud, but I could still hear Alex's name on everyone's lips. They were excited. I was excited and drunk. Jenny was just drunk. I looked around for Alex again, but I couldn't find him anywhere in the crowd. I spotted at least a dozen pale imitations, copying his haircut, imitating his easy style, but there was only one. And that one was suddenly on the stage. The background music cut and was replaced by a wild whooping from the floor. All the separated cliques swarmed forward to take their place by the stage – girls, groupies and photographers vying for space at the front, fanboys and chin-stroking musos filling up the middle of the floor, while friends of friends and reluctant dates made up the group hanging around the bar.

'Hey,' Alex said into the microphone, pulling his guitar strap over his head. 'Thanks for coming out tonight.'

The girls in the crowd screamed like he had just promised to father all of their babies. Which he definitely had not. The men muttered and nodded at each other. Craig waved a drumstick in greeting from his stool at the back of the stage while Graham fiddled with his bass, pressing various pedals and buttons at his feet.

'Is it me?' Jenny slurred, 'or does Craig look hotter?'

'It's not you and it's not him,' I replied sternly. 'It's the tequila.'

'We're Stills and we're gonna play a few songs,' Alex said. Then he turned his back to the audience, nodded at Craig three times, held up his arm, guitar pick in hand, and launched into a familiar rhythm.

The club went crazy – everyone in the house was there because they'd got the message about the secret show. They were all Stills uber-fans and they knew every word, every beat. The place hummed with one heartbeat and it was contagious. I'd been a fan of the band before I was a fan of Alex, but now, knowing everything I knew, every single word of every single song meant something new to me. Sure, sometimes that meant I had to grit my teeth and pretend he wasn't singing about his ex-girlfriend, and sometimes I had to turn a theoretical blind eye to the tunes dedicated to his time as a Manhattan man-whore, but more often than not, with the new tunes, I knew they were about me, about us. And sure I was biased, but I thought they were the best.

Alex hurled himself around the stage, crashing into Graham, the two of them jousting with their axes before spinning away and jumping up on the drum riser or leaping onto the monitors. As he moved around, eyes fixed on some point in the middle distance, he was always drawn back to the microphone just in time, like a magnet.

I was resting against the bar, my body swaying, imagining doing terrible things to him on top of that big orange amp, when I realized Jenny was missing. I scanned the room for her, but since she wasn't dressed in sequins she was hard to find. And from the looks of the Cinderella situation to my right, she had abandoned her shoes, making her both vulnerable to broken feet and an easily-lost-in-a-crowd midget. Not sure what else to do, I hopped up onto the bar and squinted into the sweaty mass of bodies before me.

'So I'm actually in town on some personal business,' Alex panted into the microphone, wiping a towel across his forehead and shimmying out of his tight leather jacket. 'I'm getting married on Saturday.'

I tried not to be offended by the mixture of high-pitched boos that underlined the crowd's cheer.

'Don't do it,' shouted one man. A man who would eternally hope I never recognized him.

'Marry me!' shrieked a girl at the front. Oh, she was just asking for it.

'Thanks for the options.' Alex looked down while he tuned his guitar and laughed. 'But I think I'm gonna stick with my girl. She's, uh – she's the one.'

Damn straight, I nodded in agreement while the crowd alternately ahh-ed and booed.

'In fact, she's here tonight.' He looked up and held his hand over his eyes to shield them against the bright stage lights. 'So if you see a super-cute girl dressed like she's on her way to Studio 54, say hi – tonight's her bachelorette party.'

He looked up and smiled. Even though he couldn't see me, I knew that smile was for me and I melted.

'This one's for you, Angela.' He combed his hair with his fingers and tried to tuck it behind one ear, but it escaped before he even got his hand back to his guitar. 'They're all for you.'

I heaved myself up onto the bar to get a better look, my sequins twinkling under the low lights, while Craig brushed out a soft beat and Graham hung back, letting Alex take the spotlight as he strummed the open bars of my song. I had heard this song a thousand times in the last few months. I'd watched Alex write it. I'd seen it go from notes on a napkin to lyrics on the page and heard it echoing through our apartment until every chord was perfect, every note was chosen and declared just right. But this was the first time I'd seen him play it live, with the band, in front of an audience. This was the first time it had come to life. And it soared. And in that moment, I wasn't just in love, I was proud. So proud that Alex was the man I was going to marry.

The crowd listened quietly, attentively, while Alex sang softly into the microphone stand, and I knew it wasn't just me who was imagining I was that stand. I was certain everyone was holding their breath just as carefully as I was; you could have heard a pin drop in the Garage for three straight minutes. Which was why it was so hard to miss Jenny as she clambered onto the stage and crawled over to Craig's drum kit. I felt my jaw drop and held my head in my hands as I watched a sound technician try to weave across the stage to beat her to the punch, but Jenny was a girl on a mission, and when she knew what she wanted, there was no stopping that girl. Plus she was pretty fast for someone on her hands and knees. Meanwhile, Alex was upping the tempo and crashing into the end of the song, and Graham and Craig were both beating the shit out of their instruments – until Jenny reached the drums, grabbed hold of a very surprised-looking Craig's skinny tie and pulled him into a deep, intense kiss. The crowd cheered, the drums stopped and everyone saw both Jenny's knickers and Craig's tongue.

Alex finished up the song, completely unaware, with his eyes closed. It was only when the last chord faded out and he turned to see what had happened to the drums that he spotted Jenny physically attacking his drummer.

'Jenny Lopez, ladies and gentlemen.' He held out his hand to introduce her to the crowd. 'Bridesmaid extraordinaire.'

Everyone clapped and whooped, and even Alex

cracked a smile, while Graham shook his head in disgust. I was with Graham.

'Uh, Jenny,' Alex shouted off mic, but his voice still carried. 'I need my drummer back. Can I get one more song out of him?'

Jenny held up her hand and gestured to Alex for one more minute before letting go of Craig's tie with the look of the cat who had got the canary. I suspected it was more likely she'd got something transmittable by bodily fluids. Mono, maybe. Strep. Who knew? She clambered upright and took a little bow to a huge round of applause and wandered over to the edge of the stage. Craig didn't take his eyes off her once.

'So this is our last song,' Alex declared to a chorus of boos. 'See you again soon, London.'

Craig shouted a countdown and all three guys crashed into their final song as everyone in the club started dancing. The lights above us spun and the last shot of tequila warmed my blood. I raised my arms high above my head and sang along, still perched on the edge of the bar. Or at least I was until I felt two strong hands on my lower back.

'I told you to get off my fucking bar,' the bartender barked, giving me a firm shove.

I heard Alex shouting goodnight and saw the lights come up overhead as I crashed to the floor, high heels first, face second. And that's when I blacked out.

CHAPTER SEVENTEEN

'The NHS is just so freaking awesome,' Jenny enthused, wrapped in Craig's parka as we waited for a taxi outside the hospital at four a.m. 'You just walked in and now you're rolling out for, like, nothing?'

'I didn't walk in so much as get carried in,' I corrected from my wheelchair. 'But yes, socialized medicine is a wonderful thing.'

'I love working for Erin,' she said, letting Craig rest his arm around her shoulders. 'But her health insurance is for shit.'

'How are you feeling?' Alex squatted down beside me, holding a bag full of different painkillers and creams for my cuts and bruises. 'Does it still hurt?'

I shook my head like a brave little soldier but couldn't help wincing when Graham turfed me out of my wheelchair and onto my crutches.

'This has to go back,' he declared, turning round and shoving it back towards the double doors. 'There. It's back.'

Graham was not amused at having his first night in London hijacked by my unscheduled trip to A&E.

Graham was not amused by Jenny hooking up with his drummer on stage. Graham was not amused by the fact he was not asleep. It was safe to say that Graham was, in general, not amused.

I couldn't remember much after being rudely removed from my seat on the bar, but Jenny assured me Alex had been quite the knight in shining armour. Someone towards the back of the crowd had recognized my disco-dolly description and passed a quick Chinese whisper down to the stage that I was out for the count. With that, Alex had leapt into the slowly dispersing crowd, gathered me up in his arms and carried me out to the exit, where about half a dozen people were already calling ambulances. Meanwhile, Jenny and Craig were dry-humping backstage, leaving Graham to question the bartender in the most aggressive manner he could muster. He'd apologized. And given him a bottle of tequila. A bottle I was now clinging to for dear life. I wasn't sure what painkillers they'd given me in the hospital, but if they didn't kick in soon, I was terrified I would lose all my willpower and go the full Heath Ledger in the back of the cab on whatever was in Alex's little white paper bag and this bottle of Jose Cuervo. My ankle killed. The doctor assured me it wasn't broken, but every second the gang spent staring at X-rays, all I could think about were my poor, unworn heels. If I had to be superglued into them, I was still wearing them on Saturday.

A black people-carrier pulled up and my phone buzzed into life, confirming it was for us. Jenny and Craig leapt into the back and continued their incredibly disturbing heavy-petting session. Graham let himself into the front passenger seat, ignoring the protestations of the driver, leaving me and Alex stuck in the two individual seats in the middle of the car. My ankle throbbed, my head ached, and I felt sick, but the doctor said that was as much to do with my raised blood alcohol level as my concussion. Of course I had concussion. I'd also had to have a very awkward closed-door conversation with a nurse regarding my black eye and subsequent injuries to reassure her that I was an incredibly clumsy cow who drank far too much and not the victim of domestic abuse. I tried to explain that, if anything, it was in my nature to be the abuser rather than the abused, but she didn't seem to find that funny. Which was fair.

We rode home to the smooth tunes of Magic FM, my eyes closing whenever the pain abated long enough for me to fall asleep; but every time they fluttered open, I saw Alex turned towards me, eyes open, face full of concern.

'I'm OK,' I whispered over the plaintive cries of Roxette. 'Really.'

'I know,' he said, reaching out and touching his fingertips to mine. 'But I really want to beat the shit out of that asshole behind the bar.'

'That is very sweet.' I gave him a hazy, drug-induced smile. 'But I don't want you in prison on Saturday.'

'I could do it after the wedding?' he suggested. 'I'm in no rush.'

'Maybe.' I brushed his calloused fingertips with my soft skin and felt the warm shiver of codeine and love trickle down my spine. 'We'll see.'

The next thing I knew, we were all huddled around my mum's front door. Alex was carrying me with considerably more care than James had shown the night before, and Jenny was negotiating the sleeping arrangements.

'You and Angie should take our room,' she said in hushed tones. 'The bed is bigger – she needs the space. Graham, uh, you want to take Alex's bed?'

'And where are you going to sleep?' Alex asked as Graham fiddled with the three different keys it took to open the front door.

'I, um, the sofa?' Jenny suggested innocently. 'And Craig can sleep on the sofa in the conservatory.'

'Or we could all accept we're adults making terrible decisions and you two can take the spare bed and I'll sleep on the sofa,' Graham said, pushing his glasses up his nose and slinging his backpack over his shoulder. 'I'm really fucking tired, guys – no games.'

'Awesome.' Craig grinned at Jenny and I tried not to puke. In the morning, I would not be defending her. In the morning I would be kicking her arse.

We crept in like naughty teenagers, Graham finding the sofa like a homing pigeon and passing out almost immediately. Jenny and Craig crept up the stairs and shut the bedroom door behind them before the sound of shoes and bags dropping to the floor was followed by the telltale give of mattress springs.

'You don't want me to share with Craig?' Alex asked somewhat reluctantly.

'No.' I shook my head sadly. 'Let her fuck up tonight. She'll feel bad enough about this in the morning. It's the only way she'll learn.'

'At least I know he doesn't have anything gross.' Alex laid me down on the bed, pulling his leather jacket from around my shoulders. I raised an eyebrow, too tired to ask why. 'I went to the clinic with him last week when he thought he had VD,' he explained. I immediately wished he hadn't. 'He's all clear.'

'Brilliant.' I raised my arms for Alex to remove my sparkly dress. As brilliant as it looked in the shop, it was bloody uncomfortable to lie down in. He replaced it with a super soft T-shirt before stripping off his own shirt and jeans. Pale moonlight leaked around the curtains, casting grey shadows over his lithe body, highlighting the tight muscles in his arms and back as he climbed into the bed beside me. His skin was warm and his hair was still damp from the gig. Usually he jumped in the shower as soon as we got home after a show, but it was too late and he was too tired. It made me so happy. I breathed in deeply, smiling with my eyes closed.

'I stink,' he said, slipping his body around mine, being careful to avoid my ankle, and kissing the back of my neck. 'I know.'

'You do,' I replied, pulling his arm around my body and lacing his fingers through mine. I'd missed his body next to me in bed. 'It's nice.'

'Your mom isn't going to agree with you.' He moved closer and I wriggled into him. 'I don't know how we're going to explain all of this in the morning.'

'That's the morning,' I said, dismissing his concerns, and felt a deep sweep of sleep pass over me. 'Tired now.'

'I love you.' He pressed his full lips to the side of my neck and my slow and steady heartbeat picked up, just for a moment. And just before I gave in to sleep, I heard him whisper the same three words again and nothing else mattered.

*　　*　　*

Coward that I was, I stayed hidden in the bedroom on Thursday morning and accepted Alex's offer to go downstairs and fill my parents in on the night's activities. I lay on my back staring up at the ceiling, at the tiny holes left by the staples that had held my cherished Mark Owen posters in place for so many years. I could hear lots of muffled voices talking over each other, and many more American accents than English ones. My dad didn't seem to be making much of an impact, but my mum definitely sounded like she was keeping up the British end of the bargain.

I rolled my head from side to side without too much trouble and tried pointing my toes down towards the floor. Ow. That was painful. My fingers traced the grazes on my elbows and the tender patches on my cheek. In fairness to me, these injuries were not caused by my clumsiness. They were possibly exacerbated by my inability to land gracefully in four-inch platforms, but I hadn't fallen, I'd been pushed. And I would wear that on a T-shirt over my wedding dress if need be.

The bedroom door creaked open on hinges my dad had refused to oil for fear of me hiding boys up here fifteen years before, and Graham slipped his long, lanky frame inside and stretched out on the edge of my bed, holding a glass of water. Out of everyone in the house, I hadn't been expecting him to walk through the door. I'd have put money on Craig trying to steal a pair of my knickers while I was asleep first.

'Morning,' I croaked, trying to push my hair into some sort of shape and rub last night's make-up from underneath my eyes. I may have been engaged to his best friend, and he might have been as gay as the wind, but I was still incredibly conscious of just how terrible I must look.

'Hi there.' Graham peered out at me from behind his heavy black glasses. He wore them every day, although Alex had let slip that they were a total affectation. He'd had laser surgery two years ago. What a hipster. 'How are you feeling?'

'Ankle hurts, face hurts, pride stings,' I smiled ruefully and heaved myself into a sitting position. 'Nothing's too bad, though. What's happening downstairs?'

'Aside from the world's greatest love story playing out all over your mom's couch?'

I knew he didn't mean my mum and dad, so I wrinkled my nose and motioned for him to skip over that part.

'Your mom is cooking breakfast for the five thousand, your dad is out with Alex, and I excused myself to bring you your pills,' he said, pulling a strip of tablets out of his pocket and handing me the water. 'Anything you don't take, I want them.'

'Still no health insurance?' I asked, popping two pills and swallowing them quickly. I hated taking tablets.

'Still no health insurance,' he confirmed. 'But also for recreational purposes. These look awesome.'

'Sorry I ruined your night.' I glugged down the rest of the water, only realizing how furry my mouth was when I took the first sip. 'But as I remember it, the show was good?'

'The show was great.' Graham's eyes wandered around my teenage bedroom and he smiled with distraction. 'The trip to the ER not so much, but hey, what's a wedding without a little drama?'

'I keep forgetting there's actually supposed to be a wedding at the end of all of this,' I said, trying another toe-wiggle. Slightly better. 'I'm not used to a solid objective, you know? Usually I'm just trying to keep myself out of trouble. Or Jenny out of trouble. Or me and Jenny out of trouble.'

'Oh, you still need to keep Jenny out of trouble,' he said. 'Or possibly take her to the clinic to remove the trouble she's already in. I don't know what's in the water over here, but those two are sitting downstairs making goo-goo eyes at each other over poached eggs. As if the jet lag wasn't turning my stomach enough already.'

'But she hates Craig.' I couldn't process what I was being told. Sure, Jenny had been upset the day before, but anyone would think she was the one who had hit her head. 'I distinctly remember her saying she "wouldn't touch it with mine because he'd put it in more hos than Russell Brand".'

'And even though you're the writer,' Graham clucked, 'she's got a hell of a way with words. But I gotta tell you, she's changed her mind. If you decide not to go through with the wedding, I don't think we'd have to cancel the ceremony.'

'Don't.' I closed my eyes and an image of Jenny flouncing around in my wedding dress popped into my mind. I popped it right back out again. 'I'll have to go through with it now just to stop her pulling a Britney again.'

'Again?'

'Long story.' I wasn't getting into that. 'Where did you say Alex is?'

'Left early with your dad,' he shrugged. 'He didn't tell you?'

'I didn't even hear him get out of bed.' I rejoiced in the power of the painkillers. 'Is he coming back?'

'You're the missus.' He climbed back off the bed and stretched his arms up, almost touching the ceiling. 'You should know. I'm gonna bounce – things to do, people to see. I haven't been in London for the longest time.'

'Well, I know it means a lot to Alex that you came,' I said, trying my best to look solemn, but that was hard with a black eye. 'And to me too.'

'Wouldn't miss it for the world,' he said, leaning down to give me a gentle hug. 'The live bed show downstairs? That I could stand to miss.'

'Me and you both,' I muttered as he closed the door behind him.

Getting showered, blow-dried and dressed took far too long, but I really didn't want to call for help. I was too old for my mum to help me, and Jenny's hands had been God knows where on Craig, so that option didn't really appeal either. After some time, the painkillers kicked in and I was able to get through my basic routine without too much trouble, just very, very slowly. An aqua-blue Splendid T-shirt dress and my leather sandals helped make dressing decisions easier, and I was applying the eighteenth coat of Touche Éclat to my shiner when I heard the front door go, announcing the return of Alex and my dad. I frowned into the mirror and hoped Jenny would be able to do a better job of my make-up on Saturday, otherwise the Photoshop bill on our wedding photos was going to be astronomical.

'Hey.' Alex opened the door, his hair windswept and his cheeks red. 'How's the ankle?'

'It's good, actually.' I demonstrated my astounding ability to very nearly bend it with added jazz hands for dramatic effect. 'Where have you been hiding?'

'Your dad took me to the market,' he said, helping me up and grabbing my crutches. 'You and I have a date.'

'And you had to go to the market with my dad in preparation?' I asked. 'Or was that just a fun treat?'

'It was related.' He put his arm around my waist and helped me down the stairs. 'I figured if I was in charge of you all day, I'd have to feed you.'

'This bodes well for our impending marriage,' I nodded, taking each step very, very carefully. 'Where are we going?'

'You'll see.' He led me through the kitchen, keeping me away from the living room. 'That you don't want to see.'

'Mew.' I took a seat at the table and accepted the hot cup of tea and disapproving glare from my mother. Both were sort of expected. 'Thank you.'

'Have you spoken to Louisa?' she asked, tight-lipped. 'In between all your adventures?'

'Not yet,' I said, eyes firmly fixed on my tea. 'And I'm all right. Thanks for asking.'

'You need to be more careful.' She fussed around me, poking my ankle and retying the bandages that I'd attempted to fasten after my shower. 'I'm not going to sleep for the next year, I know it.'

'I'll look after her, Mrs Clark,' Alex promised. 'I only took my eyes off her for a second. Won't happen again.'

'It's Annette,' she insisted with a sigh. 'And I do wonder if you two know what you're getting yourself into.'

'Angela!' Jenny threw herself across the kitchen and

landed in my arms, testing my painkillers and my patience. 'Oh my God, are you OK? You don't look OK. Do you feel OK?'

Craig lurked in the background, holding up a hand in greeting. He got a narrow-eyed grimace in return.

'It's a bit sore, but it'll be all right by tomorrow.' I was just glad I'd been able to shave my legs. My pins hadn't had this much attention in months. 'How are you?'

'Oh, I'm just fine,' she said, breezing past me in her leather leggings and another one of my T-shirts. I bit my lip hard as I remembered we'd left our day clothes in the toilets at the Social the night before. Shit. I wondered if they'd still be there if I called. I wondered if I was brave enough to call a bar and ask if they had found my clothes in their toilets. I wasn't. 'I have a ton of wedding stuff to do, though. A ton. And since I kind of lost my phone, I have to call everyone and give them a new number. Craig is gonna help, so don't you worry.'

Craig was going to help finalize the plans for my wedding and I wasn't to worry?

'For real.' She gave me what was supposed to be a reassuring look and poured herself a glass of water. 'I know we went a little off schedule yesterday, but really, things aren't so bad. We have all the clothes, and the catering is all arranged, and most everything else is booked. It's just finishing touches.'

As long as I lived, I would regret not having a camera trained on my mum's face when Jenny referred to the previous day as 'a little off schedule'.

'I just think I'd feel better if we helped out today?' I threw Alex a desperate look, but he wasn't having any of it.

'No way,' he replied. 'I have a whole day planned, and there's no way you're getting out of it. Jenny totally has this. And your mom is here to make sure everything goes according to plan.'

'Yes,' Mum agreed. 'For God's sake, go on out. I need at least half of you out from under my feet. I'm not running a youth hostel.'

'See?' Alex stood up and held out a hand, picking my crutches up with the other. 'You got your marching orders, kid.'

Against every instinct in my body, I let Alex drag me out of the front door and into the front garden, where he took a set of keys out of his jeans pocket and beeped the lock on my dad's car.

'My dad gave you his car keys?' I was gobsmacked.

'Sure.' Alex opened the passenger door for me. 'Is that weird?'

'Has he seen you drive?' I asked, too pissed off to actually get in the car.

'No?'

'What a bastard.' I would be having words with Mr and Mrs Double Standards when we got home. I clicked my seat belt in angrily and looked up at him. 'Actually, have I ever seen you drive?'

'Get ready for something special,' he said, shutting the passenger door and scooting round to the driver's side. 'I'm kind of awesome.'

'You do know what side of the road we drive on here? And you can drive manual?' I asked. Alex did not dignify my questions with a response. 'Just checking.'

'Angela, I have driven crappy old Transit vans up and down this country of yours in the snow, in the rain, in the fog and, God forbid, in blazing sunshine.

I think I can get your dad's very sensible and not at all falling apart Ford Focus to the zoo without too much trouble.'

'We're going to the zoo?' I squealed, forgetting all about my hateful parents and their antiquated, sexist driving ban. 'I love the zoo!'

'You don't say?' Alex backed the car out of the driveway, smiling, and flicked on the radio. 'You do not say.'

I did love the zoo. I loved it so much that Alex had bought me a season pass to all of New York's zoos for Christmas. As far as I could tell, there really was only one reason to go to the Bronx, and it wasn't to watch baseball, it was to hang out with a polar bear. Jenny liked to complain that zoos were cruel, that animals should be out in the wild, but since she had more than one fur coat in her wardrobe, I'd suggested she keep her yap shut on the subject. And while the Bronx Zoo was wonderful (and the Central Park and Prospect Park zoos would do in a pinch), nothing beat London Zoo, and I was so happy that Alex had picked it for our last unmarried date.

'Take that, Mark,' I thought to myself. So much for Alex not knowing me well enough.

We walked arm in arm around the enclosures, holding our breath by the hippos, narrating the lazy lions and generally avoiding the bug house. I hated spiders and Alex didn't care for anything he might feasibly have to kill in our bathroom, which, given that we lived in New York, ran the gamut of cockroach right through to crocodile. We were relatively safe with the Komodo dragons. I hoped. My knackered ankle meant we had to take the day slowly and include lots of sit-downs. The massive quantities of ice cream I consumed weren't directly related, but they definitely made me feel better. It was a perfect day. The sun was warm but not burning, and since it was a Thursday, the zoo wasn't too busy. I held tightly to Alex's hand, having abandoned my crutches in the car park – they didn't go with my outfit in the slightest – and we talked about pointless things that didn't really matter as the hours ticked by. Yesterday's drama was just a faint memory, mostly thanks to the painkillers, and all my worries about the wedding vanished. It was just me and Alex and a couple of dozen squirrel monkeys, like normal. Like it should be. Give or take the squirrel monkeys.

Once we'd done a complete circuit, doubled back to say goodbye to the red pandas and plundered the gift shop, Alex went back to get the car and we tootled up the road, climbing higher and higher above London town.

'Primrose Hill?' I asked, as we pulled up and parked. 'We're at Primrose Hill?'

'Yeah. I figured you'd been here before, but where else in London beats it for a picnic?' Alex leaned over and kissed me on the cheek. 'And I have one hell of a picnic.'

'I've actually never been here,' I admitted, climbing out of the car carefully. My injuries were starting to ache. Time for more pills. 'Is that bad?'

'It's terrible. They should take away your passport,' Alex admonished, pulling a huge wicker basket out of the boot of the car. I pressed my hand against my mouth and tried not to cry. He'd actually got a wicker basket. He looked concerned. 'What?'

'Where did you get that?' I pointed at the picnic basket. 'I know it wasn't in your backpack.'

'No, I cheated.' He took out a second bag that clinked promisingly. 'I borrowed it from Louisa's husband while you guys were out yesterday.'

My boyfriend was the best. And in two days, he would be my husband. Eek.

'Are you OK to walk a while, or do you need me to carry you?' he asked. I pondered his question for a moment, not sure whether he was joking or not because I really did want him to carry me, but before I could clamber on board he started walking away, much to my disappointment.

By the time we reached the top and spread out our blanket, I was ready to hit the deck and neck all of the pills. Instead, I just took the prescribed two and collapsed onto my back, my skin drinking up the smooth, milky sunshine. Primrose Hill was one of those London things I had read about in the magazines but had never actually experienced myself, like Mahiki and Harvey Nicks. I knew it existed because celebrities went there, but I imagined there was some sort of Harry Potter-esque spell around it designed to keep out simple muggles like me. Besides, Mark hated going anywhere in London in the car. And he hated going north. And he hated going anywhere he considered 'sceney', which covered pretty much everywhere from the Ivy to Wagamama. Basically, he hated going anywhere that wasn't the tennis club or the toilet, did the former love of my life. Thank God he'd cheated on me.

Alex, on the other hand, was always open to adventure. He knelt down beside the picnic basket, unloading plates, mini-champagne flutes and water glasses, tiny knives, little forks and enough cheese to make a cow cry. Another point to Alex. I could definitely be his specialist subject.

'Jenny told me no carbs, but we just won't tell her, right?' he said, producing two half-sized baguettes with a flourish. 'I have no idea what kind of picnic exists without carbs. That girl scares me.'

'You should have seen her at tea yesterday,' I said. 'Slightly terrifying.'

'I figured she must have hit her head or something?' Alex busied himself unwrapping a pack of giant cookies. 'I mean, Craig? Really?'

'Exactly what I thought.' And what James thought. And what Graham thought. And what my mum thought. I tipped my face up to the warmth and felt every muscle in my body relax. But that could have been the pills. 'But no, she's just gone mad.'

'More mad than usual?'

'Considerably more mad than usual. As in proper breakdown instead of bad judgement and too many cocktails. But we're working on it.'

'Banging Craig is working on it?'

I didn't answer. Instead I pulled a face and sat up to look out over London. It really was a beautiful place when you stepped away for a moment. My ideas of the city were always wrapped up in running to meetings, being held up on the tube, rushing around on weekends. It was all obligations and demands to me, but up here, it seemed to offer so much more. There was space to breathe, space to make a decision. Space for choices.

'So, we haven't really talked about it.' Alex finished emptying the basket and stretched his long legs out in front of him. They ran over the edge of the blanket and onto the grass while he twisted his torso to lie on his front and look up at me. 'But is everything OK your end? For Saturday?'

'I think so,' I nodded, feeding him a strawberry before taking one for myself. 'I have everything I physically require, anyway. Jenny has been keeping the rest of the plans far too close to her chest, but she assures me everything is in order. Everything OK your end?'

Alex nodded. 'Yes ma'am. I have a suit, your dad has a suit. I got to plan the music. I got the rings. I was allowed to write my own vows.'

'You got rings?' How had I not thought about rings? They were a pretty essential part of the process. 'How do you know if they fit?'

'There was a very involved trying-on process involving your mom, Jenny and Louisa. We're pretty certain.' He looked fairly sure of himself. 'I'm not telling you anything else. It's a surprise.'

'And you already wrote your vows?' I broke off half a cookie and tried not to let my concern show on my face. I had not written my vows. I had not thought about my vows. I had thought about getting a dress and getting drunk and my friends not killing each other and the presentation I still had to give tomorrow and hiding my hangovers from my mum. And now there were vows.

'That was the easiest part.' He ripped off a piece of baguette and chopped up a chunk of cheese. Sensible Alex going savoury first. Silly Angela, scarfing down a cookie. 'You didn't even start?'

'I've been thinking very carefully,' I said. It wasn't a lie. I had been, just not about the vows. 'Once I've got the presentation out of the way tomorrow, I'm all wedding, all the time.'

'I never would have thought about eloping, but it's kind of the best thing ever,' Alex said, staring out at the skyline. The BT Tower winked at passing planes overhead. 'Although I guess it doesn't count as eloping, since we actually ran away to your parents instead of from them.'

'Maybe consider it eloping from yours then,' I suggested. 'Since I've never met them. Have you called them?'

'I sent an email.' He shut down a little bit, clearly not wanting to talk about it. Unfortunately for Alex Reid, I want never gets in the Clark family.

'Don't you think it's a bit weird?' I tested the waters as carefully as I could. 'That they're not going to be here? Did they reply to your email?'

'No.' He squinted into the sunlight to look at me. 'They didn't reply. And no, I don't think it's weird. I don't have the same relationship with my folks that you do, Angela. They don't need to know what I'm doing every moment of every day. As long as I'm out of jail and not on crack, they kinda don't care. Not in a neglectful parent way, just in a "he's an adult and he makes his own decisions in his own life" way. They have my brother to fulfil all of their happy family fantasies. We're just not close.'

I looked back at him, slowly demolishing my cookie and processing the information. While he didn't exactly sound heartbroken, there was a hint of bitterness in there, not directed at me but just in general. And his usually easy expression looked a little tense. With the sun shining directly on him, it was hard to read his eyes. Even harder when he pulled out a pair of aviators and covered them up.

'I just don't want you to regret it, that's all,' I said,

remembering what James had said to me. Alex didn't respond, so I switched to savoury with a lump of cheese to keep my mouth busy. Delicious, delicious cheese. 'I don't want you to look back and regret anything about our wedding.'

'Not gonna happen.' His face recovered its soft smile. 'Unless Jenny and Craig really do get together, and then I'm going to feel horribly responsible.'

'Not going to happen.' I couldn't even bear to imagine it. Instead, I flopped back down onto my back and smiled sideways at him. 'Thank you for taking me to the zoo. I loved it.'

'You're very welcome,' he said, feeding me small chunks of bread. 'It was the zoo or an open-top bus ride, and actually, given your fucked-up foot, maybe the bus would have been better. But I know you like zoos and shit, so. You know.'

I did also like open-top bus rides, but I kept this to myself. Besides, I definitely preferred zoos.

'London zoo is the best.' I said. 'I used to come here all the time when I was little. My dad brought me every half-term.'

'Your mom didn't come?'

'My mother does not care for the zoo,' I replied. 'If you can imagine that.'

'I can,' he said with a laugh. 'I like your folks. I can see where you get it all from now.'

'That's such an insult,' I said, even though really it gave me a kick to see Alex fit into my family like the perfect jigsaw piece. Mark had been a piece of the furniture, always around and so familiar, but he had never really slotted in. His colours clashed; you could always feel that he was there. I couldn't imagine him and my dad splitting a spliff in the shed after hours.

Not that I liked to imagine my dad with a spliff at all, but that was beside the point.

'Your dad showed me a bunch of photographs from when you were a kid yesterday,' he said. 'You do know you were adorable, right?'

'Yes I do, and I don't want to know what he showed you,' I said, burying my face in the blanket, only able to imagine what horrors he had dragged out of the family vaults. 'Move on. Next subject. Skip.'

'I don't know what your problem is,' he said, laughing loudly. 'I thought you made a very cute Spider-Man.'

'I was seven – it was phase,' I almost shouted. When I got home, my dad was dead. 'I wore that costume every day for months.'

'And I have seen the photographic evidence to back up that fact,' Alex agreed. 'Seriously, though – super-cute. Almost as cute as Grace.'

I tried not to be jealous of a baby, but it was hard.

'You're a fan?' I asked.

'I'm pro-babies in general,' he said. 'But yeah, she's pretty cute. I saw her at Tim's place for a little while yesterday when I was picking up the picnic basket. He is not a man handling fatherhood well. I had to change her.'

'And how do you know how to change a baby?' I asked, not sure how I wanted him to answer. 'Is there something you want to tell me?'

'Ha-ha. I'm not Craig.' Alex kicked off his Converse and rolled over onto his back beside me. 'I used to change my brother when he was a baby. And I did some babysitting when I was a teenager.'

'How new man of you. Very Athena poster.' I couldn't pretend the mental image of Alex up to his elbows in talcum powder didn't hit like a kick straight to the ovaries, but it was also slightly terrifying. 'So if the band goes down the tubes, I can hire you out as a nanny?'

'At the very least, I can be a house husband while you go out media moguling,' he said. 'The Wendi Deng to your Rupert Murdoch.'

'You'll look nice in a Chanel suit,' I responded quickly.

We lay on the blanket quietly for a few moments, holding hands and looking up at the clouds. I thought about the number of times I'd done the same thing with Louisa, without the hand-holding mostly; but the number of times we'd lain on our backs staring at the clouds and trying to tell our fortunes. I felt horrible about what had happened the day before. I wanted to call her. I wanted to cry. I wanted her to tell me she forgave me and that she'd be there on Saturday with bells on. And if not bells, Jimmy Choos and a Notte by Marchesa dress.

'Angela.' Alex was the first to break the peace. 'You do want kids, right?'

'Not for dinner.' My name was Angela Clark, I tell jokes when I am nervous. Bad ones. Preferably puns where possible.

'Seriously. I know we've never talked about it, and I've been thinking about it a lot lately.'

He'd been thinking about it a lot lately.

'And you weren't super into hanging out with Grace on Sunday.' He picked up some momentum and carried on talking in spite of, or because of, my silence. 'It's probably something we should have talked about before. If you're not into it. Because I – well, I really am.'

'I'm not not into it.' I fumbled with the most grammatically incorrect sentence that had ever spilled from my lips. 'It's just not at the top of my list right now.'

'But you do want kids?' he asked.

I really wanted him to take off those sunglasses. It wasn't fair that he should have armour when I didn't.

'I've never thought I wouldn't have kids,' I explained, trying to work out how I felt while I spoke. 'But I've never been the girl with a timeline. I've never been the girl with the plan. That was always Louisa. I just went along from one thing to the next. But when I think about life now, with you, in the future, yes. There are kids.'

Alex didn't smile. He didn't frown. He didn't really do anything.

'If I were to push you on a timeline, when do you think you'd be ready to think about it?'

'Where is this coming from?' I sat up and took the sunglasses off his face. 'Has my mother been brainwashing you? Has something happened?'

'No.' He looked away. Something had totally happened. 'I've just been thinking about the future. Weddings do that, you know? And you're almost thirty, I'm almost thirty-one. After this album I'm gonna have a little bit of time off maybe, and once you've got the magazine up and running, don't you think it would be a good time to think about it?'

'What's there to think about?' I was starting to feel flustered. One minute I thought I was dragging him down the aisle, and now he was carting me off to the maternity ward. 'We carry on as normal, one day I eat a bad curry, puke, and the next thing you know, we're knocked-up. It's really as easy at that. According to everyone I ever went to school with.'

'You're hilarious.' He sat up, took back his sunglasses and dropped them into the picnic basket. I noticed we hadn't popped the champagne yet and this was not a conversation I wished to have sober, so I took matters into my own hands. 'There would be heaps to think about,' he continued. 'We'd have to move. We'd have to get better health insurance. I don't know, maybe we'd even think about having the kid over here?'

'Now I know my mother has been brainwashing you,' I said, struggling with the metal cover on the cork. Never had I wanted a drink more in my life. 'Seriously, if you don't tell me what's brought this on, I'm going to crack this bottle over your head.'

Alex utched away from me slightly and took hold of the two champagne glasses. If it came to a fight, I was worried he would break them and try to glass me. Much more manageable than bludgeoning someone to death with a champagne bottle. He was wily.

'Don't freak out, because I've been thinking about this for a while, before I found this out, but I know if I don't tell you, you'll find out and make a way bigger deal of this than it is because I'm really, really not interested.' He took a deep breath and gripped the glasses a little tighter. 'My friend Steven is still pretty good friends with the gang in Paris, and he mentioned that Solene is pregnant.'

The champagne cork popped and fizzy white bubbles spurted all over my hands.

'Congratulations, Solene,' I said flatly and swigged straight from the bottle. So Alex's Parisian ex was up the stick and suddenly he wanted me barefoot and pregnant and relocated to London? Of course the two things weren't related.

'Don't.' Alex waited for me to finish drinking. And waited. And waited. And eventually took the bottle from me. 'You shouldn't be drinking on those pain-killers.'

'You shouldn't be talking shit about us having a baby just because your ex is knocked-up,' I retaliated. 'Is that what this is all about?'

'No.' He put the glasses down and took his own glug from the bottle. I knew I wasn't picnic basket people. 'You know we have to talk about these things before we get married. It's just a coincidence.'

'I know you've never mentioned it before.' I was furious. And slightly woozy. 'Is that what all of this is about? Is this why you were so keen to go along with the wedding in the first place? Trying to beat her down the aisle?'

'She's already married,' he said quietly.

'Well, fuck a duck.' My voice was far too loud for my choice of words. 'I'm sorry you're coming in second. Maybe you should have married her in the first place. Oh wait – she said no.'

'Angela, you're overreacting.' Alex placed the cham-pagne bottle way out of my reach. 'All I wanted to do was have a conversation about having kids. It's some-thing important to me. You're the one who keeps wanting to have the family-oriented deep and mean-ingfuls.'

'Yeah, about why you're being such a creepy weirdo about not wanting your parents at our wedding.' I really wanted that champagne. 'Not about trying to get knocked-up so I can win in some pissing contest against my ex.'

'OK, I'm not talking about this.' He lay back down and closed his eyes. 'This isn't happening.'

'I don't know why you even told me,' I said, barely able to form words, my lip was sticking out so far. 'You couldn't have just let me think you were on some weird broody-boy kick?'

'Remember that whole thing where we promised to tell each other everything?' Alex snapped from across the blanket. 'Full disclosure?'

'Yeah, but that doesn't count when it's stuff that would just piss off the other one,' I ranted. 'Like, I didn't tell you when Mark tried to kiss me because there was no point.'

Oops. I cut myself off abruptly. The most important part of not telling the other person things that would hurt them was the not telling them later. Otherwise it tended to be ever so slightly more hurtful than it would be in the first place.

Alex didn't say anything. I waited as long as I could for him to speak, for him to get up and walk away, for him to do something, anything. But he didn't.

'Alex?'

'He tried to kiss you?'

'Yes.' My voice was considerably quieter than it had been five minutes ago. 'But I didn't let him. I hit him with my handbag.'

'Sounds about right.' His voice was completely level. 'And was this before or after you invited him to the wedding?'

'Before?'

'Right.'

Another minute of silence.

'So I figure you leave all your Solene shit here and I do the same with your ex, OK?' he said, still flat on his back. Still not looking at me.

'That seems fair,' I agreed, trying to stealthily grab

298

the rest of the half-eaten cookie. I didn't actually think it was fair, but wasn't marriage all about compromise? Alex getting on my case about spurting out a baby just because his ex had spawned was hardly the same as me accidentally getting into a lip-lock against my will.

But the ability to move on after an argument was another important factor in a successful relationship, so I let him sulk in silence for a few minutes before cutting off a piece of baguette, smothering it in blue cheese and handing it across the blanket. Alex took it and traded me the champagne bottle and all was right with the world again. Sort of.

CHAPTER EIGHTEEN

Alex dropped me off at Louisa's place later that evening, empty picnic basket in my arms and a huge apology in my pocket. The rest of the afternoon had been a little strained, but we'd made our peace. I hadn't mentioned Solene and he hadn't mentioned my inability not to cock things up, and it ended up being a very nice afternoon, all in all. Much nicer than the next hour was likely to be, anyway.

Tim answered the door with his usual trepidation and pointed me towards the back garden, hovering around the door and then racing upstairs to avoid the fallout. I tiptoed through the toy-strewn kitchen and out into the garden, wondering whether or not I should have kept the bottle of champagne with me as a weapon.

'Hey.' I raised a cautious hand and waved. Louisa raised a glass of wine instead and ignored me. Damnit, she had a bottle! I only had my bag, although that had proved to be a pretty handy weapon to date. 'Do you hate me?'

'Yes,' she replied, rocking Grace's cradle with her

foot. She was fast asleep on the floor, covered in soft, pink blankets. I peered inside the cradle and tried to imagine having one of my own. Couldn't do it.

'Can I sit down anyway?' I asked.

'Do you need to ask Jenny's permission first?' she replied curtly.

'Touché,' I answered, pulling out one of the metal chairs and putting my bum down before I caused any more trouble. 'I'm sorry.'

'Yeah, that's what I hear.' She leaned around the table to look at my ankle. 'Jenny said you knackered your foot up pretty well.'

'You spoke to Jenny?' I had to admit it was a surprise. Sure, Jenny had said she was sorry for what she'd said to Louisa, but I had assumed I'd have to pull some sort of romcom-worthy stunt, sending them both texts asking them to meet me in my mum's bathroom before locking them in there until they had a deep and meaningful talk and realized they both wanted the best for me.

'She came by earlier,' Louisa nodded. 'We talked it out. There was hugging. She cried. The whole thing was very awkward.'

'I can imagine,' I gasped. Hugging? Crying? Oh my. 'I'm so sorry.'

'It wasn't as horrible as it could have been,' she admitted, passing me the wine. Apparently I just drank right out of the bottle now. But just a sip. 'I don't know how you put up with her day in and day out, but her heart's in the right place.'

I nodded. The irony of the fact that I was sitting in front of a baby drinking out of a bottle was not lost on me.

'And she wants Saturday to go off without a hitch. Pardon my pun.'

'I'm not worried about her side of things.' I put the bottle down and wiped my hand with my mouth. 'Once Jenny has decided something, it happens. Doesn't matter whether it's a good idea or a bad one, as you've probably noticed – it just happens. I'm more concerned that I'm the one messing up.'

'Is everything OK?' Louisa reached down to pick up a fussing Grace but never took her eyes off me.

'Me and Alex had a bit of a row.' I felt my voice get tight and strained. This was stupid. I was being stupid. 'And he says everything's OK, but I don't know. I feel stupid and you know I really hate feeling stupid.'

'What happened?' she asked. 'I'm sure it's just pre-wedding stress, whatever it was.'

I looked at my friend, the girl I'd known since we were as old as Grace was now. She looked knackered – bags under her eyes, at least a stone heavier than the last time I'd seen her – and yet, with that ring on her finger and the baby in her arms, I couldn't say I'd ever seen her look more content.

'How did you know that Tim was the one?' I asked.

'Oh.' Louisa pulled a face. 'Well, we met when we were young, you know that. But then one day I just woke up and I couldn't imagine him not being there. Then it wasn't just the thought of him not being there in the morning, it was him not being there at the weekend and at Christmas or on my birthday. After that, it all just got bigger and bigger and I couldn't picture my life without him.'

'And did you always know you wanted babies?'

'I've always wanted kids.' She looked down at her bundle of joy. 'But it wasn't like I wanted to get knocked-up at sixteen. We'd talked about it, we knew we wanted it one day, and then, one day last spring, I woke up and I knew I wanted to do it. So we sat down and discussed it and decided to go for it. But you know me, I'm a planner. Can you imagine me just getting knocked-up? Jesus.' She grabbed her wine with her spare hand and took a deep drink. 'Anyway, are you going to tell me what's brought this on?'

'Me and Alex were having a picnic,' I started, wiping my imaginary sweaty palms on the sleeves of my cardigan. 'And he started going on about having kids and when I thought I might be ready and why I hadn't gone all gooey over Grace and how he wanted to have them soon and I sort of freaked out. A bit.'

'Well, I have been trying not to be offended by your lack of gooeyness,' Louisa said. 'I mean, she's not Blue Ivy, I know, but my baby is bloody cute. But aside from that – and I'm trying really hard not to say I told you so – I did ask if you'd had this conversation and you said it wasn't a big deal.'

'I didn't think it was,' I stressed, taking another sip out of the bottle. Classy. 'And the thing is, I don't know if it is. And I don't know how much of it is because his ex is pregnant. And married.'

'Bugger me, Ange.' She shifted in her chair, making herself and Grace comfortable. 'No such thing as an easy life with you, is there?'

I shook my head, mouth too full of wine to reply.

'So what's the story with the ex? Was it serious? Do you think he still has feelings for her?'

'It was serious,' I said, the words bitter in my mouth. 'But she is what we would refer to in the trade as a psycho-hose beast and they broke up years ago. It's that French bird who tried to get back in his pants last year.'

'Ohhh.' Louisa's face clicked with recognition. 'So no feelings, then. He's totally over her?'

'Definitely.' I was as sure as it was possible for a woman who was engaged to a man with a functioning penis to be.

'Maybe her getting pregnant just sparked something in his mind?' she suggested. 'Alex doesn't strike me as the type to be easily led, but he does strike me as someone who loves you very much. I think the real question here is whether or not you want to have kids.'

'I do,' I protested, slamming the bottle down on the table and promptly waking up the baby. I'd killed my Tamagotchi inside a week, my Sea-Monkeys inside two, and if the miracle of nature that was Sea-Monkeys couldn't hold my attention, how was a baby supposed to do it?

'Just not tomorrow. And I wasn't expecting it to come up as an immediate concern.'

'Well, apparently it is one.' Louisa stood up and handled me a little red-faced bundle. 'So let's see how you get on. I'm going inside to get her formula. You've got three minutes.'

'I thought you – you know –' I took Grace in my arms and willed every atom in my body not to break or drop her – 'did the breastfeeding thing.'

'She sleeps longer if I give her formula at night,' she shouted back from the kitchen. 'I won't be a minute.'

'She said three minutes, didn't she, Grace?' I bounced my toes, trying to lull Grace back to sleep in my arms. 'Your mummy is a complete liar.'

Grace blinked her blue eyes at me and opened her mouth, but this time no noise came out. It was amazing. I was a natural. She grabbed hold of my finger and squeezed hard. Someone was going to be a professional wrestler when she grew up. I sniffed her a little bit and waited to be overwhelmed by the instant desire to brew up one of these myself. I supposed it wouldn't be too awful. And then, from a part of my brain that hated me, came an image of Alex walking down the street with Solene on one arm and a little tiny black-haired version of himself holding onto the other. My blood boiled, my heart pounded. Imaginary Angela punched out imaginary Solene. Imaginary Alex and imaginary mini-Alex looked on approvingly. So maybe I couldn't quite picture myself having a kid just yet, but the thought of anyone else having Alex's babies caused quite the reaction. And I couldn't imagine waking up without him beside me, regardless of his clearly worrying parental issues, his inability to keep me off carbs or his insisting that he tell me the truth all the goddamn time. I wanted him there on Christmas morning, I wanted him there on my birthday, on Valentine's. I wanted him to come to the pension office with me. I wanted him to make sure I took all my pills.

'Would you look at that?' Louisa held up her phone and snapped a picture of me and Grace bonding.

'Did you get the bottle in the shot?' I asked, still rocking back and forth.

'Yes, I did,' she replied, picking it up and drinking it dry.

I smiled. 'Good girl.'

The house was buzzing when I got home. Craig had vanished, giving me a chance to keep my dinner down, but Jenny was still making calls and confirming arrangements well past sunset. Alex and my dad were huddled around his computer watching old Rolling Stones footage, while my mum was very busy watching *Coronation Street* on ITV+1 and destroying my Aunt Maureen with a 43-point word. So that was how I'd picked up the multitasking gene.

I excused myself from the fray under the pretence of going upstairs to review my *Gloss* presentation. Any animosity between me and Alex seemed to be forgotten and he wrapped an arm around my legs and rested his head on my stomach when I came over to say goodnight. My dad studiously concentrated on the screen and wished me goodnight without acknowledging Alex's and my controversial PDA. It was for the best.

'I'll come and say goodnight,' Alex promised. 'I guess I won't see you now until Saturday.'

'You won't?' I asked, stroking his back. 'How come?'

'He's spending Friday night elsewhere,' Jenny yelled, making everyone jump. 'The groom can't spend the night before the wedding in the same house as the bride. It's bad luck.'

'It is?' I mouthed at Alex.

'Apparently so,' he replied, smiling. 'But don't worry. I'll totally show.'

'I wasn't worried until now.' I tried to laugh but it didn't really work. 'If you don't come, I'll just marry Graham.'

'He's a really great cook.' Alex squeezed my hand and sent me on my way.

Upstairs, I popped two more painkillers and swallowed them down with the water Graham had left by the bed that morning, thankful that I'd kept to sips of wine since lunchtime. My head was clear and I had thinking to do.

I opened my laptop and pulled up a new Word document. I didn't need to look at the *Gloss* presentation. I knew every word of it off by heart. And looking at it would only make me panic anyway. Instead, I started writing my vows. Or at least I tried to. Every word I tapped out on the keyboard seemed hackneyed and overused. There was no way I could say what I wanted to say to Alex without it sounding like something I'd read in a book or seen in a movie or, even worse, heard in a song. And not even one of his.

I swapped the laptop for a notebook, thinking the look of pen on paper might make the process feel more personal. Might make it feel more like me. But it didn't. After several false starts and three torn-out pages, I slid under the covers for just a moment and closed my eyes, letting all my memories of me and Alex wash over me. The day we met in the diner. The show he took me to at Bowery Ballroom. Our first kiss. MoMa, the Empire State Building. Our first sleepover. That wasn't something I wanted to share with my family, friends or the officiating Uncle Kevin. I thought about the day he'd shown up in LA when I'd been interviewing James. The more romantic moments in Paris, the day I'd moved in, and more importantly, the night I'd moved in. I curled up, pulling the blanket around my chin, and wallowed in happy memories. And that was when it hit me. My vows didn't need to be about the times we'd had. That wasn't what the wedding was about. They should be about all the time we had ahead of us, all the memories we had yet to make. And if I hadn't immediately fallen asleep, I would have written that down before I forgot.

I woke to the sound of my alarm, totally confused. I hadn't heard it in a week. It was daylight and I was still in my dress, but it had definitely been dark when I'd got into bed, which meant I'd slept straight through. I wondered if Grace had done the same. And where was Jenny?

My phone declared it was eight-thirty a.m. and I had a meeting in three hours. But still, it didn't do to rush, so I lay back, watching the dust captured by shafts of sunlight fly around the room, and checked all my injuries. My ankle felt so much better already – no one tied a bandage like my mum – and while I was sure my cuts and bruises were still hanging around, they hardly hurt at all when I poked them. Someone had been into my room between me crashing out and the alarm beeping because my laptop had been closed up and placed on the dresser and my notebook and pen were placed neatly beside the bed instead of strewn across the covers. I opened the notebook and saw Alex's handwriting in place of my crossed-out clichés.

I didn't want to wake you when you have a big meeting in the morning, but know that I did kiss you on the forehead and feel you up a little. I think you liked it.
We're getting married on Saturday.
Call me tomorrow. I love you.
  A

See? I told myself. That's why you're marrying him. Because he touched you up in your sleep without waking you. That's a skill you don't find in just any man.

I stood up, tried putting my weight on my ankle and limped over to open the curtains. Jenny was in

308

the garden, directing several large men who were carrying a giant white tent. Oh my. She spotted my *Rear Window* impression and waved, giving me a double thumbs-up. So. This was happening then.

'Right.' I stepped into the kitchen with as much authority as I could muster, determined to be my most confident and professional self for the rest of the day. 'I'm going to have a quick cup of tea and then I'm leaving.'

Mum looked up from behind her newspaper, which I chose to pretend wasn't the *Daily Mail*, and shook her head.

'Unlikely,' she said, giving my outfit the once-over. 'Jenny has a plan.'

'Jenny always has a plan,' I replied, looking down at myself. 'What's wrong with my dress?'

'Nothing.' She looked back at her paper. 'It's nice. Bright.'

I sighed and went over to the fridge to pour a glass of orange juice that was almost exactly the same shade as my BCBG dress.

'Bright is good,' I told her. 'Bright signals confidence and excitement. Plus it's very on trend and I am presenting a fashion magazine.' At least, Jenny had told me all these things when I bought it.

'I know.' She sounded as disbelieving as she looked. 'Your dad and I haven't half had a laugh about it.'

'Thank you.' I sat back at the table and pressed a hand against my stomach. It always got upset when I was nervous, and I wasn't prepared to put anything in it that could cause me grief today. Mum gave me a suspicious eye and pursed her lips.

'Angela – shit, you look awesome,' Jenny said as she

blew in through the kitchen door, bringing the smell of freshly cut grass with her. 'Sorry for the swearing, Mrs C.'

Mum waved her hand, long impervious to anything but the C-word. 'I'm gonna get changed. I'll be back in fifteen. Be ready to go.'

'Go?' I looked at Jenny. 'Go where?'

'We're coming with you!' Jenny announced brightly. 'We're going to drive you into town, wait for you to do your awesome, killer presentation, and then me, you, Louisa, your mom and Sadie are going for manipedis. And you're getting your roots done and ends trimmed.'

'I just got my roots done,' I said, reaching up and touching my dark blonde hair. 'I had highlights.'

'And they look awesome,' she assured me. 'But they're going to look too harsh on camera. We need to break them up with a few lowlights. Just to bring it down maybe ten percent. Don't worry, I've asked Gina for a recommendation. You remember Gina?'

'Yes, I remember Gina.' I was starting to feel ever so slightly panicky. 'Why can't I just meet you afterwards?'

'Because we're all going to the same place,' Jenny shrugged, biting into an apple. 'What's the diff?'

'Whatever.' I didn't want to argue. I wanted to do my presentation, write my vows and drug myself up until it was wedding o'clock. 'Nice outfit.'

'Thanks.' She looked down at her second-skin neon-pink jeans and tight black sweater. 'I ran into town yesterday. Picked up some pieces.'

'And while you were picking up pieces, did you put down Craig?'

She blushed the same shade as her new jeans. 'Yeah. So that happened.'

'Yes it did,' I confirmed. 'Interesting.'

'I'm a dumbass.' She shook her hair forward and hid behind her curls. 'But maybe he's not so bad as I thought.'

'He's a filthy great slutbag and you know he is,' I said, picking up a handful of grapes and popping one into my mouth. 'Tell me it's just some holiday madness thing? Because you're in another country or something?'

'Probably,' Jenny shrugged. 'But Alex was a filthy great slutbag once, right? Maybe I should give him a chance. He is pretty damn cute.'

'Oh good, you've officially gone mad.' I stood up, nervous energy overriding the ache in my ankle. 'For a moment there, I was worried I would have both my bridesmaids at my wedding, but I should be able to get you committed, no worries. Just me and Louisa then.'

'Someone say my name?' Louisa came through to the kitchen and I was almost a little sad to see she was without Grace.

'Speak of the devil and he shows his horns,' I said, turning to give her a hug. 'Actually, while I've got you both here, I've got something for you.'

I'd spotted my Selfridges bags in the conservatory and hobbled in to grab their handbags. When I turned round and saw them at the kitchen table chatting like old friends, it was everything I could do not to cry. OK, so it hadn't been smooth sailing, but there they were, judging pictures of Cheryl Cole in the *Daily Mail* like they'd been picking celebrities to pieces all their lives. It made me so proud. Rather than kill the moment, I waited and watched while they hugged it out and Jenny went upstairs to change. So. Miracles did happen.

We were all crammed into the Yaris when my phone rang. I was trying not to sweat in my silk dress and reading my presentation to Jenny one last time when it buzzed into life with a US number I didn't recognize.

'Hello, Angela speaking?' I answered, using what Jenny referred to as my professional voice.

'Angela, it's Delia.' I heard my business partner on the other line. 'Did I catch you in time?'

'In time for what?' This didn't sound like good news. 'Where are you? Are you in Paris? I'm on the way to the meeting now.'

'Brilliant.' She sounded hugely relieved. 'I'm actually at the office in London. I noticed a couple of things in the presentation that needed updating, just a few things I've been discussing with Pops this week. I've got it on a flash drive here, so I'll just meet you in reception?'

'OK?' Shit. Changes? An hour before my meeting? I hoped there was nothing drastic. 'Are you going to make it to Paris in time?'

'Oh yes,' she replied. 'Not a problem. I've got, like, for ever.'

'You're on at four still?' I asked. 'I was going to give you a call when I'm done. Should I call on this number?'

'Still on at four.' The line crackled a little. 'But no, I'll be on my phone – don't call this number. This is a loaner. My battery died. I'm just charging it now.'

'OK, I'll see you soon,' I said, looking out of the window to see London whizzing by. 'We're almost there.'

'Cool. See you soon!' she said, hanging up.

Cool? I closed my eyes and leaned back, feeling

very carsick. I hoped my eye make-up wasn't smudging. I hoped Delia hadn't gone mad. I hoped I wasn't about to cock up the most important meeting of my life. Suddenly the wedding seemed like the easy part . . .

CHAPTER NINETEEN

'Delia!' I called across the lobby of Spencer Media UK to the Park Avenue princess, who was tapping away at a BlackBerry. She looked every inch the image of sophistication. Fitted graphite sheath dress, black pointed pumps and an Hermès Birkin that was duty-bound to take a trip back to its homeland. She was going to kill it in Paris, and for the first time I wished I was going with her. 'Delia?'

She looked up at the second mention of her name and gave me a trillion-watt smile, her lips painted scarlet, hair tied back in a low ponytail, and matching red nails clutching her Swarovski-covered phone. She glanced behind me at my entourage and I saw the shadow of a frown pass over her face before she recovered herself. I skipped a couple of steps away from the gang and rolled my eyes.

'I know,' I said, automatically kissing her on both cheeks. 'They wouldn't leave me alone, but they're waiting downstairs, don't worry. I'm not looking for Most Unprofessional Editor of The Year award by bringing my entire family into the meeting.'

'Oh, don't even worry about it.' Delia visibly relaxed and handed me a small silver USB stick. 'And don't worry about the changes, either – it's just a couple of numbers. There isn't anything different in your slides or the concept, just a few financial alterations that Pops wanted me to make, but you know me – perfectionist. Didn't want you to go out there without the final, final version.'

'I can't believe you made a pit stop on your way to Paris to physically give me this, just so I had the final numbers.' I held on to the flash drive tightly and laughed. 'Actually, I can. Really, it's going to be fine. I mean, it's just a sit-down with a few editors, right?'

'Yeah,' she said, looking at her beautiful watch. 'More or less.'

'More or less?' I did not like the sound of that.

'All you're doing is talking through the same slides we've been through a thousand times,' she said, sliding her arm around my shoulders. I tried not to choke on her perfume. She must have been more nervous than she was letting on – she'd really gone to town on the No. 5 this morning. That or she was worried about post-plane stink. Not that Delia ever stank. 'I know you're going to do just fine. Now, you go set up and I'll speak to you later.'

'Are you sure you can't stay?' I squealed as she turned to leave.

Delia gave me a pained look and then shook her head, smiling at the floor. 'I'll stay for the first five minutes. Then I have to leave. I'm meeting Pops to get the train. And you're still presenting on your own. You've got this.'

'Thank you.' I threw myself at her in a hug she

wasn't expecting. 'And please stop calling Bob "Pops".
It's weirding me out.'

'Oh.' She let out a gentle laugh. 'Of course – professional face, Delia. Bob.'

I gave her a little shove and jumped up and down on the spot, suddenly full of nervous energy. I was so happy she was there. As much as I was entirely sure I could do this – I was a strong, confident woman, after all – it felt better to have back-up. Just knowing Delia was going to be in the room reminded me why this project was going to be a success. I skipped over to the others to tell them to sit still and not touch anything.

'I just can't get over how incredibly similar they are,' Jenny said over my shoulder as she gave me a good-luck hug. 'Especially when she's all gussied up like that.'

'Delia and Cici?' I glanced over. 'Yeah. It's unnerving sometimes. But it makes sense. There couldn't possibly be someone as atrocious as Cici in this world without someone as awesome as Delia to balance it out. I know there's always one evil twin but someone really should study these two for the good of mankind, or maybe their mum. How do you get all the good in one twin and all the bad on earth into the other? I know she's saying she came to make sure I had the right presentation, but I think she just wanted to give me a face-to-face good luck.'

'Sounds like Delia.' Jenny patted down a stray hair from the top of my straight, shiny do. 'That or she just wanted to make sure you showed up.'

'Sounds like Delia,' I replied. 'OK, I'm going in. How do I look?'

'Like the editor of a kick-ass new fashion magazine

that the world is crying out for.' She gave me another half-hug. 'We've all got your back on this one, you know that, right? And I pretty much know that presentation of yours off by heart now, so I can feed you lines if you need me to.'

'My back considers itself lucky,' I said, applying a last-minute swipe of MAC lip gloss and straightening up my shoulders. 'I'm just nervous. I'm OK. But thank you.'

'No need to be nervous.' She clicked her fingers and gave me the double-guns. 'Go do this so I can get my nails did.'

'Nails, priorities,' I doubled-gunned right back at her. 'See in you in a bit.'

A harried-looking assistant was waiting for me at reception, and after strained welcomes, she dragged me into a lift, Delia following and trying not to laugh.

'Rough day?' I asked the assistant, thinking how very far away from Cici she was. Baggy boyfriend jeans, a stripy sweater and Toms made up her slouchy outfit, the kind that would make me look like I was decorating or something but managed to come off as insouciantly chic on the impossibly skinny. Her thick blonde hair was wrapped around itself in a pineappley topknot, highlighting her delicate bone structure. It was oddly reassuring to know that everyone in fashion mags in the UK was just as beautiful as those in the US. Another good reason to have Delia with me. I wasn't writing myself off as an old trout or anything, but she was a born and bred beauty. No amount of eyeliner practice could give you her level of patrician perfection.

'It's just been busy, with the sales conference in

Paris,' she nodded nervously. 'Obviously all the sales and marketing teams are over there, so the editorial team are, you know, a bit antsy – so when Mr Spencer made us slot this in, they all got a bit grumpy. And I have to get a bunch of the editors there for some event this evening. Everyone's just a bit on edge.'

'Good to know.' I flashed Delia a semi-stressed look and she squeezed my hand behind the assistant's back. My presentation had made the editors grumpy. Brilliant.

'When aren't editors on edge?' Delia replied lightly. 'The day I meet a relaxed ed is the day she retires.'

The assistant let out a hysterical cackle and then covered her mouth quickly. 'You're right,' she agreed. 'Makes me wonder why we bother? I'm always hungry, I'm always tired, I don't have time for a boyfriend, I'm always drinking Red Bull and I'm going to die of a heart attack at fifty-five. And that's if I'm lucky.'

'We are the privileged few,' Delia nodded. 'We really are.'

The lift doors slid open and we shuffled out.

'This is where you'll be giving the presentation,' the unnamed assistant said, holding open a door and shoving me through. 'If you want to give me your laptop, I'll give it to the IT guy and he'll get it cued up.'

'Can he run it off a flash drive?' Delia asked, grabbing the now warm silver stick out of my palm and passing it on. 'It's the only file on here.'

'Sure,' she shrugged. 'I've put out water and glasses, the clicker on the table will work to move each slide on, and everyone will be here in just a minute.'

'Great,' Delia replied on my behalf. 'Thanks so much.'

It was a good job that she was talking because I couldn't. My little sit-down with a couple of editors had morphed into a grand presentation in what basically amounted to an auditorium. And if the assistant had put out water for everyone who was coming, it looked like they would be bringing people in off the streets to fill the place because there was a little Spencer Media branded bottle at every one of the hundred or so seats. At the front was a little lectern, and behind that a screen that would put your average movie theatre to shame.

Mew.

'I'm going to run to the bathroom real quick,' Delia said, quietly backing away. 'I'll be two seconds, I swear.'

I wasn't sure if she was leaving the room because she didn't want to see me cry or because she was scared I had actually gone catatonic, but I was strangely relieved to be alone. If I didn't have someone to melt-down on, I couldn't meltdown. That was my logic and I was sticking to it.

Carefully, I clip-clopped down the stairs to the bottom of the auditorium and looked up at the rows and rows of seats. Half the room was made up of huge floor-to-ceiling windows, the London version of my window at home. But instead of seeing the East River with its little ferry trundling back and forth, instead of looking at the Empire State Building and the Chrysler Building, I saw all of London laid out in front of me. We were on Southbank, with the Tate Modern holding court as our statuesque neighbour and the City busily working away to the south. I liked the Gherkin. It wasn't as sunny as LA, and maybe it wasn't romantic like Paris. It certainly wasn't crazy like Vegas, and at that moment I felt a million miles away from New York, but there was no denying that London was special. Every street corner had a hundred stories to tell. It had seen it all and it wore the experience with a weary smile and a stiff upper lip.

I was still daydreaming when the screen flickered into life behind me, displaying the *Gloss* logo in six-foot-high letters. A shadow in a booth way up above on the wall opposite gave me what I took to be a thumbs-up and I picked up the clicker to test out the slides, moving backwards and forwards a couple of times. All present and correct. I couldn't even see where the changes had been made, just like Delia had said.

The more I thought about it, the more I was sure hers was a supportive trip rather than a corrective one. And I wasn't complaining. Mostly because I didn't have time to. The double doors opened dead on the dot of eleven-thirty and droves of irritatingly chic women began to trickle in, filling in the seats from the back like the cool girls are supposed to. I watched them all, hoping my black eye wasn't showing, hoping they liked my dress and hating myself for hoping, when my phone buzzed to let me know I had a text.

I immediately switched it to silent and opened the message. It was from Delia. All it said was '*Bonne chance!*' followed by a screen full of kisses. *Bonne chance*? I craned my neck around to find her, but she still hadn't come back from the bathroom. Surely she hadn't abandoned me? The mare. Now it made sense. She had found out I was going to have to present to fifteen thousand Anna Wintours and knew I'd freak out, so she'd stopped in on her way to Paris to make sure I didn't leg it when I saw the room. And now I was here, she'd fucked off to France. I wasn't sure if I was thankful or furious.

As it happened, I didn't have a lot of time to worry, since everyone had taken their seats and was looking at me expectantly. In between clicking BlackBerries and swiping at iPhones, obviously. The assistant who had shown me in popped her head around the door and gave me a tiny thumbs-up. Show time.

'So the original plan for the launch phase will take place in Q three, so we can be out for Fashion Week with *Gloss* on limited availability in New York.' I gestured towards a calendar on the screen and turned back to my audience. It was going well. Or at least I thought it was. No one had left the room and very few people were talking. I took that as a win. So far, so good.

There were only about seven or so slides left when the auditorium doors opened and I spotted Jenny, Louisa, Mum, Sadie and Delia all sneaking in and taking seats off to the side. I paused for a second, somewhat flummoxed, but Jenny motioned for me to keep rolling and Delia gave me a little triumphant wave. Did she think this was a good idea? Everyone knew parents and presentations didn't mix. It was like oil and vinegar. Or two things that didn't make a lovely salad dressing.

'Um, but what Spencer US is proposing is that we stage a simultaneous transatlantic launch and use our international leverage at Fashion Week to pull in as much support as we can – really make a splash.'

I looked over at my cheerleaders. Sadie looked like she was carrying around her own lighting as per usual, but she did look engaged and interested. I knew she

321

wanted to be involved in the magazine so it wasn't so bad if she was here. Jenny was mouthing the presentation along with me and Louisa looked impressed. It was a step up from my Year Ten report on *Lord of the Flies*. The hardest person to make eye contact with was my mum. We'd never really talked about what I did for a living. When I was in London ghostwriting storybooks about Batman she had a vague grasp on it, but since the books didn't have my name on them, I was never quite convinced she believed me. In all honesty, freelance ghostwriter would be a great cover for a high-class hooker. Or middle-class hooker. I wouldn't have been able to charge Belle de Jour prices. Not back then anyway. But this was tangible. She could actually see me doing something, something where I more or less knew exactly what I was talking about. And she looked proud. It was almost too much.

And so it was easy to understand why I didn't notice the great big image of a giant cock appear on the screen behind me nearly as quickly as everyone in the audience. My first cue that something had gone wrong was when the clicking of BlackBerry keys stopped. And then I saw the faces. And then I saw the screen. Wow. If anyone ever wanted to start the debate as to why women don't like looking at naked men as much as men like looking at naked women, they should try standing spitting distance away from a photograph of a six-foot erect penis. It was not attractive. I turned back to the audience with wide eyes and no words. Up at the back of the room, I saw Delia slip out of her seat and head for the door. Just before she vanished, she looked over her shoulder and gave me a very un-Delia-like sly grin and a wave.

Mother. Fucker.

The text. The manicure. The last-minute changes. It was Cici.

The audience began to mutter quietly, an unnerving hum that got louder and higher-pitched. And then there were the clicks of the camera phones.

'Great, so you're paying attention.' Jenny bounced out of her seat, sending my mum, Louisa and Sadie out of the door after 'Delia' and joining me at the front of the auditorium. The rows of fashionistas buzzed with confusion and probably post-traumatic stress disorder as I froze, my brain stuck like a scratched record, putting two and two together, coming up with a very ugly four.

'Sorry, guys – I can't think how that got there.' Jenny snatched the clicker and removed the offensive image from the screen. 'I keep telling Ryan Gosling not to text me shots of his junk because it's totally distracting. See? I was so distracted I put them in the presentation. I'm Jenny Lopez. Not that one. I'm working with *Gloss* as their fashion consultant, so any questions regarding the designers we're going to be working with, please direct them this way. I will also have some questions for you guys with regards to where you got all of your clothes. And shoes. And purses.'

While Jenny got the crowd back on side, I gave myself a big mental slap. I could either chase Cici out into the streets and give her the thumping she so clearly needed or I could stay here, finish my presentation and really stick it to the cow by being the mature, smart, successful human being she had no hope of ever becoming. It was genuinely one of the most difficult decisions I'd ever had to make.

I found my voice and took back the mic. 'So, to date we have the following designers in bed with us, so to speak,' Jenny squeezed my arm behind the lectern and took a step back. Still behind me, as always. 'Sadly, I do not have any pictures of their nether regions, so you're just going to have to use your imagination.'

When I got out of prison for killing Cici Spencer, I owed Jenny Lopez a drink.

Spencer Media UK was a big fan of open-plan offices. There was a lot of space, a lot of glass and a lot of light. They even had glass lift shafts which (a) made me feel a bit sick as we hurtled down twenty-seven floors and (b) meant that once I'd finished the presentation, answered all the relevant questions and even shaken hands with a couple of women I recognized from their editor's letters, I was able to see the fate of Cici Spencer from high in the sky above the atrium. Jenny had hung back to grill some of the girls about their fashion cred, but I still had business to take care of.

Much to the consternation of a lone security guard who was being kept at a distance by a very persuasive Sadie, Cici was splayed on the floor, face down, her arm twisted up her back, while Louisa straddled her waist, making sure she stayed that way. And preventing her from kicking herself out of Lou's excellent submission hold was my mother, knees together, handbag in her lap, sitting right over her ankles. They made quite the tag team. I raced across the foyer, pushing through the small group that had begun to gather around them, and tried not to wish I'd said 'screw it' to my career so I could have watched this go down in real time.

'Alright, Cici?' I asked, kneeling down in front of her. 'You're looking a bit flustered.'

'Get off me, you psycho,' she screamed, her hair

coming undone as she tried to shake Louisa off. No amount of Pilates could prepare her for a full-on scrap; all she could do was shake and squeal. It was sad. 'You're insane.'

'I must be,' I replied, checking my own manicure. 'For not putting you down before now. You're so dead.'

'Get her off me!' Cici managed to squirm her arm free as she tried to claw her way out from the torrent of tiny pummelling blows from Louisa. 'Someone?'

But no one was in a rush. This wasn't New York; there weren't nearly so many security guards to rush to her rescue, and everyone loved a girl fight.

'Angela!' Mum called. 'What exactly are we doing to do with her?'

'You're going to get the fuck off me before I have you fucking arrested,' Cici screamed.

'Oh, I say.' Mum shook her head. 'You'll never get anywhere with language like that. Your mother must be mortified.'

I loved my mum so much. So. Much.

'I suppose we'd better get her up.' I hated being rational. 'Before she has an aneurysm.'

'But she's such a cow,' Louisa wailed. 'And she went down so easily it was embarrassing.'

I pulled Louisa up and off my prey and gave her a little hug. 'I wish I'd seen it.'

Cici lay on the floor, whimpering softly with a lip fatter than Lana del Rey. Mum still had one foot on the skirt of her dress, keeping her where I could see her. 'If you wanted to give her a slap, I'm very happy to look the other way,' she said, still clutching her handbag. 'Although you know I never condone violence.'

'I think I'm all slapped out.' I let my arms drop to my sides. 'And besides, she's only made herself look stupid, thanks to you. And everything's fine with the magazine, thanks to Jenny. They seemed to think it was a big joke.'

'I hope they think the same thing in Paris,' Cici chimed in, gingerly touching her busted lip. 'I don't feel like Pops will find it so funny.'

'What?'

'It's in Dee-Dee's presentation too.'

Cici was short for Cecelia. Dee-Dee was short for Delia. But surely she wouldn't?

I looked down at Cici, who cowered. As she should. 'You put that in your own sister's presentation? What's wrong with you?'

She shrugged and sat up, still annoyingly attractive, just a little bruised. 'I don't like you?'

'I don't like Angelina Jolie, but I don't go around Photoshopping great big cocks into her films, do I?' I shouted. 'And what about Delia? She's your sister, for Christ's sake.'

'Oh, we always pull pranks on each other,' she said. She didn't even look that bothered. 'I'm just better at it.'

'Do you think that's what this is?' I asked, holding out a hand and dragging her to her feet. Then keeping hold of that hand. 'Do you think this is a joke? A prank?'

'Well, yeah, it's, like, a big one,' she acknowledged. 'But whatever. I didn't kill anyone.'

'No, but you might have destroyed my career,' I pointed out. 'And your sister's career. Something she's worked on for months. Something she cares about. Doesn't that bother you at all?'

Like a petulant child, she shrugged and looked at her nails.

'Wow, you're properly evil,' Louisa marvelled. 'You're worse than Madonna.'

'No one is worse than Madonna,' Cici scoffed. 'Are we done now? Can I leave, please?'

'Not until you tell me why you're such a mental.' I pulled on her arm hard to make sure she was paying attention. 'And what you did to Delia's presentation.'

'She shouldn't make it so easy to hack into her account. I mean, who still uses the name of her childhood pet as her password? Gag.' She stuck her fingers down her throat and then snatched her arm out of my grip. 'I put the same version of the presentation you gave on her laptop. But, you know, it's Paris. Europeans have a much more laissez-faire attitude to sex.'

'*Your grandfather is going to be in that room,*' I shouted, just to make sure she was listening. It was all I could do not to knock on her skull to see if there was a brain rattling around in there at all. 'Your grandfather. And you know he won't just cover this up for her. If she gives that presentation, he will kill *Gloss*.'

'Prolly.' She bent down to pick up her shoes. 'Maybe you should try to stop her.'

'If you even attempted to put your talents for being a massive bitch to good use, you could achieve anything.' Now I really, really wanted to hit her. 'As it is, you'll probably just end up being the president.'

She gave me a whatever face and turned to walk away.

'Um, Cici?' Louisa called.

She turned round, clutching her shoes in her hand. Big mistake. Huge. Louisa pulled her arm back and gave Cici a slap across the face so hard it echoed round the atrium. Lou grabbed her hand back and squeezed it tightly with the other, mouth wide open in shock.

'Jesus Christ that hurt,' she said, pressing her hand between her knees. 'But I do see why you've taken to doing it so often. Sorry, Cici.'

We ran out onto the street, leaving Cici in a state of shock, pushed through the crowds that had gathered to watch the show and hailed a cab.

'Right then,' I pushed my hair behind my ears and gritted my teeth. 'Next stop Paris.'

'You're not serious?' Louisa asked, handing me my handbag and shoes. Clever girl had brought them down in case I needed to make a speedy exit. Of course she'd been thinking I'd be running from the police, not legging it to France. 'But this is not my first rodeo. Don't worry.'

'Not if I can get hold of her before the presentation.' I pulled out my phone and started to dial. 'But just tell Jenny I'll call when I know what I'm doing.'

She nodded and shut the door behind me while I directed the cab driver to St Pancras. Of course Delia wasn't answering her phone, so I sent a text, an email, a Facebook message and every other kind of communication my iPhone allowed before pulling out my hand mirror to check the damage Cici had done. My mascara had smudged and my concealer had slipped, giving me a touch of the Rocky Balboas, but it wasn't too bad. My hair never looked great after a fight, but then, my hair never looked that great by midday anyway. If only I hadn't been wearing a bright bloody orange dress. Nothing said 'Look at me, I've been in a scrap' like a nearly neon.

By the time we got across town, it was past one-thirty. I was ignoring calls from Jenny and only responding to her texts with very short replies including 'fuck my manicure' and 'this is more important'. I did send a thank-you for saving the presentation, but she didn't seem to care about that one. I tried to half walk, half run to the ticket counter and ignored the sense of déjà vu that hit as the delightful gentleman behind the desk smiled and asked how he could help.

'When's the next train to Paris?' I asked as sweetly as possible, my blood pumping hard. 'Whatever class, it's fine.'

'If you can do any class,' he hummed to himself for a moment, looking at the screen and rapping his fingers on the desk, 'there's a train leaving in fifteen minutes. You could get through security before then.'

'Great.' I pushed my credit card through the tiny slot and eyed the departure door. 'Thank you.'

I keyed in my PIN and tapped my foot, impatiently waiting for my travel documents.

'Right, you're all set,' said the man behind the counter. 'If you just go through the gate to your—'

'Got it,' I called back with as much of a smile as I could muster as I dashed away. 'Thank you!'

Nothing about the Eurostar had changed in the last year, except that this time I didn't have any delicious snacks and the people sitting across from me on the train were two incredibly humourless-looking businessmen. Made me miss my old train pals. I tilted my face up to catch some sunshine through the window and told myself over and over that Paris wasn't cursed for me. Paris was a place of romance and charm and quirky dark haired actresses and musicals about bloody revolutions. Just because the last time I'd been there, Cici cocking Spencer had almost ruined my relationship and career, didn't mean it would happen again. Lightning didn't strike twice. Except in all those studies where they had proven that it did. Quite often.

Just as we pulled away, my phone rang and I answered quickly, ignoring the dirty looks from all around me. Yes, guys, I wanted to shout, I'm *that* girl. I'm going to be on the phone for the whole trip, so suck it. It was Delia.

'Angela, what's wrong?' She sounded as worried as I felt. 'I got, well, all of your messages. What's going on? Did something happen at the presentation?'

'Your batshit sister happened.' I did try not to shout, but not nearly as hard as I could have. 'She put this ridiculous slide in the presentation and she says she's put it in yours and I'm on my way, but do not show that presentation whatever you do. There's a cock in it.'

If my seat neighbours weren't paying attention to me before, they were now. They stared, clutching their Styrofoam cups of tea, utterly scandalized.

'A cock,' I mouthed, nodding at them. 'Big one.'

'Calm down,' Delia said. 'Start from the beginning. Cici did something to your presentation? How?'

'She was here,' I explained, trying to slow myself down. 'She actually came here, pretended to be you and gave me a flash drive with the presentation on it.'

'Oh, she's practically a Bond villain,' Delia said with a sigh. 'And it had a porno on it instead?'

'Porn might have been nice,' I replied. 'But no. She got the presentation off your computer and stuck in one slide with a great big knob on it.'

Again I took a moment to make eye contact with my new friends and reinforce the message quietly. 'Huge penis,' I clarified.

'And then she tried to sneak off, but I caught her, and I might have given her a bit of a slap, but she

330

said she'd done the same thing to your presentation so I'm on my way to Paris to stop you showing it because you weren't picking up.'

That was a relatively concise version of events.

'But Angie, the reason my phone was off was because my presentation got pulled forward. I just finished it,' Delia said slowly. 'And to the best of my knowledge it was cock free.'

'Ohhhh.'

I really was quite angry.

'She really is a Bond villain. She got caught, told me her evil plan and then double-crossed me to get away.'

'I do wish she'd get over herself.' Delia sounded almost as pissed off as me. 'You're really on your way here?'

'Yes!' I rested my head against the window and watched the countryside fly by. Honestly, 'I wish she'd get over herself' wasn't really a big enough of a reaction to me, but then it wasn't my sister; what did I know. Oh to be rich and find transatlantic mistaken identity pranks a hoot. 'I'm going to be in fucking France in two hours.'

'But you're getting married tomorrow!' she reminded me, entirely unnecessarily.

'You don't say?'

'Right, it's fine. You just get off the train and I'll meet you at Gare du Nord. We'll be back in London before you know it.'

It was all too much. The presentation, the cock shot, the fight, the train, my lack of a manicure, My Two Dads sitting opposite. I really wanted to have a little cry.

'Seriously. Do not freak out. I'll work out what's the

fastest way to get you home and we'll fire up Grandpa's jet if we have to.'

Ooh. Silver lining.

'Just stay calm, get something to eat and chill out. I'll see you in two hours.'

'See you in two hours,' I replied, practising being calm for her and thinking about what I was going to eat. I hung up and popped the phone back in my bag.

The man in the outside seat leaned towards me and coughed politely. I looked up, ready for another fight, but he looked surreptitiously from side to side before putting his hand over his mouth to speak.

'So just how big was this cock?' he whispered.

'Good luck with everything tomorrow,' Brian, one of my new best friends, said as we hugged it out on the platform of the Gare du Nord. 'I just wish we could be there.'

'Me too.' I wiped away a tear and swapped hugging partners to make sure Terry didn't get jealous. Terry was the jealous type. 'But you two have a lovely weekend. You deserve the break. You work too hard.'

'I tell him all the time.' Terry gave me a big squeeze. 'But does he listen?'

'Well he'll listen now I've told him,' I reassured him. 'Now go on, before you miss your dinner reservations.'

I waved them off as Delia came running over, a look of confusion replacing the air of panic about her. 'Friends of yours?' she asked.

'New friends,' I said, accepting my third hug in as many minutes. 'Good friends.'

'That's cute.' She handed me a ticket. 'Now get your ass back on that train.'

'We're not taking the jet?' I was more than a little bit disappointed.

'This is quicker.' She gave me a push. 'Don't worry, I have a bottle of champagne in my bag. I figured we'd need it.'

'I know I do.' I linked my arm through hers and looked at my watch. 'Is it really only five-thirty?'

'*Mais oui*,' Delia replied. 'I'll have you home to your mom by eight at the latest.'

Home by eight. I could only imagine what had been going on in my absence.

'And I have some good news.' She slipped her arm through mine and pulled me back towards passport control. 'Grandpa called. Your presentation seems to have gone over pretty well.'

'It did?' I made a deal with myself to ensure there was a cracking great phallus in all of my PowerPoint documents from now on.

'It did,' she said. 'And so did mine. Which means we're on.'

We're on. We were on. *Gloss* was happening. I stopped still, just to let the moment sink in. And also because I was afraid my legs might crumble underneath me at any moment.

'But you get no say in the cover design,' Delia said as she dragged me down the station. 'Grandpa told me to make that quite clear.'

CHAPTER TWENTY

It turned out one bottle of champagne was quite enough, and I was almost relaxed, full of Ladurée macaroons and the thrill of success, when my taxi pulled up outside my mum's house not long past eight, as promised. Delia was staying with friends in Mayfair and had promised to have Cici hunted down and strung up as a wedding present by morning. Or at least early afternoon. I hadn't even got my keys in the lock before the door was flung open by Jenny, complete with new Bluetooth headset, who dragged me in and tossed me into the kitchen. She gave me a warning finger and pointed at a dining chair. Apparently I was to sit down.

'Yeah, I'm sure you're heartbroken.' Jenny pressed a finger against the earpiece. 'But I need a serving staff here tomorrow at twelve. So I'll see you then.'

She shook her head and put the phone and earpiece on the table.

'How anyone gets shit done in this country, I do not know,' she grumbled. 'The caterer's mom died and she wanted to cancel. Can you believe it?'

'Shit, Jenny.' I wondered if it was cancer. I wondered if my mum knew them. 'Scrious?'

'I know – it's like, be professional.' She looked super-annoyed and had missed my point entirely. But never mind.

'But is everything else all right?' I asked. The back garden was pitch black so I couldn't see if anything had happened. 'I'm so sorry about this afternoon.'

'Jenny to the rescue.' She sat down beside me and held out her hands. 'Whatever. Did you hear from Bob Spencer? Did you hear about *Gloss*?'

I nodded, my non-manicured hands pressed against my lips. 'We got it.'

Jenny pulled me into her arms and screamed, bouncing around all over the kitchen and taking me with her. I was excited that she was excited, but I was a little bit sad that I would now be deaf in my left ear on my wedding day.

'Thank you so much.' I pressed down on her shoulders to reset the bouncing mode. 'You saved the day.'

'Hey, it's what I do.' Jenny smiled brilliantly, the perfect ad for Crest Whitestrips. 'It's who I am.'

'It is,' I agreed. 'Is everything else OK?'

'Today was not without its challenges,' she admitted. 'I probably shouldn't have thrown my phone in the river. That didn't help. But it will all come off. Louisa has been super-helpful. Your mom and dad are going to hate me by the end of this, but I kinda got everything done that needed doing.'

It was good enough for me.

'Now. What do I need to do?' I asked.

Jenny made a clucking noise and turned to a tab in her notebook marked 'Angela'. 'Since you missed all of your beauty appointments . . .' She frowned. I frowned. And then tried not to because I hadn't had Botox. Not that I was supposed to get Botox. As far as I knew. 'We need to do your mani-pedi, maybe a little mini facial, but nothing harsh, and I want to get a deep conditioner on that mop of yours.'

'What about my lowlights?' I was suddenly overwhelmed by the desire to darken the tone of my hair by ten percent. My wedding absolutely could not happen unless my hair was ten percent lower. 'Jenny, what about my hair?'

'It'll be fine.' She waved a hand at me. 'I might have been overreacting.'

It was still a concern, but if she was going to let it slide, so was I.

'Where's everyone else?' I asked. The house seemed so quiet. 'Do they all hate me? Have they buggered off on holiday?'

'Your mom and dad went out for dinner. Louisa is at home making sure Grace's flower-girl outfit fits, and shut up before you start.' She gave me another warning finger. 'Sadie is at her hotel because she couldn't conceive of crossing the river. James was gonna come over but he didn't because he's a flake. Alex is somewhere with Craig and Graham and yeah, that's everyone. It's just you and me, pal.'

'Sounds good to me,' I said. And it did. I couldn't think of anything I'd rather do the night before my wedding than veg out on the settee with Jenny, doing my nails and potentially drinking the bottle of white wine my mum hid under the sink behind the Cif mousse. 'Pizza?'

'You know, it's too late to do any damage now.' She picked up her phone. 'Pizza me.'

*   *   *

A few hours later, I was slouched on the sofa, almost at the end of *Die Hard* (my choice), having already watched *Pretty Woman* (Jenny's choice). There was an empty Domino's box on the floor and I was holding my nails held carefully away from the carpet even though they'd been dry for ages. Jenny was curled up in a corner, so fast asleep that even the untimely end of Alan Rickman couldn't wake her. Mum and Dad had snuck in a while ago and poked their heads around the door just to check we were adhering to the sleepover rules and not making international phone calls or hiding boys anywhere. It felt like any other Friday night in the Clark household. But it wasn't really. It was the night before my wedding. There was a great big tent in the garden and a boy somewhere in town who was going to come back here tomorrow and marry me. I just couldn't quite believe it.

Careful not to wake Jenny, I turned off the TV and covered her with a blanket before creeping upstairs to bed. I just couldn't take in the fact that this time tomorrow I would be married. But then I hadn't expected it. I hadn't expected to spend half an hour in Paris today. I hadn't expected to be moving to New York two years ago. And if I hadn't, maybe I'd already be married. Maybe I'd already have a baby. Maybe I wouldn't have given a presentation that included a technicolour image of a six-foot cock. Maybe I would never have lived. Just the thought of how many 'maybes' had brought me to this time and this place took my breath away. I had found Alex as a result of a thousand bad decisions made every single minute of every single day until we met. Ever since then, even the bad days seemed more manageable. He made every-thing make sense, he made everything else more bearable, and I knew that as long as we were together, everything else would work itself out in its own time. I lay down on the bed with a smile on my face and slept sounder than I could ever have imagined I might.

Morning came quickly. I woke up with the nervous excitement of every Christmas and birthday that had ever gone before bundled up in one great big ball of stomach-churning giddiness. Wedding day. Wedding day. Wedding day.

The curtains were leaking with bright sunshine – a good start, I thought – and when I pulled them aside, I spotted the marquee at the end of the garden in all its bright white glory. Closer to the house, Jenny was barking orders at a large man carrying a stereo speaker. Another large man, verging on burly, was stringing lights all over the garden. My fairy lights! I felt like such a girl.

'Angela, are you awake?' Mum knocked and let herself in, carrying a cup of tea. 'Good, you're up. I told Jenny to let you sleep in, but apparently we need you awake now if we're going to "stay on schedule".'

Hearing my mum use verbal air quotes made me very happy.

'Oh.' I clapped once and dived into my suitcase. 'Happy birthday!'

Mum pretended to look surprised, but we both knew, wedding day or no wedding day, that if I'd forgotten her sixtieth birthday I'd need more than crutches to get down the aisle. I grabbed the little blue carrier bag out from underneath my knickers and presented it to her with a little 'ta-da'.

'You shouldn't have,' she said without a trace of authenticity in her voice. I knew I should have and so did she. Inside the bag was a small box, and inside the small box was a gold chain holding a delicate Tiffany heart and a delicate little 'A' and 'C' in golden letters. 'It's beautiful.'

'And when you cark it, we've got the same initials so I'll be able to wear it!' I exclaimed happily. Mum didn't look quite as amused as I did. And she was supposed to be the practical one. 'As a touching tribute,' I added, helping her fasten the tiny clasp behind her neck. 'Because I love you.'

'Get dressed and I'll see you downstairs in five minutes,' she said. 'And thank you.'

'Thank you,' I said back. 'And I'm sure you're not going to die soon.'

'I'm glad one of us is,' she called on her way down the stairs. 'This wedding will be the death of me yet.'

'OK, listen up, flower people.' Jenny was standing in the conservatory, perched on a crate, shouting at a group of annoyed florists. 'The garden is marked into four different areas – you are each in charge of a specific area. Please go now and familiarize yourself with your location and then start bringing the flowers in. Any questions, I'm right here. Go.'

'You know they say people who choose to be florists have the same psychological profile as serial killers,' I commented, nursing my tea. 'I'd watch myself if I were you.'

'Happy wedding day!' she trilled, bouncing off the box and bounding over to me, her hair wild and her eyes terrifying. 'I have had so much caffeine. We are on fire.'

'Please don't die,' I whispered mid-hug.

'I won't,' she promised. 'So everything is going to

be fine. I'm just waiting to hear from the catering people about what time they're getting here. They're running late because of the whole dead mom thing, and then we're waiting on the cake and the dress, and after that, it's just me, you, a whole shit-ton of make-up and a good strong mimosa. Sound good?'

'Sounds good,' I said, trying to suppress my smile and calm the spinning sensation in my stomach. 'I know this is going to be an odd question, but what time am I getting married?'

'Two.' She looked at her clipboard to confirm. 'We've got four hours. Although people will be arriving from one, so really three hours. And the photographer will be here to take pictures of you getting ready from around eleven. So you have one hour, because you need to be kinda ready before he starts taking pictures of you, you know.'

'Getting ready?' My head was already spinning with the timings. 'Have I got time to have a bath?'

'Yes. But you have to eat first,' she said, turning her attention back to the garden. 'Nothing heavy! Wedding dress!'

'Nothing at all,' I said to myself, holding my stomach. I was almost certain I was going to spew. 'Bath first.'

The house was loud and busy, but no one seemed to be terribly interested in what I was doing so I shut myself in the bathroom, ran a deep, deep bubble bath and locked the door. Pouting, I looked at my phone, holding it well away from the water. There were a couple of texts but nothing incredibly exciting. I wasn't sure what I was expecting, but it hadn't happened yet. Perhaps something between a telegram from the Queen and a cavalcade of Facebook birthday wishes. Served me right for never really using Facebook.

I was afraid to stay in the bath for too long, so I took care of business, shaving my legs, scrubbing off at least three layers of skin and making a bubble-bath bikini before climbing out and turning on the shower. The ultimate indulgence – a bath-shower; and, as my mother was bound to point out, a waste of water when there was a hose-pipe ban. Before too long I was pink-skinned and fresh as a daisy. My black eye was all but gone and the scratches on my legs and arms were going to be pretty easy to cover up. My limp still threatened to add a touch of Keyser Söze to my march down the aisle, but I was fairly certain I could get away with my heels as long as I took a painkiller an hour before I needed to wear them and didn't drink for another hour after that.

I moved the solo primping party from the bathroom to the bedroom and blow-dried my hair, not sure what Jenny was planning to do with me later. I smothered myself in moisturizer and checked my mani-pedi. All perfect.

Hmm. Wrapped in my dressing gown, I didn't know quite what else to do. And it was only a quarter to eleven. Resting my chin on my forearms, I gazed out of the window at the back garden. Jenny was bounding around like a children's TV presenter, all neon jeans and headset. My mum was taking a case of champagne into the marquee. I couldn't see my dad. But I could hear him. Somewhere in the garden, somewhere I couldn't see and part of me hoped I never would, I heard a brass band begin. Wow. They were not subtle. And if I was not very much mistaken, they were playing possibly one of the least wedding-appropriate songs of all time – *I'm Too Sexy* by Right Said Fred. Without a second's hesitation, I picked up my phone and called Louisa.

'Hello? Are you OK?' she answered quickly. 'I'm coming over in, like, fifteen minutes. Grace just threw up on my dress.'

'Your bridesmaid's dress?' I asked, horrified.

'No?' I could tell she was lying. 'Not at all. Twenty minutes.'

'Don't rush. To be honest with you, there's not much I can do at the moment. I feel like Rapunzel locked in her bedroom. Well, there is this,' I said, leaning out of the window. I stuck my phone out as far as I could reach and put Louisa on speaker.

'I didn't want to be the one to tell you, babe,' she shouted over the music. 'They're bloody terrible. But your dad promised they weren't going to play their Sexy Medley, so maybe they're warming up?'

'Sexy Medley?'

'*I'm Too Sexy, Do Ya Think I'm Sexy?* and *You Sexy Thing*,' she stated. 'On brass instruments. Your dad has a solo in *You Sexy Thing.*'

'I'm going to throw up.' I closed the window but the music kept on coming. 'Alex better not have told him he can play during the ceremony.'

Louisa was silent.

'Fucking hell.'

'It's all going to be perfect, Ange,' Lou promised. 'I'll see you in a bit. Grace looks so cute, you'll want to eat her face.'

'I am peckish,' I said, trying to work out if my stomach was growling with hunger, nerves or the thought of my dad's trumpet solo. 'See you in a bit.'

The garden, unlike my bedroom, was all action. I

watched florists bring in stacks and stacks of peonies. I watched assorted burly men install the PA system and hang my lights. I watched Jenny flapping her arms around like a very attractive but angry flamingo, and I wished I could help. Sort of. When the doorbell went, I ran downstairs, determined to get involved in my own wedding.

'Hi, bride.'

It was Chloe with my dress.

'You want?' She handed over a big garment bag, and I couldn't stop myself from squealing with delight as she draped it over my arms before sliding a large, stiff cardboard carrier bag onto my wrist. 'This is all the accessories and bits and pieces,' she explained. 'I really wish I could stay and see you in it, but I've got to deliver a ton of other stuff today, and the shop is always busy on Saturdays.'

'Don't worry about it,' I said. I was bouncing with excitement again and couldn't wait for her to leave so I could go back upstairs and get into the frock. 'Thank you so much.'

'No worries.' She leaned over the dress to kiss me on both cheeks and patted the garment bag lovingly. 'Just enjoy it. I know it sounds stupid, but people forget to.'

'Thanks.' I hugged the dress tightly. 'Again.'

Closing the door, I held the bag up high and the light from the kitchen window created a halo around it. My precious.

'Is that the dress?' Mum trotted over, almost breaking into a run. 'Ooh, I'll get Jenny. We need to try it on right away, just in case.'

'Just in case what?' I wailed. 'There is no just in case.'

'Just in case,' she repeated, legging it back into the garden to grab the wedding-planner-slash-bridesmaid-slash-stylist-slash-know-it-all. 'Wait upstairs!'

'This is all your fault,' I screeched at the top of my lungs half an hour later, I'm not entirely sure at who, when I finally accepted that the dress was not going to fasten. We'd greased the zip, I'd tried on Spanx, I'd breathed in so hard I thought I was going to crack a rib, but it just wasn't going to work. There was a good inch of open zipper and no amount of sobbing, Lurpak or elasticated underwear was going to change that.

'We can fix this,' Jenny promised. 'You can't actually see the zip. We just need to pin you in.'

'I don't want to be pinned in,' I whined. 'It's my wedding dress. I want it to fit. Why doesn't it fit?'

'Just don't make this more difficult than it needs to be,' Jenny threatened. I dropped my chin and realized why she was so good at her job. She was scary when she needed to be. 'I promise we will make this work. And I promise I will kick that hipster-chick's ass for effing up the alterations.'

I dropped onto the bed in my too-small dress, feeling like a heifer. Maybe we shouldn't have had that pizza. So far, I had a dress that didn't fit, shoes I couldn't walk in and a brass band interpretation of Rod Stewart's greatest hits. Brilliant.

'Jenny?' came a voice up the stairs. Louisa had arrived. And from the sound of it so had Grace. She was the only one wailing louder than I was. 'Can you come down here? I think there's a problem with the cake.'

Jenny gave me a stern look and vanished downstairs, leaving me with my mum. I tried not to look too distraught. It was only the cake. It wasn't the dress. As long as we fixed the dress and nuked the band, things would work out just fine.

'You've got to expect a few little hiccups,' Mum said, still fiddling with the zip on my dress. 'It's not going to make any difference. You're still going to have a lovely day, and you'll be married, and that's all that matters.'

'Yeah,' I agreed half-heartedly. 'That is all that matters.'

We sat in silence on the bed for a moment before it all got too much for her.

'I'm going to go and see what's going on with that cake,' she said, patting me on the back.

I stood up and stared into the floor-length mirror. The dress was still beautiful, maybe even more beautiful than I remembered, but the fact that it wouldn't fasten was all I could think about. It wasn't so obvious that you could see it, but I just knew. It didn't sit quite as well as it had on Monday, it didn't move as well. At least it was the right length.

I sat back down on my bed and waited ten minutes before losing my temper. I wanted to know what was wrong with the cake. I wanted to know why no one was hanging out with me. I wanted to know why the bloody brass band was still playing. Enough was enough. I wriggled out of the straps of the dress and twisted it round so I could get at the cursed zip. But it didn't move. I pulled on it as hard as I dared – nothing. Not a millimetre up or down. I was stuck. Determined not to panic, I pulled my blue NYPD hoodie over the dress and made for the stairs.

'I mean, it is a cupcake,' Louisa was saying diplomatically over the sound of Jenny's angry yelling. 'And it does make a statement.'

345

'I think it's quite interesting,' Mum agreed. 'Very striking.'

'*I don't give two shits what you thought you were doing*,' Jenny was screaming at God knows who. 'I asked for a cupcake wedding cake. I sent you an email. That email had seven different photographs of cupcake wedding cakes, and this is what you came up with?'

Opening the kitchen door, it all became clear. Mrs Stevens had made me a cupcake wedding cake. Literally. Instead of a tower of little frosted cakes, there was one giant cupcake the size of a small car, smothered in enough icing to give a blue whale diabetes, with a bride and groom cake topper perched in the middle of it all. Well. It was something.

Jenny was marching up and down the kitchen bellowing into her phone. If we were in New York, Mrs Stevens would never work again. As it was, I imagined she'd feel terrible for a couple of days and then get right back on with taking her Christmas cake orders.

'Yeah, I know my number was out of order, but you had other numbers.' Jenny was starting to turn a very worrying shade of red. 'And a brain, right? You do have a brain? And eyes? And you thought this was a good fucking idea?'

'Sorry, Angela.' Louisa bounced Grace up and down in her arms. She at least had the decency to smile at me.

'All right ladies.' A bright white flash went off and blinded everyone in the kitchen. 'My name's Damien. I'll be your photographer for the day.' Another flash, this time right in my face.

'Damien? Of course you are.' I held out my hand,

hoping it was in the general vicinity of his, too blind to know for sure. 'I'm Angela.'

'Nice outfit, Angela.' He shook my hand and then turned to shoot a picture of my mum and Louisa with the cake. 'And nice cake.'

'Oh, I say.' Mum held out a hand to ward him off. Grace did not like having her picture taken and started to cry immediately. 'I think no photos for a moment?'

'Yeah, things aren't going that smoothly right now,' I rubbed my eyes and blinked several times. 'Maybe you could take some pictures outside or check the lighting or something?'

'If I'm honest with you,' Damien replied, still shooting off his flash every five seconds, 'I don't do weddings. I'm more editorial-focused, more, uh, there and then type stuff, you know? But I took this job as a favour to a friend of a friend, so I'd rather, you know, be where the action is. I like to stick my camera right in the middle of it.'

I had a paparazzo for a wedding photographer. Brilliant.

I was about to tell him exactly where he could stick his camera when Jenny hung up on Mrs Stevens with a ceremonious 'Go fuck yourself, lady', which I was certain would see my mother barred from the WI, and put her arm around my shoulders, guiding me away from the man with the camera.

'Angie, honey.' She sounded considerably more calm when she spoke to me than to septuagenarian neighbourhood bakers, even if she still looked absolutely frazzled. 'Let me talk to the man with the camera. You go back upstairs and take that mother-fucking dress off before I hit you, OK?'

'It won't come off,' I hissed. 'The zip is buggered.'

Click. Flash.

'A touching moment between the bride and her maid of honour.' The photographer looked down at the screen on the back of his camera. 'Nice.'

'Maid of honour?' Louisa said. 'Jenny's your maid of honour?'

'No,' I replied quickly. 'You're both my maids of honour.'

'You can't have two.' Jenny folded her arms and gave Louisa a look I did not want to see. 'You just can't.'

'Fine, then Grace is my maid of honour.' I grabbed the baby out of Louisa's arms and she stopped crying. 'See? Now me and my maid of honour need calm. You two stop bickering.'

Click. Flash.

'Can you stop taking pictures of us?' Jenny asked as politely as possible. 'Also, you're late.'

'But I'm dead good,' he winked. 'Trust me – by the end of the day, you'll love me.'

'By the end of the day, Auntie Jenny will probably have given him one,' I whispered to Grace. She giggled. I giggled. And then she threw up down my jumper.

'You too, Grace?' I pouted at the spew-covered baby in my arms. 'You just got demoted back to flower-girl.'

'Give her here.' Louisa took back her bundle of joy. 'Let's get you upstairs and get you ready.'

For the next hour, we pretended I didn't have a giant bun for a wedding cake, that my dress wasn't knackered and smelling of sour butter and baby sick, and that everything was going to plan, just like any other wedding.

Jenny did my hair, I did Louisa's, and no one

touched Jenny's because it was already perfect. After the hair, it was make-up. Somehow, Jenny managed to melt away any imperfections that might have been lingering and make me look every inch the blushing bride. It took half a MAC counter and enough brushes to repaint the Sistine Chapel, but I didn't care. I looked like me, only much, much prettier. My hair curled around my shoulders in loose waves with a few strands pinned back from my face. Between my glowing skin and a simple half up and half down do, I looked like I'd just come back from a very fashionable jog. It was a good look. Damien snapped at us as we fussed around, laughing and generally attacking each other with lip gloss. It felt good. It felt how weddings looked on TV, and I was relieved.

'Oh, we have to do your something old, something new!' Jenny grabbed Louisa's arm. 'Do you have it?'

'I think Annette has them all.' Louisa stuck her head out of the door and bellowed my mum's name until she came running up the stairs.

'Whatever's the matter?' she asked, panting for breath and resplendent in her DVF dress. It was awkward to admit it, but she looked hot. My dad was onto a winner.

'We were going to give Angela her presents,' Louisa mumbled under her breath, as though I couldn't hear her. 'Something borrowed, something blue, you know?'

'Oh, I thought you'd seen the nonsense with the lights,' she said, relieved. 'I'll go and get them.'

'Nonsense with the lights?' Jenny was up and at the window as fast as fast could be, and that was no mean feat as she was already wearing her Jimmy Choos. 'Oh Jesus.' She turned and bolted for the door before I could ask what was wrong.

'Right.' I pulled my puke-stained sweatshirt back over my dress and picked up my heels. 'I'm going to find out what's going on.'

'Ange, don't.' Louisa tried to stop me, but since her arms were full of baby, she was at a disadvantage and I managed to sweep by.

The garden was in chaos. The florists were running scared and the big burly men were all shouting at each other. Every ten seconds their colourful language was punctuated by an almighty cracking sound, followed by the tinkle of falling glass. It took me a couple of moments to work out what was happening, but eventually I figured out the problem. The lighting man had hooked his lights up to the generator that the sound man was using and blown the circuit. Now the lights were popping one by one and showering the garden in glass.

'Fuck a duck,' I breathed. Definitely wouldn't be going out there barefoot now.

Jenny had lost it. She wasn't just shouting at the contractors, she was now actively pushing and shoving them. Despite being half their height and a quarter of their size, I still fancied her in a fight. I turned back into the kitchen, only to be blinded by Damien's flash.

'Take a shot of this,' I said, giving him the finger. And he did. And then he laughed.

'*I don't care!*' Jenny was screaming. 'No, I don't know what the EU safety regulation is on this, and no, I don't care whether or not you're going to get electrocuted. Just fix my fucking lights!'

And then something scary happened. She started to cry.

'I can't do this.' She covered her face with her hands

and made a strange mewling sound. 'I can't. I can't believe it but I can't do this.'

'Jenny, don't.' I hung out the door and waved for her to come over for a hug. 'It'll work out, really.' I had no idea if it would. Every second we stood there, my heart sank lower and lower. The garden was a disaster zone and the electricians had already perched their barely covered arses on lawn chairs and were opening up some sort of butty. I couldn't get married in the middle of this unless we were going to pass it off as a theme wedding. And that theme was *Paranormal Activity 1, 2* and *3.*

'No, it won't.' She looked down at her perfect brides-maid's dress and then tilted her head back to prevent her mascara from running. 'I should never have told you I could do this. No one could do this. I've ruined your wedding because I'm an asshole.'

'Jenny, really, don't.' I was this close to losing it completely. If Jenny couldn't keep it together, what chance did the rest of us have?

'I'm gonna go see what I can do.' She looked as devastated as if it were her own wedding day that was hanging in the balance. 'I'm so, so sorry.'

If there was one vital thing I'd learned from Jenny, it was that when things went to shit, we drank. I opened the fridge and pulled out a bottle of cham-pagne, popping the cork without ceremony and drinking from the bottle. Because that was what I did now.

'These pictures are going to be amazing,' Damien said, clicking away. I didn't care any more. What else could go wrong? We were ten minutes away from having to have my wedding in the front room. I wondered if the caterers could serve fifty people on a three-piece suite. And actually, where were the caterers? Maybe James had been right, this was a terrible idea. But what could I do now? My mum would be heartbroken if we cancelled. The family were all on their way. Sadie had flown in. James was here. Craig, Graham, Delia, Jenny, everyone. And Alex. What would Alex think if I sent him a quick text to say I'd changed my mind? I couldn't call it off now, even if the voice in my head was whispering louder and louder with every heartbeat 'This is wrong. This is wrong.' When things went this badly, it was a sign.

I leaned against the open fridge in my wedding dress, covered by a filthy hoodie with my shoe straps slung over my wrist, and held the bottle up for Damien to get a good shot. Drinking really did help, I didn't care what anyone said. Sometimes the answers were at the bottom of a bottle.

'Angela, put that bottle down!' my mother shouted from across the room. 'This instant.'

'No,' I said defiantly. 'Shan't.'

'I know you're upset right now, but think about the baby,' she said, whipping the bottle out of my hands. 'Honestly, don't be so selfish.'

'Why is it selfish of me to drink champagne because of Grace?' I was totally nonplussed. 'She's on a bottle, I know, but not the bottle.'

'Not Grace.' She rubbed her temples and closed her eyes. 'I know you don't want to talk about it – you've made that abundantly clear – but your dad and I know. You don't have to pretend. You can stop lying – it doesn't suit you.'

'Pretend? Lying?'

'We know you're . . .' She lowered her voice to a whisper. 'Pregnant.'

352

'Pregnant?' I screeched. 'I'm pregnant?'

Click. Flash.

I wanted a copy of that photo.

'Yes.' She looked at Damien with a face like thunder. 'To be honest, you haven't done a terribly good job of pretending otherwise, no matter what you might have told us.'

'What are you talking about?' I demanded. I wanted that bottle of champagne back quite badly.

'Angela, you've had morning sickness every day, you haven't been drinking – until now – and we both heard you talking to Louisa about having an American baby.' She had certainly written herself quite the convincing story. 'Your dad even said he talked to you about it. And, you know, you both agreed to this wedding very quickly.'

'That's because we're stupid, not pregnant!' I grabbed the bottle back and took a drink. 'I cannot believe you thought I was pregnant. Is that why you pushed this? Is that why you wanted us to get married this weekend?'

'I know it's old-fashioned, but it's never a good idea to have a baby out of wedlock,' she said with a familiar self-righteous tone. 'And you got engaged. You knew that.'

'But I'm not pregnant,' I reiterated. 'Really, honestly, not even a little bit knocked-up. See?'

To prove my point, I gave the bottle a dramatic glug. 'Absolutely one hundred percent foetus free.'

And then I had to push her out of the way so I could throw up in the sink. Never shotgun a bottle of champagne on an empty stomach.

'Really?' She looked half relieved, half heartbroken. 'You're really not pregnant at all?'

'I don't think you can be a little bit pregnant.' I ran the tap for a glass of water. Brita filter jug be damned. 'I'm not pregnant. Thank God.'

'Oh, Angela.' Mum settled on relieved for just a moment. And then remembered we were in the middle of the most shambolic wedding set-up known to man and flipped straight into panic mode. 'Oh, Angela.'

'Yeah,' I said, sipping my water. 'This is happening.'

'It doesn't have to,' she said quietly. 'If you don't want to go through with it, you don't have to.'

'But it's your birthday and you'll be so let down, and we've spent so much money and everyone will be let down, and I can't,' I rambled. 'It's not just the wedding, it's your birthday party. What about Uncle Kevin?'

'Angela,' she smiled. It helped. 'Your Uncle Kevin will cope. We haven't spent so much, and I've got a feeling Jenny is going to negotiate us out of the lights. And since the caterers haven't shown up, that shouldn't be a problem. I will be eating cake for every meal for the next months, but since when was that a bad thing?'

She was right about that, at least.

'And don't worry about my birthday. All I wanted was for you to come home. I wasn't even going to have a party if you weren't coming. I bloody hate half the family. More than half the family. It's only six months since Christmas. Why would I want to see them again so soon?'

I sipped water again and looked around. The war zone of a garden. The car crash of a cake. The shit-show of a dress.

'Say the word and I'll take care of all of it.'

I held the glass tightly, cool condensation running over my fingers. 'I just need a minute.'

She walked over to me and rested her hand on my shoulder. I held my breath, waiting for the slap. This was altogether too grown-up and considerate a conversation for us.

'Whatever you want to do, we'll do.' She squeezed her fingers together very slightly and gave a curt nod. 'I love you.'

If I hadn't been completely and utterly overwhelmed before, I certainly was now.

'I love you too,' I said, having a little cry. 'I'm sorry I've been a shit daughter.'

'Oh, hush.' Mum was dangerously close to getting emotional – I could see it in her face. 'We're ridiculously proud of you. How many of your cousins have gone off to America and started their own magazine and found a husband?'

'Three?' I wasn't entirely sure but it seemed unlikely.

'Very funny.' She gave me a serious look. 'We're so proud of you. Me and your dad.'

All I wanted to do was give her a hug and go back to bed, possibly with some crisps. Definitely with a cup of tea. But that wasn't on the cards.

'Angela?' Without even knocking at the front door, my next nightmare barged right into the kitchen. 'Angela? I need to talk to you.'

'Mark?' My mum sounded considerably more surprised than I was. I was just waiting for my Year Nine maths teacher and our postman to show up. Neither of them liked me much either. 'You're either half an hour early or about two years too late.'

Ha. My mum was funny.

'Mrs Clark,' he said, nodding at her awkwardly. 'I need to have a quick word with Ange, if that's OK.'

'She'll do what she wants,' my mum said, giving

me a cautious look. 'Whatever she wants.' And with that she excused herself politely and went to sit in the conservatory, watching us like a well-dressed hawk.

'What do you want, Mark?' I asked, running another glass of water and wondering what my make-up looked like by now. I didn't feel so much like I'd been for a light jog as a sweaty marathon, and I could only imagine my make-up said the same. 'I haven't got a lot of time.' I gestured down at my frock. 'Getting married and stuff.'

'That's what I've come to talk to you about.' He took a deep breath and straightened his tie. I looked at my hoodie and bare feet. At least one of us was properly attired for a wedding. 'You can't get married.'

'Is that right?' I asked. I was tired. Was it too late for a nap? 'Well, thank goodness someone let me know before I made a right cock of myself.'

Mark grabbed my wrist. The fact that I had a glass of water in the other hand was the only thing that stopped me swinging for him. 'I've been thinking about it ever since I saw you the other day, and you can't do it – you can't marry this bloke.' He looked so sincere I almost laughed.

'Any particular reason why?' I asked through gritted teeth.

'I just can't stand by and watch you make a mistake,' he said, stepping towards me and putting both of his hands on my shoulders. He got a palm full of baby sick for his trouble.

'Don't worry, it's not mine,' I said as he held his hand up and pulled a face. I tore off some kitchen towel and wiped it off for him. Maybe I would make a good mum after all. 'Do carry on.'

'I've known you a long time, Angela,' he carried on, starting what sounded very much like a prepared speech. 'And I know I made a mistake and that cost me my future with you, but I can't sit here and watch you do this. Watch you throw your life away over some silly rebound crush.'

And now I was mad.

'Silly rebound crush?' I repeated quietly. 'Can you hear yourself? You can't mean it, surely.'

'We were together for ten years,' Mark replied. 'And yes, I know I cocked up, but just because I broke your heart doesn't mean you should mess up your life.'

Just because he broke my heart? Oh dear. Oh dear, oh dear indeed.

'Right. I haven't gone mad or fallen into a coma or woken up to find out the last two years have been a dream, so I'll assume this is actually happening,' I said, taking his hands off my shoulders and dropping them right back by his sides. 'So I'll be brief and, if I may, blunt. Mark, are you here to declare your undying love for me?'

'Not exactly,' he stuttered. 'But I, um, there are still some feelings there, aren't there?'

'And so you think, what – I should call off my wedding to the American loser and move back to England for you?' I asked, using every ounce of self-control I had to manage my rage.

'You're going to come back eventually,' he said, starting to look a bit less sure of himself. Which was a first. 'And I'm not saying we should get back together, but maybe we should, you know, see what happens?'

'You want me to come home and be your bit on the side while you decide whether you want to drop your other bit on the side and get back together with me?'

Anger rising, control slipping. 'Jesus, Mark – you were so much better at cheating on me than you are at the grand romantic gesture. In case you were wondering, this is neither grand, nor romantic.'

That was the push he did not need. For the second time that week, Mark lunged at me with an ill-advised kiss, catching me off guard. But this time I didn't have a bag in my hand. I had a shoe. And I was lethal with a shoe.

'Fucking hell!' he shouted as I grabbed my Louboutin heel and flattened his knuckles with the heel. 'You've broken my fucking hand!'

'And I should have done it two years ago,' I shouted back. 'You owe Tim an apology. Now fuck off home.'

'Angela, Alex is here! He cannot see you in your dress! Get out of the kitchen,' Jenny yelled down the stairs. 'Now!'

My choices were behind the settee or into the garden. Lady that I was, I chose the garden. With one last seething glance at Mark, I took off. Running across the only glass-free part of the lawn, I headed straight for Dad's shed, snatched open the door and slammed it shut behind me. I was breathing hard and heavy, my hair was now coming loose, and I still had my shoe in my hand. People could say whatever they wanted about the price of Louboutins, but you could not argue against the fact that they made a fabulous weapon.

The shed was far more inviting in daylight than it had been a few nights before. Dad had done a nice job of kitting it out. If the worst came to the worst, I could probably hide out in here for what, a few months? The first thing I did was open the contraband drawer. I ignored the tin of terror and instead grabbed the little bottle of whisky he had hiding in there. Just in case.

I watched Mark emerge from the conservatory, presumably looking for me, clutching his shattered hand. I shrank away from the window and waited for him to leave. But he didn't leave. He just stood in the middle of the garden like, well, like a spare prick at a wedding. It was apt. But he didn't stand there on his own for very long. A couple of seconds later Graham appeared. Followed by Craig. Followed by Alex. I wished I could have been distracted by how handsome Alex looked on his wedding day, because he did. His suit was the perfect shade of blue and fitted him perfectly. Graham and Craig were equally well put together, both wearing sunglasses, both laughing. Only Alex wasn't laughing. Alex was too busy staring at Mark.

'Can I help you?' he asked, walking over to my injured ex. Alex cocked his head to one side, letting his hair fall out of his eyes to get a better look.

'Please don't recognize him, please don't recognize him,' I whispered, gripping the windowsill with one hand, the flask of whiskey with the other.

'Um, I was just . . . well now,' Mark blustered, doing his very best Hugh Grant impersonation. 'You must be Alex.'

'Mark, right?' Alex pointed and smiled. 'Angela's ex.'

'That would be me.' He held out his hands and laughed.

Alex laughed too. And then he punched him in the face. Mark fell to the ground and stayed there. I jumped up from my hiding place and flung open the shed door.

'Alex,' I shouted, legging it across the lawn. 'Jesus Christ.'

'Angie.' Alex looked at me and then looked away,

covering his eyes. 'I'm not supposed to see you before the wedding.'

'And neither of us is supposed to be punching people,' I pointed out. 'What are you doing?'

'What am I doing?' He turned away from me while he was yelling. 'What was he doing here?'

'Yo, Angie.' Craig raised a hand in greeting. Graham did the same before I could answer. 'Great dress.' They grabbed the prostrate Mark under the arms and dragged him back into the house without another word.

'It's all just such a cock-up,' I said, poking a bit of glass with my foot. 'And now someone is unconscious. Amazing.'

'I'm sorry.' He still had one hand over his face. 'Shit. I'm sorry.'

'It's just that you didn't need to.' I waited for him to uncover his eyes. 'I'd already done him once.'

'Yeah?' Alex pulled a half-smile. 'You hit him?'

'Broke his hand with my shoe.' I waved my shoe in the air with embarrassed triumph. 'It's officially my signature move.'

'That's my girl.' He stuck his hands in his pockets and squinted. 'Is that whiskey?'

'Oh.' I hadn't realized I was still holding it. 'Yeah.'

Alex held out his hand and I tossed it over. 'So what's going on?'

'Um, my dress is broken, the lights exploded, the speaker system blew up, the cake is a big fuck-up, the caterers have gone AWOL and my mum only wanted us to get married because she thought I was pregnant.'

'Wow.'

'Yeah.'

We stood in the garden looking at each other for a moment.

'Why is there a man asleep on the kitchen floor?' I heard Jenny yell from the kitchen. 'I quit! OK? I quit. I can't do this.'

'And Jenny quit,' I added.

'So it's not total smooth sailing?' Alex asked, looking around the garden at the glass in the grass. When the sun caught the shards, it really was quite pretty. Shame it would probably kill someone.

'When you thought about our wedding before we came to London . . .' I said.

'Uh huh?' Alex threw the bottle of whiskey back to me.

'Is this how you imagined it?'

'I don't think I had you in an NYPD sweater,' he shrugged.

'Seriously.' I tried not to smile. 'How did you imagine it?'

'Seriously, I guess not like this.' He gestured towards the building site of a garden. As if on cue, the brass band kicked in with a curious version of something I believed was *SexyBack*. Justin Timberlake would spin in his grave. If he was dead.

'It's not really what I'd imagined either.' I looked at my shoes and frowned. 'Maybe the shoes. The rest of it not so much.'

Alex took a step closer and held out his hand. 'Hey, Angela,' he said in a low voice. 'Wanna get out of here?'

I paused, looked back at the garden, looked into the house.

Click. Flash.

I took his hand.

'Let's go,' I nodded.

CHAPTER TWENTY-ONE

Three months later . . .

The aisle looked really, really long.

Can you put weight on around your ankles? I wondered. Have I got muffin-top on my toes? My shoes really hurt. Should have worn flip-flops.

But it was a pretty day for a wedding.

The heat wave we'd had for the last couple of weeks had broken and New York had given me the gift of perfect seventy-degree weather. I stood in the doorway blowing out cool, calming breaths and switching my weight from foot to foot. I never wanted to take these shoes off, no matter how painful they might be.

'You doing OK?' Jenny looked at me with a soft smile and straightened a curl. 'Need anything?'

'Nothing.' I shook my head. 'Got everything I need.'

'Well, you look pretty good,' she laughed. 'And that's really all that counts.'

'You look OK yourself,' I replied, squeezing my bouquet. 'You both do.'

'I'm just glad that dry-cleaner could get the baby

sick out,' Louisa said, pawing at a non-existent stain on her dress. 'I have to find out what they used to remove it – that stuff is like tar.'

'I'm just happy my dress fits.' I looked down at my brand new, made-to-measure Sarah Piper dress and gave a little shimmy. 'No jumper necessary.'

'No jumper, no ex-boyfriends, no fucked-up lights, no giant cupcake and no absent caterers,' Jenny confirmed. 'I'm on top of it this time.'

'I still think that cake was pretty brilliant,' Louisa said. 'And, quite frankly, delicious.'

'It was delicious,' I admitted. I would know. I had eaten a lot of it. I will accept that no one was expecting to spend that afternoon sitting cross-legged on my mum's living room floor in formalwear eating a cocked-up wedding cake, but as Saturday afternoons went, it was actually one of my favourites. After Mum and Jenny had turned all our guests away, using the delightful excuse that I had food poisoning and 'it was coming out of both ends', we all managed to calm down a little bit. Uncle Kevin was heartbroken, but everyone else was terribly English about the whole thing. I didn't imagine I'd be on a lot of Christmas card lists in December, but I didn't imagine I really cared.

Once we'd seen everyone off, Delia and I had toasted the magazine, Graham and James had got along far too well for boys that already had boyfriends, Sadie demonstrated her secret talent for the trombone, and she and my dad treated us to a little duet of some of my favourite show tunes. Jenny and Craig made sure someone made the most of the honeymoon suite, while Louisa and my mum kept everyone up to the eyeballs in hot tea. They were in their element. Which just left Alex. He and I had spent a couple of hours bonding with Grace, and I had to admit it had gone some way towards recharging the batteries in my biological clock.

'Are you girls finished gossiping?' My dad knocked on the door with a smile. 'I think they're ready for you.'

I nodded, suddenly lost for words. This was it. It was happening. I felt nervous and scared and almost certain that Alex was going to dive into the East River at the last minute. Dad held out his arm and I took it, trying not to cry. If I messed up my make-up now, Jenny would kill me. The girls went out ahead, Louisa with Grace in her arms, Jenny with a skip in her step. Their escorts, Graham and Craig, were waiting outside and I tried not to notice Craig slapping Jenny's arse as they went by.

'Saucy,' my dad commented. I had not inherited my sense of blind denial from him. 'Shall we?'

'We shall,' I nodded, taking my first step into the sunshine. 'Um, Dad, thanks for all this.'

'All of what?' he asked.

'Coming out here, being OK with the whole abandoned wedding thing. Not bringing the rest of the brass band.'

'I've got my trumpet back at the apartment.' He patted my hand and led me out. 'Don't tempt me, madam.'

'Noted.'

'But you know your mum and I are just happy you're happy,' he went on as we walked towards the music, towards the water. 'That's all that matters to us, love.'

'And happy I'm not pregnant,' I added. 'Yet.'

'Maybe in a couple of years, eh?' he replied as we reached the small group of friends gathered around the aisle. 'Here's your man. The future Mr Angela.'

'Can't imagine he'd appreciate being called that.' I

blinked into the light and wished I had the balls to be one of those wanky city brides who wore sunglasses. 'But he'll get used to it.'

Everything was perfect. Under the shadow of the Brooklyn Bridge, I locked eyes with Alex and all my nerves went away. Part of me saw my friends and family lining the aisle I was about to walk down – Erin and Thomas and their tiny baby. Sadie, James, Mary, Delia, Uncle Kevin, Vanessa, Alex's manager and his creepy old roommate – but they could have been complete strangers at that moment. All I saw was Alex. Part of me saw the Manhattan skyline behind them, the Statue of Liberty waving her torch to try and get my attention. She was failing. I could only concentrate on not falling over and getting to the end of the aisle.

'Hey.' Alex looked as happy as I'd ever seen him as we reached him. 'You look nice.'

'You look all right yourself,' I said, relieved that my voice was still working. 'Bit overdressed, maybe.'

'I was going to say the same to you,' he whispered.

The sun bounced off his hair until it shone almost blue, and he already had pink spots on his pale cheeks where he'd forgotten to put on his sunscreen. I was almost surprised how strongly I felt as I took him in. I woke up next to him every day, he was mine already, surely? But it felt as though I'd been holding him by the edges, just pinching the corners and hoping he wasn't going to blow away. Here, now, it felt like I was holding on to him with every ounce of myself and he was doing the same.

'This old thing?' I couldn't manage more than a choked squeak. 'Had it ages.'

'Bloody kids.' Dad gave me a kiss on the cheek and shook Alex's hand. 'You're a pair, that's the truth.'

'Thanks, David.' Alex was solemn for a second. 'It means a lot to us that you're here and that you've been so welcoming. I feel like I'm not just getting Angela, I feel like I'm getting a family that I never had before.'

'For the last time, Alex,' he said, slapping his arms round his back in a big manly hug, 'it's Dad.'

And that was when I started crying.

'Alex and Angela have asked you all to be here today to witness their wedding,' the officiant declared to the crowd. 'Because you have been part of their story. You have been there for them in the good times and the bad.'

Alex gripped my hand and squeezed. I nodded, biting down on my lip, destroying my gloss job and trying not to sniff too loudly. Sniffing wasn't hot. I also hoped this guy wasn't going to dwell on the 'bad' part. Move on, already.

'I love you,' Alex whispered while the officiant went on.

'And I quite like you,' I whispered back, getting a slap on the arm for my cheek. 'Fine,' I tutted. 'I love you too.'

'Today they start their adventure as husband and wife, promising to stand by each other, to care for each other and to love each other. Today they start a new chapter of their story together here with you, here in New York.'

I looked at Alex and then out at the city. It twinkled more brightly in the summer sun than any number of fairy lights.

Well, I thought to myself, if you were going to start a story anywhere, where else would you go?

THE END

Angela's
Guide
to London

HOTELS

The Sanctum

For real rock and roll luxury in the heart of London town, The Sanctum is pretty hard to beat. They get a lot of celebs (apparently) lured by the huge bathtubs popped in the middle of the bedrooms and the abundance of mirrored surfaces. There is also a hot tub in the open-air rooftop bar. I wanted to throw a telly out of the window but that's frowned upon.

sanctumsoho.com

Number Sixteen

Pretty much my favourite hotel in London, Number Sixteen is impossibly classy and elegant while still being super homey and comfortable. It's the fanciest B & B that has ever existed with delicious breakfasts, super-swanky rooms and a lovely, lovely little garden. Plus they had an in-room lavender pillow spray. AMAZEBALLS.

firmdale.com/london/number-sixteen

Charlotte Street Hotel

Charlotte Street Hotel is a dream. It's right off Oxford Street (ie: very close to TopShop, Beyond Retro and M&S for Percy Pigs), it's ever so pretty and all kinds of fancy types hang out at the bar. Plus I once saw Jake Gyllenhaal standing outside. For me, that is enough.

firmdale.com/london/charlotte-street-hotel

Avo Hotel Dalston

If you're awesome enough to head east, make sure you book in at the Avo Hotel. It's a home away from home, if your home happens to be so incredibly super cool that it has Elemis toiletries, in-room wi-fi, Sony iPod docking stations and a memory foam mattress. So actually, it's much better than my home.

avohotel.com

BARS & RESTAURANTS

Bourne and Hollingsworth
Super-cute twenties style speakeasy with gin cocktails in teacups? Um, yes please. This is my favourite place to pop in for a cocktail on a Friday night, it's cool but not in a 'cooler than you' way. Make sure you get there early enough to bag a table.

Rathbone Place, W1
bourneandhollingsworth.com

The Book Club
My favourite Shoreditch hangout, aka the only place I go in Shoreditch. The cocktails are deliish, the fresh fruit juices are yummy and the food is great. If you're feeling active, there are board games and table tennis. Otherwise, it's a great place for a good old-fashioned bitchathon. Plus you can marvel at hipsters – always a fun way to while away the hours.

Leonard Street, EC2A
wearetbc.com

The Lexington
The Lexington not only serves a million different whiskeys in a good old-fashioned pub setting (which would be enough for most people), they also serves FISH FINGER SANDWICHES. Oh, and upstairs you can catch some of the most exciting up-and-coming bands in the world on their way through town. It's an indiepop hipster crowd so make sure you dig out your big black glasses and cardigan, boys and girls.

Pentonville Road, N1
thelexington.co.uk

Karaoke Box
I love karaoke. I love Soho. Can you even imagine how much I love Karaoke Box in Soho? There's a great song selection and most importantly, you can dim the lights. This is essential to a good karaoke experience.

Frith Street, W1
karaokebox.co.uk/soho

The Diner
America has made me a complete fatty when it comes to burgers but in becoming a fatty, I have also become much more discerning than I used to be. The Diner has some of the best burgers in London, as well as chilli fries and awesome cocktails. More than two A Boy Named Sues and I'm on my back. Amazing.

goodlifediner.com

CLOTHES & ACCESSORIES

Beyond Retro
I never used to understand vintage. Searching for clothes that fit in a jumble sale environment just seemed a lot like hard work but once you've found your first dream vintage dress, it all changes. There's something great about finding a special piece that's one of a kind. Plus, compared to my other love, it's dead cheap.

beyondretro.com

TopShop Oxford Circus
I know this is news to no one but America has exactly TWO Topshops. Two. One in New York (thank GOD) and one in Las Vegas (pretty far away). Therefore I beg you, do not take this wonder for granted. Be still my beating heart. Sigh.

topshop.com

Tatty Devine
The fabulous ladies at Tatty Devine create jewellery and accessories with a heart and a soul. They're quirky and cute plus they do awesome collaborations with bands like Camera Obscura and Belle & Sebastian. What's not to love?

tattydevine.com

TREATS

Mrs Kibble's Olde Sweet Shoppe

I can't even attempt to explain to you how happy I was to find this place. The way I feel about Sherbet Fountains is the way some people feel about crack and they had boxes and boxes and boxes here. It was a dark and wonderful day. Long live Mrs Kibble.

mrskibbles.co.uk

Liberty

Liberty is one of those incredibly fancy shops that used to be on my list of 'good places to go to the toilet while out shopping'. These days it's been promoted to 'good place to blow an entire month's paycheck' but only after I've been to the toilet.

Great Marlborough Street, W1
liberty.co.uk

Benefit Cosmetics

Benefit make-up has been on my favourites list for the longest time. I'm so happy that they have quirky destination boutiques now – I can browse merrily while applying a variety of sparkly concoctions to my face and then get a brow wax. Since I'm not allowed to tweeze my own eyebrows, this is a Good Thing.

benefitcosmetics.co.uk

Elemis Spa

London is a busy city, fact. Elemis is a wonderful skincare brand, fact. So the fact that an Elemis spa exists right in the middle of that city is a wonderful, wonderful thing. It's basically like going on holiday without actually going on holiday. Brilliant.

Lancashire Court, W1
timetospa.co.uk

CATCH UP WITH

I heart

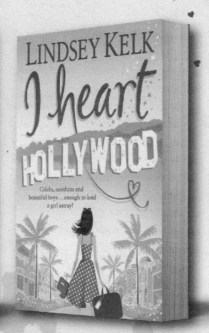

THE REST OF THE SERIES!

Log onto
iheartlondon.co.uk

You'll also have a chance to enter competitions, keep up-to-date with Angela's adventures through her blog, read top tips for where to eat, drink, shop and sleep in London, and much much more!

to find out more about all the
I heart titles

 Catch up with her on
facebook.com/LindseyKelk

Follow her
@lindseykelk

Check out her blog
lindseykelk.com

ALSO AVAILABLE
FROM LINDSEY KELK

The
Single Girl's
To-Do List

Newly heartbroken Rachel Summers must
complete a Top Ten list compiled by her best
friends to kick-start her fabulous, new single life –
but nothing can prepare her for the adventures
that unfold…

'Laugh-out-loud'
Heat

'Very entertaining'
Sun

'Fab'
Star Magazine

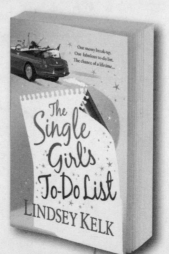